DREADFUL SANCTUARY

If someone put the question to you, "How do you know you're sane?", and told you that your life depended on your giving the right answer, could you think of what to say? This is only one of the situations the hero of this novel finds himself in—a novel that is full of scientific extrapolation and philosophical conundrums.

Dreadful Sanctuary is one of the classics of science fiction, first published in 1948 during the "golden age", and out of print for many years. It is the second novel by one of the best writers of science fiction, Eric Frank Russell, whose own imaginative style has made him one of the field's most popular best-selling authors.

Eric Frank Russell has long been an admirer of the writings of Charles Fort, that strange philosopher who recorded so many unexplained mysteries of history. In a fictional guise, *Dreadful Sanctuary* deals with problems that would have fascinated Fort: Are there aliens among us? Can we really control our own destinies?

The answers to these questions come out in this novel, which is a superb example of imaginative plotting and mounting tension. A story that has been concocted by an expert author at his best.

TOM BOARDMAN, JR.

Dreadful Sanctuary

ERIC FRANK RUSSELL

LONDON

DENNIS DOBSON

Published in Great Britain in 1972
by Dobson Books Ltd., 80 Kensington Church Street, London W8 4BZ

Printed by Straker Brothers Ltd., Whitstable

ISBN 0 234 77825 3

CHAPTER ONE

The premature explosion of the seventeenth Mars-rocket ushered in the year 1982. There was nothing spectacular about the big bang, but the event caused something of a turmoil.

Reasons for the sensation were twofold. Firstly, nothing more sensational occupied the headlines at that time. Secondly, the rocket had been manned. Prior to this, sixteen failures had got the public used to it. The little man in the street accepted that Mars-rockets crack up just as he accepted that airplanes often crack down, official reassurances notwithstanding. Of the sixteen flops, eight had been American, five Russian, one British, one French and one Canadian, all crewless and automatically controlled. Dollars had been burned aplenty, but no lives lost.

Public opinion, reacting from repeated dollops of pre-launching propaganda, sought explanations for continual failures. The public found two: either the technicians weren't as technically infallible as they pretended, or else they were being craftily sabotaged by some crackpot organization determined to stop rockets from reaching Mars. Propagandists encouraged the second theory, not from political hatred or any real faith in it, but as a means of diverting attention from the first and less desirable idea. Obediently, those thus diverted looked around for possible saboteurs.

When thirty million roubles blazed momentarily in space, and Mikichenko along with them, the complex became inhibited. It couldn't be the Russkis after all. Some other reason must be found. The taxpayer, miserably conscious of his taxes, swung right back to reason number one. Leftist log-rollers, financial theorists and others helped boost the swing by talking about capitalistic destruction of surpluses. That annoyed John Doe. He pictured his own wad on the bonfire and began to scream.

Such was the situation when John J. Armstrong read an article by Professor Mandle in the *Herald*. The professor was in favour of a Mandle Layer. According to him, this was a lethal electro-magnetic envelope surrounding Mars at a distance which varied from day to day, possibly between ten and twelve thousand miles from the surface. Here was a new notion moderately supported by what little data was available.

Armstrong was a big, tweedy man, burly, broad-shouldered and a heavy punisher of thick-soled shoes. His thinking had a deliberate, ponderous quality. He got places with the same unracy, deceptive speed as a railroad locomotive, but was less noisy. Straining his chair to its limits as he leaned his two hundred pounds backward, he eyed the glowing television screen on which the *Herald's* cogent page was reproduced, stewed the theory in his mind.

Finally he dialled his phone, got Mandle. The professor's face swam into his screen, young, swarthy, curly-headed.

"I don't suppose you know me. My name's John J. Armstrong," he told Mandle. "I've a finger in the eighteenth rocket now building in New Mexico. Whether it'll ever get finished is another matter, seeing that the public's starting to howl about it. If Congress also starts, guess we'll have to give up or go elsewhere."

"Yes, I'm aware of the position." Mandle looked sympathetic.

"I've been reading your bit in today's *Herald* recording," Armstrong went on. "If there's anything in your theory we might as well scrap the ship and have done with it. So I want to ask you a couple of questions. Firstly, can you think of any means whereby we can get the measure of this layer without destroying a ship? Secondly, do you think it might be possible eventually to combat this snag and drive through?" He paused, added, "Or are we banned from Mars for all time?"

"Now, look," answered Mandle, "all the data radioed back by auto-controlled rockets proves beyond doubt that there's an ionized envelope around the Earth. Ergo, around Mars may be another, superficially similar, but not the same. Its nature is speculative. But eleven of the seventeen ships exploded between ten and twelve thousand miles from the planet when they'd covered ninety-five per cent. of their intended journey. That's coincidence too many times repeated to be coincidence; it's a phenomenon with some law back of it."

"Humph," grunted Armstrong. "The other six never got

6

that far. In fact two of them blew to blazes at the moment of launching."

"We must make allowances for the human factor, for faulty design, flawed workmanship, errors of judgment and so forth. All those rockets, as you must know, were crewless and auto-controlled because we're still feeling in the dark and must recognize hazards. I consider it inevitable that with the best will in the world a few of the first rockets should prove failures long before they reach this critical point near Mars."

Armstrong rubbed his heavy chin with a thick and hairy hand. "Yes, maybe. But since they've boosted through the Appleton and Heaviside Layers with no more trouble than a rise in temperature and an upped cosmiray-count, I don't see why they should blow apart at this Martian layer, if it exists."

"Because it's not the same," Mandle asserted with a touch of impatience. "I can conceive its existence without knowing its nature. Maybe it causes spontaneous disruption of the fuel, or the entire fabric of the ship. I don't fancy that notion, myself. My guess would be that it causes overheating so intense that the ship gets burned apart like a meteor plunging through our atmosphere. If the overheating comes from some queer radiation which is inherent to the planetary field, I don't see what can be done about it. But if it comes from friction, then you might penetrate by reducing velocity below the critical point."

"This eighteenth rocket is designed to be manned," Armstrong pointed out grimly. "A crackpot named George Quinn is going to squat in its nose. We don't want him burned up. How're we going to prevent it?"

Mandle hesitated, his features showing thoughtfully in the little screen. "The only useful suggestion I can make," he said slowly, "is to have an auto-controlled pilot rocket running ahead of him. If the two are fitted with sympathetic recorders, and . . . and——" His dark eyes looked at Armstrong steadily, unwinking. Then his face slid gradually from the screen.

Staring into the empty area of fluorescence, Armstrong waited for him to reappear. His watch lasted a long time. In the end, he frowned, pressed the emergency button.

When the operator came on, he complained, "I was talking to Professor Mandle at Westchester 1042. What's happened?"

She disappeared, returned in a minute with, "Sorry, sir, your correspondent does not answer."

"What is his address?"

Her smile was courteous, apologetic. "I regret, sir, we are allowed to reveal subscribers' addresses only to the police."

"Then get me the Westchester police," he snapped.

To the official who answered, he spoke swiftly: "This is John J. Armstrong, Greenwich 5717. Something's gone wrong at the home of Professor Mandle, Westchester 1042. You'd better get around there fast!" He switched off, switched on again, got the *Herald*, asked for extension twelve, and said: "Morning, Bill! No time to waste—I want something quick. Can you give me the address of Professor Mandle whose article you ran in the last edition?" He listened awhile, got it, rumbled, "Thanks! I'll call you again, later."

Grabbing his hat, he raced out front, heaved his great bulk under the steering-wheel of his car, jabbed the powerful machine into action. Within him was the queezy feeling that Mandle had nothing more to say—ever.

Definitely Mandle had nothing further to voice. He was deader than last month's bottles. He reposed extravagantly on the carpet beneath his phone, his features calm, composed, his body cold.

An authoritative, grey-moustached individual moved around the body, said: "You're the Armstrong who rung us up? Quick-witted of you. We came right away but were too late."

"What caused it?" Armstrong inquired.

"Can't say yet. Looks like he kicked the bucket quite naturally. The autopsy will tell us why." His glance at the other was keen and calculating. "Was he very excited when talking to you, or apprehensive, or in any way abnormal?"

"No—he seemed O.K. as far as one can judge from those dime-sized screens." He studied the body morbidly. "Quite a young chap. In his late twenties, I'd say. Bit unusual for young ones to shuffle off like this, isn't it?"

"Not at all," the other scoffed. "They do it every.day." He shifted his gaze from his listener as a uniformed policeman entered the room, barked at the latter: "That the meat wagon?"

"Yes, Cap."

8

"All right. Lug it away. There's nothing to interest us here."
He turned back to Armstrong. "If you want the result of the autopsy, I'll phone it to you. Grenwich 5717, you said?'

"Yes, that's right."

The police captain grew slightly curious. "You a relative?"

"Oh, no. I was consulting him about a technical matter. It gave me a jolt when he slid out on me like that."

"I suppose it would." The captain pendulumed his hat, took a final, morose look around the room, tossed the hat carelessly on to his head. "Some of us get used to it, though." He went out.

Armstrong made it to the *Herald*, called for Bill Norton, took him to lunch. The café was small, homey, its rare steak excellent. He ate his way through the menu before saying anything.

"Mandle's dead. He went off while talking to me. It's a lousy trick to play on somebody before the conversation's finished."

"I've heard of lousier," Norton informed. "There was the case of the guy who suddenly went nuts and——"

"Never mind the journalistic reminiscences," put in Armstrong. "This event has left me sort of suspended in mid-air. I don't know whether Mandle really had got something or not. If he had, I want it."

"Too late, alas, too late." Norton nodded his head in mournful disinterest. "The stream of time has passed you by." He eyed his plate. "Thanks for the steak, anyway."

"Darn the steak." He made the table creak as he rested brawny arms upon its rim. "What's Mandle worth? Was he regarded as an authority in his field, or just a minor noise?"

"Ferguson could tell you that. He's the science ed, and he bought the article. From what I know of Ferguson, I'd say Mandle was big enough to say things that get inscribed on tablets of stone and handed down through the ages. Fergie specializes in scientific last-words, and he's so scientific himself that he buys his liquor in litres instead of quarts."

"Thought you once told me he doesn't drink?"

"Aw, you know what I mean." Norton was politely bored. "He's particular."

"Look, Bill, do me a favour, will you? I'm out of touch with all these layer-inventors and I'm beginning to regret it. Get me Ferguson's estimate of Mandle's scientific status plus the name and address of any other local boy he thinks is qualified to take up where Mandle left off."

"Anyone would think you're in danger of losing money."

"I might lose seven new and extremely expensive gadgets, including the world's only one-millimetre film recording apparatus. Apart from other brain-children in his ship, Quinn's toting around a fifty-pound camera that'll take a tremendous footage of film in full colour. It set me back twenty thousand bucks, for which I get Mars-trip projection rights. Those items represent all my headaches and half my fortune rolled into a lump." He mused a moment. "I'm gambling the lot at long odds, but I sure hate to lengthen the odds unnecessarily."

Norton grinned and said: "So you want to make sure Quinn gets back with all the dingbats and the stupendous epic?"

"Of course! But quite apart from that, I don't want Quinn vaporized." Armstrong was serious. "He's a screwball—as is any guy who prefers to shoot for Mars while there's still a crossing to sweep. But I like him. Even if he loses the camera and all the rest, I want him to get back with his pants unscorched."

"Nice of you!" Norton stood up, patted his stomach, sighed with pleasure. "The curse of all these rocket-ship disasters is that they occur too far out for us to get action shots of them. You couldn't persuade Quinn to bust-up somewhere handy and, say, bring down the Empire State with him?"

"If he does come down, I hope it's smack on Joe's Joint where all your bloodthirsty photogs hang out," growled Armstrong.

Norton laughed. "O.K., keep your hair on! I'll bait Fergie for you and give you a ring."

"Make it as soon as you can." Ordering a second coffee, he sipped it meditatively as Norton departed.

A coincidence too many times repeated, Mandle had declared, was not a coincidence: it was a phenomenon with a law behind it. That was logical enough. Haphazard chance had room for sequences, as any gambler knew, but hardly for sequence that long. Mandle had something there . . . but what? A law? What law? *Whose* law?

The last notion made him blink uneasily. Whose law?—how silly! Must be a remnant of the Russki complex. No *real* laws were man-made; they were products of nature, fixed, unalterable. The so-called laws of man were ethical accommodations, understandable, modifiable. Man-made edicts couldn't blow up eleven ships more than forty-eight million miles away. Of course not. Something far outside of this world was responsible for that.

Outside of this world? What was outside? That's what the rockets were trying to discover. That's what his super-camera was intended to record. Anyway, one thing now seemed a safe bet: new worlds harboured new laws.

Or new people operated new laws.

Or old people operated old laws!

Scowling at where his thoughts were taking him, he gulped the remainder of his coffee, left the café. He caught a mirror as he went out, paused and studied his own features. His face, big-boned, brown and muscular, framed dark grey eyes which regarded him steadily. Nothing abnormal there.

"My! what great big teeth you have, grandmamma," he said.

The image grinned and answered back: "All the better to eat you with, my dear."

"I dream too much," he grunted. Dreaming had produced the super-camera, the solar-compass and his other ideas, but for the moment he was too disgruntled with himself to think of that. "Time I got wise to myself!"

The last lugubrious comment was prophetic, decidedly so. He didn't realize it, of course, neither did he consider that ancient crack about true words being spoken in jest. Not that anything made any difference; bull-bodied people oft are bull-headed.

Norton was the first to agitate the phone. He came on with, "According to Fergie, the late Bob Mandle was an up-and-coming astrophysicist whose speculations are as good as anyone else's. He showed me Mandle's last paper. It was full of crazy drawings and a lot of Greek to me; all about Mandle's Patterns, which are supposed to modify some other nutty scrawls called Lissajous' Patterns in a way that shows why photons have weight. Pussonally, I don't care why any durned photon has weight, or even if it floats weightlessly, like a balloon. Still, Fergie seems to think it approximates to divine revelation."

11

"What of the other data?" Armstrong pressed.

"Oh, yes. Mandle's nearest prototype is Professor Mandle."

Armstrong gazed patiently at the screen while Norton gazed back, then he rumbled: "Say that again."

"The only local big-brain of Mandle's type and status is Professor Mandle. This phone's O.K. at my end. What is wrong at yours?"

"I heard you the first time. Quit horsing. It isn't funny."

"I'm not trying to be funny. I've more sense than to try to buck your competition." He smirked in the screen. "Fergie said anyone with enough brains to slosh around in his skull ought to know of Mandle's collaborator without being told."

He smirked again. "Claire Mandle."

"A girl!"

"His sister. Her hair has square roots. If she condescends to listen to a wolf whistle, it's solely to study the Doppler effect."

"Hm-m-m," contributed Armstrong, impressed.

Norton became earnest again. "But Fergie insists she's as good an authority as was her brother, in fact the only better one he can think up is a mighty-domed old dodderer named Horowitz, who lives in Vienna. This Horowitz, affirms Fergie with enormous awe, actually weighed a photon to the one hundred twentieth place of decimals by juggling a lot of mathematics around a chlorophyll reaction—whatever that may mean. D'you know what it means?"

"Since one of my gadgets employs photosynthesis, I ought to have a faint idea," Armstrong told him, dryly.

"Good for you! Me, I'm so ignorant I think colonization is personal hygiene. Want any more info?"

"I guess that's all I need. Thanks a lot, Bill."

"No thanks. I've paid you for the steak. When'll you be ready to buy me another?"

"I'll call you when telepathy tells me you're starving." He cut off, brooded until the instrument woke up and nagged at him again. It was the captain this time.

"The medic pronounced it cardiac thrombosis," he informed. "In real language that means a blood clot in the heart."

"A natural cause?"

"Of course!" The police captain showed signs of irritation. "Why not?"

"I just wondered, that's all," Armstrong soothed. "It's a case

12

of a little knowledge being worse than none. I happen to know that blood can be made to clot by employing the diluted venom of Russell's viper. From that fact I jumped no-place."

The captain's irritation increased and he waxed officious. "If you know anything which gives you cause for suspicion, no matter how remote, it's your duty to tell us."

"All I know is that rocket-shots have a hoodoo on them. So when the first guy likely to get us some place promptly turns up his toes, it makes me wonder whether there's more to it than a mere hoodoo."

"Such as what?" the captain riposted.

"You've got me there!" Armstrong confessed. "I'm playing blind man's buff."

"Mind you don't break your neck over a chair," the other advised.

"Not if I can help it."

After the captain had switched off, he pondered the problem of interviewing Claire Mandle. This would be a poor time to pester her, with a funeral on her hands. Better wait a bit. Better give her at least a week. That would allow plenty of time for a trip to New Mexico and a useful check-up on progress down there. Besides, the journey might help him to get rid of his elusive obsession, his silly notion that rocket number eighteen would get nowhere if he left undone those things which ought to be done—without knowing what things.

He got the phone again, called the airport, booked a seat on next morning's jet plane for Santa Fé. Disregarding the car, he went out on foot for his evening meal. One could see more and think more when walking.

His choice of an eatery was careless and unfortunate. The food was good, but they shot it around on an electro-skate serving system as if they were stuffing cattle in a pre-marketing fattening battery. There was a small dance floor on which, half-way through his meal, a dozen pairs commenced the latest shiver-jig to the steady, nerve-jangling thrum of six double-basses and one electric harp. The pom-ting-pom rhythm was supposed to be a tune titled "Skiddin' with My Shiver-Kid." It whumped up and down and to and fro like a Mephistophelean metronome. Pop-eyed and open-mouthed, the couples clung together and shuddered from knees to head. The harp and

13

basses skidded them into a state of near-hysteria. If they stuck it out for twenty minutes, some of them would be borne from the floor jerking and twitching like marionettes. Sonolepsy! Armstrong walked out in disgust.

Window-shopping along the road, he came to a small art shop. There was one piece centred behind the glass which caught his attention, a curiously curved lump of wood faintly resembling the body of a lobster. From its upper surface projected two thin, rhodium-plated rods, one bent, the other straight. The ticket beneath it read: "Elevation of the Psyche, by Tamari. $75.00."

His strong jaws lumped as his grey eyes lifted their gaze and caught his own reflection in the window glass. For a moment he stared at himself as if at a complete stranger.

"Who's been sleeping in *my* porridge?" wailed the teeny-weeny bear.

He stamped one foot hard as if somehow to shake off something that wasn't there, made for the nearest bank of recorder booths. Only the *Daily* booth was unoccupied, so he entered it, reclined in its easy-chair, metered his nickel, and scanned the *Daily*'s evening edition as it glowed into the screen.

There was nothing about rocket ships apart from the item stating that the Russian Government acknowledged and appreciated the many expressions of sympathy received from all countries in the world. No word of public clamour against rockets appeared. Maybe the papers were keeping it out as long as possible. National pride, if nothing else, demanded that rocket-shots persist.

The whole edition was unusually innocuous, giving most prominence to the Mississippi floods and the Wentworth murder case. Young Wentworth had been declared insane and the *Daily* hinted that if he hadn't been young Wentworth he'd have burned. But three alienists had spouted learnedly about combative neuroses and saved his dissipated body. Elsewhere, perhaps in Balikpapan or Bungo Bungo, somebody was being hung by the neck until dead because he really was nuts. It wasn't what you did so much as where you were when you did it.

"Darn!" said Armstrong loudly. "There I go again! What the heck's up with me today?" Emerging from the booth, he diagnosed his own complaint as a disordered liver, promised himself some salts. If he'd diagnosed it as athlete's foot, or œdipus complex, or extra-sensory perception, he'd have gone no farther from the truth.

"Truth is a jewel with many facets," defined Prince Gautama. But the Buddha forgot to add that the farther you get from one, the nearer you get to another. Armstrong didn't think of it, either. Leastways, not then!

CHAPTER TWO

The New Mexico construction and launching site lay some fifty miles north of Gallup. From the viewpoint of those operating it the only thing to be said in its favour was that it had come cheap. Rocket number two had taken off from here twenty years ago, and when it burst in space, like a monster squib, its saddened builders had abandoned the site. Better financed, partly with government funds, the constructors of rocket number nine had taken it over, improved it, extended it, then discarded it. Now number eighteen was hoping for better luck.

Armstrong found the place strangely quiet. Laconic guards let him through the big, triple-locked steel gate and he met Quinn when half-way to the administrative block.

Looking up at him from shoulder height, Quinn said: "Hello, Shorty! What brings you here?"

"You never write to your benefactor," Armstrong pointed out.

Quinn grinned. "Benefactor my foot! Now Lawson isn't playing around with his eternal mathematics I chivvied him into calculating your rake-off. He says that if the film runs no more than ten minutes, it should bring you ten million frogskins."

"Of which the government takes seventy per cent. and you get fifteen." His answering smile wiped off as he continued: "What d'you mean, Lawson's not working? What's going on around here—is it the local saint's day?"

"All work ceased yesterday because Washington has cut the dollar flow until some question of high policy gets settled. That scared our private supporters and they followed suit. There's a trickle coming in which is sufficient to meet the weekly pay-account, but that's all. On top of this, Ribera Steel is held up by lack of beryllium for body plates." He grinned again. "Hence the siesta."

"This is tough."

"I don't agree. The longer it goes on, the longer my lease on life."

Armstrong eyed him carefully. "You don't have to go, George. You can step out of it any time you want."

"I know," Quinn's small, pugnacious face lifted as he gazed at the sky. "I was only kidding. Wild horses won't drag me out of that boat once she's flaming to go. The job's mine and nobody else's. Don't you forget it!"

"Whenever she gets completed."

"They'll finish it some time. There are technical snags and bureaucratic obstructions which slow down the job, but it will get done eventually. I feel it in my bones."

"Well," praised Armstrong, "thank heavens for one optimist."

"It isn't that I'm optimistic at all. You felt the same way last time I saw you. Why, you told me yourself that number nine took two years and that this one's well ahead of it." He studied his listener curiously. "I'd say you've got a temporary touch of pessimism. You've got the blues. Snap out of it!"

John Armstrong mused a moment. A worker in oily denims wandered by whistling "Skiddin' with My Shiver-Kid." He heard it writhing among his thoughts, wriggling like a worm.

"Maybe you're right," he acknowledged. "I seem restless these days, and my notions shoot off at the queerest tangents."

"The reason is simple," Quinn offered with an assured air. "You worked like nohow to develop some skeezits in time for this ship. You beat your brains around until the job was done. Now you've time on your hands while your mind is still spinning. It gives you the fidgets. You ought to take up something to occupy your thinkbox, something high-pressured and healthy, such as bank robbery."

"Thanks for your advice, Dr. Quinn," he smiled. "Well, let's go bait friend Fothergill."

They stopped as they came to the part-built rocket, surveyed it silently. It posed within its surrounding framework, a dull black cylinder eighty feet high. The framework soared another eighty above it, indicative of the total height after the nose got fitted. That meant the shell was half-completed, and not much of the innards put in. There was a lot of work yet to be done, a lot of work.

Continuing on to the administrative block, they found Fothergill in his den, a dark, dapper individual who liked flowers on his desk.

"Ah, howdy, John!" He offered a smooth, well-manicured hand. Then he signed to chairs, sat carefully in his own, primped his perfectly knotted tie, moved the flower vase an inch to one side. "Well, well, well," he said with unctuous joviality, "to what do we owe this pleasure?"

"I was bored," Armstrong informed. His stare at Fothergill was steady, unblinking.

"Indeed? Fancy that!" He fluttered his hands helplessly. "You couldn't have picked a more unfortunate time. What with supply difficulties and governmental indecision and whatnot, we're all tied up. But it's only temporarily, I hope."

"What's the 'whatnot'?" inquired Armstrong, bluntly.

"Eh?"

"You mentioned 'whatnot' as one of the things tying us up."

Fothergill swallowed, looked at the flowers, then the ceiling, then the flowers again.

"Well?" Armstrong rapped. At his side, Quinn eyed him speculatively, but he disregarded it, kept his attention fixed on the other.

"Little things," said Fothergill, feebly.

"What little things? Anything which can hamstring a project as big as this can't be little. Who says they're little?"

Flushing, Fothergill sat up. "You can't talk to me like that. I don't like your attitude."

"Go easy, John," warned Quinn, anxiously.

Armstrong leaned forward, grey eyes aglow. "Why do Ribera Steel have to keep us waiting for plates when Bethlehem have got enough beryllium to sink a battleship?"

Fothergill jerked in his seat and said: "How d'you know that?"

"Because Bethlehem are soliciting beryllium armour plate orders in the advertising columns of all the trade sheets."

"Even so, I can't cancel a contract." Fothergill protested.

"I'm not suggesting that you can. But there's nothing to stop Bethlehem supplying on behalf of Ribera. It's a common trade practice. Who decided that Ribera was to have the contract, in the first place?"

"Womersley."

"Senator Womersley?" Armstrong's bushy eyebrow arched upward.

18

Shifting the flower vase another inch, Fothergill nodded. His expression was that of one crucified.

"Now, what about the 'whatnot'?" Armstrong persisted.

"Oh, for Pete's sake!" Fothergill's optics made vain appeal to the ceiling. "They switched the atomic fuel from plutonium to thorium on some abstruse grounds of top-velocity controllability. That didn't matter much, seeing the engines aren't finished. But North American Tube were advised of it, looked into the matter, then asked to have the venturis back. They say the silicone plastic linings are no longer good enough. They'll have to be thickened or toughened somehow."

"Anything else?"

"The X-ray scanner went haywire, leaving us unable to examine welding lines as they're completed. We had to order another. It hasn't come yet."

"Is that all?"

"A strike of lorry drivers held up supplies for several days, but we got it settled. We settled it by threatening to bring in a railroad spur." Fothergill was beginning to recover. He looked at his questioner. "What's up with you this time? You act like you've been appointed official progress-chaser. You got a diamond mine on Mars?"

Armstrong stood up. His smile was large and lopsided. "It may be a case of mischief being found for idle hands to do," he said, enigmatically. "Thanks a lot for all the news—and so sorry I got in your hair."

The other's hand went up and smoothed his glossy, well-oiled pate as if to stroke Armstrong out of it. "I've got troubles enough without reciting them to all and sundry," he complained. Then he switched on his most hospitable look. "Glad to have seen you again, anyway."

Outside the block, Armstrong said to Quinn: "You're doing nothing, George, so how about giving me a hand?"

"What d'you want me to do?"

"I'd like you to snoop around and dig me up some names. Mail them to me as soon as you've got them. I want the name of the guy who's in charge of that scanner, also the one who advised changing the fuel, also the one at North American Tube who wrote in asking for the venturis back. If you can manage it, I want to find out who stirred up the lorry drivers."

19

George Quinn gaped at him incredulously, and said: "I think you're nuts!"

"Most of the world thinks you're a darned sight nuttier!" Armstrong retorted. He squeezed the other's arm, making him wince. "We lunatics have got to stick together."

"Oh, all right." Quinn became moody. "If you want to play Sherlock, I'll stooge along."

He patted Quinn on the back by way of approval and encouragement. We've got to stick together—pat-a-cake, pat-a-cake, baker's man.

All the purple mood crowded on him again, suddenly, heavily. It was as if some fourth-dimensional pseudopod had reached forth to compress his brain. Shoving hands deep into his pockets, he tramped to the gate. Best to get away before Quinn's analytical stare started uncomplimentary comments. Shoo-shoo, baby!

Back in New York he settled himself in his apartment and considered matters afresh. In Connecticut he'd got as nice and compact a laboratory as any man could desire. There, many of his best hours had been spent in profitable development of some germ of an idea. It was an enticing place providing one hastened to it bursting with idea-generated enthusiasm. It was equally unenticing if one went seeking no more than refuge from the world.

At the present moment he had nothing to develop, nothing in any scientific sense. His record stood at a dozen fruitful notions in as many years, which was good going for any freelance experimenter. But he couldn't produce a flash of genius to order. He couldn't indulge a burst of laboratory activity without first being fired by inspiration—and such inspirations came as they chose, unforeseen, uninvited. Quinn, therefore, had made a shrewd estimate: his trouble was that he hadn't enough to keep his mind busy.

Defeated by the closure of its natural escape channels, his brain was seeking elsewhere. It was conjuring phantoms for him to chase, summoning nameless spectres for him to pursue through the darkness and the night.

Reaching that dismal point of introspection, nine men out of ten would have decided to see a mental specialist or take a foreign vacation or, at least, join a golf club. Armstrong's reaction was individualistic and typical of himself. If his brain wanted to run after visions, well, let it run! It should be a harmless pursuit and possibly amusing. A change is as good as a rest. Why not try track down the imaginary dragons? Through the darkling wood might really lurch something with a breath of flame. He decided to give his obsession free rein. To him, such a personal decision verged on the irrevocable. Once made, he stuck by it stubbornly.

"Or would you rather be a mule?"

Relieved by the prospect of openly enjoying his own eccentricity, he got out the car, drove into New Jersey, called on Eddie Drake.

"Hey," exclaimed Drake, to thin air. "Look what's here! The Man-Mountain!" He made a gesture of welcome. "Take that chair—it's the strongest one in the house. How much d'you want to borrow?"

"I'll borrow a cigarette, seeing you're charitably disposed." He lit up, crossed thick legs, surveyed his big shoes. "Seven years back, Eddie, you worked on rocket-ship number nine."

"Don't remind me of it," Drake mourned. "It was also flop number nine."

"That wasn't your fault."

"It wasn't anybody's fault," remarked Drake.

"You sure of that?"

Drake dropped his automatic lighter, scooped it up from the carpet, and protested: "Don't wallop me on the noggin with a sudden one like that!" He examined the lighter for damage, shoved it into his vest pocket. "Number nine went *bam!* halfway to Mars. Everyone had made as good a job of it as he knew how. Evidently the job still wasn't good enough. Somebody's best hadn't proved sufficient. Was that his fault?"

"No, of course not. But I'm not so much interested in what happened ultimately. I'm curious about the snags you hit before that, and the nature of them."

"I see." Drake's regard was keen and understanding. "You're having trouble with number eighteen and are looking for a tip or two?"

"In a way."

"Doesn't surprise me. I'll be glad to give what help I can." He ruminated while his memory searched back. "Our biggest trouble was when the engines cracked. They'd proved top-

21

notch on the test bench. They functioned beautifully at the first tryout after instalment in the ship. They cracked at the second test and we had to replace them with a heavier job. That cost us five months and a lot of moola."

"Who built the engines?"

"Southern Atomics."

"D'you know who designed them?"

"I've not the remotest idea. Probably I could find out."

"I'd be obliged if you would," Armstrong told him. "Any other troubles?"

"Only minor ones."

"Remember them?"

"The auto controls had to be aligned again. Two tubes burned out on test and had to be replaced. We had a good deal of bother with local civic dignitaries who objected to a bang in their bailiwick and wanted us to go to China. The government's half-interest in the boat enabled us to fight them off."

His eyes narrowed in reminiscence as he studied Armstrong and carried on. "The biggest trouble occurred *after* the thing blew up. It took off, as you'll recall, in the full glare of world-wide publicity. Later came the premature bang. That was followed by an uproar I can still hear today. Every tax-payer, foreigner, religious crank, financial pundit or political extremist seemed to write pungent letters to the papers, to Congress, and to every individual remotely connected with the ship. A dozen guys wrote me offering to reveal who'd blown it up. Two more confessed to doing it. Ten said it was God's judgment. One mailed me his income-tax demand and invited me to pay it." He chuckled knowingly. "When number eighteen falls apart you'll soon find out who did it—they'll all write in and tell you."

"Who d'you think they'll say?"

"The Catholics, the Jews, the Negroes, the Freemasons, the Ku Klux Klan, the Salvation Army, the Veterans of the World War, Jehovah's Witnesses, the British, and Russkis, the capitalists, the anarchists, the bankers, the oil combines"—he paused, out of breath—"and so on."

"That'll tell me a heck of a lot!"

"It'll tell you the world's chock-full of petty hates and cock-eyed prejudices and warped judgments."

"Not quite full," Armstrong differed. "No, I wouldn't say

22

it's quite full. There's calm reasoning in some places. But let's get back to what I'm after. Ed, who supplied the auto controls and the tubes?"

"Remote Engineering made the controls. North American Tube supplied the venturis."

"Hm-m-m! One more item—d'you know who started that civic agitation against you or, if not, could you find out?"

"I know," said Drake promptly. He pulled a face. "I had more than one wordy battle with him. He was Mervyn Richards, a hollow-eyed, lantern-jawed busybody from Farmington. He could talk the legs off a running duck, and he scared the local folks plenty."

"He's not bothered us so far."

"I don't think he's likely to, either. Last I heard of him, he was in 'Frisco lording it over some cult which wants to boost its ectoplasmic vibrations, or some such twaddle."

"I see." Armstrong mulled things over a minute. "D'you know where Clark Marshall is these days?"

"Somewhere in Florida, I believe. Want to question him as well?"

"Yes. I'll get hold of him somehow." He got up, shook hands. "See you again, Ed. Don't forget to let me have those names."

Driving home, he stopped at a Jersey City library, spent some time searching through reference files and several books on rocketry. This gave him nine names, two of which he traced in the Manhattan telephone directory. These two he rang up and cross-examined with a persistency which brought him a shower of wisecracks and friendly abuse. But he extracted reluctant promises to co-operate, and was satisfied.

From the library, he finished the run home, dumped the car, made a written record of all he'd got to that moment. Then he read it through, weighed its worth. Not so much. Just a lot of meaningless stuff. However, there was more to come in as Quinn, Norton, Drake and the others dug up data.

Even if it did get completed, the jigsaw might not present an intelligible picture, and it was a certainty that he couldn't concoct as much as a suggestion of a picture out of these few pieces. He'd have to do a lot more loping around and, in the end, was more than likely to find himself with a crazy pattern compounded of bits of a dozen pictures. Still, as a time-passing occupation it was better than chalking slogans on walls. "Vote for Moriarty." Not likely!

What next? There would be the other seven names to chase on the morrow and perhaps the day after, too. After that, the time should be ripe to interview Claire Mandle. Thinking over all possible sources of information, it suddenly struck him that there was nothing to prevent him going the whole hog. If he was determined to practise systematic lunacy, he might as well be thorough about it.

Extracting his typewriter from its case, he hammered it heavily, made up several air-mail letters, four for Britain, three for France. They were clear, cogent, and invited assistance, but he wasn't sanguine about them. Urgency tends to dissolve with distance. Petty troubles look considerably pettier from three or four thousand miles away. Maybe the Europeans would come back with data, maybe they wouldn't, but it was worth a try.

Taking the letters out on his habitual think-walk, he mailed them, strolled downtown. Electric signs winked and blinked and glowed at him from every angle: "Rose Bourbon," "Perlitz's Snackery," "Vitalax Will Give You Life," "Taxi Dance," "Kit Rooney in 'The Luck of the Irish,' " "Vitalax," "Gildé Brau," "Vitalax," "Vitalax." Persuasion, invitation, insinuation, repetition, repetition, repetition. A fundamental truth is anything proclaimed often enough to be believed. God is love. Rah-rah for good old Rutgers. Peace—it's wonderful. All the news that's fit to print. What's meant by "fit" and who says so? Vitalax will give you life. Strong arms will protect the peace. All the news . . . Vitalax——

Unconsciously he must have spoken aloud, for a passer-by stopped, stared at him, and said: "I beg your pardon?"

"Nothing," he assured. "I was chatting to Twillip." The other looked puzzled, and he explained: "He's tiny and green and wears a knot in his tail. I keep him in my vest pocket." He grinned, showing his teeth.

"Oh!" The pedestrian became vaguely frightened, gave him a peculiar glance, hurried on his way.

Turning into a nearby snackbar, Armstrong picked a corner table, ordered a pint of extra-strong java. He nursed his head in his hands while waiting for it. There ought to have been little blue bubbles expanding in his brain and steadily going *plop-*

plop-plop. The queerest part of it was that there weren't any bubbles. His brain felt fit and fat and full of sin. He didn't want to play with feathers and treacle, neither had he any desire to fill his shoes with butter.

The coffee came, he sipped it, watched the passing crowd. The blaze of light from the windows lit them up like actors on a stage. Cold faces, hot faces, long faces, squat faces, snappy faces, happy faces, dark faces, fair faces, smug faces, bare faces, blubber faces, rubber faces—and none of the lot alike. Yet they all rotated around an elusive norm. And that norm was the keystone of democracy.

What democracy? Lincoln's? Lenin's? Queen Elizabeth's? The democracy of Robespierre? Of Confucius? Oh, anything from the companionship of misery to the airy enlightenment of the Duc de Morny who didn't mind the people so long as they didn't come at him downwind. They'd all got it in some shape or form, in mode as variegated as themselves.

An attendant back of the counter switched on the radio and the Philharmonic Orchestra oozed forth with Handel's "Largo." It was soothing. It snored out with a slow, majestic beat that cleared away the mental blurs like the metronomic sweep of a windshield wiper. It killed the Shiver-Kid, and poured all the Vitalax down the drain, and lent grace to the stream of faces.

Then the music faded out; a cold, precise voice took its place. "Newsflash! A major disaster occurred half an hour ago in the Ural Mountains where Russia's largest atomic fuel plant is located. The shock of the explosion registered on all the world's seismographs and it is feared that the death toll is heavy. Further news will be broadcast as it comes in." He paused, added: "This comes to you by courtesy of *Gildé Brau*, the better beer." He departed. The "Largo" drifted back. It sounded different now; a dreary dirge.

With a muttered imprecation, Armstrong left the place, joined the throng outside. Darkness was now complete and all the firmament was sable save where the Moon leered down like a great white eye. There was a continual flow of powerful fast-moving lights along the whole length of the Manhattan Skyway and far up into the Bronx. Somewhere between the light-stream and the Moon, high atop an invisible building, a crimson worm crawled slowly and formed words:

25

SHE WILL LOVE CHICLEMINT!

Behind him, the radio in the snackbar changed stations and blared with enhanced volume. Someone started to croon a song called "Mudder Shudder Wump" while a hot band beat 'em down into their boots.

"Then suddenly they knew that they had died, hearing this music mock their shadow land." Armstrong couldn't remember whence he had got the words, nor could he imagine when they had popped into his head. But they unsettled him. Grabbing a passing taxi, he raced away from the scene, a fugitive from he knew not what.

Seven wasn't such a lucky number. He got up from a sound, untroubled sleep which contrasted strangely with his daytime meemies, showered, shaved, switched on the morning's *Herald* recording. The Russians had announced that fifty square miles of land surface had been desiccated and that the central pit was nearly two miles deep. Cause unknown. The Society of Friends had offered twenty air-ambulances and were rushing them in from the Chinese border. Young Wentworth had sold the movie rights of his life story.

Savagely he switched off the recording, spent the rest of the day tracking down the seven. Two, he learned, were dead. One was in Europe, whereabouts uncertain. Three he reached on the phone, found one of them lightheartedly willing to humour him, the other two surly, impatient, scornful and at no pains to conceal their opinion that he was a crank. To the last one, the seventh, he mailed a letter. That was that. Until fresh items turned up he'd exhausted all lines of approach, excepting Claire Mandle.

Mid-morning of the following day he motored to Tarrytown, following the last line. Claire Mandle proved to be small, dark-haired, pert-featured, and quite unlike her brother. She wore an expensively tailored suit of myrtle-green corduroy, her hair-do was precise, and she bore herself with quiet self-confidence. Looking at her, Armstrong decided that her most attractive feature was her eyes; they were dark and slightly tip-tilted, giving her an elfin appearance.

She sat at ease on an antique wheelback chair, her hands resting in her lap, and listened as he spoke.

"Then your brother had just got to the point of enlarging his suggestion when . . . it happened." He brooded for a few seconds. "I felt I couldn't very well bother you about it before now."

Her finely arched brows rose a fraction. "You think I might be able to give you the information you've missed?"

"I have been assured that you're about the only one competent to do so."

"Bob and I worked together, but not entirely," she said thoughtfully. "We had separate interests, too. I'm afraid I'd have to look through his papers and give the matter some thought before I could offer you a worth-while opinion."

"I'd be grateful if you'd do just that," he assured.

"Can I phone you?"

"Of course." He fixed her with grey eyes as calm as her own. "But I'd prefer to see you in person. Say, in town. We could discuss things over lunch."

She released a low tinkle of laughter. "You don't let the moments run idly by."

"I have an ulterior motive," he told her.

"Really?" She was femininely curious. "What is it?"

"I'd like to show you to a newshawk friend of mine. He told me that your hair has square roots."

Her laughter was the same as before, soft and low. "Very well. I am quite willing to demonstrate the truth, if it will upset a newsman." Her look reminded him of a pixie peeping around a larder door, liquid-eyed, a little amazed. "I'll phone you when I'm ready."

"Bless you!" he said, conscious of the gruffness of his voice.

Back in the car, he started the engine, got well out of earshot before he performed an underbreath yodel. Brother, it pays to be nuts. Look where it gets you! *She will love Chiclemint!* He clipped his yuralayetee off in mid-song, glowered at the windshield, did the rest of the journey in silence.

Quinn shiver-jigged the phone in the afternoon, gave him four names. "Here they are, Sherlock, and much good may they do you." In the screen he squinted violently and protruded his tongue. "Lookit me! This is what you'll be like in a week's time."

"What's supposed to happen in a week's time?"

"Nothing. That's why you're going to look like this."

Armstrong emitted a disdainful grunt. Carefully he noted the names on his scratch pad, then asked: "Anything doing down there yet?"

"We've started a local chess tournament."

"What, are they still held up?"

"Held up ain't the words for it. Senator Carmichael has sonorously enunciated the total number of greenbacks spent on Mars shots to date. Also the number yet to be spent. He says it's all a darned shame. Senators Wright, Embleton and Lindle joined in and chorused that it's a shame. They're still talking about it."

A copy of "Runbaken's Political Zoo" was among the tomes on his shelf. Getting it down, he read the profiles of Senators Carmichael, Wright, Embleton and Lindle. Then he remembered Womersley, looked up that worthy's also. It didn't get him anywhere; that is to say, he didn't find the feature for which he was looking. The profiles' slick phrases and diplomatic adulation were plastered over the usual successful-business-executive and poor-farmboy-makes-good stories. The five men differed in quite ordinary ways, agreed in quite ordinary ways. On the face of it, they were nondescript. What he was after, if it could be found, was some strange or unusual or peculiarly significant feature which they shared in common. For all that the Zoo book revealed, what they shared in common was the habit of wearing pants.

The most foolish feature of his will-o'-the-wisp hunt after imaginary and perhaps non-existent rocket-busters was, he suspected, that he was conducting it practically single-handed and without adequate facilities. He was trying to outdo the F.B.I., and with less on the ball. But the hunt itself wasn't foolish, not to his experimental mind. He'd run after phantasms before and had found them astonishingly solid-looking at the end of the chase. When, by one of those rare, Edisonian accidents, a midnight stroke of lightning super-gausses an iridium-cobalt needle which promptly stands perpendicular to Earth's magnetic field and drifts slowly from right to left, and when you spend two years pursuing the phenomenon until you can nail it down and tag it a solar compass, well, by that time you've developed a hound-dog nose for any curious odour. Thus he compounded with his eccentricity and rationalized it in familiar terms of research. The argument was a welcome prop for his mind; he never did like his mind being shoved around until it stumbled.

The next logical step was to peel a few off the wad and buy an extra brain or two. When you're having fun, you must expect to pay for it, and should the fun turn deadly—a dark and vicious game of stab——!

CHAPTER THREE

Hansen was a likely ally; his reputation was good, by all accounts. It took Armstrong only a short time to drive up-town to the brownstone block on the second floor of which was Hansen's Agency. There, a tall, languid blonde took his card, disappeared for a minute.

Presently she came back with: "Mr. Hansen will see you now, Mr. Armstrong."

Hansen himself proved to be a hard party almost as tall as his client but not as beefy. Giving Armstrong a chair, he sat erect behind his desk, his sharp optics taking in the other from head to feet. The examination was slow, deliberate and unconcealed.

"Summarizing?" smiled Armstrong.

Without dropping his scrutiny or changing expression, Hansen inquired: "What can I do for you, Mr. Armstrong?"

"I want an accurate report on several people." Pulling the list from his pocket, he handed it over. "Those people."

Hansen scanned it. "Five of these are senators."

"Does it matter?"

The gimlet eyes went over him again. "It depends upon what sort of a report you have in mind. If you want their conventional life-stories, O.K.! But if you want material for a smear, I must know exactly who you are and what sort of a smear it's going to be. If I don't like it, I won't take it." His thin lips clamped shut, opened again. "That's the way I do business."

"And a very proper way," Armstrong approved. "Evidently you don't know me. If you doubt my motives, the solution is a very simple one—all you need do is put another name at the head of that list."

"What name?"

"John J. Armstrong."

"Yeah," Hansen agreed. "That's good enough." His right hand fiddled with the gold signet ring shining on his left, twisting it round and round. "Say more."

"I don't want an expensive book-length report on each of those individuals. I'm not interested in their birthdays, bath-nights or blonde troubles. All I do want, as fully and completely as possible, is data on organizations to which they belong, businesses, clubs, brotherhoods, fraternities, political, religious or ethical bodies, or any other puddles in which they may be jumping frogs."

"That'll be easy," Hansen commented.

"Then it ought to come cheap." He smiled broadly as the other flinched. "The more thoroughly you can do it, the better it'll be for future business."

"Oh," said Hansen, poking the list. "This isn't all?"

"No—that's just the beginning. You'll have another list before long, and another one after that. If my money and patience last out, and if none of my friends subject me to a mercy-killing in the interim, I may want you to investigate a battalion."

"We'll do our best. I'm sure you'll be satisfied." He played the ring again. "It'll cost you forty each to get us going. All extras above that will be detailed in full on the bill. No major expense will be faced without first consulting you."

"For which heaven be thanked!" remarked Armstrong, with fervent humour. He handed over the money.

Pressing the stud on his desk, Hansen said to the blonde when she appeared, "Put this lettuce in the safe, Miriam, and give Mr. Armstrong a receipt."

The car took it slowly back to the *Herald* while he lounged behind the steering-wheel and called a mental roll of the troops. On the professional side he'd now got Hansen and whatever cohorts he commanded. The volunteers, willing or merely obliging, consisted of Norton, Drake, Quinn and several others—to which he might be able to add The Pixie. It wasn't bad going seeing that none of them knew just what they were doing, himself included. It wasn't such good going considering the huge, world-wide organizations of people who'd no better idea of what they were doing. But, of course, from orthodox viewpoint it is not of any importance that one should be going somewhere; it is enough only to think that one is doing so, or imagine it, or believe it. Or be persuaded of it.

Norton was busy when he reached the *Herald*, and he had to wait awhile. They gave him the visitors' lounge to himself, a large room furnished with garish opulence and littered with recent recorder copies printed on paper. Idly, he looked through them.

The first copy got him on the stumble again. Page seven announced that "Airways Eat Up Distance" while page ten showed lurid pictures of the Iowa City airmail crash in which were fifty dead. The distance to the grave! He ripped the page over. "Vitalax" . . . "the Coolskin Hour" . . . "Gildé Brau" . . . "Ivory Tower Gloss Contains Benadium, the Wonder Polish for Your Teeth." Benadium—common baking-powder. Why didn't they call it bolonium? Don't you know? Silly man! Toora-loora-loora, hush, now don't you cry!

Whut! went the page as he whisked it over. "The Four Freedoms." "Mercer Indicts Arcadia In Able Speech." "Greek Protest." "Copper Shares Scramble." "Thought for Today . . . Thought for Today——" he blinked and read it, tiny letters in a little box.

"Verily, verily, I say unto you, what shall it profit a man though he gain the whole world and lose his own soul?"

Just then Norton bounced in yelping cheerfully, "Boy, have I got a telepathic appetite!" He stopped, stared, added in more sober tone: "What's up with you, Misery?"

"I can't make out why my dander takes switchback rides over my brain-crenellations," said Armstrong, slowly. "If I shouted the reactions I get in this dump, I'd be put down as a red-hot radical. If I bawled them in Herald Square, I'd be lynched as a fascist. I think the real trouble is that I ought never to have crawled out of the lab."

"Nope," Norton contradicted. "You've got the same trouble as yon Cassius—you think too much." Dexterously, he topped it with, "And don't eat enough, in company."

"All right. I can take a hint. Where d'you want to guzzle this time?"

Norton shuddered. "Need you be so coarse?"

"I talk to suit the local atmosphere."

"Let's get out of it then. Let's try Papazoglous' dump—he's got a new way with steaks, so I'm told."

Going out together, they took the car to the Fiftieth Street subterranean car-park and left it there. A short walk of two blocks brought them to the Greek's place, a modest eatery full of warm kitchen smells. The new way with steaks proved to be gobbets of meat sandwiched around mushrooms and roasted on a spit. Norton, as usual, worked his way through a load of it as if he'd been hungry for thirty years.

Finally, he said, "A-a-a-ah!" and lay back. He gave Armstrong a dull, surfeited eye. "O.K. Now you've got me helpless and incapable of rising, you can shoot the works. What d'you want me to do this time, while I'm still too weak to refuse?"

"Clark Marshall seems to have disappeared. Eddie Drake thought he was down in Florida, but I've not been able to trace him. I thought maybe some of your Floridian newshawk pals might be able to get a line on him. He was in Key West a few days ago."

"Sure it's not a copper job?"

"I can't go crying to the police without just cause for suspecting that something's happened to him. As far as I know, he's packed up and ambled on in his usual aimless way. But he's a newsworthy character, and probably one of your fellow steak-killers has gone the rounds with him and knows where he is."

"Yes, he's newsworthy all right—or was! He grabbed the headlines three times with rockets numbers one, ten and fourteen." Norton shook his head sadly. "Poor old Clark! He sure went to pieces when the last one busted." His look at the other was distant, reflective. "You never met him, did you?"

Armstrong shrugged and said, "I've only seen his photo and read some of his old articles. I also read his letter to the papers in which he prophesied that number eighteen was doomed in advance. I reckon disappointment has soured him a lot."

"It more than soured him. It got him scatty."

"In what way?"

"I dunno exactly. Let's say he developed a sort of persecution complex. Yeah, that's about it. He took on the fixed expression of an early Christian martyr and started to shift around, first here, then there, tomorrow some place else. As if he was running from something."

"Or chasing something?"

With difficulty, Norton sat up. "Now look here, I don't mind you pursuing Irish phoonigans and getting me to run after them with you with occasional pauses for steak. But don't add to your delusions the notion that Clark Marshall and paint-drummers and bigamists, and everyone else who dodges around, are all pounding steadily along with you, going where you're going, looking for whatever you're seeking. Don't think the whole tomfool world is solidly behind you." He flopped back, exhausted. "Because it ain't!"

Armstrong said: "I am aware of the fact. I am also aware that the world is not solidly behind anything."

Tangling his fingers in his lap to form a sling for his distended stomach, Norton let his mind struggle with that last remark. "Cheesecake?" he murmured. "No—some people object to it. Peace? Nope! If nations don't larrup nations—which at present they don't—then families larrup families and guys larrup guys." He closed his eyes. "And sometimes they larrup dolls, just for the ducks of it." He opened his eyes. "Eats," he pronounced pontifically. "The world is solidly behind its fodder. All the world eats—it has to."

"Except when it fasts or goes on hunger-strike."

"Darn!" ejaculated Norton, tiredly.

"It fasts for religious reasons, hunger-strikes for political reasons, and sometimes destroys food for economic ones."

"Go on, rub it in! All right, we'll agree that the world isn't solidly behind anything. Do you know why?"

"Do you?"

"Sure I do. Everyone in my line of business knows why, and so do a good many more. It's because the world is stupid."

"I wouldn't say that," Armstrong opined.

"I would." He gave the stomach a comfortable, satisfying hitch upward. "You've incarcerated yourself too long to know how all-fired stupid it is. Why, a few years back one of our guys asked a hundred people the name of President Jackson's mother. Forty-seven correctly replied, 'Mrs. Jackson.' Fifty-three said they didn't know or couldn't remember." His glance at his listener was self-satisfied and cynical. "Last year, two hundred thousand Russkis paraded past Lenin's Tomb as if it were God's hiding-place. About the same time, Frenchmen started tattooing their ear lobes with three dots for liberty, equality and fraternity. The year before, when the King of Siam broke his leg, his entire court stumped around on crutches because royalty had set the fashion. There was one period when most of the British aristocracy wore snakeskin suspenders for the same reason."

"Maybe, but——"

"Lemme go on," insisted Norton, beginning to enjoy himself. "By the time you've been twenty years in my game you'll realize that nothing's too crazy to be impossible. Have you ever read Pitkin's 'A Brief Introduction to the History of Human Stupidity'?"

"I can't say I have."

"Believe me, the governing word is 'brief.' Pitkin and his sons and grandsons couldn't live long enough to write the whole of it! The marathon dancers and peanut pushers and flagpole squatters of your childhood were all centuries behind the times. Stupidity goes back, way back to the dawn of history. Why, the Pyramids are such mighty lumps of stupidity that stupid people have been evolving stupid theories about them ever since."

"Perhaps so, but——"

"For the love of Japhet," complained Norton, "will you let me get a word in edgeways? The degrees of stupidity are varying. For instance, I think I'm pretty clever because I've encountered plenty of people a good deal more stupid than myself. But it's only a relative cleverness. Really, I'm stupid too, though not so utterly and completely as some dumbclucks. Similarly, there are people in the world with sufficient glimmerings of intelligence to perceive the greater stupidity of their fellows and take advantage of it. If they can get hold of the law they use it to throw a cloak of legality over their machinations, and thus become politicians. Or they get under the cover of some convenient, ready-made law and become journalists, patent medicine vendors, armaments makers, crystal gazers— or even rocket shooters. Some will go so far as to operate outside their fellow racketeers' laws, which makes them lawless or, in other words, crooks." He smiled dreamily. "It is an ancient adage that Nature made crooks to educate fools."

"Have you finished?" inquired Armstrong politely.

"Yes." He gave his stomach another hitch, wriggled it pleasurably. "It's the steak. It makes me supinely bellicose."

"Well, then," Armstrong continued, "it seems to me that your reasoning is topsy-turvy: you start with effects and work your way back to an assumed cause."

"Assumed?"

"Certainly. How d'you know it's stupidity?"

"If it isn't stupidity, what is it?"

"I don't know."

35

"There you are, see?" Norton was triumphant. "You don't know!"

"What of it? Does my ignorance prove anything?"

"No, it doesn't prove anything," he admitted reluctantly, "but it leaves my theory standing alone, with no competition: the theory that the world is, and always has been, and probably always will be hopelessly stupid. No other notion fits in so well with the facts."

"I can think of ten," Armstrong told him. "And they all fit better!" He stood up, facing the other's look of dumbfounded surprise. "As you remarked, the trouble is that I think too much." He picked up his hat. "If you're not too stupefied to remember, see if you can get a line on Marshall for me." He waved a big hand. "So long, Gusty."

"Pleasant fellah!" Norton called after him, loudly. Glooming at his empty plate, he licked his lips, suddenly became gloomier still. "Oh, suffering snakes, he's left me with the check!"

It took Hansen five days to dig up the details. From Armstrong's viewpoint, this was speed, and his estimate of the tough, lanky agent went up six notches.

Opening out the neatly typed report which Hansen had mailed, he went carefully through it, murmuring its phrases as he scanned them.

"Irwin James Lindle, partner in Reed-Liddle Autobinder Company, of Wichita, Kansas. Member of the Senate Catering Committee, and the Latin Relations Committee. Belongs to the Association of Farm Machinery Manufacturers, the National Association of Manufacturers . . . um . . . um . . . Second Avenue Episcopal Chapel of Wichita, International Rotary, Kansan Bowling Union, Post 414 of the American Legion, Sharpshooters' Club . . . um . . . patron of American Youth Movement's Wichita Hostel . . . um . . ."

There was a lot of it. Hansen had done the job thoroughly. Armstrong counted the items after he'd perused them, found that Lindle belonged to no less than thirty-eight organizations of one sort or another. On the next sheet, Womersley beat the score with a total of fifty-four. Embleton went down to twenty-nine. Marking each report with its appropriate score, he found Womersley's fifty-four at the top, while Mervyn Richards held the bottom with a mere eleven.

Anyway, this lot was far from sufficient. He needed the reports on Quinn's list of names which he'd received and passed on to Hansen the day before. He also needed the information yet to come from Norton, Drake and the others. It was sheer waste of time to fiddle around with only one-tenth of the puzzle. One had to have many more pieces to gain some clue to the picture, to deduce what bits were missing and, perhaps, where they were concealed.

He gave it up as the phone shrilled. Claire Mandle's face swam into the screen when he switched on.

"Good afternoon, Mr. Armstrong!"

"Good afternoon, Claire," he responded with bold enthusiasm. "When do we dine?"

"My!" she chided. "Have I kept you waiting?"

"About a week," he pointed out.

"I'm sorry. I didn't think the date was so urgent."

"Of course you didn't. Modesty becomes you!" He favoured her with a mock glare. "But now that the waiting period is over, and you've satisfied yourself that my intentions are honourable——"

"Oh, so you have intentions?" she interrupted mischievously.

It caught him off-balance. He screwed up his face while he walloped his wits into submission. The way her tip-tilted eyes watched his performance added nothing to his comfort.

"I told you of them," he said feebly. "I wanted you for an exhibit."

She smiled and carefully stabbed him again. "Where do you wish me to make an exhibition of myself?"

"You pick the most awful words," he complained. "How about Longchamps?"

"This evening?"

"Oh, boy!" he yelped.

"Tut!" she reproved. "That isn't at all scientific of you."

"Have you had a look at yourself?" he shot back.

"I was not referring to your appearance. I meant your behaviour."

"Oh, that!" His grin was broad. "That was designed to prove that action and reaction aren't equal and opposite."

37

"We can discuss the point later," she said. "Eight-thirty at Longchamps. Will that suit you?"

"I'll be there." For some queer reason his voice seemed high and squeaky, and when he pulled it down it dropped into his boots. "At eight-twenty—just in case you're early."

She was not early, but she was prompt. A taxi dropped her outside the main door at exactly eight-thirty, and he met her, conducted her inside, found her a seat. Under her fur coat she was wearing a frock of shimmering green stuff, and her fault-less hair-do was topped by an object too small for a hat, too big for a flower.

Noticing his fascinated gaze fixed on the top-piece, she informed, "It's just a finisher-off."

"I'll say!" he endorsed, with total lack of tact.

With a slight frown, and a delicate nibble at her bottom lip, she switched the subject. "I've looked through Bob's papers."

He dragged his eyes down, said: "What did you find?"

"He'd made a systematic collection of data on the eleven ships which exploded fairly near to Mars, such as their distance from the planet at the time they blew up, and the last instrument-readings radioed back. The evidence he assembled makes one thing seem certain: they didn't disrupt because of fortuitous appearance of different causes in the same area. The disasters had a common cause."

"This layer of his?"

She hesitated. "Maybe." Her elfin eyes grew troubled. "One of those ships developed an off-swing, probably due to the burning out of a side venturi. Its observed path curved a great deal before the gravigyros turned it straight. The result was that it approached the planet's eastward limb and got a couple of thousand miles nearer than did any of the others. Then it blew apart."

"And so?"

"So that fact bothered Bob considerably. It created the only flaw in his layer theory, which can't be reconciled with a two-thousand mile plunge before disruption. He stewed it over, found himself faced with two conclusions. If the data on this boat wasn't accurate, and if in actuality it had exploded at about the same distance from the surface as had the others, then his theory was O.K. But if the data was correct"—she

38

paused doubtfully—"it looked very much as if that ship had been beamed out of existence."

"What," he exclaimed, "from here, forty-eight million miles away?"

"Obviously not. There is no disruptive beam of that efficiency on this planet, as far as I know. In fact, I can't see how it would be possible to make a beam with one per cent. of the required efficiency." She pondered a moment. "The alternative is a beam from Mars, which is said to be devoid of any sign of life. The notion is so patently absurd that it's hardly worth considering. That leaves only Bob's layer theory, which is faulty if all the data is correct."

They ceased conversation as a waiter brought them their order, resumed when he had gone beyond hearing.

Armstrong told her, "All this mystery about what's causing it is due to lack of data at this end. The ships have radioed back a lot of stuff, temperature, cosmiray-count, fuel consumption, gravity pull involved, and so forth, but it's not been enough." She nodded in response to his glance, and he went on, "How're we going to dig up the extra information? Have you got any ideas?"

"A convoy might get it."

"A convoy?"

"Yes—and the more ships, the merrier." She sipped her drink delicately. "A manned mother-ship controlling several auto-jobs running in echelon ahead of it. The leader should be the decoy duck. When it bangs, its follower curves off short, radioing data. If that one proves to have skidded too near and likewise goes kerplonk, the third ship curves away. Meanwhile, the mother-ship, lagging well to the rear, turns for Earth at the first blast, picking up all the data it can get from the others as it retreats." She twiddled her glass around on the white cloth, her eyes meditative. "Even if that technique fails to bring in enough information, it will, at least, settle one point."

"Such as which?"

"It'll settle whether they're being beamed or sabotaged in some remote way. If they're being sabotaged, then no fast getaways will save them. But if only one makes safe return, then the cause may be assumed to be a layer."

"Easy, so easy," he mourned. "It won't cost more than a mere couple of hundred million dollars."

"Yes, I know." She was genuinely sympathetic. "But since the required details are millions of miles away, I suppose someone will have to spend a fortune to get them. There doesn't seem to be any other way." Her pert features brightened and she gave him an encouraging smile. "I can lend you ten, for a start."

"Thanks, but I don't think I'll need them," he told her. "If a couple of hundred million smackers were wanted for the purpose of blowing up most of civilization, they'd be found in short order. But not for a project like this, oh no! Ten million for a battleship; ten cents for astronautical research—that's the way the world wags."

Her cool hand rested gently on his big paw. "Moody man!" She smiled again as he fidgeted restlessly. "It's not that the world's sense of values is wrong, you know!"

"No?"

"Not at all. It's quite natural that money should be found for war more easily than for adventure. After all, fear is an emotion deeper, ghastlier than any other. Insurance against fear is so much more imperative than is satisfaction of curiosity. Nobody's home will be preserved, nobody's life saved or freedom secured by conquest of Mars."

"Freedom," he scoffed. "What atrocities are committed in thy name!" He fidgeted again, his heavy jowls lumping muscularly. "It all depends on what is meant by freedom." Then he changed tone and added, "Pardon me—we didn't come here to argue with each other, did we? Let's get away from the subject."

"All right." Gazing around, she surveyed the people at neighbouring tables. "Where's the newshawk who was supposed to look me over?"

"He won't be along. I changed my mind and didn't call him."

"How come?"

He tried to leer at her, but hadn't the features for it. The resulting grimace sent her eyebrows up. "Two's company," he informed.

"And that horrible face you just pulled was supposed to express menace?"

"If you like. I guess I'm no durned good at putting on an act."

40

"Do you think it necessary?"

He warmed to her, and assured, "Of course not! I was trying to run away from my earlier thoughts and I ran too far. Like someone who laughs heartily after a dental extraction, just to show he didn't feel it."

"The masculine mind is strange indeed and tortuous are its ways," she quoted philosophically. Idly her glance went over his shoulder. Her eyes sharpened, she leaned forward and spoke in low voice. "My brother Bob had one bee in his bonnet. Maybe he told you of it. He suspected coincidences."

"Yes, he mentioned it. Why bring it up now?"

"It just occurred to me." Her trim head came still nearer. "Four tables behind you is a sandy-haired, freckle-faced man in a light grey suit. He was strolling past my house this morning when I went out. I looked at him quite casually, of course, and would have forgotten him except that he crossed the end of the road when I started out this evening. Now he's here. Three times in one day—how's that for coincidence?" She chuckled softly. "If he's half as nosey as Bob was, and notices me, he'll think I've got designs on him."

"You're sure that it's the same fellow?" asked Armstrong, without looking around.

"I'm positive."

"And you've never noticed him before today?'

"Not that I can recall."

He pondered it a moment, then shrugged. "Your timid admirer," he hazarded, "worshipping you from afar."

"Don't be silly," she reproved.

He shrugged again, consulted his watch. "Will you excuse me a moment? I'll be back very soon." He got up as she nodded, strolled casually to the entrance, still without looking around.

Outside was a phone booth. Stepping into it, he slipped it a coin, watched an ipsophone dial grow into his screen.

Mechanically, the ipsophone enunciated, "Hansen's Agency! You may switch to night-line at the stroke of four or record your message at the stroke of ten. One . . . two . . . three . . . four——"

"Switch!" snapped Armstrong.

A small blue light began to wink steadily at point four on

the distant dial, while to the listener's ears came the persistent *brrr-brrr-brrr* of the calling-tone.

Followed a sharp click, the ipsophone-dial faded out, was replaced by Hansen's dour features. The agent had his hat on. He looked expressionlessly at his caller, saying nothing.

"Going out or coming in?" inquired Armstrong.

"Going out. It makes no difference. The line gets answered whether I'm here or not." He stared bleakly from the screen. "What's the matter?"

"I'm at Longchamps with a lady friend. Maybe she's being tailed."

"What of it? There's no law against tailing someone, especially a dame."

"How about loitering with intent to commit a felony?"

"Bunk!" Hansen's eyes glittered in his dead pan. "You've been reading the wrong books. If the guy has no criminal record, it won't hold water. You can't get him until he cuts your throat."

"All right." Armstrong grew pugnacious. "I don't call you for nothing. Sing me a lullaby."

"You can drop him by doing some fast skipping around."

"Skipping's a girl's game."

"Or," Hansen continued, disregarding the crack, "you can lure him some place nice and quiet and systematically kick him in the teeth."

"I've thought of that. It doesn't tell me anything."

"Or," Hansen went on, as imperturbably as ever, "you can do what I'd do—tail the tailer and find who's back of him. I like to know the score."

"That was my idea. Since I'm staying with the lady, I can't track a guy who's tracking her—especially while I've got her on my mind. This is where you come in."

Hansen said: "Can you stay put until I get there?"

"Sure. We were going to the Television Exhibition on Sixth, but we can stick around until you're with us."

"Give me fifteen minutes." He shoved his hat backwards on his head. "When you see me, you don't see me—get it?"

"I don't know you from Adam," endorsed Armstrong. Cutting off, he saw the screen fade out, went back to Claire.

She was dabbing her face with a handkerchief little larger

42

than a postage stamp and her upward glance was bright as he reached her table.

Seating himself heavily, he complained, "That fourth table is not occupied."

"Goodness me!" she exclaimed, openly surprised. "Are you thinking of that man? Why, you're as bad as Bob!" Sobered by his calm, level gaze, she added: "He went out right after you."

Waving the subject aside, he summoned a waiter. Best to dismiss the matter. Let her settle down and be happy for the necessary fifteen minutes. But who was Sandy-hair after now, Claire or himself?

Only one minute late, Hansen arrived in company with Miriam and a squat plug-ugly whose jacket creaked across his back. The trio paraded loftily past Armstrong, looked at him as if he were a pane of glass, took a table far over to his left.

Chatting to Claire, and keeping one eye open for the still absent tail, Armstrong gave the arrivals time to deal with a round of drinks, then got up, helped his companion on with her coat.

They made it to the exhibition, spent a couple of hours mooning over the imposing collection of stereoscopic jobs and watching a demonstration by a rural travelling model with a ten-foot screen mounted on a truck. Full colours and stereoscopy didn't leave much further room for improvement, they agreed. Television, as such, was mighty near the limit of development.

From there, he took her to a midnight snackery, then got out his car and ran her home. Nothing untoward happened and by the time he'd reached his apartment he'd seen no sign of Hansen's company or of any other shadow. Feeling disgruntled about the unexpected normality of events, he wondered whether he was afflicted with an infantile tendency to over-dramatize mere incidentals.

Looking backward deep into his childhood memory, it did not seem that he'd been in any way abnormal. His active mind had been no more active than that of any other healthy child, his fancies no more fanciful, his excitements no more unreasoning. It was only of late that he'd developed his peculiar obsessions and dark suspicions. Why, why, why? He glowered at the wall which silently echoed: "Why, why, why?"

With the dawn and later in the morning he was still thinking it over, and the echo still lingered. Restless and disturbed, he mooched around the apartment until Hansen called him on the phone at ten-thirty.

"I've been in the business a long time," Hansen announced, "but this is the first occasion on which I've ambled around with a cavalcade like last night's."

"What do you mean, a cavalcade?"

"There was you and your girl friend. There was a guy tailing you. After hanging behind him for an hour I suddenly discovered someone was hanging behind me. So I switched with Pete and thus dropped this last snooper. He stuck to Pete, being unimaginative. I joined behind him. That made you, then your tail, then Pete, then the other guy, then me. Good job you didn't decide to make a night of it—you'd have been leading half of New York around by now."

Armstrong frowned. This recital puzzled him completely. "What happened?"

"The first tail dropped you when you got home. He went to the sub-park on Eighth, dug out a car, took it to this address in Cypress Hills." He read out the address, then continued, "Of course, the rest of the parade reached Cypress Hills, at which point Pete threw it up and went home. Pete's tail then followed him but got dropped half-way. Miriam had to put in some circus antics with our car to help Pete get rid of him. That left this last tail and me, and I stuck to him. Ten guesses won't tell you where he led me."

"Where?" Armstrong demanded.

"Fourth floor of Bank of Manhattan. He took the night elevator up by himself, as if he owned the place. I couldn't follow him any farther."

"D'you know who's on the fourth floor?"

For the first time, Hansen's lean face took on an expression; a queer mixture of dissatisfaction with the revelation he was about to make, and satisfaction with the anticipated effect upon his listener.

"I watched the elevator indicator. It stopped at the fourth floor. I looked outside, saw lights on the fourth floor." He paused tantalizingly. "The entire fourth floor happens to be the local headquarters of the F.B.I."

"What?" Armstrong bawled.

44

"You heard me." Hansen went dead pan again. "So I reckon I'm entitled to know what this is all about, and what I'm being dragged into."

"How the heck do I know?" For once, Armstrong felt lost for words.

"If you really don't know," suggested Hansen, with grim scepticism, "you'd better go round and ask the F.B.I." Giving the other a hard stare, he cut off.

Armstrong sat down and nursed his head. It'll settle whether they're being beamed or sabotaged in some remote way. Skipping's a girl's game. Vitalax will give you life—or will it? Better go round and ask the F.B.I. Strong arms will maintain the peace. Fifty square miles with a crater two miles deep. I am Ozymandias, the king of kings—gaze on my works, ye mighty, and despair! Gildé Brau . . . Vitalax . . . better go round and ask the F.B.I.

Better go round and ask the F.B.I!

CHAPTER FOUR

The F.B.I. man had the widest and boniest features Armstrong had ever seen. He looked like a wrestling champ with sartorial tastes. Sitting solidly behind his ebony-topped desk, he propped his visitor's card against a small calendar, studied the other with cool, slightly greenish eyes.

"What is your trouble, Mr. Armstrong?"

"I'm dragging someone around. He's a member of your mob. I want to know why."

"Of course you do!" The F.B.I. man smiled faintly. "We hoped you'd come here after Hansen tipped you."

Armstrong rocked back in his chair, and said sharply: "How d'you know Hansen tipped me?"

"Our man reported that Hansen had followed him most of the evening and finally trailed him here. He made no attempt to drop him, since Hansen is quite well known to us." He smiled again. "And doubtlessly he gained some mild amusement in leading your agent to this place."

"Ugh!" growled Armstrong, disgustedly.

"However," the other continued, "I can tell you that you've nothing to worry about as far as we're concerned. You acquired a tail solely because we're keeping a fatherly eye on Miss Mandle."

"Then why the hope that I'd come here?"

"Because your coming would prove that you've not the slightest notion why you were followed. That, in turn, would prove that you don't know why we are interested in Miss Mandle." He gazed absently at the calendar. "Have you told her about last night's episode?"

"No, I haven't."

"Is she aware that she was followed?"

"I don't think so. She came near to suspecting it but put it down as coincidence." Armstrong began to feel a little irritated. The mystery of his own making was threatening to become a mystery of considerably wider scope. "Just why are you keeping an eye on her, anyway? Of what do you suspect her?"

Blandly ignoring the questions, the other eyed him keenly

and inquired, "Were you quite satisfied with the way in which she dismissed her momentary suspicion as coincidence? You don't think she was putting on an act? Did her manner convince you as natural and innocent, or was she in any way apprehensive?"

Armstrong answered: "Anyone could see with half an eye that the last thing she'd dream of was being shadowed. She'd no reason to be followed. Why should anyone trail around with her?"

"Why do you trail around with her?" the F.B.I. man thrust.

"That's my business," he snorted.

"Quite! And this is ours!" The federal agent stood up, legs braced apart. "All I am able to tell you is that we're keen to discover whether Miss Mandle is aware of a particular fact which we'd rather she did not know. Also whether—if she does know it—she is passing it to anyone else. What you have told me suggests that she does not possess the information in which we're interested."

"Why not ask her in a straightforward manner?"

"Because Miss Mandle, having a scientific mind, could not be questioned without perceiving the significance of the questions. She would, I am afraid, be swift to deduce the very truth we wish to keep from her."

"Then this information is of a scientific nature?"

"You may draw that conclusion, if you wish." Picking up Armstrong's card, he handed it back. It was a polite gesture of dismissal.

Armstrong got up, stuck the card in his vest pocket. "Has it anything to do with Mars rockets?"

The F.B.I. man did not bat an eyelid. "I am sorry, I'm quite unable to give you any indication at the present time."

"Supposing I tell her that the F.B.I. has got her tagged?"

"We would much rather that you didn't. But we can't compel you to say nothing." The federal agent studied him levelly. "We may be satisfied and drop our interest in her pretty soon. But if you chip in, we'll treat it as a hostile act and keep a tag on you, too. Please yourself—it's up to you."

"Oh, heck!" Armstrong was puzzled and far from pleased. "You talk in riddles and tell me nothing. At least, you might say why that guy from Cypress Hills also shadowed us."

The other frowned. "That's something we've yet to discover.

If Hansen's doing his job, you'll probably get the reason as soon as we shall."

"All right." Armstrong walked hard-heeled to the door. "We'll leave it at this."

"Sorry we can't tell you more," the agent called as he swung the door behind him.

Reaching the street, Armstrong wended his moody way to the nearest phone booth, called Hansen, told him in detail of what had occurred. "So," he finished, "they're tagging Miss Mandle in case she discovers that Santa Claus is only her father and starts a revolution among disillusioned kids."

"You mental deadbeat," said Hansen politely.

"What?" He blinked, glared at the agent's impassive face in the little screen.

"That fat Fed told you plenty."

"Did he now, Bigbrain? What did he tell me?'

"One, they can't ask questions in case Miss Mandle mulls them over and sees the light. Two, that means they don't suspect her of getting the facts by her own astuteness. Three, that tells you they think she may have got hold of them in some other way. Four, that suggests they think she may have been told by somebody known to have been in possession of the information."

"Go on," Armstrong encouraged.

"For some reason, they can't check up on whoever might have told her. Why can't they? Answer: because he's dead. O.K.! What person now dead might have been so close to her that he'd blab something he shouldn't ought to?"

"Bob Mandle."

"However did you guess?" Hansen's dark eyes stared from the screen, steady, unwinking. "Bob Mandle had some officially provided information which he was supposed to keep to himself. No doubt it concerned something in which he was directly involved, and in which his sister was not involved. Maybe another Manhattan Project. Maybe the government is trying to make a wavicle-bomb some place. I dunno. Darned if I care, either, so long as I can keep this business in the clear."

"You're in the clear, you needn't worry about that," Armstrong assured.

"No need to tell me. I rang up the F.B.I. before you got there. They said they'd nothing against you." He looked down

48

at his desk, not visible in the screen. "I've three more reports just come in. Will you pick them up, or d'you want me to mail them?"

"Mail them," Armstrong ordered. Cutting off, he went to his car, got in, but did not start the engine. For some minutes he sat in the driving seat and pondered the problem. He had a faraway expression as he stared through the windshield and let his mind wrestle with the facts.

Suppose he contacted Claire and asked her flatly how come —what then? Anyway, how could he ask her? "Have you got any official information which you should not possess?" Darned silly, that! "Did Bob ever tell you anything he shouldn't have done and, if so, what was it?" Hey-hey, that would get him shown the door in double-quick time!

If she were ignorant of whatever she was suspected of knowing, his questions would be resented no matter how tactfully put, and all he'd get for his pains would be a negative response. On the other hand, if Bob had passed her something strictly in brotherly confidence she wasn't likely to hand it over to a comparative stranger at the first asking. He'd still get a negative response. Definitely, cross-examination of Claire Mandle was out. He immediately dismissed it from his mind.

How, then, to dig out the cause of the F.B.I.'s interest? It wasn't that he was unduly inquisitive about something which was no business of his, but rather that he was obsessed with an irresistible feeling that here was a missing piece belonging to his own peculiar puzzle. It might be a key piece. If he could get hold of it, an entire corner of the picture might appear.

The matter needed further stewing, since it was evident that he was not going to get at the truth in any direct way. What Claire Mandle was not supposed to know was also something which he was not supposed to know, and if the F.B.I. wouldn't tell him anything it was a safe bet that no other bureaucrat would confide in him.

Temporarily, he released the problem from his thoughts, decided to visit a newsreel theatre and give his over-active imagination a rest. Taking the car uptown, he parked it, went into the Fiftieth Street Newsflash.

Blinking in the semi-darkness, he found his way to a seat, sat down, cast a jaundiced eye at the screen. Glowing in full colours, the brilliant oblong depicted the North Dakotan gallows wedding which many of that morning's news-records had criticized as being in the worst of taste.

There, swinging side by side from a pair of scaffolds, the bride and groom hung with the fateful nooses around their chests and under their arms. A goatee-bearded justice of the peace, similarly suspended, muttered his way through the prescribed formula while the betrothed couple smirked inanely at the camera.

Edging uneasily in his seat, Armstrong scowled at the picture. Obligingly, the scene changed. Indian riots, this time. Moslems charging a Hindu procession, and police armed with lathis beating up both. Close-up shots of sweating, fanatical faces, of bodies sprawling in the gutters. A brief glimpse of a burning temple with its ages-old walls collapsing around the smoke-obscured figure of the Great God Ganesha.

Next, the launching of the *Iron Duke*, Britain's latest and biggest battleship. Bang went a bottle, up went a flag, and a horse-faced individual saluted to distant strains of martial music. Strong arms will protect the peace. Then the first flight of Russia's new bomber. Cheers, more music, and the shot of a column of marching feet. Strong arms will protect the peace. After that, the picture of a tiny, shapeless dot racing at tremendous speed across the fuzzy horizon; America's two-thousand-miles-an-hour stratosphere fighter. Glory, glory, hallelujah! Strong arms will protect the peace.

Followed a swift whirl of new fashions in hats, frocks and swim suits, then some useless gadgets from a trade exhibition. The programme settled down to a eulogy of the latest juke box, with press-button changes, a twelve by twelve screen depicting the appropriate performers, and adjustable focus to pick out individual instrumentalists. Get an eyeful of this: Runny Runbaken's Runnerbeans playing "Skiddin' with My Shiver-Kid." It's solid, sister, eight beats to the bar. C'mon, slip me some skin and let's beat 'em down a bit. Stab button two and it'll really send you. Hep-hep!

His eyes now accustomed to the half-light, Armstrong looked sidewise, studied the faded blonde sitting next to him. Her jaws were working rhythmically, her eyes fastened to the screen with a sort of dull intensity, her left foot tapping in time to the blaring juke box. Introductory stage of sonolepsy.

50

Averting his gaze, he transferred it to the opposite side, found there a vapid youth, his mouth hanging open, his eyes bugging straight ahead, his well-padded shoulders twitching to the same crazy beat.

> *Bang 'em for a zulu,*
> *Slam 'em for a lulu:*
> *Riddin' all the rhythm rats,*
> *Skiddin'—skiddin' with my shiver-kid!*

Nudging him with a heavy elbow, Armstrong snapped, "Poostermoolies!"

The vapid one gave a violent start, ceased his twitching, turned his popping optics to the other. "Eh?"

"Poostermoolies," growled Armstrong, standing up.

"Oh, sure!" The youth drew in his legs to let Armstrong pass. After the brawny figure had gone, the youth returned his attention to the screen, his mouth hung open again, never a thought about what poostermoolies might mean entered his mind. As Armstrong had known, any word would have done to obtain the required reaction.

Armstrong went home. Something deep in his brain was curling and contorting like a mutilated snake. It was a weird and worrying evasiveness which he couldn't pin down, a nagging thought which recurred at the most unexpected times. Whenever it got him bothered, his technique was always the same: first he tried to identify it, then, failing, he tried to get rid of it.

What enabled him to lose it this time was the sight of the tiny pinhead glowing like an insect's eye in the centre panel of his door. Standing before the door, key in hand, he examined the fluorescent speck, then looked swiftly up and down the landing. Without touching the door, he pocketed his key, stole silently away.

Outside on the sidewalk he glanced up at the windows of his apartment, noticed that they were in darkness. Crossing the road, he went to the corner drugstore, phoned Hansen.

"I've got an ant-eye cathode ray tube buried in my door. It lights up if the door is opened by any means other than a special non-conducting key. It's alight now. Somebody's in there."

"Call the cops," Hansen suggested.

"That was my first thought, but now I've got a better idea. I want you to phone my apartment. If anyone answers, tell them it's the hourly police-check and demand to see me. If they've got the scanner covered when they answer, tell them the same and order them to uncover it." He grinned belligerently. "That should send them out on the run. I'll be behind to see where they run to."

"O.K.," Hansen agreed. "I'd like to know what all this is about, but I'll do it." He cut off.

With a casual air, Armstrong mooched out of the drugstore, made his way along the street, slipped into a dark doorway almost facing his apartment. His wait proved longer than expected. Fifteen minutes crawled by, then twenty. Nobody came out of the place, nobody went in. His impatience mounted. Darn it, had the invaders seen through the bluff? If so, it could only be because they knew Hansen by sight. That was a clue, of a sort.

He glanced frequently at his watch while waiting for results. The vigil had lasted twenty-two minutes when a couple of cars suddenly swung into the street, raced along it, stopped before the doorway he was watching. Four uniformed cops tumbled out of the first machine. Hansen emerged from the second, looked searchingly up and down the street.

Coming out from his hiding-place, Armstrong crossed the road. "What went wrong?"

"I phoned three times," Hansen told him, "and could get no reply. Neither could I get hold of you again. So I called the cops."

"Humph!"

"I thought maybe by this time you'd bulled your way in and got bopped, so I brought along some muscle. Come on, let's see what's doing."

The sextette marched up to the inner door on the panel of which the tiny tell-tale still glowed. Inserting his key, Armstrong eased the lock, flung the door wide. A beefy cop promptly shoved him aside, got through ahead of him, gun in hand, his other hand feeling for the light switch. The lights went up. The cop took four paces, stopped and ejaculated, "By cripes, a stiff!"

Pressing through behind him, the others had a look. The entire apartment was an unholy mess. Cupboards and drawers stood open, their contents scattered over the floor. Loose papers fluttered in the breeze through the door. Even the carpets had been torn up and tossed to one side.

In the middle of this litter a corpse reposed in an armchair, its leisurely sprawl being in eerie contrast with the general upset around it. The body's attitude was one of careless indifference, there was no blood visible upon it, indeed nothing to indicate that it lacked life except that its head lolled forward upon its chest.

Putting one hairy hand under the cadaver's chin, the leading cop lifted it gently and revealed its face. "Dead, all right!" He ran his gaze over the others. "Anyone know him?"

Frowning at the lean, blue-jowled features and the thick, tousled hair of the corpse. Armstrong said: "I'm not positive about it, never having seen him in person, but I think he's a guy named Clark Marshall."

"The rocket nut?" Hansen put in quickly.

Armstrong nodded. "If you'll call Bill Norton of the *Herald* and give him an eyeful over the phone, he might identify him— he knew Marshall well."

Trying the phone, the cop jiggled it repeatedly, then put it down with, "Out of action. Disconnected some place." His eye was professional as it went over the disarray. "Whoever did this was in a heck of a hurry." He shrugged, said to the other officers, "O.K. I'll go down to the car and call the homicide boys. I'll tell them to pick up this Norton." He went out.

One of his fellows said to Armstrong: "Generally speaking, prowlers don't bump and bumpers don't prowl. Looks like you've had both here, for once. Any idea of what they were after? If so, you'd better look and see whether they got it."

"I've not the remotest notion of what they were seeking," Armstrong confessed. By his side, Hansen smiled and emitted an exaggerated yawn. Turning to the sceptical agent, he went on, "It's a fact. I've not the slightest idea of what they were after." He paused, added with vicious satisfaction, "But, with luck, I'll soon know who did it."

"Your confidence in me is most flattering," said Hansen.

"Modesty, thy name is Hansen," he scoffed. "If I leaned solely on other guys, I'd never get any place, even though they do hold my dough. I wasn't thinking of you, nor of the police. What was on my mind was the main stem of the wall clock."

"Oh." A little disconcerted, Hansen went to the big time-piece fixed to the farther wall. Now that he was close to it, he could see that its stem was thicker than usual and that something lens-like gleamed within its cap. But for the other's remark, he realized, he could have gone over that room a hundred times and never noticed this feature. He licked his thin lips in anticipation.

While the three cops looked on in unconcealed surprise, and the corpse reposed languidly in its chair, Armstrong gently pulled the clock outward until something behind it emitted a sharp, metallic click. He then turned it round and round, as if unscrewing it, got it free from its fastenings, laid it face upward on the table. Examining it curiously. Hansen noted that its stem was now an empty tube; he could see right through it.

Working at the wall-cavity formerly concealed by the clock, Armstrong carefully disconnected several wires, drew out a small, silvery instrument fronted with a thin, lens-capped tube, This he put on the table beside the clock.

"Inside that," he told them, "is seven hundred feet of one millimetere talking film. It may have been exposed. Whatever works that tell-tale on the door should start this going as well. We'll get it developed. If the gods are with us, this affair is in the bag."

"Boyoboyoboy!" whispered one of the cops, then added even more reverently, "Oh, boy!"

He started on the job immediately, and was still at it when the homicide crew poured in with Norton. The latter came at him excitedly.

"It's Clark, sure 'nuff! For Pete's sake!—I was talking to him earlier in the day."

"Were you?" Dexterously he clipped the developed magazine to the fixing tank, commenced winding it through. "Did he say he was coming round here?"

"I sent him round here. I got in touch with him yesterday, told him that you'd gone just as daffy as he was and that you wanted to see him, as one loony to another. He turned up this morning. I tried to phone you about six times to tell you that he was in town."

"I was out. I spent most of my time at F.B.I. headquarters."

"He was like a cat on hot bricks," Norton went on. "Restless and leery. He acted like he was haunted by his grandfather's ghost. In the end, I gave him your address and he said he'd look you up later today." Norton ran a hand through his untidy hair. "I didn't think he was naming his death spot!"

With an eye on the watch, Armstrong kept the tank rotating. "What d'you mean, he was restless and leery? Did he behave as if in danger of his life?"

"Well, no, I wouldn't say that. He was more like a guy who expects to be strapped in a strait-jacket the first time he blows his nose. He seemed like he was nursing something he'd rather not have known, something decidedly frustrating." Norton peered at the tank. "What the blazes are you doing—making butter?"

"I hope so. I'm trying to grease the skids under someone!"

A police captain lumbered in, edging Norton to one side. "Are you John J. Armstrong?"

"That's me."

"The medic says that guy's been dead about three to four hours. Cause unknown—but we'll find it later." He stared at the tank which Armstrong was still revolving. "Where were you between three and four hours ago?"

"At F.B.I. headquarters."

"Huh?" The captain jerked as if given a mild shock. "If the Feds have an interest in this case, I'd better give them a ring pronto."

"It would be just as well," Armstrong endorsed. Pulling the film's dummy end from the tank, he inserted it into the electric dryer, began to wind it through. He winked at Norton as the captain went out.

Hansen stuck his head through the doorway. "How long?"

"Five minutes."

"I've rolled down the screen and connected the projector."

"Thanks." Still winding, he heard the phone ring in the next room, said phlegmatically to Norton, "Looks like they've managed to reconnect it. Bet you that's Mrs. Saunders calling from Hartford to say there's hell to pay. You go take the call and tell her not to worry."

As Norton turned to go, a cop entered and announced, "The phone's O.K. now. There's a caller on who says she's been trying to get through for hours, a Mrs. Saunders, ringing from Hartford. She says your laboratory has been broken into and it's in a deuce of a state. She's got the Hartford police there now."

Norton gaped at the cop, then at Armstrong, then back at the cop. He swallowed hard. "Dump me in the den and call me Daniel!" he said to the cop. Then he made for the phone.

Reeling through the last of the film, Armstrong spoke to the openly mystified police officer. "He's taking that call. I guessed that the lab would have been tossed around, after seeing the mess here. Not likely that they'd give one place the works and overlook the other." Sliding a random section of the film into the microreader, he stared through its convex glass viewplate, whistled between his teeth. "Verily, the trap was sprung!"

Taking the evidence into the other room, he threaded it into the projector. There were now five uniformed bulls in the room, plus four plainclothes ones and Hansen and Norton. The latter finished soothing Mrs. Saunders, slammed down the phone.

"She says the whole place is upside-down, and she doesn't know what's missing, if anything."

Armstrong grunted, switched off the lights, switched on the projector. Its brilliant beam cut sharply across the room, lit up the little screen on the opposite wall. A tiny picture of the room, three feet by two, appeared on the screen. It showed the door slowly opening.

A man slipped cautiously through the door, closed it behind him, made certain that it was properly fastened before he gave the room a swift appraisal. Of medium height and build, he was sandy-haired and wore a grey suit.

"The guy from Cypress Hills," breathed Hansen, poking Armstrong in the hip.

Crossing to the small oak bureau at the left-hand side of the door, Sandy-hair deftly forced it open, went through its contents as if he had not a second to spare. Papers and documents were ripped out, scanned hastily, thrown down at random. Evidently he did not find the mysterious item for which he was seeking. With the bureau empty, he raked it for hidden drawers, tapped it on all sides, upended it and examined its base. Satisfied that nothing more could possibly be concealed within it, he turned his attention to the duralumin writing-desk, dealt with it at the same frantic speed. He had no luck there, either.

For a moment, he paused and faced the little lens hidden in the clock. His pale-blue eyes stared directly into the camera

56

without showing any suspicion of the thing's betraying watch. His face was alert, calculating, and contained a hint of impatience.

With renewed energy, he set to, removed all books from the bookshelves, shaking them thoroughly one by one, examining the empty spaces thus left on the wall. From there, he turned his attention to the chairs and settee, upending them, tapping them all over. A few ornaments were scrutinized, the carpets torn up, and he got down on hands and knees to study the floorboards beneath.

Dissatisfied, he disappeared into the bedroom at left, removing himself from range of the lens. Though he had gone off the screen, the film continued to reproduce the noises of his moving around and the occasional shift of furniture as he gave it a going-over. This continued for a couple of minutes, at the end of which someone rapped heavily on the door.

Sandy-hair reappeared. With quick, catlike step, he approached the door, stood warily at one side of it, his pale eyes on the lock, one ear close to the jamb. From his pocket he extracted an object resembling a small, brightly plated torch, and this he held ready in his right hand.

The invisible caller knocked again. Sandy-hair waited without moving. A pause, then a third knock. For about three minutes Sandy-hair stood there, his eyes and ears alert, the torchlike object still in his grip. Then the film ran out. Armstrong upped the lights.

"Jeepers!" wailed the police captain. "If only there had been more footage!"

"That was the punk we traced to Cypress Hills," Hansen asserted. He looked gloomily at the body which had been moved to the settee and which reposed there under a sheet. "Pity you couldn't pick up the scene after he came in. I wonder what happened?"

"Ten to one, he didn't go away, as that sandy guy thought he would," hazarded the captain. "He knocked three times, gave it up, wandered off for a paper or cigarettes or something, came back in short time, sat down outside the door and waited for Armstrong to return. So when this sandy-haired snooper opened the door to go out, the waiting guy had him red-handed. What happened after that is anyone's guess, but this sandy guy is the one we want." He eyed Hansen. "You know where he lives, eh?"

"I know where I followed him to the other evening." He gave the address in Cypress Hills. "The Feds followed him there, too. Maybe they know where to pick him up."

"We'll see about that." The captain turned to Armstrong. "You'll have to hand over this film of yours—it's essential evidence. Momma, what sweet evidence it is!" His beefy features were admiring. "As nice a trap as I've seen in a naughty lifetime. I congratulate you on it. Pity you hadn't another one like it at your place in Hartford."

"There is another one. I'll tend to it directly you're finished with me here."

"Then you can get on the job right now. I'm durned if I see any reason to detain you."

"O.K." Feeling in one pocket, Armstrong found his door key, gave it to Hansen. "Lock up for me, will you? I'll call at your office immediately I get back." His attention shifted to the police captain. "If the Feds turn u,p, you'll have to do the explaining."

With a nod to the unseeing Norton, who by now was hurriedly scribbling data on a pad about the late Clark Marshall, he went out, got into his car.

His driving was very fast without being furious. His thoughts were mixed but not muddled. His grey eyes steadily watched the road ahead with a casualness which belied his alertness; now and again, briefly and without expression, the eyes flickered over the rear-view mirror, then returned to the streaming road.

He had been running little more than an hour when he reached the roundabout where five roads converged. This was as good a spot as any. Disregarding a heavy lorry thundering in from his right, and putting a sudden strain on the brakes of two sedans speeding in from the leftward road, he whirled his big machine right around the circle, regained the road from which he'd just emerged. There, he swung his car sideways across the path of the green tourer which had been following him for the last half-hour.

Swift as this tactic had been, the green tourer's driver was not disconcerted. Finding his path so suddenly blocked by Armstrong's automobile, and the other half of the road occupied by the oncoming lorry, he braked in the nick of time, stopped within a yard of the obstruction, rammed into reverse gear, backed in a half-turn.

He made the turn all right, his rear wheels well over the verge, but as he again switched gear to go forward, Armstrong reached the driver's door, jerked it open, grabbed the sandy-haired man's left arm.

CHAPTER FIVE

LIKE many of his buffalo-build, Armstrong seldom realized his own strength. He snatched Sandy-hair out of the car as if the fellow were a rag doll. His huge fist slammed Sandy-hair straight in the pan. The victim soared a couple of yards and went out like a light. It was as easy as that.

Mildly surprised that one of his haymakers should prove so slumbersome, he licked his knuckles, looked around, discovered that he had an audience. The lorry had stopped fifty yards down the road, its driver leaning far out of his cab and gaping back curiously. One of the two sedans had pulled up on the farther side of the road, and from it an immensely fat woman and a load of kids were giving him bug-eyes as if he'd done it for the movies. A long, racy-lined black limousine was easing to a stop behind his own stalled machine, and the two men therein were making to get out.

Finding a handkerchief, Armstrong rolled the unconscious Sandy-hair on to his face, got his hands behind him, prepared to tie his wrists together. The pair from the car reached him, studied the scene with quiet interest. Both were big and burly, though not quite as big as Armstrong himself. One of them put out a foot, nudged the reclining captive.

"You beat us to it, Mr. Armstrong," remarked one of the pair. He flashed a gold badge in the palm of his hand. "We're federal officers." He gazed thoughtfully at the recumbent form. "We picked him up immediately he picked you up. It's unfortunate that you bopped him, though. Might have been better if you'd let him string along—he'd have gained enough string to tie himself up."

"You're somewhat behind the times," said Armstrong, curtly. "He's tied up already. He's wanted by the police."

"Oh, well, in that case you've done a mighty neat piece of work," the other acknowledged. "We could have grabbed him ourselves, only they don't always remember to tell us these things." He pulled out a set of handcuffs. "Leave him to us— we'll take him in for you."

"I'd be very much obliged to you," pronounced Armstrong, carefully, "were it not for the fact that I dislike the way your ears stick out."

With that, he smacked the other in the teeth. The kick of a stung horse might have been milder. The fellow laid flat with a spine-tingling thump.

Armstrong ducked coincidentally with the thump. The fat woman, who was still watching open-mouthed, must have credited him with eyes in the back of his head, for the stricken one's companion swiped his blackjack through thin air, stumbled, half-fell over Armstrong's broad back and promptly was tip-tossed the rest of the way to ground. Armstrong made a dive for the first one now struggling to rise, and his heavy foot trod on the second one's stomach as he jumped. It was accidental but at least would serve to keep him prostrate a while.

Sheer speed, unusual in so large and heavy a man, had brought him swift victory but now proved his undoing. As he pounced upon the one striving to rise, Sandy-hair came suddenly to life, stuck out an intervening leg at precisely the right moment. Armstrong tripped, went down with a weighty wallop.

Breathlessly, he rolled on to his back, heard the fat woman emit a queer, high-pitched yelp. Somebody snatched at his feet. There came a short glimpse of pale-blue eyes staring into his own, then his noggin seemed to explode. An unknown comet arrived in the depths of his brain before all faded to utter blackness.

His senses crept back slowly and reluctantly while he lay flat on his back in the grass, with a rising lump on his cranium. A dull, pulsating ache registered painfully at the back of his eyes. Blinking to clear his vision, he saw the lorry driver and a motor-cycle cop bending over him. He sat up, nursed his throbbing head, looked around. The fat woman's sedan had disappeared, as also had the machines of Sandy-hair and the other two. His own car had been straightened up and a police motor-cycle stood behind it.

"Ugh!" he grunted, fondling his head tenderly.

"Them three guys slugged you and beat it," the lorry driver informed. He looked apologetic. "They did it so quick and got out so fast that I wasn't able to get their numbers."

61

"My buddy's after them, anyway," put in the cop. "We came along a minute later, so maybe we'll be able to put the bee on them yet." He eyed Armstrong with an air of official speculation. "Maybe you can identify them?"

"I don't know them at all—or not yet!" Armstrong replied lugubriously. Struggling erect, he held his head to stop it splitting in halves. "Two of them tried to kid me they were federal agents detailed to follow me around. Looks like they were really an escort for the third guy."

"How did you know they weren't Feds?"

"I've never heard of F.B.I. boys tearing around in foreign sports models or using European-type cuffs."

"There goes another charge," mused the cop. "It's a serious one ; impersonating a law officer. I'll have to make a report in any case. Give me your name and address." Turning to the lorry driver, he added, "Yours, too—you're a witness." Having noted the details, he said to Armstrong, "How far are you going?"

"To Hartford."

"It's out of the bailiwick, but who cares? I'll tag along. If someone's laying for you they're liable to try again."

Sliding into his driving-seat, Armstrong started off, the police motor-cycle hammering steadily behind. Driving wasn't so good with one's head bulging like a toy balloon at every stroke of the pulse. His aching eyes strained at the windshield and he felt more than soured on himself. It hadn't proved so smart a move after all, grabbing Sandy-hair like that. All he'd got out of it was a knob on the pate.

Or was that all? Come to think of it, there was one item he didn't possess yesterday—he had the sound assurance that his seemingly eccentric search for pieces of a seemingly imaginary puzzle was no longer either pointless or senseless. Somewhere there was a picture of some sort if only he could build it up, if only he could find and assemble the various pieces. His home and his laboratory had not been searched in a spirit of good, clean fun. He had not been tailed by Sandy-hair—and said elusive person had not been dragging a rescue party—merely to lend verisimilitude to crackpot notions. Behind all this was a purpose, a motive that might be made manifest if he persisted in his fad long enough and had a small measure of luck. Dark the purpose might be, and perhaps deadly, but *it was there*!

These thoughts soothed him so much that he arrived in Hartford in much better spirits. The motor-cycle cop dropped him with a double toot on his horn and zoomed back for his own territory. Mrs. Saunders met him, wringing her hands nervously and assuring him that she'd gone out for only a couple of hours. "And this is what happens immediately me back's turned."

Easing her agitated mind with a few words, he extracted the hidden camera from its lair, processed the film, ran it through the projector.

What he got was very similar to the scene recorded on the other film except that here the searcher proved to be a thin, sunken-cheeked individual who raced through his task without being disturbed by any knocker on the door.

Two Hartford plainclothes-men arrived and he ran the film again for their benefit. But neither of them recognized Hollowcheeks. They departed with the evidence, after which he tidied the lab, checked its contents, decided that nothing of any importance was missing.

Everything suggested that both searchers had failed to find the mysterious object they were seeking. What were they looking for? Was it something he carried on his person? If so, he'd better watch out!

It was three days before Hansen saw him again. The languid Miriam showed him into Hansen's office where he sat restlessly in a squeaking chair.

"I'm dumbfounded by the speed at which we get no place," announced Armstrong tiredly.

Hansen frowned, fished inside his desk, found the key to Armstrong's apartment, tossed it across. "Whenever I get somewhere it's because I know where I'm going. How the blazes d'you expect me to make progress when I'm working in the dark? All you want are reports, reports and more reports, except occasionally when you scream for help."

"Too bad," Armstrong sympathized. "I wouldn't keep you in the dark if I could see any light myself."

"D'you seriously mean to tell me you're barging around like a drunken hippopotamus without knowing what it's all about?"

"Certainly I don't know! I wish to heck I did!"

"Ye gods!" Hansen was incredulous. "You push your nose into places, and dumps promptly get torn apart and people get slugged and others get bumped—and you don't know the score!"

"Look, all that happened was that I got a bee in my bonnet. The rest just naturally came along."

"Natch," said Hansen. "Some day a meat-wagon will come along." He frowned at his listener. "You will be in it." His frown grew deeper. "And nobody will know why." He leaned on his desk and scowled. "Neither will anyone know who's next."

"You've made a point there," Armstrong admitted. "It would be nice to know who's got to wait his turn while I get buried." A bright thought struck him, and he added enthusiastically, "Why, Hanny, it might be you!"

"I have not overlooked the possibility," said Hansen, grimly.

"Besides," Armstrong went on, "if I kick the bucket, people ought to know why I kicked it. The knowledge might persuade someone to take up where I left off. Then he'll get bumped and I'll have a friend in the hereafter."

"My business is confined to this earthly sphere," Hansen informed, stiffly. "Astral planes don't interest me unless they pay hard, solid, mundane cash."

"All right." Armstrong waved a hairy paw in bored dismissal. "I'll tell you what little I know, and a fat lot of good will it do you. I got the idea that repeated rocket failures were too many for accident or coincidence. Maybe there's something deliberate about them. Maybe somebody's doing it."

"Who?"

Armstrong favoured him with a look of scorn. "Why the devil d'you think I'm jouncing around like a caged monkey if I knew that?" He waited, but Hansen said nothing, so he went on. "That was a premise I adopted mostly for my own amusement, or for some other reason I'm quite unable to explain. If that premise is wrong, all my conclusions will be wrong no matter how logically I proceed from one to the other. Let me say again, I took as my premise that rocket failures are being arranged by persons unknown. What's the logical consequence of that?"

"Go on—it's your talk."

"The failures belong to different times, different experimental groups and different countries. Ergo, even a superbly clever crank could not be responsible for the lot. That, in turn, sug-

64

gests an organization which, since its sabotage is so widespread, must be truly international and quite without any patriotisms. This is where the first snag comes in." He rubbed his broad chin in thought. "Those Russkis might like to prevent us reaching Mars ahead of them; the French similarly would like to delay the British; and so with practically every count you can think up—but why should any international organization want to stop anyone getting there no matter who it is? What do they gain by that? Where's their motive?"

"Search me," said Hansen, shrugging.

"I don't see the sense of it," Armstrong admitted, "and this lack of motive is the main thing which has got me bothered. A week ago, I could conceive two solutions: firstly, that they're selling their services to each country in turn, in which case they'd have been found out for a gang of double-crossers by now. Or, secondly, that I'm nuts and am imagining things." He rubbed his head vigorously. "However, I didn't imagine this cracked skull."

"Maybe you're digging for something that doesn't exist and unwittingly unearthing something else," suggested Hansen. "Like the guy who started digging for water and got up a corpse."

"Possible, but not probable." He mused a moment. "All the same, if there is an organization in existence, the technique is to look for it among all possible suspects, and expect it to be in some innocuous guise. That's why I'm keeping you busy with reports. I want to rake the suspects for a common denominator."

"Ah!" commented Hansen, his eyes sparkling, and again, "Ah!"

"Trouble is that I've not yet got enough reports and that complications keep catching up on me. Did you get any British and French letters, by air mail?"

Hansen extracted four from a drawer. "Sorry, I should have given them to you right away. They came yesterday afternoon." He twisted his signet ring around and around while contemplating the other. "I take it you want reports on the eleven guys mentioned in those letters?"

"Yes, sure!" Armstrong finished reading the last one, handed them back. "Well, a few of them responded. It was more than

I expected. You've only got to say, 'Boo!' to some people to make 'em clam up." Shoving his hands deep down into his pockets, he stretched out his legs, and sighed. "All I need is the butt of a monogrammed cigarette from the scene of each crime and a dramatic showdown with the guy who smokes them. That's what happens in the movies." He gloomed pessimistically at his listener. "Have you ever proved that crime doesn't pay with the aid of a monogrammed butt?"

"Things don't happen that way," scoffed Hansen. "Or not while I'm around. I have to swim my way through a sea of sweat—but I get there just the same, eventually."

"That's the hell of it. Every time we think we're getting somewhere, we find we're getting nowhere. Sandy-hair disappears, along with his rescuers, and nobody's seen a hair of them since. The Cypress Hills address proves to be a rented apartment stripped of all clues. Nobody can get a line on the punk who raked my laboratory. Clark Marshall dies of cardiac thrombosis, just like Bob Mandle, and all the medical experts tell me to think nothing of it."

"Now there's something," put in Hansen. "Aren't they doing anything about it?"

"What can they do? They swear that all the evidence satisfies them that neither man's condition could be brought on by artificial means. Neither had eaten, drunk or been injected with anything that might cause it. So far as can be ascertained, both deaths were entirely natural in spite of the fact that the last took place in highly suspicious circumstances. So that is that!"

They were silent a long time, brooding while their thoughts worked at top pressure, then Hansen remarked: "Come to think of it, all these guys about whom you want reports have one thing in common."

Armstrong sat up, drawing in his legs. "What's that?" he inquired, sharply.

Hansen said, "They're all alive."

Shoving out his legs again Armstrong relaxed. "Of course they are. Fat lot of use getting data on dead men."

"Why not? Some of them might have shared this elusive common denominator of yours when living."

"True enough."

"In addition to which, some of them may have died naturally."

"Meaning what?"

"Some of them may have curled up with cardiac thrombosis."

"Boy, they might, indeed!" He tossed the idea to and fro. "Supposing we tracked down a dozen who died that way—what of it? Any medic will tell us that a dozen kick the bucket the same way, every day, in New York alone. Mind you, I'd still think it means something. But what does it mean?"

"You've a notion of what it means," suggested Hansen shrewdly. "You pulled a fast one on Sandy-hair with that camera of yours, but the camera itself showed that Sandy-hair pulled a fast one, too. You're not half-blind and dopey. Dollars to doughnuts, you saw what I saw and have thought about it fifty times since." He twiddled the ring again. "And since officialdom has confiscated the film it's a dead cert that the cops are ruminating the same notion, or soon will be."

"Yes," Armstrong admitted slowly. "That thing Sandy-hair was holding as he stood by the door. It looked like a torch, but who'd face the light behind an opening door with a torch ready in his hand? It's illogical. Nevertheless, he went for it just as if he were going for a gun—and it wasn't a gun." He stared at the other. "That fellow's very stance and expression told that the object was a weapon of some sort. My guess is that it was a gas projector."

Hansen nodded. "That was my conclusion. When he came face to face with Marshall, he gave him a squirt that laid him out." He licked thin lips. "I can theorize about that weapon only in terms of the known, although the known isn't always the familiar. I don't accept that it could be any absolutely novel gadget. I concluded that it was a pocket gas projector. So yesterday afternoon I rang up Dr. Lowry, and asked if he knew of any gas that could cause cardiac thrombosis."

"And what did he say?"

"He said the idea is absurd."

"There we go again—nowhere," Armstrong grumbled.

"He poured out a flood of ten-dollar words that all meant the same thing—no gas could cause it." Licking his lips again, he added, "But——"

"Go on! You're not tongue-tied!"

"But a gaseous irritant powerful enough to bring on respiratory convulsions might cause death to a person already in a certain condition of thrombosis." He carried on to explain it more ghoulishly. "The victim would heave his pulse sky-high and pump the clot into his heart."

"That tells us a heck of a lot," declared Armstrong, down in the dumps again. "I saw Mandle slide out. I saw him with my own two eyes. He didn't even cough."

"I know. I checked up on Mandle myself. I checked on Marshall's autopsy, too. He wasn't gassed, or not with anything that left a trace in his lungs. Neither had he had convulsions—that's definite."

"So we're back at the start. Sandy's gas-projector didn't project gas." His bushy brows drew together. "Here we go round the mulberry bush."

"You owe me a century," Hansen reminded. "That's the way the money goes—pop goes the weasel."

Armstrong stood up, paid it over. "Momentarily, it's an impasse. I'll bust out of it somehow, even if I have to stick out my neck until someone can't resist taking a chop at it. However, I may be able to strike a new line when I've got all of your reports. A few aren't enough for my purpose. I need the lot—and the sooner the better."

"Leave it to me," said Hansen, easily. "I'll get the job finished as soon as possible. I'm combining it with a line of my own."

His hand holding the door half-open, Armstrong paused on his way out. "Mind telling me?"

"The search-line. Those guys didn't go through your apartment and your laboratory just for the ducks of it. They were looking for something even though we don't know what. Now if any others on these lists of yours have been searched or slugged, it might give me a pointer. I'm digging data on that angle."

"You're wasting your time." Armstrong watched interestedly as Hansen opened his mouth, then closed it without saying anything. He continued: "I've played that angle until I'm pretty sick of it. It always gets me the same place, namely, that the Feds know the object of the search, but won't tell. Those guys were looking for something I haven't got and am not supposed to possess. Either they wanted to discover what it is, or else they wanted to make sure I haven't got it."

"And the Feds refuse to blat?"

"Yes."

"Then it's Old Whiskers' biz." Hansen rubbed his forehead wearily. "Hell's bells! We sink deeper and deeper every minute without knowing what we're sinking into."

Hunching his broad shoulders in phlegmatic resignation, Armstrong closed the door, went to his apartment.

Hansen or someone had tidied up the place before locking it, a fact for which he was duly grateful. Shucking his overcoat, he slung it on to a hook, dug out the spy camera, reloaded it, set it for action, fitted it back into its hiding-place.

Then he phoned Claire Mandle. She bloomed into his screen as neat and as pert as ever.

"Oh, it's you, Mr. Armstrong!"

"John!" he insisted.

"Tut!" she came back. "We haven't been introduced."

"That's why I insist on John. It's rather too early for anything more endearing."

"From which I gather that you're not calling me in any official capacity, but because of the flowers that bloom in the spring, tra-la. Once again you have an ulterior motive." Her sigh was annoyingly melodramatic. "Very well, you may pursue the matter—John!"

"Look," he ordered, "I called to see whether we could meet again some place."

"Undoubtedly we could. I don't know that we should."

"I wanted to ask you an important question."

"Gracious! So soon?" She gazed at him in mock surprise.

He went on, his voice rising: "If you won't give me the opportunity to discuss it in person, I'll have to ask you now."

Her response was to lower her eyes modestly, an able performance which he observed with gradually reddening face.

Taking a hold on his emotions, he gritted: "Has anyone cased your place and gone through your papers of late?"

Startled, she looked up. "How on earth did you know?"

"So someone has!" he observed grimly. He made full use of the heaven-sent opportunity to get tough with her. "If you want the whys and wherefores, it's got to be over a cuppacawfee and not over this phone."

"That's your ultimatum?"

"It is."

"Bully!" she defined. "All right, I'll give in. I'll come quietly. Tonight?"

"Wow!" he enthused, thinking it childish and not caring.

Her smile was genuine. "Same place, same time?"

"Or sooner!'

He watched her fade out of the screen, then kicked a cushion across the room, bounced it a few times on his head. Then he smacked his hands together, said "Wow!" a couple of times, and sobered down sufficiently to have a shave.

Dead on time again, she turned up in a slick, tailored costume and a little deerstalker which was recognizably a hat.

"Well," she began, when they were seated, "are you going to let me in on the mystery?"

He sat facing her, arms crossed on the table, and gazed at her intently, without answering. The gaze went on a long time and, after a while, her tilted eyes widened slightly, she produced a compact, opened it, inspected herself in its mirror. She failed to find the suspected smut on her nose. Replacing the compact, she leaned forward, gave him a smart rap on the knuckles.

"Animate yourself! I asked you a question!"

Shaking his head slowly and profoundly, he said: "Fancy, all that and brains as well!"

"What's the matter?"

"Nothing's the matter. That's the point. Why should you alone be perfect?"

"You need glasses," she scoffed. "Besides, would you rather have me dopey?"

"Heaven forbid!" he prayed fervently. "But even if you didn't know the day of the week, I would still——"

She rapped his knuckles again, harder this time. "This is the Longchamps, not the Zoo! Pull yourself together and tell me about these prowlers."

Opening his mouth, he intended to retort, "You started it," but changed his mind and said: "Oh, yes. My place got a rake-over three or four days back. So did my lab in Hartford. What they were looking for is a mystery which has got me bothered." He eyed her carefully. This was delicate. He'd have to be careful not to ham the job. "Since this occurred soon after our last talk, I wondered whether there was any connection. That is to say, maybe we were suspected of sharing information of some sort—in which case you should have been victimized, too."

"I see." She was frankly mystified. "What on earth could we share which would justify a search?"

"We might have shared whatever they sought at your place," he riposted.

It didn't faze her. On the contrary, she was more puzzled than ever. "Somebody sneaked in yesterday, went through all my documents, left my desk and my library in a mess, but took nothing."

"You're sure that no item is missing?"

"I'm positive."

"None of Bob's papers, for instance?"

"None of those, either." Her glance was quizzical. "What has Bob got to do with it, anyway?"

"All I know is that he was concerned in a government job which is a top secret."

"Who told you that?"

"The F.B.I."

There was no way of telling whether this information hit home. She had excellent self-control, and took it coolly. Her manner was deliberately reflective as she thought it over.

"Bob was involved in something concerning space-rockets. I do know that. Just what he was up to is not apparent from any papers he left behind, except that he'd developed his Layer Theory. Evidently he kept nothing which concerned work for the government; presumably he passed his stuff straight to the government and destroyed the rest. Bob always was very methodical and extremely cautious."

"As he should be if mixed in a top secret job," Armstrong approved.

"Since rocket number eighteen is under construction at the present moment," she went on, "it looks very much as if Bob was busy with something concerning it. Possibly number eighteen will be an extra-special construction incorporating a revolutionary idea which the authorities are keeping to themselves."

"Number eighteen is practically a dead duck," he contradicted. He told her all he knew of the rocket, detailing his recent visit to New Mexico, his sparring match with Fothergill,

71

and what he'd since learned from Quinn. "I don't know what you think," he concluded, "but to me those hold-ups look somewhat deliberate, as if the rocket is being delayed as much as possible without making the fact too obvious."

The information gave her subject for thought which occupied her mind quite a while. Her elfin eyes were serious with concentration as she examined the evidence.

At length, she said: "This poses a curious paradox. The ship is government-sponsored and yet some, though not all, of the snags look government-inspired. The government is trying to build the ship and, at the same time, to delay its completion. Maybe someone else wants to delay it also, and that complicates the situation, but let's ignore that factor and concentrate on the governmental aspect. Why should the powers-that-be try to build the vessel but not too soon?"

"It isn't lack of money for one thing. Ask me an easier one!"

"We've got to ask it. There's logic somewhere in this seeming illogicality."

"The only other solution I can think up isn't as plausible as it ought to be."

"What is it?"

"Maybe this top secret—whatever it is—needs futher development before it can be applied to the ship. So the vessel's construction is being held back in case of necessary alterations. But why start it one way and change it to another when, just as easily, they could have timed its commencement to fit in with new plans embodying new notions? I know that bureaucrats do nutty things, but not as nutty as that!"

Her small nose wrinkled in disapproval. "For my part, I don't think you've got it."

"Neither do I. You concoct me a better one."

She mulled it over again. He ordered drinks, and she was still occupied with the problem when her glass was empty. He spent the time studying her face. He was still gaping at her when suddenly her eyes brightened.

"Supposing that eighteen isn't a dead duck at all."

"O.K., suppose it isn't—then what is it?"

"A decoy duck."

"What!" he yelped.

"*Shsssh!*" She glanced around at the nearest tables. "Don't bellow like that!" Her voice became low, confidential. "Half the world has pondered the idea of systematic rocket-sabotage in its usual lackadaisical, apathetic way. The authorities are certain to have given the theory a lot of consideration. Now let's suppose they're ready to put a super-rocket on the stocks but are leery about all the queer things that have happened to its predecessors." Her look was sharp, penetrating. "What would *you* do?"

He smacked the table with a huge hand. "By gosh! I'd build it quietly and surreptitiously some place like the North Pole. And I'd build another, well-publicized one in New Mexico, for the saboteurs to play with."

"Brainy boy!" she admired.

Ignoring that remark, he went on, "One item has got me worried."

"You may open your soul to me."

"It's the way you gnaw at problems. Some day, some guy will have to think up some awful good excuses—or else!"

"That'll be his worry, won't it?" she pointed out.

"Sure! I told you I'm worrying already!"

For the first time, she pinked a little, a phenomenon he observed with lordly satisfaction. She was conscious of it, for she dug out the compact, dabbed at her face with a piece of lace. This, too, he studied with the same expression.

When she had finished, she said, tartly: "You can't con-certrate on two problems at once and get somewhere with both."

"That remains to be seen," he contradicted. He waved a waiter, and when fresh glasses had been brought, leaned forward confidentially. "Let's drop the cross-talk while I consult you about the state of my liver."

"Good gracious!" she murmured, taking a slow sip from her glass.

"These days I get the wackiest feelings," he went on doggedly. "I can't help wondering whether other folk get them too, or whether it's that I'm abnormal in some way."

"What sort of feelings?"

"A peculiar mixture of apprehension, irritation, suspicion and general nerviness."

"And when do you get them?"

"Most any time. I read the press-recorders and the feelings promptly come on. I look at the sky-signs and they come on.

I listen to the radio and they crowd in upon me. One moment I can be on top of the world—then the most insignificant thing suddenly hems me in. I'm getting more temperamental than a prima donna."

"You need a good dose of Vitalax," she diagnosed.

His scowl was heavy, ferocious. "That's precisely the sort of remark that does it! Every day and in every way I'm reacting more and more!"

Putting her glass down, she looked serious. "If I may say so, John, you should have a long rest."

"I don't think so. I was joking about my liver. Physically, I'm topnotch. The trouble is a mental one. It's got a cause." He regarded her levelly. "I don't know the cause but something keeps telling me it's an important piece of the puzzle I'm trying to put together."

"Do you really suggest that your irritability is connected with these rocket problems?"

"Claire, for the life of me I can't imagine how the one can possibly be connected with the other—nevertheless I am as certain of that link as ever I've been certain of anything."

"Have you tried to identify any causes and analyse them?"

"Yes, sure—but it doesn't work out. It only leaves me wondering what the heck's the matter with me." He glanced around moodily, and his eyes were slightly baffled when they returned to her. "For example, while watching the crows the other evening I noticed a dark-skinned, smooth-looking guy wearing a green turban. Obviously a swami; Shri Bannerji, or some name like that. Immediately my mind leaped to Hindu ascetics. I thought of those who stare fixedly at the sun for years and years until they go completely blind—then continue sightlessly staring for the remainder of their miserable lives. I thought of others who hold up one arm until it withers, and others who squat cross-legged until their nether limbs become shrunken and deformed and they have to be carried around. The feeling came on me. It came on in overwhelming strength. I felt jumpier than a cricket on a hot stove."

There was a queer light in her eyes as he came to the end of this recital. "How do you feel when with me? Seriously now—no wisecracks."

"Soothed," he told her. "Soothed and calm and placid."

Her laughter tinkled gently. "As if I were not of this world?"

74

"You're not quite an angel, thank goodness," he evaded. "You're a woman. I prefer you that way."

"That doesn't answer my question."

"I'll answer it," he said, surprisingly, "when I've managed to get hold of the facts."

Their eyes remained level, looking straight into each other's, while her phrase drummed in his mind as regularly, as rhythmically as a pulse. Not of this world . . . not of this world . . . not of this world. There was an idea, now! People not of this world!

She was the first to lower her gaze.

CHAPTER SIX

It was noon of the fourth day after Hansen's last report had arrived when Armstrong shoved aside the mass of papers littering his table, rubbed his heavily bearded jowls and reached for the phone.

"Is Hanny there?'

Miriam drawled: "I'll put you through to him, Client."

The dour face of Hansen grew into the screen. The agent said: "Did you get the bill?"

"Yes. The cheque's in the mail."

"O.K.! Anything more?"

"More? Ye gods, we've hardly started yet! I fancy I've found something in these reports. You'd better come round."

"Give me twenty minutes." Hansen faded out.

A quick shave refreshed Armstrong but failed to remove the lines of tiredness around his red-rimmed optics. He washed his eyes with an eye-bath, was blinking them when Hansen arrived. Towel in hand, he admitted the caller.

Grabbing a chair, Hansen slumped into it. "Well, Sherlock?"

"Out of one hundred seventeen reports I've found thirty-four suspects sharing one feature in common. What they share is membership in the Norman Club."

"Humph!" Hansen was not at all impressed.

"Ever heard of it?"

"Never." The agent waved a hand airily. "There are as many clubs in the world as fish in the sea. Most of them are no more than petty ego-inflatories. What's peculiar about the Norman Club?"

"Several things. For a start, it's international, although few people seem to know of it. There's a Norman Club in every country in the world and in practically every city of any size. It is extremely exclusive. Only its members know what it's about and the reason for its existence."

"Where did you dig up that dirt?"

"From the Central Registry. All clubs and organizations have to be registered, as you know. This one is said to be literary and strictly non-political. It's the bunk—there's something more behind it."

"Ho-hum," said Hansen. "So you want me to investigate this crowd?"

"No, I don't. I'm going to barge right into their local dump and get it myself, if possible." Giving his eyes a final rub, he tossed the towel on to its rack, sat down facing his listener. "I believe there's something to be got. Sandy-hair took his own escort around with him and I think it's a good notion."

"Run it your own way," said Hansen imperturbably. "So long as I get cash on the barrelhead."

"I want you hanging around back of me in case I get some place too tight." Leaning to one side, he stretched, opened a cupboard, took out a small, dull-black instrument with a tiny, cone-shaped mesh of fine wire swivelling on its top. Giving the thing to Hansen, he added a long, careful list of instructions and ended, "Make it six o'clock this evening, corner of Sixth and West Fifty-eighth. Once you've picked me up you're on your own—use your own judgment."

Hansen stood up, toyed doubtfully with the instrument, thrust it into his right-hand pocket. "So be it. I'll be there. But if you peg out with a blood clot I'll be some place else mighty fast! The Norman Club—pah!" He went to the door. "Probably a gang of punks who collect French literature—I hope!"

Grinning at him, Armstrong said nothing, watched him go out. He hadn't overlooked Hansen's half-jocular guess. The name of "Norman" suggested French origin or some sort of Frenchy connection. And there was a branch in Paris. But there were branches in other places where French literature would smack of coals to Newcastle. One city's poison was another city's meat. The Norman part of it, he concluded, had some significance quite different from the obvious. It wasn't necessarily French, or even European, or even—what?

Darn it, his brains were starting their antics again. Away his mind wandered, all on its ownsome, from proposition to proposition, each one successively wilder, and threatening to hand him some conclusion so elusive that he could get it in his grasp but not within his grip. It was the maddening dance of that conclusion which gave him the meemies; he knew that, knew it instinctively without being able to identify the cause.

Barely outside the realms of consciousness, just beyond the

border of comprehension lurked a shadowy theory which mocked his mind and jeered at him repeatedly.

"Come on, pal—come and get me! I spy, with my little eye! Yoo-hoo, big boy—you can't see me! Hidey, hidey, where do I bidey?—nobody knows but Old Mother Tidey!"

It was a ghostly idea. Or a ghastly idea. Or even a fact, a tremendous, world-shattering fact which deftly skipped out of his reach every time he made a snatch at it. It gibbered at him in the sky-signs; it hooted at him through the radio; it blared and blatted among the mobs in the streets; it gibbered derisively in the pompous speeches of leading figures; it whispered sibilantly through the lips of stone-blind ascetics, and it cackled amid a multitude of prayers.

"Some jeer at me for leaning all awry—what, did the hand then of the Potter shake?"

He was perspiring again. Heavy-footed and cumbersome, like a caged bear, he prowled up and down the carpet, up and down, up and down. The floorboards squeaked beneath his weighty tread. Up and down. What times does the Zoo open? Have they let the visitors in? Have they brought any buns? Who is the Potter, pray, and who the Pot? She will love Chiclemint. Chew-chew, baby. Violently, he kept punching his right fist into the palm of his left hand. Six o'clock—roll on six o'clock!

The Norman Club suggested a million dollars without being obtrusive about it. It had a huge, arched doorway set in an imposing greystone front which soared ten floors up. Within the doorway was a plate glass revolving door, and beside the door posed a commissionaire attired like a ten-star general in the Ruritanian army.

Mounting the wide marble steps leading to the door, Armstrong reached the top, at which point the general extended a white-gloved, gentlemanly hand and spoke in well-modulated, gentlemanly tones.

"I beg your pardon, sir."

"It is granted," said Armstrong with unhesitating generosity.

"Admission, sir, is permitted to members only."

"Oh." Armstrong tilted his hat forward, scratched the top of his neck. The general observed this indelicate operation with well-bred forbearance which told that membership of the club positively did not include people who scratched. Armstrong eyed him calculatingly. "How does one become a member?"

"One must be recommended, sir."

"By whom?"

"By a present member, sir."

"Ah, yes, of course." He gave the door a tentative jerk which started it spinning slowly. "It seems that I'll have to go inside and persuade my most influential friend to recommend me."

The general permitted himself a martial frown, took a step forward, put out a restraining arm. "I regret, sir——"

Carefully Armstrong put a big foot on the other's glossy boot and gave him an equally careful push in the chest. The general sat down suddenly and hard. With a swift glance up and down the street, Armstrong went through the revolving door, found himself in a thick-carpeted foyer.

Here, a distinguished individual with mirror-polished hair met him, took his hat and coat, gestured gracefully to the door at the farther end, and said: "That way, sir."

"Thank you." Wading through the carpet's high pile, he reached the door, looked back, noted that outside in the street the uniformed squatter had regained his feet and resumed his original pose. He was not attempting to come in, evidently being unsure of himself, or perhaps content to let those inside cope with the brusque invader. Smiling his satisfaction, Armstrong opened the door, entered the room beyond.

Softly the door closed itself behind him, emitted the faintest of clicks. The room's sole occupant—a man seated behind a distant desk—looked up. He was a swarthy, highly groomed individual with very black eyes.

Expressionlessly regarding his visitor, he spoke in cultured tones. "Glad to see you, Mr. Armstrong." His manicured hand indicated a chair. "Please take a seat." Then he pressed a stud on his desk.

Sitting cautiously, Armstrong rumbled: "So you know me?"

"Of course, of course." The other's laugh was short and artificial. "We have been expecting you. Our Mr. Rothman will be here to see you any moment. He won't be long, I assure you."

"All right." Armstrong crossed thick, powerful legs, glowered at the swarthy man who, quite unconcerned, began busily to attend to the papers on his desk.

We have been expecting you—how in the name of all that's holy could they possibly expect him? Nobody knew that he was coming except Hansen and, perhaps, Miriam. Unlocking his legs, he stood up, went to the door by which he had entered. He tried it. As expected, it was locked. He returned to his seat. The swarthy man hadn't bothered to look up, and continued nonchalantly to deal with his papers.

"Where's our Mr. Hansen?" Armstrong asked him.

The other glanced at him, black eyes quizzical. "Mr. Hansen?" He pondered a second or two. "Oh, yes, Mr. Hansen. We shall attend to him in due time, and if necessary." His eyes shifted to the second door at one side of his desk. "Here is Mr. Rothman."

Armstrong was on his feet, one hand in his pocket, as Rothman entered. The newcomer proved to be a big, heavily built man tending to fatness. He had a florid face, surmounted by a mop of curly white hair. Nodding affably at the swarthy man, Rothman advanced eagerly towards Armstrong with extended hand.

"My dear Mr. Armstrong! Delighted to meet you!" His grasp was firm and strong, his shake the essence of cordiality. Chuckling his pleasure, he slapped Armstrong on the back. "D'you know, I had a small wager that you would be here before another ten days had passed."

"Really?" said Armstrong glumly. This reception was the nuttiest item in the entire nutty set-up. It had him puzzled. "Who told you—Hansen?"

"My goodness, Mr. Armstrong, you wouldn't expect *that* of us, would you? We have sources of information so much more reliable." Chuckling again, and talking with friendly enthusiasm, he conducted Armstrong to the second door. At his desk, the swarthy man got on with his work and ignored them. Rothman went on: "I don't doubt that you'll find our outfit very different from what you may have anticipated—but so does nearly everyone who gravitates to us. We are quite a sober crowd, yes, quite a sober crowd." Reaching the door he opened it wide.

Armstrong, bang in the middle of the doorway, caught only the briefest possible glimpse of a group of half a dozen men around some unfamiliar piece of apparatus faintly resembling a gigantic movie camera. It gave him no time to ponder the scene, to do anything about it; not even to swing the clenched fist he had ready; not even to spring aside or flop to the floor.

The picture of the gadget and its waiting team registered in his eyes a split second before the machine emitted a tremendous blue flash, upon which his senses shot skyward and his big body collapsed. He lay as relaxed as a bundle of rags while a smell of ozone pervaded the room. Behind him, the swarthy man calmly shuffled his papers and continued with his writing.

He came to in a sumptuously furnished cell, dry-mouthed but unharmed. There was a bed, an inlaid table, a small bureau, a couple of deep, springy armchairs, a large electric radiator, a rack of expensively bound books and many other items not normally found in cells. Surveying them blearily, he ran a tongue like tinder around his parched palate, went to the corner wash-basin, worked the cold faucet for most of a minute.

There was no door to the cell, its place being taken by a heavy grille of inch diameter beryllium-steel rods. Going to the grille, he shoved his head between its bars, had a look along the passage outside. The facing wall was blank, but there was a cell on each side of the one he was occupying and presumably there were more still farther along.

Shaking the grille, he called: "Anyone at home?"

Somebody moved in the cell immediately at his right. Its occupant came to his own grille, but neither were able to see the other. Armstrong's invisible neighbour spoke, his voice that of a much older man.

"So you've recovered your senses, eh? I wondered how long it would take you to snap out of it. I've called you about ten times these last couple of hours. How did they get you?"

"I'm not sure. Something burst into a big blue light and I went out like I'd been slugged. Where are we?"

"That's what I wanted to ask you." The other was silent a moment, then said: "Anyway, now you're up and awake you can answer another question for me—an important one."

"Go ahead," invited Armstrong, straining futilely to peer farther through the bars.

"What is life?"

"Eh?"

"What is life?" repeated the other.

"Who cares?"

"I do. I care a lot. I've got to answer this one question at all costs. Upon my answer depends my neck. It may get broken. Or something worse, if there's anything worse. I don't know. But I've got to answer one question, and that is, 'What is life?'"

Taking a fresh grip on the grille, his knuckles whitening, Armstrong said between his teeth, "Who's put that question? Who wants the answer? Who's threatening to break your neck, and why?"

"If I tell you all those things," retorted the unseen man in the next cell, "you'll start thinking about them and won't seek the answer to my question. You find me an answer, a good one, and then I'll tell you what little I know." He stopped, emitted several deep, racking coughs, then continued: "You might as well sharpen your wits while you still possess them. It'll be your turn next. One question!—and for your sake I hope you find the answer!"

"What's this—a quiz game?"

"That's what they've made it. The losers get buried!"

"You're nuts!" defined Armstrong, positively.

Leaving the grille, he reclined in a chair, stared with jaundiced eye at the wall. Had he been smuggled into an asylum? By all accounts they were places easy to enter and almost impossible to leave. If so, who had put him in, and on whose authority? Was this the supremely smooth and crafty method by which pernicious influences got unwelcome snoopers out of the way? Or were his own many recent obsessions proof that he was not—normal?

Maybe that monstrous blue flash had been only a dream, a delusion. Maybe he'd flopped right into the surprised arms of an innocent and pally Rothman, the victim of an overdue nervous breakdown or something as bad. A tumour on the brain, perhaps. No, it couldn't be that—his brain could whirl and do side-slips, but it could still think, and he felt mentally fit despite all his past cerebral surgings.

His ruminating gaze shifted to the row of books, but his eyes did not see them, and his ears heard only faintly and inattentively the low, constant mumbling of the prisoner in the next cell. If they wanted to bump him they'd have done it before now—unless they wanted to get something out of him before slapping him down for ever. Perhaps they were after the mysterious information for which Sandy-hair had searched in vain. It wasn't likely that they needed only a satisfactory answer to one question. To make a victim purchase his life with a single pearl of wisdom was the height of imbecility. This quiz-palaver was the sheerest hooey!

"What is life?"

Despite his mental rationalizing, the question insisted on popping up repeatedly within his mind. It nagged at him until he got out of his chair, paced his cell several times, and eventually found himself back at the grille.

"Hey!" he called to his unseen neighbour. "What do *you* think life is?"

The other ceased muttering, came close to his bars. "When I was a kid I was taught that life is a stepping-stone to higher things. That's the answer I ought to give. But supposing it's not the one which satisfies them? Supposing they get that answer, and take me out and . . . and——"

"Well?" Armstrong prompted.

"I don't know. I'm not sure the answer's right—and it's *got* to be right! You'll know how right it's got to be when they ask you yours!"

Ignoring that sinister comment, he demanded: "How many other likely definitions have you thought up?"

The other hesitated, said doubtfully, "Life is growth."

"Crystals grow," Armstrong pointed out.

"That one's wrong then. How about life being motion?"

"Trees don't move of their own volition."

"They grow, though. And growth's a form of motion."

"Planets move. So do satellites, asteroids and various other whatnots which aren't exactly alive."

"Oh, for heaven's sake, if you can quibble they can quibble, too. I've thought of dozens and they've all got snags." His weary voice betrayed nervous strain. "One snag is enough." He was quiet for a while, then came back with, "If you had been asked it, what would you have said?"

Armstrong gave it considerable thought before he replied. slowly: "I'd say that life is a predicament of matter—and stand pat on that."

Unenthusiastically, the other murmured: "Thanks! I'll think

it over." Volunteering no further information, he went away from his grille and began muttering again.

He didn't have long to think it over. Within ten minutes a pair of burly, hard-faced men appeared in the passage, paraded past Armstrong's cell without so much as a glance inside, unlocked the grille next door. Armstrong stood behind his own grille to watch them return.

A moment later they came past, a stoop-shouldered, wizened man between them. Peering myopically over low-slung pince-nez, the prisoner stumbled as he walked along. The guards on either side of him were as impassive as a pair of sphinxes.

Armstrong said pleasantly to the nearest guard, "About two hundred pounds—you'll need eight feet of rope."

They might have been deaf mutes for all the effect it had. They went grimly on, the prisoner mumbling querulously between them. At the end of the passage the sound of their steps and the captive's voice cut off abruptly with a noise like that of a slammed door. All was silence. Evidently there was nobody in any of the other cells. Armstrong was alone with his thoughts.

He spent the following hour searching his cell for modest microphones, button-scanners or any other snooping oddments which might be installed. No soap. Upending the furniture, taking down all the books, seeking in every spot of which he could think, he had a busy time which kept him amused but brought no reward. If they'd planted anything of a spying nature, it was buried in the plaster. He'd have to tear down the walls and ceiling to find it.

Satisfied that there was nothing which he could uproot, he washed, brushed his teeth, tidied himself, glanced over the books. Momentarily, none of them interested him.

One of the guards came along shortly, pushed a supper tray under his grille, went away without a word. Breakfast arrived in the same manner the following morning. The food would have done credit to the snootiest hotel. It seemed that whatever fate they had in store for him included fattening up before the kill. Eating the lot with open relish, he decided that the menu provided his only cause for gratitude.

By dinner-time his appetite was spoiled by mordant thoughts about his still-absent neighbour. The old fellow—whoever he was—had not reappeared. Maybe he'd given the wrong answer and had suffered all that he'd anticipated. Maybe this lunatic stunt of making one's fate depend upon a single question was somebody's sardonic way of dealing with those who had asked too many questions. An eye for an eye.

But the Norman Club definitely was part of the mysterious picture, a cogent part, a key piece. Knowing it wasn't doing him much good, but Hansen also should know it by now—unless the dour agent was one of the best actors and the most accomplished liar Armstrong had ever encountered. Though his mind long had been obsessed by suspicions, he was not inclined to suspect Hansen. The arrangement between them had slipped up somewhere. It was due to his own foolhardiness. Fools rush in, and all that.

Lugubriously he felt in his vest pocket for the twentieth time. The something which should have been there was missing. They'd beaten him to the draw there! If only he'd been able to retain it, half the cops in New York would be bursting into this dump by now. The fact that they weren't was proof that the item was no longer functioning—they had known how to deal with it.

A few moments later all speculations were put away. His dinner was shoved under the grille and went cold before him. There was a clean white envelope propped against the carefully laid plate of fried chicken. Picking it off the tray, he tore it open, read its neat typescript aloud:

"Dear Mr. Armstrong: What may happen to you ultimately will be decided by the manner in which you find an answer to the simple question inscribed below. Of course, you will give it serious thought since your fate is a serious matter. Take your time about it—you will have at least two days in which to give it your most earnest consideration."

There was no signature. He looked at the six words printed in large block letters at the bottom of the note. His brain sideslipped, swung around in mad abandon so that his thoughts became a chaotic swirl. Dampness crept over his back. A multitudinous host of all the eerie feelings he'd ever experienced swept upon his revolted mind with the frightening impetuosity of a ghostly cavalry charge. A full quarter of the mystery-picture blazed before his grim, unseeing eyes, brilliant, in infernal colours. A vision of hell itself.

This was the pay-off! Gradually, draggingly, almost hypnotically, his eyes wandered back to those six fateful words.

"How do you know you're sane?"

CHAPTER SEVEN

Six words totalling a mere twenty-one letters yet demanding a response on which depended an unknown fate. True, the type-written note had made no direct mention of death; it derived its menace from what it left unsaid, from that which it left to the reader's imagination. What the quizmasters had in store for him could be anything, anything at all—but if they were powerful enough to defy world governments and delay the conquest of Mars by at least a couple of decades, then they were big enough to have no scruples about the way to deal with one man. Six words—they weighed as heavily as a corpse on a rope!

He scanned them for the third time, his eyes troubled, speculative, a little uncertain. The sentence was printed in blue pencil, boldly, confidently, challengingly, as if the writer had gloried in the satisfaction of posing an unanswerable problem.

How do you know you're sane?

Flipping the paper on to the top of the bureau, Armstrong sat himself at the table. He pushed the tray and its meal aside, held his head between his hands, his elbows on the table. Contrary to his earlier reactions he was no longer interested in the fried chicken. The sight of it didn't as much as stimulate his salivary glands. His reflex had been inhibited. That typed note was the Pavlovian bell—and the dog refused to drool!

Between his hands he let his thoughts play as they wished. If sane, they might get him somewhere even yet. If insane, they'd play despite him. Norton was right—yon Cassius, that's me! I think too much. Can I exist without thinking? "I think, therefore I am!" I am . . . what?

I am John J. Armstrong, or so it is alleged. I have made ingenious things conceived by John J. Armstrong. Some people have praised those things, have recognized them as products of sanity, have been kind enough to ascribe to me a touch of genius. And . . . and . . . genius is akin to madness! There I go again! Am I a borderline case? Have I prospered one side of the border and now slipped over to the other side? Is this the nut-hatch?

Anyway, what makes them think I'm not sane? How do they know that they're sane themselves? What is sanity? Is there any positive definition of that? If there is, who defined it—and how did he know that *he* was sane? How does *anyone* know they're sane?

HOW DO YOU KNOW YOU'RE SANE?

Answer: Of course I'm sane!

How do you know that?

I *must* be sane!

Why?

Because I'm sane in my own estimation.

So is every other lunatic!

They shoot horses, don't they? And they put lunatics away, don't they?

Oh, yes, the lesser lunatics incarcerate the greater ones. It has been said that the difference between those in jail and those not in jail is that the latter have never been found out. The difference between those in asylums and those not in asylums is——

"*Shut up!*" Armstrong was dumbfounded by the sudden and savage shout of his own voice. It shocked him outright; he left the table, began to pace his cell.

Don't worry about that, sonny boy. It's nothing—nothing at all. Crazy people often talk to themselves. Sometimes they shout. Sometimes they scream. Sometimes they shriek way up on the high notes, where only dogs can hear. Sometimes they whisper, whisper, whisper, while their red-lit eyes watch the thing which is not sitting on their shoulder. They do other things. They carry a talisman so they won't be run over in the street. They have a lucky number which controls their lives and, sometimes, when they do a thing, they repeat it the same number of times to "make sure." They touch door-knobs when they think nobody's looking, because it's a terrible thing to let a knob go untouched. They avoid stepping on the cracks between paving blocks because to step on a crack would split your soul. They make faces at themselves in the washroom mirror when nobody else is there to see. The lunatic needs solitude to expand his lunacy, to bring it to full bloom. But you don't do any silly things like those, sonny boy—or do you?

HOW DO YOU KNOW YOU'RE SANE?

Do you consider it incumbent upon you—in fact, imperative—to adopt a special attitude whenever a collection of brass instruments produce sonic vibrations in a certain sequence? What, you wouldn't do anything so ridiculous? Fifty million Frenchmen do it every time the band plays the *"Marseillaise"* —and fifty million Frenchmen can't be wrong, can they, sonny boy? Would you hold your right foot in your left hand every time you heard "Skiddin' with My Shiver-Kid" if a hundred million others did it too, and if they expected you to follow suit?

You would not?

You're a liar!

"Loonies are liars," said Armstrong to nobody. "They lie to themselves, persistently and glibly, because they can deceive themselves—because, being loonies, they live in a dream-world of their own. I am not a liar to myself. I am not a blithering imbecile. I talk to myself the better to co-ordinate my thoughts, as other people occasionally do. It is a symptom of introspection and has no bearing upon the question of sanity."

The little speech soothed him, but it failed to convince. He erred on the side of scepticism because he knew how remarkably easy it is to convince those who want to be convinced, and he had no intention of substituting emotional brain for mental reasoning. One must think with one's brain, not with one's glands. That should have some bearing upon this tormenting problem—the *mode* of thought determines sanity. If the cerebral processes follow a particular pattern then, by virtue of that, one is sane. If they follow some other pattern, and especially if they're biased by emotions, one is insane.

But what is the sane pattern . . . and who says so . . . and how does he know *he* is sane?

He returned to the table. Pulling the tray towards him, he surveyed it without enthusiasm, and grunted irritably: "Darned if I feel hungry, but I'm not going to let them think they've got me scared—because they haven't!" Whereupon he wolfed the lot.

After that, he turned his chair to face the grille, let his mind toy with not very scientific notions regarding Claire Mandle. He could picture her tip-tilted eyes peeking at him right now. With optics like those she ought to wear an emerald-green pixie-hat with a ridiculous little tail sticking out of its top. Yeah—nice! A time might come when he'd buy her one and make her wear it.

Meanwhile, he kept his own eyes on the grille. When the guard came to swap a full tea-tray for the empty dinner-tray there would be another sort of emptiness waiting for him. The stunt might prove futile, but it was worth trying and at least would break the monotony. Foo-foo merchant or not, he'd give them as much food for thought as they'd given him.

Silent and impassive as ever, the guard duly appeared with his tray. Removing the coffee pot, he handed it through the bars, slid the tray under the bottom of the grille, waited for the empty one to be returned.

Armstrong jeered at him: "Bet you can't prove it either."

The guard made no response, didn't as much as bother to glance at the speaker.

Carelessly shrugging his broad shoulders, Armstrong commented: "You must have been to see Consuelo Eguerola's latest movie. It was red-hot, so I'm told. Guess you've been petrified ever since. Snap out of it, kiddo—she was made for another."

The guard made an impatient gesture. Armstrong looked him over slowly from head to feet, then from feet to head, an examination that produced no effect whatever. Giving it up, he brought the empty tray, passed it under the grille. He was careful to hold it an inch above the floor, but as it got through and the guard bent to pick it up, he let it drop.

Something fixed under the tray's farther end broke with a sound of splintering glass and, as Armstrong backed hurriedly away, a spurt of misty vapour shot from the floor into the guard's face. The surprised victim remained bent for several seconds during which his body jerked as he tried in vain to straighten up. Then he toppled forward and lay with his face in the tray.

Snatching the cloth from the table, Armstrong flapped it vigorously. Pausing, he sniffed the air, flapped again, advanced gradually towards the grille, had another sniff. For a short while he fanned at the grille itself until satisfied that the fumes were dissipated. Reaching through the bars, he lifted the guard with one powerful arm, held the fellow erect.

It was at this point he suddenly became aware of two more guards standing in the passage. They were four or five yards away, and he could see them only because they were lounging against the opposite wall. Negligently they leaned on the wall, side by side, their hands deep in their pockets, their hard features devoid of anger, alarm, or any desire to interfere. The eyes of both were on him, watching him with a strange air of aloof interest.

Still holding up his senseless victim, and keeping a wary eye on the two onlookers, Armstrong snaked his other arm through the bars and frisked the guard. He made a thorough job of it, trying every pocket. The procedure took some time, during which the others studied his actions academically. It was the wackiest situation in which he'd ever been.

In the end, he lowered the guard, let him slump gently to the floor. He felt disgusted with himself. Not a key, not a weapon, not one object worthy of the effort. The waiting pair came to the other side of the grille, picked up their unconscious comrade.

The one nearest to the grille looked into the cell and said: "You've been searched. Where did you get that knock-out bulb?"

"Ah, a kind word at last!" approved Armstrong. "I thought you'd all had your tongues cut out. How about coming around for a cosy gossip some time?"

"You won't tell us?" the guard persisted.

"You're not old enough to be told that sort of thing yet. When you've eaten all your spinach and grown up a great, big man, pappy will tell you."

It was like water off a duck's back. The fellow betrayed no annoyance, resentment or any other human reaction. Veritably, whoever chose the guards must have hand-picked the world for its most phlegmatic types.

Accepting his refusal as if it were of the least consequence the guard hefted the victim's head and shoulders preparatory to carrying him away. He asked: "How long will he be out?"

"About twenty minutes," Armstrong told him. "He'll be O.K. after that."

The other nodded in understanding, and the two moved off bearing the body between them. Armstrong mooched around in his cell. He was decidedly disgruntled. Not a key, not a weapon—and it wasn't hard luck, either. Luck had nothing to do with it. The guards had nothing because the powers-that-be ordered that he have nothing, of malice aforethought. They'd been ahead of him there.

And the attitude of the witnesses had been unnatural, to say the least. He'd have enjoyed it more if they'd acted like enraged apes, and made for him breathing fire and slaughter. If he'd been able to grab one of them, he'd have lugged him clean through the bars, thinning him down and stretching him out in the process. They refused to grant him even the satisfaction of a little horseplay.

Why do you want horseplay, you wondering, wandering, muddle-minded nitwit? Why do you crave violent action? *How do you know you're sane?*

There was a dictionary in the row of books. Pulling it out, he leafed its pages. It said: "Sane (L. *Sanus*.) Sound. Not disordered in intellect; in one's right mind; of sound reason." Of course, this brought up the inevitable points for the hundredth time: What is not disordered, or is right, or is sound, and who says so, and what are *his* qualifications for determining what is or is not nuttish? Are asylum regulations, rules and laws determined by any special one of its inmates? Not on your sweet life! Who is to say that one is mad if none can prove that they are sane?

Slamming the dictionary back into its place, he extracted the adjoining book. "The Snake Pit," by Mary Jane Ward. He looked it over. It was about life in a jello foundry, a feather-and-treacle wavery, a nut-hatch.

Studying the last page, he read, "I'll tell you where it's going to end. When there's more sick ones than well ones, the sick ones will lock the well ones up!"

That book also shot back into place with a bang as he growled an underbreath imprecation. The sick ones will lock the well ones up—or had they done so already? What if people in asylums really were sane? But that was absurd. How to find a positive standard of sanity if there were no positive way of identifying insanity? Why could an emphatic individualist be considered insane if poor, but merely eccentric if rich? Did the possession of a million frogskins determine the balance of the brain? To suppose so was nonsensical.

Psychologists and psychiatrists had been seeking a positive standard for years and had compounded with their inability by making decisions based on public interest, and sometimes on private interest. And if said psychologists and psychiatrists were merely profounder examples of the general, all-pervading nuttiness, who was entitled to say that this murderous maniac should go free or that liberty-lover should be locked up?

"Let him that is without mental flaw snap the first padlock."

There had to be an answer to this question, an answer which could be found if he remained cool, calm, collected; if he refused to be fooled by its outrageous pertinence. Yet an answer satisfactory to himself might be anything but satisfactory to his inquisitors, in which case he would take a dive with his feet set in a tub of concrete, or something just as effective. Possibly it might be best to give them an answer contrary to whatever they expected, to look at them cross-eyed, to giggle and make extravagant gestures, to tell them, "I am not sane and never was sane. I am the daffiest character this side of Hades." Then, in low, confidential tones, "Know who I am? I'll tell you—I'm Hutsut Rawlson on the Rillerah!" After that, a triumphant chortle. That would give them something to think about. But what would they *do* about it?

"They'd do no less than if I'd responded wrongly," he told the wall.

He wondered how the old dodderer had got on with his what-is-life question. Perhaps he knew the answer by now, having found it in death. There was no way of telling whether the oldster had been the first or the fiftieth victim in this quiz game, nor what sort of questions the others had been asked before they stepped into the eternal unknown. Questions, questions, questions, they'd drive a guy nuts—if he wasn't nuts already.

Approaching the bookrack, he eyed it warily. If these tomes cunningly had been chosen to suit the situation, he'd best lay off them. "The Snake Pit" suggested deliberate selection, a work carefully calculated to unsettle his bothered mind. On the other hand, if they were permanent and haphazard adjuncts of his cell they might come in useful. Temporarily, he could get away from his problems and find relief in the depths of a book.

His questing gaze found Stuart Chase's "The Tyranny of Words" and he pulled it out and scanned it. All about semantics. Well, that should be helpful. Anything would do to unfrock imaginary devils. Since he was experiencing the psychical tyranny of six fateful words he would lose nothing by gaining a better understanding of the tyrants.

Settling in a chair, he drove his problems aside, disciplined his thought-stream and concentrated on the explanations and ironical comments of Chase. They held his attention partway through, at which point he reached a cogent passage which made his mind resume its hateful cavortings. Blinking. he read it again, murmuring the words distastefully.

"A good semantic discipline gives the power to separate mental machinery from tangible events; makes us conscious of abstracting; prevents us from peopling the universe with non-existent things. It does not dispense with poetry, fiction, fantasy, imagination, ideas, intellectual emotion. It checks us from acting as if fantasies were real events worth fighting and dying for. It checks a kind of dangerous hypnotism, abnormal reversals of nerve currents, *mental states approaching insanity*."

Violently, he slung the book into a corner. "Mental states approaching insanity." Was Chase peculiarly qualified to say, "That is sane," or, "That is not sane"? Are all authors arbiters in this matter? If not, who is?—goldfish-gulpers? What was it the old farmer said to his wife? Oh, yes, "All the world's mad except thee and me—and thee's a bit queer at times!"

Returning to the rack, he snatched the next book, began to read it with an air of grim fatalism. If this one had a similar touch, he could conclude that these tomes had been chosen specifically for this occasion. Three in a row would be too much for coincidence. Choice would mean preparation, and that in turn would signify that his mysterious captors had anticipated his coming as, in fact, they had suggested when first he'd walked into the Norman Club.

He found the touch all right. The book was Bertrand Russell's "Let the People Think," and he tossed it after Chase's volume when he got to the point where he said: "There are some who think that psychoanalysis has shown the impossibility of being rational in our beliefs, by pointing out the *strange and almost lunatic* origin of many people's cherished convictions."

Swearing with unashamed vigour, he sought a switch to cut off the lights, failed to find one, lay down on the settee and tried to sleep. At midnight, the lights went out of their own accord, but it was long, long afterwards before he slid into uneasy slumber. Without meaning, with no significance that he could understand, a phrase kept recurring to him as he drifted away, ". . . and in some corner of the hubbub couched, make mock of that which makes as much of thee." The same quotation came to him immediately he awakened later in the morning, tired, bleary and ready for trouble.

They gave him a further thirty-six hours to fight with his problem, by the end of which he appreciated how much even the strongest mind can be worn down by an obsession. *How do you know you're sane?* Don't think of it. Take your mind off it. Think of something else, anything else. *How do you know you're sane?* Think of Quinn waiting for his chance at Mars. Think of Fothergill. Think of that time you caught a black bass not as big as a whale. Think of the day you planted the solar compass for ten thousand smackers and a fat dividend. Think of the dinner Ma Saunders made last Thanksgiving. *How do you know you're sane?* It was a psychic form of water torture; the steady, unending *drip-drip-drip* of a question which came back and came back and kept on coming back.

By the time the guards arrived he welcomed them with relief. There were six of them, burly, blank-faced, as alike as brothers. Unlocking the grille, they beckoned him out, conducted him along the corridor, through four small rooms and into a great hall. As he went with them his pace was heavy and unfaltering, betraying nothing of the nervous stumbling of his predecessor. His eyes were alert as they weighed his surroundings. His chief regret was that his escort had not been a little smaller in numbers. Any two of them would have been fair prey for his outsize muscles, three might not have been too many, and he'd have taken a chance with four. Whoever had decided on six had estimated the requirements to a nicety. It would be sheerest folly to start something he could not finish.

Outside the big double doors at left of the hall, the escort stopped, and one of the guards ordered: "Take off your shoes."

"What's this—a mosque?" Armstrong asked.

"Take 'em off."

Bending down, he removed them, placed them against the wall.

A guard pushed open the doors, signed him to enter. He went through defiantly, his stockinged feet treading silently on the thick carpet. Taking a chair facing a huge, ornate desk, he plumped himself into it, stared belligerently at the man seated behind the desk.

The latter gazed back with polite interest. An aristocratic individual, his iron-grey hair was perfectly barbered, he had shrewd, dark-brown eyes and a thin, sensitive nose, slightly beaked, giving him a hawklike appearance. His lips were full, a little pursed, and his mouth was good-humoured.

Tossing a brightly plated object to Armstrong, who caught it deftly, he spoke with a voice both deep and rich: "You may have your cigarette lighter back, Mr. Armstrong. It is very ingenious if I may say so. What is its range?"

"About seven miles," Armstrong told him curtly.

"Indeed? Its little battery interested us most. A remarkable job, in fact quite revolutionary. So, too, are the couple of tiny button-tubes." He rested well-manicured hands on his desk and smiled. "We extracted the crystal, of course. We couldn't have you oscillating wherever we took you, with friend Hansen dutifully following us around. A pity, such a pity, but we have to consider ourselves. You radio people call that gadget a squagger, I believe?"

"A bleeper," Armstrong contradicted grumpily. "It goes *bleep-bleep, bleep-bleep.*"

"Dear me! We might have been bleeped into an embarrassing state of affairs if we hadn't had the foresight to search you for booby-traps, mightn't we?"

"You aren't out of the woods yet," Armstrong assured him. "Not while I'm still wearing my pants."

For some incomprehensible reason, this remark appeared to please the other. Chuckling his approval, he surveyed his captive with a friendly air. Then he pressed a button on his desk, spoke into a little visivox.

"Find anything?" A voice responded tinnily, and he said, "In the heel of his left shoe, eh? And a pack of incendiary leaves in his right? We should not have overlooked those!" Red sparks leaped into his amiable eyes. "*Who* overlooked them?" Getting the reply, he snapped, "Send him in to me immediately I've finished with the case in hand." Taking his finger off the desk-stud, he leaned back in his chair. The harshness faded out of his features as he regarded Armstrong blandly.

The latter said: "I guess you're going to smack his diapers."

"It is of more importance to decide how we're going to cope with you," retorted the other pleasantly. His face remained smooth but his eyes grew hard. "We asked you a question. Have you found an answer, or do you crave further time in which to consider it?"

"I crave nothing from anyone—much less you." Armstrong gave him a look of equal hardness. "I have the answer."

"What is it?"

"I don't know that I'm sane."

"That is your definite and final reply?"

"It is," asserted Armstrong. "And I don't care a hoot whether you like it or not. So far as I'm concerned, you can go play it on your bagpipes."

"Tut!" reproved the other. "Let's not be unsociable. What I, personally, may think of your answer has nothing to do with the consequences thereof. For your own satisfaction, I may say that I consider your reply a most excellent one."

"That's mighty white of you," jibed Armstrong. His gaze was challenging. "I doubt whether you could have thought up a better reply yourself, or anyone else for that matter."

"A reasonable assumption considering the very misleading circumstances under which you've been living," the other observed. "But an assumption which is totally wrong."

"Eh?"

The inquisitor sighed reminiscently and said: "As it happens, I know that I'm sane. The fact has been ascertained beyond all shadow of doubt, and it can be proved afresh any time I wish."

"Bunk!" put in Armstrong explosively.

Disregarding the comment, the other went on, his rich voice even-toned, unhurried, unemotional. "Furthermore, every person in this building differs from most people in that he is demonstrably sane. Every member of the Norman Club is completely and indisputably sane." His eyes were cool and confident as they levelled upon his listener. "A person needs one major qualification for membership in the Norman Club. He must be a sane man, a *normal* man—*a Norman!*"

"What?" Armstrong stood up, his big fingers twitching.

"He must not be one whose brain is contaminated by certain of his own body fluids," pursued the other, imperturbably. "That is to say, he must not be a *humoral* man—a Human."

Armstrong said carefully: "Are you trying to tell me that you are not human?"

"Sit down, sit down! Calm yourself! Unwarranted excitability tells against you." He waved a soothing hand, watched Armstrong sink reluctantly into his chair. "I am human only in the sense commonly accepted in this unfortunate world, namely, in the sense that I am flesh and blood, structurally and organically no different from yourself. But in the sense commonly accepted elsewhere—the proper sense—I am not a Hu-man, thank heavens! I am a Nor-man!"

"What do you mean, commonly accepted elsewhere? Where else?" Armstrong demanded.

"That is something you've yet to learn." He put his finger on the desk-stud. "And the moment is not quite ripe." Taking his attention from his listener, he spoke into the visivox. "This case is ready for Room Ten."

Armstrong stood up again. He was ruffled, untidy and conscious of the creases in his slept-in suit. "So I've plenty of moments to come and still stand a chance of discovering what's behind all this melodramatic balderdash?"

"I should hope so."

"Then why all this daffy play with questions, backed by vague hints of death?"

The other smiled broadly. "The question was designed to tempt your mind to a state of exhaustion necessary for what is about to follow, for a tired mind is both receptive and uncombative. As for what you describe as threats, well, I can only assume that you've been misled by the pessimism and apprehension of the rather weak individual in your neighbouring . . . ahem . . . apartment."

"Cell," corrected Armstrong.

"All right then—we'll call it a cell. But it was a little foolish of you to permit yourself to be so misled, don't you think?

Our message to you bore no threat. Indeed, we wish you no harm at all."

"O.K., I'll take you up on that—give me my shoes so that I can walk out of this dump."

"Not yet." He glanced at the doors as they opened and the guards came in. "Not yet, Mr. Armstrong. We hope first of all to grant you the immense satisfaction of knowing that you really are sane. I sincerely trust that we shall not fail!"

"Supposing that you do fail?"

The red gleam crept back into the other's eyes. "I shall be immeasurably saddened."

"You bet you will!" promised Armstrong. With a warning look which was in blatant defiance of all the odds, he joined the guards, went outside, put on his shoes. He didn't bother to shake the shoes before donning them; that brief conversation over the visivox was enough to show that the hollow heels had been emptied.

Straightening up, he gestured towards the double doors, said to one of the guards: "Who was that smoothie?" He didn't expect a reply, and was surprised when the guard answered.

The fellow said: "That was Senator Lindle."

Armstrong gaped. "Lindle? For Pete's sake! Hasn't he read the Constitution?"

"You should have asked him," the guard shot back. He pointed across the hall. "There's where you're wanted next —Room Ten."

"What goes there?"

With utter lack of expression, the other replied: "That's where we'll have a look at your thinkbox and decide whether——"

He did not finish the sentence, he clipped it short and ducked swiftly to avoid Armstrong's sudden and vicious punch. The blow aimed for his jaw was too fast to dodge; it landed on his forehead. He switched from the perpendicular to the horizontal and stayed there.

Once again it was demonstrated that these fellows were not quite as other people are. None of the other five guards showed any undue excitement. Not one of them so much as indulged in a startled exclamation. They accepted the situation philosophically and instantaneously, and their reaction was rapid and concerted. In complete silence, and with appalling efficiency, they jumped him together, bore him to the carpet, held him there. Heaving mightily, he tossed one of them off, but the fellow bounced back again. The one first smitten recovered his wits and also joined the fray.

The lack of noise was unnatural as the whole seven struggled furiously on the carpet, the heap occasionally rising and falling as Armstrong's immense muscles lifted the entire pile. But six were too many. Pinning him down, they took expert grips on his big limbs, bore him bodily into Room Ten.

There, by main force, they strapped him to a horizontal metal rack set in the middle of a gigantic mass of apparatus. They made him as ready for the roasting as any turkey on a spit.

CHAPTER EIGHT

Even the five big straps binding him to the rack were barely enough for a victim of Armstrong's unusual build. There was a broad strap around his ankles, another just below his knees, another across his broad hips, a fourth around his waist and a fifth running over his chest. The veins stood out on his neck and his heavy face went red with strain—then the chest strap broke with a loud snap. The tremendous effort to burst two-inch leather was impressive and spectacular, but it did him no good. They added four more straps, making eight in all. After that, they rubbed their bruises, regarded him with neither admiration nor animosity, and left the room.

Alone on the rack, Armstrong twisted his head around as far as it would go and estimated his surroundings. For a torture chamber, it bore some resemblance to a radio station. Amid the close-packed and highly complicated litter of junk which was all around him he recognized several fixed condensers of imposing size, an array of vitreous high-wattage resistors, several hydro-cooled, carbon-anode tubes larger than goldfish bowls, a number of mercury vapour stabilizers, and several wire-bound double-spheres set one within the other like ancient variometers. A lot of the wiring, he noted, was not done with solid copper but with slender silver tubes carefully brazed at all junctions. Some parallel runs of these tubes were threaded through large glass beads and directed between parallel strips of aluminium-foil which he presumed to be parasite-suppressors.

This similarity to a radio junk-pile was entirely superficial; as far as he could trace the wacky circuits, they bore no relation to accepted practice. No radio technician in his right mind would link the suppressor grid of a big, multi-screen tube to an extra and seemingly useless terminal embedded in the plastic electrolyte of a fixed condenser. He could see this particular condenser just above his strapped feet. Without any outer casing, it was a cube twenty inches on the side, its thick, lead-coloured plates separated by slabs of transparent, amber-hued stuff like yellow glass. The terminal in question was buried in the glass, no doubt of that! It was daffy!

Behind his head, where he could get no view of it, was still more of this incomprehensible array. The apparatus surrounded him on all sides excepting the one employed to fix him to the toaster. Partly over his head, and partly behind it, he could just glimpse the rounded rim of a shining, bowl-shaped object like a huge helmet. This, he concluded, was the brain-picker. Glumly contemplating what little he could see of it, he theorized about his fate. By the looks of it, they had discovered some electronic way of driving people nuts without leaving physical scars or mauling the cerebellum; a method effective enough to dispose of unwanted snoopers as certainly as if they'd been slaughtered outright; a method sufficiently new, strange and crafty to allay the suspicions of any mental specialist who might examine the victims later on. Yes, that was it—when they'd finished with him they would let him go—too crazy to know Friday week from breakfast-time. Vainly he heaved at his straps again. They creaked, but refused to give.

A voice said softly: "You find this a little more complicated than your bleeper, Mr. Armstrong?"

Turning his head, he saw Lindle standing at his side. The man's sharp, well-shaped features looked more hawklike than ever, yet contrived to hold a queer suggestion of basic amiability and good humour.

"Have your fun while it lasts," Armstrong growled. "Any cock can crow on its own dunghill. Later, comes the knife!"

"My dear man, I would not presume to crow." Lindle made a gesture of protest. "I have the utmost admiration for you as well as for all your works which, let me say, are more ingenious than is this apparatus if one considers the grave handicaps under which they were devised."

"Thanks for nix. In due time, I'll admire you the same way ⸺strapped down."

Lindle smiled, and asked: "When you were very young, did your pappy have to drag you to the dentist, or did you run to him willingly, of your own accord?"

"I dragged pappy," Armstrong said sourly.

"You *are* bellicose," commented Lindle, still smiling. "However, it is not your fault. I shall be delighted to resume the

conversation later on, when you've been suitably treated."
Raising his hand, he beckoned. An old, white-haired man wearing bottle-lensed glasses and a long, white coat, came into view. The latter peered short-sightedly at Armstrong as if he were a rabbit pinned on the board and ready for dissection. Lindle said: "This is Dr. Horowitz. He will operate." Then to Horowitz, "All right—carry on!" With a final smiling glance at the victim, he went out.

Going to the control board, Horowitz closed a big copper switch. The bank of mercury vapour tubes popped, spluttered, emitted flickering purple light. The carbon anodes of the largest tubes gradually grew cherry-red, then golden. A strange and steady hissing like that of escaping steam came from the apparatus as it warmed up, and some invisible part of it beneath the bottom end of the rack began to warm Armstrong's feet with the quiet, dutiful efficiency of an electric radiator. There was a slowly strengthening smell of hot metal, roasting plastics and ozone.

Straining uselessly, Armstrong promised Horowitz: "Some day I'm going to choke you with your own ears."

The other turned, surveyed him glassily. His eyes were huge and owlish behind their powerful lenses. He said not a word. Taking hold of the rim of the helmet, he lowered it gently over Armstrong's head and face. The latter caught a momentary view of several eccentrically wound coils within the bowl, then darkness fell. He heard a few quick steps, the sharp click of a second switch being thrown. Something snatched his brain right out of the brainpan and started to do things with it.

There was no physical pain but much physical unpleasantness resembling that of when one dreams of falling immense distances and awaits in terror the inevitable bump. An eerie sense of separation was the worst part of it, a sort of splitting which was violently unnatural and somehow blasphemous. He seemed to be a fleshly, mundane and rather dopey Armstrong watching the ruthless examination of another, spiritual, supermundane Armstrong. The one was as much part of him as the other, and the limited senses of both were revolted by the severance which violated every law.

A million questions rained upon his isolated mind with such incredible swiftness that his purely automatic responses were registered before any of them had time to impress themselves upon his muddled memory. A million pertinent problems thrust at him and probed his intellect to every extreme. How do you react to this? How do you react to that? Does this statement mean anything to you? Do you believe this, that or the other—and why? Do you reject this, that or the other—and why? Are you sympathetic towards this? Does that repel you? Do you think you might still be sympathetic or repelled if reconnected with your glandular system? A million per minute, thousands per second, hundreds per fragmentary moment. No time to think, to ponder, to reason, to argue, no time to call in latent prejudices, preconceptions, conventional acceptances or any other part of his native conditioning. Time only for immediate and automatic reactions. It was like poking an amoeba. Does it quiver—does it shrink—does it crawl?

The flood poured on, an immense stream. Is this hot or cold? Light or dark? True or untrue? Weigh this fact—or is it a fact? Calculate this sum. Would you say that this is ethical? *In certain circumstances, eh?* Well, is *that* ethical? *In certain circumstances, eh?* Do the circumstances determine the ethics of any deed? *How do you know you're sane?* What is the difference between right and wrong? Could this be right here but wrong there? Could this be right today but wrong yesterday—and wrong again tomorrow? Could this be right for you but wrong for me? Is anything wholly right or wholly wrong, everywhere, in all circumstances, now and for evermore? Is reason reasonable? Is faith reasonable? *How do you know you're sane?* What meaning, if any, do you attach to the following words . . . ? Is intuition reasonable? Is logic dependable? Is thought really rational?

Down, down, down he sunk into a deep, dark sea of appalling cogency, his mind producing obedient jerks to every one of the multitudinous thrusts and probes. How long it continued he had no notion, for time and space had ceased to be and there was nothing in the cosmos but his naked spirit explaining itself to an electronic god.

Warmth and complete bodily exhaustion were his first sensations on returning to consciousness. Limp upon the metal rack, he lay with his dazed eyes staring unseeingly at cooling tubes and shrinking inductances. The strength within him made him feel as mighty as a wet rag. His arms were quivering and he had a tremendous headache. Slowly he became aware that the straps no longer clung to his body and that Horowitz was posed by his side studying him silently.

In poor English, with a guttural accent, Horowitz said: "Here, drink this—it will make you feel better."

A hot fluid raced down Armstrong's willing throat and made a glow inside him. Swallowing the lot, he licked his lips, closed his eyes. Semiconsciously he realized that the stuff was drugged, for he could feel it working on him already, but such was his exhaustion that he gave himself up to it without protest and soon fell into slumber.

At the scientist's call, the guards came in, lifted the big body from the rack, bore it back to the cell. There they composed him and left him to sleep it off. The way they did the job was as phlegmatic as ever, as though carting bodies was a daily chore. But they, too, had had a taste of the psychotron.

He slept right around the clock, washed, shaved, had a meal and was feeling himself again when the escort arrived to take him out for the second time. Again they paraded along the corridor, across four rooms and into the hall. Again he went through the double doors, took a seat and stared over the desk at Lindle. The latter gazed back, his expression one of pleased satisfaction.

"Well, Mr. Armstrong, it looks as if you've struggled to the end of the trail. It was long and winding and full of traps and stumbling blocks, but you got there just the same. I congratulate you."

"The end isn't yet! And it won't come until——"

Lindle raised an arresting hand. "I know, I know! You want to tell me just what you think of me—but let's forget personalities for a little while, eh? There are a lot of things you wish to learn, and the time's now ripe to tell you of them. There are no longer any good reasons to conceal them from you; and there's one good reason why you ought to be told."

"What reason is that?"

"You are sane!"

"Just fancy!" said Armstrong, with false delight. "I can hardly believe it myself."

Bending forward, Lindle eyed him sharply. "Now look, I can give you some very important facts, some facts which should astound you no little. Indeed, they may strain your

105

credulity to the utmost, though that makes them none the less true. But I am willing to give you this data only under certain conditions."

"State them," invited Armstrong, flatly.

"You must abandon your quite natural feelings of antagonism which arise from your emotions rather than from your mind. I do not ask for forced cordiality. I do not ask for friendship—yet! But I do insist that I must be heard unemotionally, impartially, without prejudice. Let us forget recent events and talk frankly, as man to man."

Armstrong mulled it over. From his viewpoint, the other was demanding that temporarily he cease to be human, to become as cold-blooded as a fish. He must sit and listen as phlegmatically as a graven image. Well, perhaps he could manage it. They'd kidnapped him, and they'd annoyed him, and they'd subjected him to some crazy experiment, but the basic fact remained that he still had his health and strength and a whole skin. No court would uphold a prosecution for assault on the evidence of his physical body. Maybe he could manage to control his emotions, to forget for a while that he was anything other than a friendly confidant. At least, he could try.

"O.K., I'll do my best."

"Good!" approved Lindle. Folding his arms on the desk, he started with, "As you've noticed and perhaps have thought about sometimes, the peoples of this world can be divided into various kinds in various ways, also that some methods of classification cut squarely across other methods. You can, for example, divide them according to the colour of their skin. Or you can do it phonetically, according to the languages they speak. Or politically, according to their economic adherences. Or religiously, according to their theological beliefs. You can divide them into male and female, or the old and the young, or the rich and the poor, or the ignorant and the educated. The methods of classification are very great in number, very great!" He slowed his voice in emphasis. "But there is one method of classification which is the least employed yet is the most significant of all—in fact it is of supreme importance to the whole of mankind."

"Go on," Armstrong encouraged.

"Every Terrestrial is either a Hu-man or a Nor-man!" He

studied his listener speculatively. "That is to say, he is either mad or not-mad; he is either insane or demonstrably sane!"

Shifting uncomfortably in his seat, Armstrong observed, "I'm saying nothing. I'm leaving this to you."

"The sane are few in number," Lindle went on. His voice now had a peculiar quality, sombre and ponderous, as if he were trying to imitate a recording angel reluctantly reading the scrolls of fate. "The insane are many—in fact they represent the huge majority of the people upon this unfortunate world. In considering this, do not be deceived by relative appearances; some are less insane than others, so much so that they may appear sane by comparison. It follows therefore that nobody upon this world can be declared sane unless actually found so under test, according to a definite and positive standard."

"Which standard you, in your supreme ingenuity, have devised," suggested Armstrong sarcastically. "The loonies define the loonies!"

"Now, now!" Lindle reproved. "We agreed to suppress antagonism, didn't we?" He gazed quietly at the other, then continued, "I did not devise it. Neither did any living man. It was not devised by anyone of this earth."

"They invented it on Mars, I suppose?" guessed Armstrong jocularly.

"Correct!"

Armstrong emitted an involuntary yelp of "What?"—then bit his lip and lapsed into silence.

"I warned you. I told you that you're going to get more than you'd bargained for!" Lindle's finely cut features grew reminiscent. "It was designed on Mars by our own forefathers one hundred and twenty thousand years ago. It is called the psychotron. It is the only means by which sanity can be determined beyond dispute."

"You say our forefathers invented it. Are you trying to tell me that we came here from Mars some time way back before recorded history?"

"Not all of us. Only the white-skinned ones. By direct descent the whites are Martians, all of them, whether they know it or not, whether they like it or not. The yellow-skinned peoples are the only true Terrestrials—they have been here all the time. In a way, we are their guests very much as some broad-minded Americans consider themselves guests of the Red Indians. The brown-skinned peoples are Venusians. The black-skinned are Mercurians. Every Negro is a Mercurian, in his own right, by direct descent."

"Sounds to me as if you're out to start a new religion," Armstrong commented sceptically. "Where did you get all this stuff—did you read it in a crystal? Or did someone pass you some sacred tablets?"

"One does not have to start anything already so ancient that Terrestrial history contains no record of it!" He made the retort in manner confident and assured. There was nothing about him to suggest the cultist, the fanatic, the crazy advocate of a crazy creed, the phony harbinger of a phonier destiny. He spoke as certainly and as matter-of-factly as if he were saying that roses are red and violets blue. "These things I am telling you are facts of extra-Terrestrial history, the records of which are far older and infinitely more accurate than the footling legends of this world. They are facts fixed and unalterable—and they can be reasserted any time."

"Oh?" Armstrong took him up on that. "How?"

"In many ways. For instance, I can show you three-dimensional records of actual events, including the first Martian explorations of Terra and Luna. I can let you play with the psychotron until you've satisfied yourself that it resembles nothing existing in this world. However, the most spectacular and indisputable proof will come when the first Terrestrials land on Mars—if they ever get there—and if we fail to prevent them!"

"Ah!" Armstrong rested broad hands on broader knees and looked belligerent. "So you admit that you're involved in systematic sabotage of rocket-shots?"

"Admit it? My dear man, we boast of it!"

"That," defined Armstrong, "is an almost perfect example of sticking out one's neck. Will you still boast of it when the F.B.I. toss your pants in the clink?"

Lindle's chuckle was one of amused tolerance. "There speaks the would-be Terrestrial—and one hundred per cent. American at that!"

"Maybe. But I like being an American. I'm sane, see? You said so yourself. I'm sane enough to enjoy retaining some

108

remnants of self-respect. I don't go around peddling my loyalties to the highest bidder."

"Naughty, naughty!" laughed Lindle. He wagged a corrective finger. "No animosity—remember? The whole purpose of this conversation is to enable you to decide where your loyalty really lies after you've heard the whole. As an intelligent individual, and something of a scientist to boot, you wouldn't base a decision on insufficient facts, would you?"

"No, I guess I wouldn't. Let's have the rest of the gabble. I'll listen—but don't take it for granted that I'm believing it!"

"I'll give you as briefly as possible a sketch of history unknown to most peoples of this world. It is unknown because it has been kept from them for reasons which will become obvious, though a few distorted smatterings of it, and some vague suggestions of it are the prized secrets of certain esoteric circles such as the Freemasons and the Rosicrucians. The facts I am about to give you are the truths which must not be mentioned, the pearls that are not to be cast before ordinary, nondescript people. They are for the few—*the sane!*'

"I'm listening."

Lindle said, "You will have to do more than listen. You must also think. Afterwards, you must remember. And, remembering, you must observe the daily features of this world through new and enlightened eyes." He watched the other keenly, then started his story.

"More than one hundred and twenty thousand years ago the white-skinned and highly advanced peoples of Mars conquered space and sent their rocketships to the Inner Planets of this solar system. They found all of them inhabited by beings superior to the animals, being of their own shape and form though not of their precise lineaments or colour. Incidentally, the Martians evolved an interesting solar-potency theory to account for this similarity of shape, but I won't go into that here. Let it suffice that all superior forms of life on the four worlds nearest to Sol proved to be bipeds resembling yourself. The inhabitants of Mercury were black-skinned, those of Venus were brown, those of Terra were yellow. There is a very simple explanation of these colour-gradations, the depth of coloration being in direct relationship to the intensity of photon-bombardment from the Sun. The Martians therefore were white because they *had* to be white."

"I'll give you that much," acknowledged Armstrong. "It could be—if it were true."

"Now we come to the point where planetary fertility influenced the course of history," continued Lindle, ignoring the interruption. "All planets were fertile, as is obvious from what I have said, but none were so amazingly lush as Terra. To its own misfortune, Terra was torn and racked with restless, dynamic life, a sphere in torment of labour pains. Thus the Martians found the Mercurians and Venusians only little less advanced than themselves, so little that either of them would have conquered space within the next ten centuries had not the White Ones of Mars beaten them to it—but the yellow peoples of Terra were very primitive, mere aborigines with time to concentrate on nothing but the awful struggle for survival against the monstrous life-forms which spawned in multitudes all about them. Their potential advancement and ultimate greatness was no less than that of peoples on neighbouring planets, but they had far tougher obstacles to overcome, their hold on life was more precarious, and their progress naturally was very slow. Terra was the most violent, most backward and least desirable of the four planets solely because it swarmed with fierce, vibrant, brutally competitive life. None of the inhabitants of the other three planets had been compelled to beat down so much opposition, and thus their progress had been rapid by comparison; the Martians most rapid of all. The yellow people, the Terrestrials, had a stiffer uphill climb. The bounding fertility of their world, in some ways a blessing, was also a curse."

"So?" Armstrong prompted unnecessarily.

"So under the tremendous impetus of Martian space-conquest and the resulting contact of cultures, Mercury, Venus and Mars grew spiritually close to each other and progressed in friendship and peace—while Terra, the world of jungle and swamp, of stings and poisons and ravening carnivores, was ignored, neglected. Terra was not ready for trans-spatial communion. Terra was too young and too bloody to join the Solarian Brotherhood. Though their potentialities were recognized, and their equally great destiny taken for granted, Terra's small number of yellow men were then regarded as little better than the apes."

"Against which is the fact that our oldest known form of

civilization happens to be Chinese," put in Armstrong shrewdly.

"Quite true," Lindle admitted. "It's a fact which will be found to support my story by the time I'm through! You'd better bear that item in mind." He studied his listener for effect before he went on. "Thus, for a long, long time Terra was neglected much as America was disregarded between the times of its discovery by Eric the Red and its rediscovery by Columbus. Meanwhile, the peoples of the other three planets grew nigh to gods, and only one feature denied them perfection—they had within them the seed of their own destruction, a malignant strain which repeatedly had tried to convert their peace into futile wars. It was an inherent strain of mental imperfection which continued to breed and which there was no sure way of identifying. Lack of means of identification was due mostly to lack of inducement to seek a means, and that in turn was due to realization that a solution to the problem would be worthless unless they could also solve the still greater problem of eradication. There was no point in separating the sheep from the goats unless they could first decide what to do with the goats. Nobody knew what to do with the imperfect ones after they'd been sorted out. There was no question of killing them off, or of removing them from existence in any imaginable way, for a people become almost godlike—by virtue of that—are generous and merciful. All that was needed to bring true perfection to the near-perfect races of the three planets was some non-lethal method of ridding themselves for ever of impurities. And, for a long time, for many, many centuries, the wisest of them could not find a solution."

Pausing, Lindle leaned over his desk, offered Armstrong a cigarette. Accepting one, the latter remarked: "Even the angels resort to drugs, eh?" Grinning, he stuck the tube between his lips, felt for his lighter, absently sucking at the tube as he did so. The cigarette's end suddenly glowed without any flame being applied, and what flowed into his lungs was not tobacco but a vapour more aromatic, more soothing.

"Even the angels love solace!" cracked Lindle. "However, to continue, the time came when the solution arrived. Every problem has its secret hidden in infinity. This one came when Prahada, a Martian electronics specialist, perfected the

111

psychotron. It was an absolute solution. Beyond all manner of doubt, it distinguished the mentally rational from the irrational. It could do nothing to remove the cause which is hidden in the make-up of the individual blood stream, but it could and did identify the mental effect. Its analysis was solely a mental one; it ignored physical imperfections which are not and never were of racial significance. The mentally faulty were the ones withholding near-godlike status from the biped trinity, and at last they could be identified."

"Nice for them!" commented Armstrong.

"Soon after publication of the news of the psychotron a Venusian philosopher completed the solution of the problem by producing a plan which fitted in perfectly with the triune's code of ethics, a non-lethal scheme, fair, merciful, and so designed as to admit the right of the imperfect to their own destiny. In brief, he proposed that the mentally unfit be sorted out and dumped on Terra."

Armstrong dropped his cigarette, snatched it up from the carpet. The fingers with which he held it trembled ever so slightly although he exerted all his will-power to control them. His mind, already kicked around too much for his liking, seemed to have split itself in two and was speaking to him with contradictory voices, one of which said: "Hey-ho, what a liar is Lindle! The crankiest of cranks! The nuttiest of nuts! Listen how he hands you the good old phonus bolonus!" The other voice droned with damnable persistence, "This is what you've suspected all along but have refused to admit even to yourself. You've known all the time that humanity as a whole is not rational but you have never found the courage to face the fact. You've lacked confidence in your own judgment because all around you lunacy is the norm!" Determinedly thrusting both suggestions aside, he concentrated on absorbing the hawk-like man's astounding version of ancient history.

"In effect, what he proposed was the mightiest purge known to the history of this solar system—and maybe the mightiest in this neck of the galaxy. Strangely enough, the plan was little different from that of Terra's later and inadequate history when, for example, the British followed their explorations of Australia by turning it into a penal colony to which they exported their criminals and various kinds of trouble-makers. France did the same with Guiana. Terra was conceived as a

112

sort of cosmic Australia, and the plan won much favour. Let us, argued the Mercurians, Venusians and Martians, let us rid ourselves of every Hu-man without denying him the right to life. Let Nature be the judge of whether the mentally defective may or may not survive. So they did it. They paid the price in work, materials and tears, and it took them six hundred years to shift the lot—but they did it!"

"You make Hitler look a piker," Armstrong contributed.

Undeterred, Lindle went on, his eyes reflective. "At great length, with complete thoroughness, all three planets sorted out and rid themselves of every mental defective regardless of age or sex, regardless of the degree of imperfection, and regardless of pleas or prayers. It was a case of having to be hard to the minority in order to be just to the majority. It was far better than euthanasia, and more soothing to the conscience." His gaze fixed again on his listener. "Thus Terra became populated by the outcasts of the Mercurian blacks, the Venusian browns and the Martian whites, plus, of course, its native yellow races who, being unpurged, alone were neither wholly insane nor wholly sane. It is still a matter for debate whether this purge was just to these yellow races, the only true Terrestrials. Maybe it was a dirty trick, or maybe it was greatly to their benefit—which, only time will show. But the fact which you have mentioned and which I asked you to remember, namely, that the Chinese built the first Earthly civilization, was no mere accident, for they alone of Terra's motley mobs had sane influences to counterbalance their insane ones. All other peoples, by the decision of the psychotron, were wholly or partly mad—and most of them still are!"

"Anyone dopey enough to swallow all this would have some cause for suicide," Armstrong suggested. "Even loonies don't like being reminded that they're incurably nuts."

"The point is well-put but quite wrong," Lindle contradicted. "As I have told you, these fundamental truths are known to very few—and ignorance is bliss. Secondly, the tremendous stretch of history over these scores of centuries has given birth to a fact of great significance, a fact which gives cause for optimism and may be regarded as justification for the purge—the fact that sanity is the dominant strain."

"Eh?"

"Sanity is the dominant," Lindle persisted. "As time rolls

on and generation succeeds generation, so do mental flaws gradually weaken and die out until, some day, sanity becomes ascendant. The hordes of the mentally flawed are not on a path different from that of their forebears. They're on the same path, and merely lagging behind. Some day they'll catch up!" He watched the other for effect before he went on, "The great misfortune of the present time is that they're catching up scientifically—and especially astronautically—far faster than they're progressing psychologically. They now threaten to invade the resting-places of the gods long before they've attained their own godhood. They are developing the brains of the Nor-man while still retaining the mind of the Hu-man. They insist on running a race for a prize which is not theirs to grasp —or not yet. Unless by one means or another we can delay space-conquest by Terrestrials, the Martians, Venusians and Mercurians are going to have their original problem dumped right back in their laps."

"Won't it be a shame!" said Armstrong.

"Will it?" Lindle's query was sharp and pointed. "Think again. You regard yourself firstly as an American, secondly as a Terrestrial, because you've been conditioned that way exactly as once you were conditioned to believe in Santa Claus and the Easter Rabbit. But you are white and sane and by definition are a Martian! With whom does your true loyalty lie?"

Armstrong snapped back: "That's an easy one. What has Mars ever done for me that I should owe it anything?"

"Plenty! In the first place, Mars granted you life when just as easily you could have been denied your very existence. You live because your ancestors were exported instead of slaughtered. Had they been purged as some of Earth's maniacs might have purged them, you would never have been born!"

"But——"

"And secondly," Lindle pressed on, "by their occasional and well-disguised interventions in this world's affairs, the Martians have done their best to encourage the swifter growth of sanity on this planet. That means that you are living in a world not quite so outrageously insane as otherwise it might have been."

"Interventions?" Armstrong's look was quizzical. "What do

114

you mean by interventions? I thought you said they'd dumped us and deserted us?'

"They held a purge, but they did not wash their hands of us entirely. There was never any ban on infrequent visits to the asylum by high-minded persons interested in its progress. Some of them came and did their best. Super-missionaries! Many of them are still remembered even today—the North Venusian Gautama Buda, for instance. They call him Buddha! In their peculiar day and circumstances their teachings moved mountains in spite of the fact that they've been greatly distorted and were never more than half-understood. Today, their origins are wrapped in mystery so far as the common herd is concerned, and their minor demonstrations of superior science are still spoken of as mighty miracles. On a pillar of fire they came, and in fiery chariots they ascended into heaven!"

"You mean——?"

Lindle nodded. "Almost every great one of whom you can think. Excepting Confucius—his was the natural wisdom of the native Terrestrial, unpurged and sane. But almost all the others . . . almost all." His voice trailed off, he was silent awhile. "There are no such things as miracles, as many Earthly scientists know—since many of them are sane. When Isis conversed with the speaking Memnon that great statue no more than sounded its resonant note whenever Isis struck the proper chord. When Mohammed moved the Khaaba Stone he teleported it as easily as zonal fruits are teleported across the red deserts. But neither demonstrations of superior science nor simple tutoring in ethics could restore sanity to the witless; indeed, upon these things they built insane cults which added to their insane rivalries and created further antagonisms between them which have lasted to the present time. So those ceased some sixteen or seventeen centuries ago, and other, more secretive, more effective forms took their place. Now, in this critical time, the Martians, Venusians and Mercurians find themselves at the point where they're more concerned with protecting themselves from the consequences of Terra's scientific progress than assisting the Terrestrials psychologically and sociologically."

"Most interesting," conceded Armstrong. He leaned back, stretched his long legs out. "As a story it has all the power and vitality of Goldilocks and the Three Bears." Drawing the legs in, he stood up. "Myself, I could have improved on it. I'd have put a sting in the tale by declaiming dramatically, 'Behold! *I* am a Martian!'"

"Which I am," Lindle retorted. "As also are you! By birth I am a Terrestrial. In sentiment and loyalty I am a Martian. I don't expect you to look at it the same way just yet, but I've planted the seed in your mind and sooner or later it will bear fruit. Whether you like it or not, you're going to find that you can't stick stubbornly to Earth-inspired prejudices and cock a snoot at the most advanced peoples in the system. You, along with the rest of the sane, are a guardian in the nut-hatch and it's your duty to stop the craftiest and most determined of the inmates from climbing over the wall."

"My duty? Who says so?"

"Not me! Not anybody! You're going to say it yourself if, subconsciously, you've not done so already. You can't help being sane because you *are* sane!" He arose from his chair, his height as great as the other's. He looked more like a prosperous defence attorney than a prominent politician. "You are free to go, Mr. Armstrong."

"Pretty sure of yourself, aren't you? Unwarranted interference with the liberty of the subject is an indictable offence, if I remember my law. How do you know I won't make plenty of trouble for you when I go out?"

Walking to the door, Lindle held it open invitingly. "My very words. I said precisely the same the moment they released *me*. So did a hundred others. They all come back after due thought. We gain strength because they seek us out, they gravitate to us of their own accord. There's a reason for that, too, though you wouldn't understand it. You might call it birds of a feather flocking together, or similar hunches of similar personalities, or psycho-gravitation. The Outsiders of other worlds call it tele-sympathy."

"I call it herd instinct," said Armstrong sourly. "And I'm a rogue elephant!"

Lindle grinned. "A characteristic of the sane is that they can't help thinking. They actually enjoy it and it causes them no pain. They think and think and think with a perspicacity and a determined insistence from which hardly anything can divert them. Eventually they think themselves right into membership of the Norman Club. Like clings to like—and I'll be seeing you again." He waved an inviting hand towards the doorway. "So here is the liberty we're granting you, Mr. Armstrong—the freedom to walk right back into the cosmic looney-can!" A strange gleam sparkled in his eyes. "See how you like the madhouse *now*!"

Armstrong studied him doubtfully and with a touch of irritation. His strong teeth gnawed at his lower lip while his emotions urged him to say something which his cooler mind found difficulty in putting into words.

Finally, he murmured: "All right. This is where I go build up my muscles. Next time we meet it'll be on different territory." He eyed the other forbiddingly. "Watch out!"

With that, he departed.

CHAPTER NINE

Miriam was lounging lackadaisically at her typewriter when he bashed the door open and barged straight through her room with no more than a surly grunt of acknowledgment. Treating Hansen's door in the same way, making its glass panel shudder in its frame, he entered like an invading rhinoceros, slammed the door behind him, sat down and fixed the saturnine agent with baleful gaze.

"Fine escort you turned out to be!"

Hansen's left eyebrow rose a fraction, he felt in a drawer of his desk, extracted a paper, tossed it across without remark. Armstrong picked it up, scanned it.

It said: "This is a boy scout joint. I won't need you on so soft a job. You're wasting your time. Beat it—I'll phone you when I want you again. John J. Armstrong."

"Your signature," said Hansen emphatically. "I even double-checked. I got Sid on it, at police headquarters. He said it was your writing and your signature."

"When and where did you get it?"

"An hour after you entered that dump. I was in the snackery across the road, fourth table on the left counting from the door, exactly where you told me to be. That rear-admiral guarding the Norman Club came straight to my table, handed me the envelope and said: 'Message from Mr. Armstrong.'"

"I don't know a thing about it." He threw the note back with unconcealed disgust.

"When I'd read it," continued Hansen, "I compared it with a signature of yours which I was carrying in my wallet. It looked genuine. So I took it to Sid. He said it was genuine. I'm not so dopey that I'd fall for a gag, but this isn't a gag—*you* wrote that note!" He made a gesture of defeat. "It left me no choice but to pack up and scram."

"Nevertheless, I didn't write it."

Hansen permitted himself a deep, heartfelt sigh. "Then the age of miracles has not passed." He poked the offending missive away from him. "I suggest you take it and drag it around the banks. After the fiftieth paying teller has compared it and told you it's genuine, you'll have to believe in miracles."

Picking it up again, Armstrong folded the note, put it in his pocket. "I'll look it over myself. If it definitely is mine, then I must have written it at their dictation, while unconscious—somehow, I don't know how."

"Oh, so you were unconscious?"

"I went right in and they gave me the business and I flopped on the floor, all within a few minutes. I got dumped like a sack of goobers while you squatted on your hump and listened to the bleeper bleeping. They discovered that, too. Only you and I knew of it, and I didn't tell them." He bent forward, hands on knees. *"Did you?"*

"Of course I did! You bet I did! I do things like that. I burn all my cheques, and I spit in clients' faces and spend most of my time thinking up ways to bankrupt the biz." His voice became sharp. "If you can write letters in your sleep, you can answer questions in your sleep."

"Questions!" Armstrong emitted a groan. "I've answered a million of 'em."

"See!"

"Maybe I did talk too much. I don't know what I said or what I wrote or what I did, nor how they persuaded me to do it." He glanced around. "Where is the bleeper?"

"In the safe. Miriam will give it to you when you go. That dingbat continued to squeak for four hours after I returned here. Every time I gave it a whirl it indicated a different direction. It jiggled all over the shop, but ended up pointing across the river to New Jersey. Then it cut off."

"Yeah, I found myself on the other side of Jersey City when they let me go."

Hansen studied him. "You've been gone four days and you look as if they gave you the willies among other things."

"They did." he brooded solemnly awhile. "I suspected it wouldn't be easy to slam back at that smooth mob, but just for the ducks of it I went to the cops immediately I could steer my feet where I wanted. What they told me was much as I'd expected. My prison is an address known to them as a clinic for neurotics run as a charitable interest by the Norman Club. All they know of the Club is that its members include some influential people. At various times, about twenty nervous wrecks

119

have bothered them with complaints of illegal detention at the clinic. Sixteen thought a second time and subsided. Four got tough, pressed charges, went to great expense, and lost their case. Too many eminent lawyers and too many eminent witnesses made nonsense of their evidence. Besides, they gabbled wildly about gallivanting Martians, and any court knows that a guy who drags in Martians isn't a reliable witness."

"Martians?" Hansen's eyebrow crawled up again.

"Sure!" Armstrong regarded him with malicious satisfaction. "You're a Martian and I'm a Martian and Miriam's a Martian too—or Martianess. You aren't of this world unless you've got a name like Ah Koo. The Norman Club can prove it."

"Nuts!" said Hansen succinctly. Then he added: "How can they prove it? Anyone who can prove that can prove anything —which makes the whole world crazier than a coot."

"That's precisely the point. It is crazy. Almost everyone's crazy but me."

A hint of expression crept into Hansen's immobile features, a faint touch of alarm. Bending down, he felt at random under his desk, brought up a bottle of bourbon, offered it to the other. "Here you are. Take a good, long suck at it—it'll make you feel better."

"I'd be as daffy as everyone else if I refused." Tilting the bottle, Armstrong gargled heartily, said, "Ah!" and gargled again. Then he polished the neck, handed the bottle back. "Knowing that I'm *compos mentis,* I'm faced with a hundred problems resulting therefrom. The most immediate one is to determine just how nutty *you* are."

"Me?" Hansen was both surprised and pained. Snatching at the bottle, he took a long and noisy swig. "The only times I get the heebies is when I'm driven into them by slap-happy clients."

Ignoring the point, Armstrong offered generously: "Of course, there is a slight chance that you're sane. It would be nice if you were. If two of us have enough sense to pull up our socks, we'll be company for each other amid all these imbeciles." He waved a hand to indicate the world at large.

"What did they do to you?" inquired Hansen, anxiously. "Did they pour beer over your naked brain?"

"I'll tell you. No kidding this time—here's what happened."

120

He gave Hansen the lot. It took him an hour of steady talking. By the time he finished, the agent's face expressed a curious mixture of emotions.

"And that is all," Armstrong concluded. "According to them, this is a world of native Terrestrials plus the descendants of outcast Martians, Venusians and Mercurians, and practically none of them know it. Most of them still are crazy to varying degrees, and they don't know that either."

"Do you believe all this twaddle?" Hansen burst out.

"I don't accept it. I don't reject it. It's too ego-deflating to believe; too plausible to disbelieve."

"But, man, what would it do to this planet if its inhabitants suddenly discovered that they were just so many chronic psychopaths locked in a cosmic foo-house? Heck, they'd go really nuts!"

"The really nutty can hardly go more really nutty," Armstrong observed, cynically. "Besides, you forget that sanity is the dominant strain. Insanity can't last because it's a characteristic congenitally weak—it's doomed to die out, though very gradually. This world can't help but become completely sane in time, by which time the other planets will be ready to welcome us like long-lost brothers. But we're not ready yet."

"Bilge!" snapped Hansen. "Bunk! Piffle! Balderdash! A dollop of pseudo-historical hooey!"

"Maybe—or maybe not. You miss the point, though. The point is that I've discovered two things I've been anxious to learn."

"Such as what?"

"First, the rocket-shots *are* being sabotaged by various methods yet to be found. Second, that the sabotage is being organized by Norman Club members of all sorts of nationalities, members who, rightly or wrongly, insist upon regarding themselves as Russo-Martians, or Anglo-Martians, or Franco-Martians or what have you. They consider themselves Martians or Venusians or Mercurians first, and British or Russian or Portuguese last." He pondered a moment, his eyes abstract. "Doubtless if a rocket were to be built in India it would ultimately be wrecked by Indo-Venusians. An African one would be dealt with by Afro-Mercurians. We're up against a powerful and ruthless organization of world-wide scope and of otherworldly loyalties. That their faith may be founded on a mass of gibberish makes no difference to the effect with which we have to deal—somehow. The Koran may have no foundation in fact, but that doesn't rid this planet of its millions of faithful Moslems. The belief, the faith, the loyalty are all that matter."

"I know, I know," admitted Hansen, glumly.

"So we're confronted by a supreme illogic which denies that truth is that which is demonstrably true and asserts that truth is that which is believed with great fervour. What is worse, the illogic justifies itself quite logically in so far as its acceptance proves its own premise—that the world is mostly crazy." He studied the bourbon bottle morbidly as he went on, "So the illogic says that if fifty million people believe in Rumpusbumpus, firmly, fanatically, even unto death, then Rumpusbumpus *is*! It's only in an asylum where they'll accept as self-evident that fifty million Frenchmen can't be wrong—therefore the illogic is established and justified. Looney laws for looney people!"

"I'll be drunk before this night is out," Hansen said.

"Therefore the question of whether these Norman Club fanatics are right or wrong is of no moment whatsoever. What is of moment is the effect their beliefs have on them, the things it's making them do. What is of equal or greater importance is the problem of what *we* can do to upset their game."

"Why should we bother?" Grabbing the bottle, Hansen took a long gulp. He put the bottle down, gasped, said: *"Whew!"* gasped again and wiped his mouth. "If some crackpots want to blast into space and other crackpots want to prevent them, why not leave them to fight it out between themselves? If anyone ever does get to Mars it won't earn me a bad dime."

"It's the bourbon talking." Armstrong looked at him severely. "You're not used to it. You forget that I'm on the side of the Mars-boys and that I'm paying you cash for helping me limp along."

"Yesh," Hansen admitted. He was faintly surprised as his tongue skidded. "Yesh . . . I mean *yes* . . . sure! Anything you say!"

"Then leave that bottle alone and pay attention. This episode at the Norman Club got me somewhere in one huge jump. But I'm dissatisfied. The jump was so big that I skipped right over stones I don't like leaving unturned."

"Meaning the deaths of Mandle and Marshall?"

"Those, and other things as well, such as who searched my flat and lab—and why. Who's Sandy-hair, for instance? Where's he got to now? What was he seeking?"

Carefully, Hansen put both hands on the desk and stood up, his features taut, his eyes narrowed. Watching him, Armstrong planted big feet squarely on the carpet and braced himself.

Behind him a quiet, silken voice said: "A back-somersault will do you no good at all, Mr. Armstrong. Please relax. And you, Mr. Hansen, kindly be seated."

Came the sharp click of a closing door and three men entered Armstrong's field of vision as slowly he twisted his head around. He recognized all of them. The first was Sandy-hair. The second was the gaunt-featured individual who'd frisked his laboratory. The third was one of the pair of bogus F.B.I. operators.

Sandy-hair and Gaunt-face held strange, torchlike objects identical with the thing revealed by the secret camera. The third man kept his hands in his pockets.

Strolling easily across the room, Sandy-hair hitched one leg over a corner of Hansen's desk, sat with his back half-turned to the agent, spoke smoothly to Armstrong. "I trust that you will attempt nothing foolish or precipitate, though I don't think you're likely to, seeing that you're said to be sane."

"You've got the drop if that gadget of yours is lethal," Armstrong answered. "So it's all your talk."

"I have been most interested in your visit to the Norman Club," Sandy-hair continued. "The way in which your deductions led you there does you great credit."

"Thanks. You don't know how much you hearten me."

"Some credit is also due to Mr. Hansen for his able support."

"Nuts to you!" rasped Hansen. "What have you done to Miriam?"

"She is perfectly all right. She's got company. No harm will come to her, I assure you." His pale blue eyes held a cold light as he continued to watch Armstrong with steady, unwinking gaze. "It was very nice to learn of your sanity, but what pleases us more, far more, is your refusal to be influenced by the facts of which you've been informed, and your determination to continue to meddle in opposition to the Norman Club. Such a reaction is unusual and most gratifying."

"If you know so much already, you must have a mike planted here."

"There is one under Mr. Hansen's calendar. It is unfortunate that he should be involved in this way, but it's not his fault at all—he did not suspect that it was there. Of course, we had your apartment and your laboratory similarly fixed up, since there was no way of telling in which of these places you would choose to reveal what's on your mind."

"Very thorough of you."

"We have a habit of being thorough."

"We?"

"I shall not rise to the bait, Mr. Armstrong. Consider that I refer to my comrades and myself and let it go at that." His thin mouth betrayed mild amusement while his eyes remained cold and expressionless. "But we're not here to swap testimonials. We're here because we like your attitude towards rocket experiments, knowing what you now know. Despite all you've learned, despite the contrary opinions of the Norman Club, despite any extent to which you secretly credit their assertions, you are still in favour of space-conquest as quickly as possible?"

"I am."

"Why?"

"Mind your own business," invited Armstrong.

"Essentially this is our business and we intend to mind it. We, too, want space-conquest as soon as can be."

"By whom?" He surveyed the other shrewdly. "By Americans or Russians or Eskimos or whom?"

"By Terrestrials. Any Terrestrials at all will do—their nationality is of no importance."

"That's broadminded of you. I could like you a lot if you'd had a bath this year. You're an anarchist, I presume?"

Sandy-hair remained calm and cold, refusing to be baited. "I am not interested in any of Earth's religious or political isms. I am a native-born Martian."

Behind him, Hansen muttered, "Eek-eek! Off we go again!" As Sandy-hair half-turned to study him with snake-eyes, Hansen added, "I might as well be in the fashion. Know who I am? The Wizard of Oz!"

"Very witty," pronounced Sandy-hair in tones like splintering ice. He swung back, returned his attention to Armstrong.

Armstrong said: "You've got bingles in the shingles. You're crazy."

"Most certainly I am. That's why we're here. The psychotron pronounced us crazy, all of us. That's why we're stuck with this lousy planet. That's why we want to bust out!" He bent forward.

A hint of eagerness warmed his pale optics. "Once the floodgates are opened there will be no question of a mere mass of apparatus arbitrarily deciding who lives where."

"That's a cockeyed story. It's phony on several counts. First, the great purge was supposed to have been completed umpteen years ago, and therefore——"

"It was completed," Sandy-haired interrupted, "but rare cases kept on popping up every now and again within succeeding generations and they all got tossed out as soon as found. You've had them here time and time again—Princess Cariboo —Kaspar Hauser—the Man Without a Name—dozens of them!"

"Second," pursued Armstrong, disregarding him, "no guy, not even an idiot, would boast of his idiocy without an ulterior motive. Where's your motive?"

"What's your guess?"

"My guess is that you're trying to kid me that space-conquest will further the insane aims of demonstrated imbeciles— and thereby turn me against it. The way the Norman Club wants me to go! My guess is that you're just another drummer for the Norman Club out to get at me from a different angle. The only thing I can't understand is why the heck you and they consider me of such all-fired importance."

"Your assumptions are completely haywire. We'd rather see the whole Norman organization blown sky-high than be made Indian rajahs. Your importance lies in the data you've been digging up, some of which affects us personally." Slowly he swung his foot to and fro, bumping his heel against the desk. His torchlike weapon remained levelled and steady. "I can't make you believe what you're determined not to believe. If, in refusing to credit basic facts, you also refuse to surrender what we want"—he gestured with the torch, and ended—"we'll get it any way we can."

"You're not telecasting a whodunit," Armstrong reminded him. "Get what?"

"The data."

"What data?"

"Don't act dumb!" swore Sandy-hair. "You know that we want the data on rockets nineteen and twenty."

"Oh!" said Armstrong, refusing to let his face betray his surprise. "Oh, that! As a matter of fact, I've buried it."

"Where?"

"Under the Statue of Liberty."

"That is not amusing." Sandy-hair put his feet on the floor and stretched himself to full height. Coming out of their state of semi-relaxation, his two companions stiffened into alertness. "We're fed up sparring with a mule like you. We're going to give you exactly one minute——"

A sudden uproar in the outer office drowned his voice completely. A door crashed open, there was a rush of heavy feet, a high-pitched squeal from Miriam, and four shots in rapid succession. The glass in Hansen's door splintered and flew in all directions as a big-calibre bullet came through and bedded in one leg of the desk. At the same moment, Armstrong's swiftly upswinging foot cracked Sandy-hair on the wrist and sent the menacing torch arcing to the carpet.

Not giving himself time to come erect, Armstrong remained in sitting position, lashed out a brawny arm and snatched Sandy-hair to him. The fellow found himself whisked irresistibly forward by power too great to oppose. Armstrong growled like an angry bear as he got him.

Then came a sharp blast and a spurt of flame from the region of Hansen's middle, and Armstrong saw the agent's dark, intent eyes watching Gaunt-face bowing like a Japanese general. Two more explosions sounded from the doorway behind, but ignoring all these, and disregarding his victim's sinuous writhings, Armstrong rammed a ham-sized mitt in the small of Sandy-hair's back, planted the other over the victim's contorted face, pulled with the first and shoved with the second. Sandy-hair's head shot violently backwards and gave out a sound like the snap of a rotten stick. The body dropped to the floor.

Breathing heavily, Armstrong stood up. He dusted his hands, looked down at the still twitching corpse.

"By hokey, I busted his neck! I pushed and I busted it. He was easier than a chicken." In mild surprise, he stared

126

around the room, noted that Hansen's face was still taut and that the agent had an automatic gripped in his right hand. Hansen's plump stooge Pete was peering in the doorway with a pair of uniformed cops gaping over his shoulders. Gaunt-face lay limp on the floor, and the third invader sat in one corner exhibiting a hole in lieu of his left eye.

Pete mourned, "Reckon we overdone it. These guys won't tell us anything now." Ambling into the room, he nudged Gaunt-face with his foot. "Deader than last week's bottles."

Slowly placing his automatic on his desk, Hansen looked at the pair of cops and signed to his phone. "There you are if you want to use it. Better phone the F.B.I. as well—they've got some sort of stake in that ginger-haired cadaver." His expression was one of tired resignation as he watched the cop grab the instrument. To his side-kick he added, "Nice work, Pete."

"Hey, what d'you mean, nice work?" demanded Armstrong, waking up. With a leery eye on the two cops, he slid a foot forward, edged Sandy-hair's torch out of sight under the desk. "Did you know he was going to barge in?"

"I didn't know he would—but I hoped he would."

"How come?"

"I've got my own routine, see? So when I received that lay-off note of yours I packed up and went, like I told you. But Pete took over. Then another guy relieved him. I've had that place watched right until you turned up here, and it's just as well I didn't mention it earlier. The watchers had orders to stick with you whenever you came out, to follow you wherever you went. They lost you when the bleeper quit bleeping."

"So?"

"So I was in the eatery," Pete took up, "when Miriam phoned to say you'd just turned up here. I left, came back here, hung around waiting to pick you up when you left. I saw those mugs go in, recognized that guy from Cypress Hills. That was enough for me—I called the cops and we busted in after them. That's all there was to it."

"That's all," echoed Armstrong. "A few bangs, and three cadavers, and we know all the answers—like heck we do! Oh, well, maybe we're mighty lucky." Mooching around, he knocked a basketful of papers from the desk, swore, bent down and scrabbled among them on the floor. He put them back tidily. The torch-thing slid safely into his pocket, unobserved by the cops, but noticed by Hansen who maintained his dead pan and tight lips.

Putting down the phone, the cop said: "They're on their way." Noticing Gaunt-face's torch lying at his feet, he picked it up, studied it curiously, said to Pete, "Is this the dingbat you warned us about? Doesn't look much to me. Just a hand-torch."

"Try it on yourself," Pete invited. "It'll give you the funniest feelings before you find yourself gripping your harp."

"Humph!" Sceptically, the cop dumped it on the desk. Going over to the third body squatting in the corner, he frisked it, found another torch, placed it beside the first. Taking his cue from this, the other cop went to the outer room, returned a moment later with a third weapon. Jerking his thumb over his shoulder, he said: "Smack in the eyebrow. Nice shooting, though I says it myself. I was in form when I popped that one at him."

Hansen breathed heavily and bawled: "Miriam!"

"Nothing doing," Pete told him. "She grabbed her hat and went out as we went in. She was all hips and elbows and going fast. She was historical."

"Hysterical," Armstrong corrected.

"Historical," maintained Pete. He nodded towards Hansen. "She was saying things about his ancestors."

"She'll get over it," Hansen opined. "She'll be back in the morning. I pay her to work here, don't I?"

"Maybe she figures she ain't paid to die here," Pete offered.

"Neither am I!" Hansen snapped. He turned his attention to his client. "The rates go up with the risks."

"Natch!" Armstrong squatted on his heels and brooded over Sandy-hair's body. "Anything you say. I'm not broke yet!"

He looked closely at the corpse's features. In death they were calm and had lost much of their coldness of expression. The nose, he observed, was freckled and the skin had that fine, almost transparent texture characteristic of red-haired people. But there was nothing in any way remarkable about that face. Indeed, if the fellow had been a native-born Martian—as he had claimed to be—he had needed no disguise to conceal his other-worldly origin. His protection lay in his being so very ordinary. You could pick a dozen like him out of any Terrestrial crowd.

Was Sandy-hair's startling claim based on real, hard facts, or was it yet another piece of confusing twaddle such as had bedevilled this case all the way through? Lindle arbitrarily had divided the world into the sane and the insane, all of Terrestrial birth, and he'd made no mention of present-day Martians, either perfect or daffy. True, he had hinted at Martian interventions, vaguely, as if he didn't know much about them. It seemed that Sandy-hair's mob had the advantage there, for they knew plenty about Lindle and the Norman Club.

It was beginning to look as if this crazy sheep-and-the-goats theory was too simplified; the situation was more complicated than that notion would suggest. And the trouble was that the evidence led you to the same conclusion whichever way you looked at it. If all the data were correct, then this planet was a glorified madhouse. If it was incorrect, then it became a mass of gibberish so fantastic that only the nuttiest of people would find it convincing or try to convince others—and that, too, meant that there must be an awful lot of lunatics hanging around.

Another difficulty lay in ascertaining the degrees of whatever might be defined as lunacy. Those detained in Earthly madhouses maybe were so far gone in their insanity that their condition was obvious even to other, lesser lunatics who were swift to keep them out of sight. But here, right here in this room, was a form of imbecility not readily recognizable as such.

Lindle, who asserted categorically that he was sane, looked sane, only his superior pose and his obsession with so-called ancient history giving any hint to the contrary. Sandy-hair, who had another but confirmatory angle on the same crackpot story, had well-nigh boasted that he was insane—yet looked just as normal as Lindle or anyone else. Except for his touch of emaciation, Gaunt-face also looked normal. The third one in the corner was so normal that he might have been precisely what he'd once pretended to be, namely, an F.B.I. agent. Very ordinary and in no way peculiar were these three dead even though mentally damned by the evidence of their own mouths. Damned either way, whether their story be true or untrue—that was the hell of it. How then to distinguish the insane? Couldn't it be done without the psychotron? Come to that, could the psychotron really do it?

This Prahada, who was said to have invented the psychotron, had *he* been sane and, if so, how did he know it, how had he proved it? Had he employed his own invention to provide his own proof? If so, what real proof was that? One has to be sane to devise real proof of sanity. One has to prove sanity to be sane. Round and round and round—it was like running in circles. The old hen-and-egg problem in a new guise.

Suppose that Prahada's form of insanity had been peculiar, highly individualistic, totally different from the general forms of insanity of his fellows, might he not have mistaken it for sanity? In which case all that his psychotron could achieve would be to sort out the nuts like Prahada from the nuts not like Prahada, authoritatively defining the former as balanced and the latter as unbalanced now and for ever after. Thus everybody in Creation—Martians, Venusians and Mercurians included, purged or otherwise—might be as daft as they make 'em!

How do you know you're sane?

Armstrong uttered a hearty, "Double-damn!"

"Just how I feel," agreed Hansen. "Only I could do with some words to express it." His gaze drifted towards the door. "Here comes the thud-and-blunder squad."

They poured in heavy footed and eager; two plain-clothes-men, a photographer, a medico, a fingerprint expert and the same police captain who'd investigated the death of Clark Marshall.

Seeing Armstrong, the captain exclaimed: "Oh-oh! Look who's here! You got a movie-reel of all this?"

"No, not this time."

"A pity." He glared around the room. "Three stiffs in here and one outside. They would be defunct! How can we drag evidence out of defunct guys?" His shoulders jerked to indicate his helplessness. "Oh, well, we'll get on with the job. What happened?"

Carefully, Armstrong said: "I was here consulting my agent when this crowd busted in and demanded some information which I don't happen to possess. For no reason that I can imagine, they remained convinced that I'd got it and was being stubborn about giving. Pete, who was hanging around outside, saw them entering, recognized them as wanted and called those

130

two police officers. They came in just as these three were about to get tough. There were some fireworks. It was all over in less than a minute. What was left was what you can see."

"It'll do for a preliminary yarn, though you've left nine-tenths of the details out. What sort of information did they want from you?"

"They demanded details of our latest rockets."

"Ah!" breathed the captain. "Then it's a hundred to one that these babies are foreigners. A heck of a time we're likely to have trying to identify them. It should be an F.B.I. job at that—reckon I'd better call them."

"They've been called. They're on their way."

"O.K. We'll go through the routine and leave them to deal with their part."

He presided morbidly until the F.B.I. men turned up ten minutes later. There were four of them. Three remained with the police. The fourth beckoned to Armstrong.

"I'm to take you to headquarters."

In short time they got there and Armstrong found himself faced by the same wide-featured official whom he had tried to cross-examine about Claire Mandle.

"So your friends are getting hard, Mr. Armstrong. What occurred?"

Armstrong explained it exactly as he had done to the police captain.

The other mused a moment, then asked: "Specifically, what did they want to know about rockets?"

"They demanded details of rockets numbers nineteen and twenty."

"As far as I know, nineteen is a French job hardly yet begun. Who will build twenty remains to be seen—maybe we shall, if eighteen proves another flop."

"The way you keep your face straight is magnificent," Armstrong told him.

"Meaning what?"

"Meaning you're telling me nothing."

The other was politely puzzled. "What do you expect me to tell you?"

"Oh, let it lie," growled Armstrong irritably. "I know the cold shoulder when I'm given it."

131

"You mystify me. I am at a loss to imagine what you think I'm withholding. If it comes to that, you're not so talkative yourself. You've not told me one quarter of what you know."

"Then it's tit for tat."

"Yes," the official conceded. "On the face of it, it may be. But you don't appear to appreciate the difference in our respective positions. You, as a free citizen, not charged with any crime, are at liberty to reveal as much or as little as you like. On the other hand, I may tell you only that which is permitted by higher authority. Naturally, such permission would not be granted merely for the sake of satisfying your curiosity." He tapped a finger to emphasize his words. "But if you see fit to give us information which obviously you are holding back, we may be satisfied that your personal stake in this affair is of sufficient importance to justify taking you into our confidence."

"I'd like to think that over."

The other betrayed a touch of impatience. "This may be a matter of some urgency."

"Judging by the snail-like progress on rocket number eighteen, I'd say nothing's urgent in this cockeyed world."

"Don't be too sure!"

"The day's long past when I was sure of anything—including that the F.B.I. is precisely what it purports to be."

"Are you suggesting——?" began the other angrily.

"I'm suggesting nothing except that of late I've taken a fresh look at Mother Earth—and found that the old grey mare ain't what she used to be. The fact has made me muddle-minded. I have to concentrate more to get through my thinking. That's why I'd like time to think things over before deciding what to do for the best."

"But, man, this is not a problem requiring long and involved thought. It is an obvious duty. That gangs of foreigners should interfere in our rocket experiments is serious enough without American citizens being reluctant to recognize their duty, and——"

"Don't you tell me of my duty!" put in Armstrong, sharply. "Things have got to the state where it's up to every man to decide his duty for himself, and not have it defined for him by seeming patriots whose real loyalties may lie sixty million miles away."

"Sixty million miles away!" pooh-poohed the official. "Idiotic!"

"Yes, idiotic," agreed Armstrong. "Like Hindus putting their sacred cows before their fellows. Like a stockbroker valuing his wallet above his own mother. Like——"

"Are you cracking at me?" The other's face was hard.

"I'm cracking at people like Senators Lindle and Womersley and a whole host of powerful and influential friends of theirs. Good, solid citizens who salute the flag and sing the national anthem—yet want nothing better than to see every American rocket blow itself apart."

"Is this an official accusation against Senators Lindle and Womersley?"

"Treat it any way you like," Armstrong stood up. "Dig deep and you'll strike pay-dirt—if some higher-up doesn't chip in with an order that you're not to dig!"

Compressing his lips, the other thumbed his desk-bell, said to the individual who responded, "Please show Mr. Armstrong out." His air was one of ireful speculation.

Smiling to himself, Armstrong turned, followed his escort through the door.

CHAPTER TEN

Reaching his apartment, Armstrong cautiously locked himself in, gave the place the once-over. Knowing the microphone was there, it didn't take him long to find it though its discovery proved far more difficult than he'd expected. Its hiding-place was ingenious enough—a one hundred watt bulb had been extracted from his reading-lamp, another and more peculiar bulb fitted in its place. It was not until he removed the lamp's parchment shade that the substitution became apparent.

Twisting the bulb out of its socket, he examined it keenly. It had a dual coiled-coil filament which lit up in normal manner, but its glass envelope was only half the usual size and its plastic base twice the accepted length.

He smashed the bulb in the fireplace, cracked open the plastic base with the heel of his shoe. Splitting wide, the base revealed a closely packed mass of components so extremely tiny that their construction and assembling must have been done under magnification—a highly skilled watchmaker's job! The main wires feeding the camouflaging filament ran past either side of this midget apparatus, making no direct connection therewith, but a shiny, spider-thread inductance not as long as a pin was coiled around one wire and derived power from it.

Since there was no external wiring connecting this strange junk with a distant earpiece, and since its lilliputian output could hardly be impressed upon and extracted from the power mains, there was nothing for it than to presume that it was some sort of screwy converter which turned audio-frequencies into radio or other unimaginable frequencies picked up by listening apparatus fairly close to hand. Without subjecting it to laboratory tests, its extreme range was sheer guesswork, but Armstrong was willing to concede it two hundred yards. So microscopic was the lay-out that he could examine it only with difficulty, but he could discern enough to decide that this was no tiny but simple transmitter recognizable in terms of Earthly practice. The little there was of it appeared outlandish, for its thermionic control was a splinter of flame-specked crystal, resembling pin-fire opal, around which the midget components were clustered.

Putting this puzzling assembly on the table, he lugged out of his pocket the torchlike object formerly carried by Sandy-hair, looked it over. This thing was two inches in diameter by six long, with a stud set in its side, and a fat lens of transparent plastic at one end. It was smooth, had the colour of rhodium-plating, and was very heavy.

Since the entire casing was of seamless, brightly plated metal without an aperture of any sort, and since the lens effectively sealed its own end, it was obvious that he had erred in thinking it was a gas projector. Pointing it out the open window, he pressed the stud. Nothing happened—at least, nothing visible. No noise came from the torch, no light sprang from the lens. He aimed at a glass pane with no better result. The glass remained intact.

Extracting a sheet of paper from his desk, he pinned it to the window, crossed to the opposite side of the room, aimed at the paper and pressed the stud. He might as well have menaced the sheet with a walking-stick for all the good—or bad—it did. For five minutes he sat down and considered the problem. Returning to the wall, he again aimed at the paper, walked slowly towards his target while keping the stud pressed. No result.

Maybe the gadget was a piece of bluff, or no more than a torch with dead batteries inside. The most certain way to get at its secret was to pull it to pieces, but he didn't want to do that without first discovering how it functioned. Getting a big six-mag glass out of his desk, he ran its powerful lens over the paper target. At a point a little below centre he discovered a mark in the shape of a perfect disc less than one-tenth of an inch in diameter. Light brown in colour, it resembled a scorch-mark.

Finding another sheet of paper, he gave it a careful once-over with the glass and satisfied himself that it was devoid of blemishes. He put that up as a fresh target, walked towards it with stud pressed, examined it. A brown disc again. The discoloration was the same in tint, the same in size.

Ten minutes and a score more sheets of paper enabled him positively to determine that the mark appeared only when the target was a precise distance from the lens, said distance being five feet nine inches. Whatever power the torch ejected was effective only at that focal point: no reaction could be detected before that point, none beyond it.

Fixing another sheet at the critical distance, he tied down the stud of the torch, watched the target. Very slowly the brown spot appeared, grew darker in colour, finally became black, as if charred, though there was no flame, no smouldering. Switching off the torch, he blew away the disc of ash, stared wonderingly at the small hole left in the paper. It had taken the torch four minutes and twenty-two seconds to make that mark; far, far too slow for effectiveness as a weapon.

Setting a cup of water upon the table, he put a clinical thermometer into it, focused the torch on it. The mercury crawled sluggishly up its tube and reached peak in seven minutes, at which point it read 107° or well above blood-heat. Now thoroughly absorbed in his task, he tried the effect of the focal point on everything of which he could think, and all the time regretted that here he lacked the facilities of his own laboratory in Hartford. In four and a half minutes the torch charred the end of a cigarette without making it glow. It melted a speck of paraffin wax in exactly seventeen seconds. It lit the head of a match in eleven seconds. Half an hour later he got his first clue from what it did to a drop of gum arabic. The drop hardened and dried in eight seconds.

It looked as if the heat generated at the focal point was quite incidental. Some other sort of energy-field was concentrated there, and the heat was no more than evidence of mild thermal properties or perhaps an unimportant part of the reaction it got from materials it was not designed to influence. He was beginning to get a shrewd idea that what it could do to some specific substance might be startling in the extreme.

Following this line, and influenced by suspicions half-born and soon stifled many days before, he nicked his arm with a sterilized razor blade, got a few drops of blood on to a spatula, edged it into the focal point. The crimson liquid congealed instantly. He tried it again. Same result. The time was a mere fraction of a second. He stuck a piece of adhesive plaster over the small cut in his arm, switched off the torch, flopped into a chair and sweated heavily.

That two-inch-by-six instrument on his table was a weapon of tremendous might. He pondered its devilish efficiency while the perspiration flowed freely. The more he thought of it, the deadlier it appeared. Its supreme power was derived from a feature uncommon to weapons in general, uncommon even to detectable poisons—it was so surreptitious!

If you used a revolver or automatic pistol to kill a man in public, you committed the crime under every conceivable disadvantage, for it was a deed loudly advertised. The gun went off with an attention-attracting bang, the bullet whined and made a clunking sound, the victim dropped, sometimes with a yell and with dramatic gesticulations, and the wound ejected blood.

But with this infernal gadget you could walk past a man and give him the works without him knowing it, without anyone nearby suspecting it. If you had an excellent knowledge of anatomy, and especially of the venous system, and if you were a topnotch marksman with this torch, you could sentence a man to death with almost any time-delay you chose. Silently, slyly and beyond the ken of passers-by, you could plant a blood clot in his heart and see him die of coronary thrombosis within minutes. Or you could create the clot farther along the inflowing blood stream where it would take a day, a week or a month to travel to the fateful point where followed swift collapse and swifter death. Unfelt and unsuspected by the victim or by anyone else, you could put the bee on him in such a way that he'd drop of seemingly natural causes, some time in the future, when you were on the other side of the world enjoying an unimpeachable alibi.

Pulling out a handkerchief, Armstrong mopped his forehead. How could he be certain that Sandy-hair had not pressed that stud while in Hansen's office? Supposing that a crafty and unnoticed compression of this thumb already had sentenced Armstrong to death in the near future? How many other victims might still be walking around unaware that their days were numbered, and that the number was dreadfully few?

Now that Sandy-hair had joined the ranks of the blank-eyed boys prone in the morgue there was no way of telling whether he'd booked his revenge in advance. An X-ray examination wasn't likely to prove effective. There was nothing for it but to wait and see whether one remained perpendicular or suddenly assumed the horizontal—gasping—clutching—and inevitably going out.

Like Mandle.

Like Marshall.

Like an unknown cohort of others.

Realization of the appalling menace of this torch caused his mind to recoil and move its attention back to the first gaget, the microphone. Instantly it struck him that in his preoccupation with the other instrument he'd overlooked a fact so obvious that a child should have noticed it: that mike made no direct contact with the power lines. It got its energy by induction. If the lamp were not lit there could be no current-flow in its lines, no alternating surges to activate the tiny coil and start the mike's circuit working. The mike was dead so long as the lamp was dead; it functioned only when the lamp was lit.

The conclusion stuck out a mile. His opponents had accurate knowledge of his habits, knew that rarely he occupied the apartment during daytime but often could be found in it at night. They also knew that it was his invariable habit to switch that lamp regardless of whether or not it was needed. The switching was his fad.

He was thinking rapidly and lucidly now. Sandy-hair and his crew had burst in on Hansen with remarkable promptness. They'd been listening and had not come far; evidently their eavesdropping post had been near. It wasn't likely that they'd abandoned the post the moment they decided to take a hand. In all probability, another as yet unknown member of the mob had remained on the job, listening, listening until a veritable blast of sound had driven him to flight.

The news would have got around. Wherever they were, and whatever their numbers, the rest of the crazy clique would know by now that their attempt to ally themselves with Armstrong had cost them three men. They wouldn't like it, not one little bit. No matter how much his views on rocket-shots coincided with their own they'd accept him as a foe—and take measures accordingly. Likely enough they'd take them anyway, as a matter of necessary vengeance.

This meant that he found himself in as paradoxical a jam as any man could be. Hansen, who knew the least, had told him the most. The F.B.I., who were well informed, had given him nothing. Sandy's crowd, who supported his aims, were his enemies. The Norman Club, who opposed him grimly and fanatically, had made overtures of friendship. The whole situation was madder than a polecat's convention, smelled just as bad, and was a lot more threatening. In fact, it was the sort of contradictory state of affairs one should expect to find—inside an asylum.

The most immediate problem was that of the most immediate peril, namely, when, where and how the dead Sandy-hair's avengers would strike. So far as they were concerned he was a sitting duck. They would listen for him with the darkness, pick up his last and most significant words, bide their time and let him have it either while exiting or entering, or perhaps actually in the place.

To go out was asking for trouble. To stay in was praying for it—except that here he had a sturdy door with a strong lock. But if that mike worked when the lamp gave forth light . . . ah . . . hum . . . they wouldn't listen for him before sunset. There was time to beat it before daylight faded. If he got out fast and moved too rapidly for any tail to keep up, he could drop the lot of them and remain secure in a hide-out some place else.

The notion lay in his mind like a stink. He even wrinkled his nose at its odour. Running like a rat! Seeking a funk-hole! The idea offended his self-esteem, made him ireful. It was contrary to his nature. Substituting sentiment for sense, he decided that he'd no objection to scuttling out of reach providing he could paste them one on the schnozzle first. Finding a bolthole would be a more dignified affair if he sought it after handing them a slap. Could it be done?

Maybe it could. The listeners would arrive at their posts with the dusk. Said post was likely to be within two hundred yards' radius of the apartment. A small enough area, small enough to cover, and grab all eventide arrivals, searching them for torches or any other outlandish gadgets they might be bearing. Such a snatch would mean that the counter-trap had operated to his satisfaction, the paste on the schnozzle good, strong and effective.

No use summoning Hansen for a job like that. They'd be watching the agent as closely as himself and maybe with motives just as deadly. Hansen's men preparing the trap would be like advertising it over the visivox.

Summon the cops?

Summon the F.B.I.?

A queer, nagging voice within him said: *"To blaze with the cops and the F.B.I. You don't know who's on which side in this daffy mix-up."*

"Then what the heck——?"

"You know who you are! Do it yourself! Give them a moose-call—they'll come running!"

Startled, he picked up the cracked microphone, examined it carefully. A gleam crept into his eyes.

If he'd still been capable of the contortionist feats of his babyhood, he'd have kissed his right heel. Good heel, nice heel —you didn't come down too hard. Just enough to crack the casing without busting the works. It'll still operate—this time, for me!

The lamp portion was broken, of course. That didn't matter. No use reconnecting the broken ends of its filament to restore continuity; the wiring came in parallel, and a resistance as low as that would be as good as a short, good enough to blow a fuse. His solution was easy: he brought in his bedlamp, bared the ends of its cord, joined the broken wires to that. Then he took out its bulb and substituted a one-hundred watt job. Functionally, the dingbat was as ready for action as in the first place.

Next, he found his ·38, checked its mechanism, made sure that it had a full magazine. After viewing that torch, the ·38 looked as antiquated as a crossbow. All the same, it had its advantages, it was not as insidious a weapon as the torch but its deadliness was immensely swifter. He was more accustomed to it, too. He could wallop three nickels in a row at twenty yards, and that was no parlour game.

The wait until sunset was the worst part. Mooching around, he tidied things up, untidied them, thumbed books and muttered with impatience. He was as restless as a rhinoceros who has scented but not yet seen the foe—and as heavy-footed.

He switched on his *Herald* recorder. Nothing new. No mention of the fracas at Hansen's. Too early for that. Nothing about rockets, either. A slump on Wall Street, two suicides, a domestic massacre and another instalment of young Wentworth's life-story held the field. Murder in the financial marts, murder in high society, murder in the dirtier dumps. News values. What the public wants. Boy bites débutante.

All the fits that's news to print.

Vitalax.

"Skiddin'——!"

"See how you like the madhouse *now*!"

He glowered out of his window. There were purple fingers in the sky, creeping from a rising and broadening bowl of darkness. Already two skyscrapers a mile away were brightly illuminated and another seven were patchy with lights. Dropping the window shade, he switched on his reading-lamp, watched the mike warm up. The process was visible, for the splinter of crystal in the mike's centre glowed a deep, rich pink. All set now for the unseen snoopers—Martians, maniacs or whatever they might be.

More waiting. He gave them until nine o'clock, confident that they would burst in without some preliminary eavesdropping. They'd hope for a last golden egg of information before killing the goose.

At nine precisely he broke the silence by picking up his phone and dialling it with the stud out. That wouldn't get him anything, but if the hidden listeners were shrewd enough to count the clicks they might recognize Hansen's number. Leaving the phone, he reposed in an easy-chair facing the door, carried on a conversation with nobody.

"Harumph!" He cleared his throat, pictured an ipsophone dial, mentally counted four, and said: "Switch!" He gave it suitable time, then went on with: "Hello, Hanny. So the cops didn't drag you in?" Pause. "No, I had a difference of opinion with the F.B.I. and we parted the worst of friends." Pause. "Yes, a bad business. I've only realized how bad now that I've had time to think it over. Those cops completely balled up the works."

Eyeing the door, he stopped a moment, raised his voice slightly. "How? For the love of Mike, have you lost your wits? Here's me at long last making contact with the only guys who're going my way—maybe the only ones who can help me —and they get shot up."

Pause. He let it last, as if listening. Then, in sourer tones, "Sure I stalled them. I wish now that I hadn't. But I don't take up any proposition the moment it's dumped in my lap. I like to look it over to see whether anything I pick up is going to bite me." Pause. "Now, at this time, several hours too late, I can see that Pete and those cops have bust things to heck and away.

I've lost contact. It's up to you to regain it if you can." Pause. "Yes, I know, but what am I paying you for?"

Another mock listening-wait. His voice dropped back, but was till clear. "All I ask is that if you get a line on them somehow, anyhow, keep it from the authorities and give it to me. I've got to find this crowd before somebody starts beating both of us over the noggin." Pause. "Yes, you bet! I had to warn you about this. And you warn that dumbcluck Pete to keep his trap shut, too." Pause. "All right, I'll see you tomorrow."

Reaching out, he made the phone emit a cut-off click, lay back in his chair, watched the door. The old moose-call!

He was still sitting and waiting three hours later when a large clock in the distance solemnly struck the hour of midnight. Three hours and no response. He mulled the possibilities while grimly determined to wait even if he had to squat there until dawn. There was a remote likelihood that Sandy-hair's fate had scared them off, nobody had come along to snoop, and his vocal performance had been in vain. Or maybe the four corpses really did represent the lot—there were no more either to flee or to seek vengeance. He rejected that latter possibility on the ground that fanatics form circles bigger than mere quartettes.

If the phone itself had been tapped, they'd know his call to Hansen was a call to them to come and get it. That might have been done years ago, in times of external lines, but not now. The most plausible explanation for the unexpected delay was that the listeners lacked authority to change tactics to suit his sudden change of front. Doubtless the intended victim's display of co-operative spirit had disconcerted them, they'd had to report his about-face elsewhere and get instructions. In that case, they might be along any time during the night—if they were coming at all.

They came.

Unheralded by footsteps in the corridor outside, a sharp knock sounded on his door. Coming to life, he got up, opened the door, gazed inquiringly at the two men standing on the threshold.

The first said, coolly: "Mr. Armstrong?"

"That's me."

"Sorry that we're calling on you at so late an hour." His eyes deliberately raked what they could see of the room over

142

Armstrong's shoulder. "We want a chat with you. It's about this afternoon's events, and it's rather urgent."

"Come in." Standing cautiously to one side, Armstrong watched them enter.

They moved forward, easily, confidently, one behind the other, their hands deep in their pockets. Again their eyes searched the room before they took chairs.

Closing the door, Amstrong said: "You're police, I presume?"

"Not at all." The first intruder permitted himself a hard grin. "We represent the victims, in a way."

"In what way?"

"That depends," responded the other, carefully, "on what we consider best preserves their interests at any given moment."

"You're talking a lot and saying nothing. Get down to brass tacks."

"Those were the very words I was about to use to you. You've done quite a lot of talking yourself just lately—a few hours ago. But you didn't say anything." He stared steadily at Armstrong who noticed that his eyes were the same light blue as Sandy-hair's had been. This fellow's hair, though, was mousy. "If you've something really to say, then say it. Get down to brass tacks yourself."

Armstrong said, morbidly, "You people go about things in a sloppy way. No attempt to gain the confidence of the customer. In fact you take pains to push up his sales-resistance before trying to sell him." Planting his broad beam on the corner of the table, he pressed his hands palms downward on the table's surface, close against his sides. "You invade my apartment at an ungodly hour, demand that I talk, but give no indication of who's doing the listening. I'm not going to shoot off my mouth to the first guy who comes along saying, 'Give!' That's why I stalled the three I saw this afternoon. Before I start talking, I want to know who you are, where you're from, and where you stand with reference to me. And I want proof."

"Fishing, eh?" The other's grin came back. "We treat you like a father confessor before you condescend to bless us with information?" The grin grew craggy. "You've got a darned cheek seeing you're here with us—alone!"

"Yes, that's what bothers me," admitted Armstrong, primly. "And we're not even married."

"Funny!" said the other, unpleasantly. He showed his teeth. "Very funny!" He glanced at his companion who was sitting tensely on the edge of a chair and saying nothing. To Armstrong, he continued, "Come off the high horse. We know you've been talking of wanting to dicker with us. We suspect your motives. Your attitude does nothing to allay that suspicion. So far as we're concerned, the proof of the pudding is in the eating; if you're sincere in your desire to join with us, you can prove it by dishing out the essential dope."

"Be more specific," growled Armstrong. "It's too late in the night for riddles."

"Come out with all the information you've got about rockets nineteen and twenty." His look was challenging. "If you give us that, we're satisfied. We're brothers-in-arms or however you care to look at it. But if you don't give——"

"Say on," Armstrong urged. "I don't mind cuss words."

"You won't mind anything very much," retorted the other. His hand moved suggestively in his pocket.

Armstrong shot him where he sat. Two pellets, one hard after the other, *blat-blat*. He saw the fellow kick back as if sledge-hammered, but didn't pause to watch. He was off the table and around it while reverberations whacked to and fro within the room. Ability to move so swiftly usually upset the calculations of people accustomed to the ponderous motions of big men, and he was trusting to that to enable him to avoid the silent, invisible flare of the second man's torch. Both of them, as he'd realized from the first, had stationed themselves strategically, distancing themselves so that he would be precisely in focus. A quick jump behind or beyond that focal point would save him even if the stud was pressed.

So he dived hell-for-leather around the table even as the second man came erect. The fellow's hand was out of his pocket, and the torch shining in the hand. Armstrong popped a fast one at his wrist, missed, and triggered again. The other lurched backwards, swore, dropped the torch but swung up his other hand with something gleaming bluely in its grasp.

This was no time to ponder the obvious merits of bringing 'em back alive. Regretfully, Armstrong plugged him one inch below the hair-line. The victim leaned backwards against the wall and slid down. He released his grip on the blue object which promptly shattered and spewed a hellish shower of hot, scintillating sparks.

For a moment, Armstrong stood there gaping uncertainly at the small volcano on the floor. The next instant it hissed like a locomotive and a pillar of intense flame spouted from it. The flame roared up to the ceiling. It was like a monster blowlamp aimed through the floor by someone in the room beneath. The roar built up until the room trembled, and the sheer intensity of its heat drove the watcher to the door.

Pocketing the gun, he got out fast. The edge of the table and a corner of his desk burst into flame behind him. Racing upstairs, he tried to warn the occupants of the apartments above his own, found nobody there. There were no floors still higher. In the fastest time he'd ever made he got down to ground level, sent in a fire call from the nearest box.

Within a few minutes the street would be crammed with firefighting paraphernalia, cops and spectators. A late night crowd, massing and murmuring, would be ideal cover for small-time thieves—and big-time torches. To seize and search every member of that audience would require a full division of police. It wouldn't be wise for him to stick around; the sensible thing was to get going while the going was good.

Hastening up the street, he signalled the first taxi he encountered. There were no external signs of the fire as the machine whirled him away from the scene. For twenty minutes he made his puzzled driver do two up and one along, circle several blocks and backtrack three or four times while carefully he watched the rear view. Uptown, he switched taxis, repeated the performance, switched again to the subway, jumped trains, and finally felt satisfied.

This performance landed him a few blocks from Bill Norton's place. He walked it under a full moon which smirked down upon him tantalizingly.

After long delay, Norton answered his knock, appearing at the door in old pyjamas. Scratching his tousled hair, the scribe blinked at him blearily.

"Oh, you! Whassermasser?" He gestured wearily. "Come in, anyway. Dontcha ever go to bed?"

"Not when I might be fried in it." Armstrong lumbered inside, looked around, sniffed distastefully.

"Eh?" Norton eyed him vacantly and enjoyed a wide yawn.

"I go to bed to sleep, not to be cremated."

"Yes, sure." Finding a tattered dressing-gown, Norton struggled into it. "Don't like getting too hot myself." He fiddled dozily with the gown's cord, yawned again, patted his mouth. " 'Scuse me. Durned if I'd go wandering around this time of night, just to cool down."

Armstrong frowned at him. "They've set my apartment on fire."

"Must've been some party!" Norton strained lacklustre eyes at him, blinked, nearly fell asleep. "Who did you say?"

"I didn't say who."

"I thought you didn't." He managed a semi-somnolent leer. "Dames, eh? Frisky ones?"

"Oh, get back to your hay," said Armstrong, shortly. "Give me some place to flop. You'll hear all about the big fire in the morning."

"*What?*" Norton woke up. "Did you say a *fire?* When? Where?"

"Nuts!" Armstrong snapped. "You're not on duty, so what do you care? Find me a big rug, or lend me a sofa or something."

"There's a spare bed in there." He pointed to the room on his left. "But what about this fire?"

"Good night!" bade Armstrong, impolitely. "You can bill me another steak in the morning." He went into the room, surveyed the small camp bed, shoved his ·38 under the pillow, commenced to undress.

Watching him from the doorway, Norton said: "Let Dooley have it. I done enough for one day." Stretching his mouth, he added a weary *yeouw!* and ambled off, his pyjama trousers flapping around his legs.

CHAPTER ELEVEN

Norton shook him at seven-thirty and posed by his bedside scowling.

"You big, ugly, dumb bum! They had eight fire-squads on the job. Half the street was gutted."

"Anyone hurt?"

"No. It was the biggest fire in four years, but no one has been hurt as far as is known at present."

"Thank goodness for that!" Rolling over, Armstrong tucked the bedclothes around his ears.

Snatching them off, Norton bawled: "Why didn't you *tell* me?"

"Oh, for Pete's sake!" Armstrong lugged the clothes back again. "Let me catch up on what I've lost, will you? I did tell you. You were too dull-witted to hear even your own snores. How'd you find out, come to that?"

"I phoned the *Herald* and asked."

"That's the best way to round up news," Armstrong approved. "Phone the paper and ask."

Norton said, nastily: "I could strangle some guys!"

"Me, too. I've a private list of them." Closing his eyes, Armstrong sighed luxuriously. "What's for breakfast?"

Pushing his face unpleasantly near, Norton snarled: "You don't get breakfast, see? I haven't got time, see? I overslept and I'm late on the job already, see! I always oversleep when guys come dragging me out of the sheets, see?" With considerable ire, he observed his listener's total lack of expression. "And even if I did have time, you wouldn't get any. Not unless I slapped it over your pan. Moreover, when you do get it, I hope you have to go five miles for it and then it chokes you."

"The perfect host," murmured Armstrong dreamily. "Close the door when you go out. I'll tidy up before I leave."

Favouring him with an evil look, Norton took the hint. He stamped angrily into the next room, looked back through the doorway a moment later, the scowl still on his face, and his hat pulled down to his ears. Then he departed, breakfastless. Alone at last, the sleeper snored on for another two hours.

It was mid-morning before Armstrong was ready to leave. He washed, shaved, did the promised tidying, finally used Norton's phone to call him at the *Herald*.

"How're you feeling now? Any more angelic?"

"I feel better," Norton admitted. "I got something to eat across the road and I've had an hour's doze in the office."

"Good! I'm just about to pull out and wanted to say thanks for the flop. It was nice of you."

"I am nice," said Norton. "Sometimes I get tired of hearing my admirers mentioning it. But I'm a heck of a lot nicer when guys pick better hours for craving my charity." He smirked craftily. "If you'd come along at a more reasonable time, I'd have given you a suck at my half-bottle of whisky."

"I've had it," Armstrong told him. "I found it in the bathroom cabinet."

Norton's face swapped expressions, and he yelped: "Hey, you——!"

"No use crying over lost bourbon! What's the latest news about the fire?"

"Same as earlier. They got control of it and put it out. Lot of damage to property, but nobody hurt."

"Nobody?"

"That's what I said."

"Not even one teeny-weeny corpse?"

"Did you expect a corpse?" asked Norton pointedly. "Maybe you *started* that fire, huh?"

"I expect anything these days. A regiment of cadavers wouldn't surprise me." He mused a moment. "All right, Bill, I'll phone you anon."

"When'll that be?"

"Sometime," he gave, ambiguously. He cut off, went out, making sure that the apartment's door was securely locked behind him.

He strolled rapidly down the street, grimly aware that he was enjoying the personal view of a man on the lam. That mob of Martian deportees—or whatever they really were—now had him marked as Enemy Number One, to be dealt with as swiftly and efficiently as possible. Knowing the details of his habits, they'd have ideas about where to pick him up: Papazoglous' restaurant, or Hansen's place, or the Hartford laboratory, or even via Claire Mandle. Ten to one they'd be counting on him reporting the episode to the police, and they'd be laying for him near the precinct station and general headquarters. Probably they'd have an eye on F.B.I. headquarters as well.

There didn't seem to be any satisfactory way of reporting to the police while avoiding a demand that he come in for questioning. Such a report, phoned, mailed or given in at some distant station, was bound to produce a peremptory demand for his personal appearance on what might prove to be the spot marked X. Any refusal by him wouldn't look too good, especially if the cops were trying to account for two unadvertised bodies. The choice lay between disregarding the police and risking the sorry consequences, or doing his duty and thereby walking into an ambush.

According to Norton, there were no corpses to be explained. If that were true, it made his solution easy. But was it true? Either the bodies were yet to be discovered, or, less likely, the fire had consumed them utterly, or they'd been snitched from the holocaust, and despite it, by persons unknown. Too, there was the possibility that the police had found the dead pair but had kept the fact to themselves for the time being.

To dive out of sight right after a double shooting would be enough to make any jury of solid citizens form prejudices in favour of his guilt. "Self-defence? Don't give us that! Then why didya beat it? Why didya fire the dump and take it on the run, eh, tell us that?" It was a sticky situation.

But the alternative remained—to be torched without knowing it until the last dreadful moment of collapse. Which reminded him—that fire had cost him the specimen torch. He could go no farther with that potent instrument unless sooner or later he could capture another.

His decisions crystallized one after the other. First, he must leave the car in its garage; it was too much a part of his personal life not to be under observation by others. Next, he had to avoid the bank he patronized regularly, and cajole some dough out of another of its branches. Money was needed, since he had nothing but the clothes in which he stood plus the contents of his pockets.

The bank proved easier than expected. At the local branch they held his cheque before the telephone's tiny scanner and the teller at the other end identified both the signature and its writer. They gave him a wad without demur.

Possession of adequate funds made him feel good. He celebrated with a meal in a small dive near Bowling Green, disposed of it hurriedly, then tried to phone Hansen's office. No reply. He tried again twenty minutes later, still without result. A third attempt half an hour afterwards proved equally futile.

When calling on Hansen he'd noticed the nameplate of some other outfit on the ground floor of the same building. What was it? He hung around the phone box until the name came back into his mind—"Spearman's Mantles." They were in the directory. He dialled their number.

A fat-featured and extremely swarthy individual loomed into his screen and said: "Spearman's! You want what?"

"I want Hansen's Agency, but I've not been able to raise them on the phone. Can you tell me whether anything is wrong?"

"That I should know, eh? Is for me to find out, hah?"

"If you would be so kind."

"Kind I am," said the fat man. "Wait. Don't go away. You hang on. I send somebody to see." His moon features turned sideways and he bellowed, "Asher! Asher! Is for you to go upstairs and to Hansen speak. People can't get through his phone. You tell him a gentleman wants him down here." He turned full face again. "You hang on. Don't go way, Asher won't take not more one minute."

"Thanks very much." Armstrong looked stolidly at Moon-face who gazed back until both became embarrassed by the silence. "Nice weather we're having," Armstrong offered, helpfully.

"Stinking!" contradicted Moon-face. "Is not good for business. You like a good fur? We got plenty. Come and look them over."

"Sorry."

"Is cheapest to buy out of season," the other urged. "Down goes thermometer—up goes prices. Give you ten per cent. off today." He stopped, turned to listen to someone not in the scanner's view, looked back at his caller. "Is locked. Hansen's office. Nobody there."

"All right. I'll find him some place else. So good of you to go to the trouble for me—I appreciate it."

150

"Is no trouble," Moon-face assured. "Don't you forget—ten per cent. off."

Smiling, Armstrong cut off. His expression slowly changed to a thoughtful frown. Nobody at Hansen's, not even Miriam. Looked very much as if the wily agent had drawn the same conclusions as himself, had ducked out of sight for the same reasons. If both of them were lying low, they were going to have a deuce of a job finding each other. To add to the fun, the cops would want both of them fairly soon since their evidence before the district attorney would be required to close the case of Sandy-hair and his fellow stiffs. The cops were inclined to be liverish about witnesses who took vacations.

The Norman Club was yet another item. Lindle and his associates had freed him and left him unmolested only because they were confident that he'd return to them of his own accord after thinking things over. Eventually they'd realize that he was not about to enter their fold, that he was remaining stubbornly in opposition despite his proved sanity. Once they got that into their heads they'd be tough. Providing that they could catch him, they'd deal with him in some characteristically cunning way which would arouse the suspicions of no one. Instinctively, without knowing exactly why, he credited the Norman Club with more finesse than Sandy-hair's gang. He suspected that whereas the latter's victims died of apparently natural causes, the former's did not die at all—they became incurable goober-jugglers and were locked away. After a taste of the psychotron, it wasn't difficult to imagine what an overdose of it might do!

Without the fabled preliminary of inventing the perfect mousetrap, the whole world would be seeking him before long. Hansen and his boys undoubtedly were trying to regain contact with him right now. Sandy-hair's mob would be wanting him more badly than Antony wanted Cleopatra. Tomorrow, or the next day, the cops and probably the F.B.I. would have a call out for him. Some time after that, the Norman Club would generate a yen for whatever was left of him. A motley field of hounds—but he'd give them a good run for their money!

Tramping to another phone booth half a mile from the first, he called Idlewild, chartered a two-seater plane for New Mexico. They booked him a fast sports model, a jet job, complete with experienced pilot, and entered his booking in the name of Thompson. Next, he called Claire Mandle.

"This," he said, unnecessarily, "is me."

"So I see." Her impish features grew clearer in his screen. "And sober again, too!"

"Am I?" He registered astonishment. "Love must be fading!"

She looked momentarily confused, recovered her self-possession and said tartly: "You've been sleeping with the cutlery. You're too sharp for me today, Mr. Armstrong."

"John!"

She ignored it.

"John!" he persisted.

"Go on—bully me from a safe distance."

"If you refuse to call me John, I'll stop calling you Claire, and I'll substitute"—he thought it over, finished with malicious triumph—"Tweetie!"

Her responding shudder was gratifying. "All right—John!" She changed her manner to one severely professional. "I don't suppose you have called me merely to bandy small talk. About what do you wish to consult me this time?"

Watching her closely, he shot back: "The Norman Club."

"Oh, that!" she said, indifferently.

Slightly amazed, he snorted: "So you *know* of it?"

"Don't snort at me like a warhorse! Of course I know of it! Who doesn't?"

"About ninety-nine point nine per cent. of the world," he retorted. "What *do* you know about it?"

"Only that it exists," she answered, vaguely, "and that some very important people belong to it. They came after Bob once. They wanted him to join."

"Did he do so?"

"Really, I don't know—but I doubt it."

"Who was to sponsor him?"

"Senator Womersley." She became curious. "Why the sudden interest in this club? It's only another club, isn't it?"

"I'll say it's a club," he told her, dryly. "The sort of club that's used to batter people's brains out of their noggins."

She laughed. "You don't seem to like them."

"I've no reason to! They tried to persuade me to join, and their methods of persuasion were a good deal too autocratic for my liking. In addition, they're sabotaging rocket shots."

He studied her pixie face as it registered incredulity, scepticism. If those reactions weren't genuine, then she was a topnotch actress.

"That's silly," she protested. "Rocket failures have occurred for quite a long time, all over the world."

"By a most astounding coincidence, the Norman Club has existed for quite a long time, all over the world."

"But, surely, they'd be arrested, imprisoned?"

"You bet they would," he agreed, "if fellow members in high positions of authority gave the order!"

"You've got a bee in your bonnet," she diagnosed.

"I know it. And it's not going to sting me, either—not if I can help it."

"Oh, dear!" she sighed. "Sometimes I wonder whether the whole world is going queer."

"Ah!" he said, knowingly. "Ah!"

"What's that for? Has somebody put a stethoscope to your chest?"

"Someone put a ditherscope to my bean." He sucked in his cheeks, distorted his mouth, squinted his eyes violently. "That's why I am like I am—queer!" He straightened his face again. "Most everything has a value which is relative, you know. I'm queer relative to the nuttier nuts, or so I'm told."

"I take back what I said in the beginning," she decided. "About being sober, I mean."

"Judge me in person," he invited. "Can I meet you again when I get back?"

"So you're going away?"

"Yes." He watched her closely, waiting to see whether she'd ask *where* he was going. It was important, that! It was essential to know the extent of her interest in his destination, and it should be enlightening to observe her face as she asked.

"For very long?"

"No longer than I can help," he evaded.

She smiled at him. "Then call me again when you return—you may catch me in a sociable mood."

"All right," he agreed. " 'Bye, Claire!"

He was thoughtful as he cut off and saw the little screen cloud over. She had not asked. Her omission was unflattering, yet it cleared some of his vague suspicions. If she had inquired, he would not have known whether to feel gratified or warned.

153

It all depended upon whether his movements interested her personally, or interested others with whom she might be in cahoots, and from the latter viewpoint it was just as well that she had shown no curiosity. Unless, of course, her wits were two jumps ahead of his own, and she had perceived the trap!

A taxi took him to the drome where he found his jet-job awaiting him on the tarmac. The pilot, a lean, lanky, yellow-curled youth, grinned down at him form the streamlined cockpit, gave the port and starboard turbines a preliminary spin. A strong smell of paraffin permeated the air as spurts of vapour shot backwards from both wings.

Tossing up a large lunch-box, Armstrong heaved himself after it into the small cockpit, squashed himself into the port half of the side-by-side seat.

"Mr. Thompson?" the pilot checked. Armstrong nodded. He went on, "I'm Captain Oliver Moore. The boys call me Ollie." He eyed the lunch-box appreciatively. "That was mighty good of you." His gaze shifted to the tarmac. "Are we all set?"

Armstrong said: "Take her away."

They trundled over to the east-west runway while their radio yammered instructions from the control tower. Reaching the limit of the strip, they paused while the turbines revved up, then slowly they began to edge forward. Suddenly they rocked from side to side as somebody snatched the world away from beneath them. The planet fled from their tail.

"Nice jobs," enthused Ollie. "I love 'em!" Dexterously he gunned her over a fat cloud.

"They hold only two," Armstrong commented. "That's what I like about them."

Ollie looked mystified.

"I'm running away from my wife," Armstrong offered, solemnly.

The plane dropped on something soft, gradually rose again, swaying as if suspended by a string. Ollie's face was disapproving.

Putting his feet on the lunch-box, Armstrong titled back his head, closed his eyes, went to sleep. The jets emitted only a faint, slumbersome murmur since their real uproar was not less than half a mile behind. Ignoring the hearty snores at his side, Ollie nursed her while she swung and sank and rose lazily —yet at tremendous pace. His eyes flickered continually from windshield to instrument panel, but his mind was on a certain strawberry blonde. If ever he ran away from her, he would be nuts!

With the lunch-box empty, and the darkness of night all about them, they picked up the repeated *pipper-pop* of a radio beacon, and shortly swooped into the flare-path at their destination. They touched down neatly, raced half-way along the strip, waddled the rest of the way to the perimeter, Armstrong climbed out, stretched his arms, exercised his stiff joints.

"A sweet hop, Ollie. It does you credit." He put on a mask of anxiety. "If anyone asks you about Louie Thompson, you took him to Chihuahua or any other foreign part you fancy."

"I'm a flier, not a liar." Ollie glowered his reproof from the cockpit's sliding window. His face withdrew from sight, his machine ambled through the darkness towards some distant dispersal point. The navigation lights gleamed red and green on the wingtips as the plane swung round in its far parking place, then they winked out.

Armstrong smiled to himself, decided that Mrs. Ollie wore the pants in a most becoming way.

After a fidgety night in a ramshackle hotel, he was up with the dawn and arrived at the rocket site so early that he had to wait half an hour for the technical staff to appear. The guards who had admitted him on previous occasions were not on duty, and the tough, belligerent specimens functioning in their place were disposed to doubt his credentials. Bluntly, they refused him admission. Until Quinn turned up and vouched for him he kicked his heels outside the main gate while the guards kept him under beetle-browed observation.

Quinn yipped at him joyfully: "Well, well, the world's mightiest midget!" He led Armstrong through the gates. "To what do we owe the pleasure, Ugly?"

"Just come to have a look at what's doing, and pick up any fresh information."

"Still sleuthing, eh?" He punched the muscle of the other's arm. "What about those names you persuaded me to dig up for you? Have you exposed them, and slung them into the calaboose?"

"Not yet."

"Not yet?" George Quinn echoed. "You're still on the trail? The Mounties get their man, eh?" He chuckled his amusement. "How many corpses have littered your path?"

Armstrong pulled out a big pipe, sucked at it without bothering to fill it, and said, curtly: "Only eight."

Quinn fell over his own feet, and yelped: "You're ribbing!"

"Professor Bob Mandle, Clark Marshall and half a dozen members of some crackpot gang," Armstrong continued, evenly. He had a noisy suck at the pipe. "I'm supposed to be the ninth. Probably a guy named Hansen is to be the tenth. Providing they can catch us!"

"Who are 'they'?" demanded Quinn, becoming goggle-eyed.

"That's what I'd like to know."

Wig-wagging his arms as if playing ducks, Quinn said: "Now look—death isn't funny. It doesn't make me laugh myself silly. If this stuff is your idea of making conversation——"

Taking his pipe from his mouth, Armstrong rasped: "I tell you that eight guys have died, to my knowledge. There may be dozens of others of whom I don't know. There may be many more yet to die, including myself—and including you! I don't give a care whether or not you believe it." He rammed the pipe back into his face, his strong jaw tilting it at a sharp angle. "The main thing is to keep from under the chopper, for as long as one can."

"Thank heavens I'm beating it to Mars just as soon as the ship is ready," Quinn said, piously. "Next time some dope asks me why I'm risking my neck to get out I'll ask him who wouldn't."

They stopped as they came to the tall, silent metal tower that was the unfinished ship. Its smooth, cylindrical shape was black save where the morning sun struck a crimson gleam down one side. Its body had gained a mere ten feet since Armstrong had last seen it.

"A bit more has been done," observed Quinn, without much enthusiasm. "They've fitted the hindmost impact-ring, as you can see. There are four more rings yet to be put on along with the nose-cap. A set of newfangled carborundum stabilizing vanes arrived yesterday and should be fitted before the week's out. There's a little more of the plumbing been done inside. About half the guts are installed."

"At that rate, it'll be ready for instrument tests the other side of Christmas."

"I dunno. I can't make out what's going on in Washington. One time they're rushing us along, the next they're holding us back. They start out feverishly to get the job done as quickly as possible, then they ball up the works and delay the task hopelessly, then they put on another frantic spurt, then ball it up again. The way they act, it looks like they can't make up their own minds whether they want to grab Mars or not."

He glanced at his listener, obviously inviting comment, but getting none, he carried on: "Sometimes I can brace myself sufficiently to bear the acute agony of thinking. When I do, I think up some queer notions."

"Such as which?" Armstrong encouraged.

"I get the idea that among that political mob in Washington are rival gangs fighting for and against spaceships. Both of them have lots of power and influence, and both use it for all they're worth. So here, in New Mexico, far from the scene of conflict, we speed up or slow down according to which way the tide of battle goes at any given moment."

Armstrong said, disarmingly: "Rocket shots eat money. They are champion moola-guzzlers. I never heard of a money-swallowing project that wasn't the subject of a political row." He gave the ship a final once-over. "Let's go."

They found Fothergill in his office. The executive's glossy hair looked as if it had been gummed down and left undisturbed for a least a month. As always, a vase of flowers occupied one corner of his desk.

Forcing an expression of pleasure into his unwilling features, Fothergill murmured: "Back again?"

"I come and I go. Do you mind?"

"Why on earth should I care what you do?"

"I'm glad that you don't," Armstrong informed, dryly. "Too many people seem to be caring these days. I'd rather not enjoy their attention."

Fothergill opened his mouth, changed his mind, closed it without saying anything. He gloomed dumbly at the flowers.

"I'd like to ask you a question or two," Armstrong said.

"For the love of Mike, don't take up where you left off last time you were here. Progress on the ship is held up for substantially the same reasons as I gave you before. I've no more

157

information to add and, to be candid, I'm getting fed up with the subject."

"Then we'll change the tune." He fixed Fothergill with an unpleasantly penetrating eye. "Can you tell me anything about rockets nineteen and twenty?"

The other's face quirked. Swiftly, he asked: "Who's building them?"

"That's what I'm asking you."

"Me?" Fothergill was prettily surprised. He smoothed his hair confusedly. "So far as I know, number eighteen is positively the latest. I know of no others. What makes you think there are others? Who told you about them?"

"Minnie Finnigan."

Fothergill was pained. "Who's she?"

"You don't know her, of course. She gets around. When she gets here, I'll introduce her to you. She cultivates flowers."

Quinn snickered. He shut up when Armstrong looked at him.

"Does she now?" Fothergill displayed sudden interest. "What kind of blossoms?"

"Precious ones. I forget the species. But never mind that—it's beside the point." Studying his big boots, he thought a moment, said to Fothergill: "Is Healy still working here?"

"Yes."

"And Muller, Centrillo and Jacques?"

"Yes—what's wrong with them?"

"They're the boys likeliest to bust the ship if ever it gets busted."

"How do you know that?" Fothergill challenged.

Ignoring the question, Armstrong snapped at him. "Ever heard of the Norman Club?"

"Never! Am I supposed to have heard of it?"

"Not necessarily. Neither are you supposed to admit it if you have. I wanted your reaction rather than your reply."

Flushing a deep red, Fothergill said: "Each time you come here you bait me with petty insinuations. There is no reason at all why I should answer any of your questions, truthfully or otherwise. You've no authority over me."

Butting in, Quinn pleaded to Armstrong: "Let's not start mussing one another's hair, John. It's plenty bad enough in this dump without souring the inhabitants still further."

"It wasn't my intention to push you around," Armstrong told Fothergill, soothingly. "I'm afraid you emote too readily. When a guy gets excited his face tells things which he refuses to voice—and I've got to get information somehow."

"So far as I'm concerned, you're not entitled to any information from me. You've no authority over me, as I've told you."

"None whatever," Armstrong agreed. "It had never occurred to me to apply for any—not as long as I can manage without." He smiled as he noticed the touch of uncertainty which crept into the other's face. Getting up, he strolled to the door, Quinn following. "All the same, thanks a lot for giving me so much of your time."

Outside, and well away from the building, Quinn ordered: "Come on—give! Who's this Minnie Finnigan!"

"What do you care?"

"Well, what's all this stuff about two more rockets? Is someone getting ahead of us? Who is it—the Russkis, the British, the French or who?"

"Them danged Northerners."

"Eh?"

"This hyah is a Suth'n rocket, suh," declared Armstrong, waving a hand to indicate the landscape, "and them Yankees is scheming to outsmart it, shor nuff!"

Quinn said, loudly and emphatically: "You're nuts!"

"It's this way, George." His voice grew serious. "Somebody is mighty interested in rockets nineteen and twenty. Said parties appear to be convinced that I know as much about them as anyone—and maybe more than most. Nothing I can say to the contrary is good enough to make them believe otherwise. Yet I don't even know that such rockets exist, much less who's building them."

"If there are any such, they'll be European," opined Quinn.

"Then why pester *me* about them?"

"I'm not pestering you."

Armstrong growled: "Dope! Why should *they* pester *me* about them?"

"I give up. The whole world's daffy, anyway."

"They chivvy me—and probably certain other people unknown to me—because they've good reason to believe that they're American rockets!"

Swallowing an invisible lollipop, Quinn voiced his objections in high tones. "Baloney! They could hardly build two more rockets without someone here knowing about it if only as a rumour. Besides, why should they build three, one here and two elsewhere?"

"Somebody here, my little innocent, does know about them. Fothergill does!"

"He denied it."

"Yeah—and I was watching him as he denied it. He knows about them, but he's supposed to keep his trap shut. He also knows that I ought not to know about them. Doubtless he's now wondering how much I've learned and is crediting me with more than I've got. He'll have to take action about that. He'll phone his immediate superiors, or maybe the nearest lair of the F.B.I. if only to cover himself against any suspicions that he talked too much. His mouth said nothing, but his face said plenty. I'll now stake my life that two more rockets are being constructed in secret some place else, and that they're American ones!"

They were passing the shell of the unfinished number eighteen as they made towards the gates. Looking at it beseechingly. Quinn put his hands together as if in prayer.

"Sweet Lulu," he begged of it, "get me there ahead of all the competition that's piling up!"

"What've you got against Mars that you should want to help dump a dollop of loonies on it?"

"As the lady-dog said," Quinn retorted, "if I'm first to trot along the road can I help how many follow me?"

Standing by the gates, he watched his visitor depart, and continued to brood long after the other was out of sight. Finally, he mooched back to the huge column of the rocket. He addressed it like an aborigine addressing his metal god.

"Men have been killed because of you, and more may yet be rubbed out. It wouldn't be so bad if you didn't just sit impassively on your rear end and stare at the sky as if next century were soon enough. I may not live that long, even if I die naturally—and according to that big clunker, plenty of people are dying unnaturally." He spat in its general direction. "The earlier you blast off and get me there, the better it'll be for you and me and a good many more besides."

CHAPTER TWELVE

Back in New York, Armstrong phoned the *Herald,* made contact with Norton.

In the screen, the scribe greeted him with a mock scowl. "So you vanish for a couple of days, and now your conscience tells you to give yourself up."

"What are you talking about?"

"You're wanted," Norton informed with relish. "I lent my bed to a fugitive from justice—which makes me guilty of compounding a felony or some such devilment. I won't forget that. You always were a pal!"

Armstrong said, pleasantly: "If you weren't safe at the other end of a phone line, I'd wring your unwashed neck. Come out with the news, in plain language."

"My, my! Murderous threats!" He bugged his eyes in horror and jiggled the stud of his phone. "Were you listening-in to that, Blondie? If so, you're a witness!"

"Good-bye!" Armstrong bawled at him, making to cut off.

Semaphoring frantically, Norton yipped: "Wait a minute. What's your hurry?"

"You fail to amuse. If you've anything to say that makes sense, then say it."

"So that's how you are—liverish again? Oh, well——" He scratched his head wearily. "The police are looking for you and Hansen so's they can formally tie up the case of four stiffs. They can't do it without official evidence from both of you, signed statements or some such red tape. The F.B.I. want to know why you've both chosen to disappear at such a juncture. They can't make up their minds whether you've lammed or not. Pretty soon they'll start dragging the East River for you. A smoothie named Carson contacted me yesterday and cross-examined me regarding your possible whereabouts."

"Carson, Carson?" Armstrong searched his mind. "Don't know him."

"Said he was Randolph K. Lindle's aide-de-camp, whatever that may mean. He acted liked your carcass was worth a million smackers to this Lindle who, I presume, runs a freak show.

Of course, I wasn't able to tell him anything except that with luck you might be in the crematorium." Finishing the scratching, he began to run his fingers through his dark hair, making it stick up in puckish spikes. "A little later, Ed Drake phoned to ask if I knew where you were. He said some guy like a frustrated vivisectionist had been worrying him for the information. Ed seemed apprehensive for some reason; he thought maybe you'd gone the same way as Clark Marshall."

"Perhaps I have," said Armstrong, calmly. "Next time I talk to you it may be via a Ouija board."

"What with one thing and another," continued Norton, completely missing the point, "I decided to *cherchez la femme*. So I called up your heart-throb."

"Claire?"

"Yup. She seemed to think most of New York was after you. She said I was the seventh in the queue that afternoon. Six others had been on before me, asking the same questions."

"What else did she tell you?"

Norton glanced slowly and apprehensively to both side before saying, "That just between ourselves, you were the Albany hatchet murderer and she was hiding you in her cellar." His face went sour. "Just like a dame. Knows nothing, and tells lies about it." Feeling in his vest pocket, he took out a slip of paper. "There was one thing more. Her fourth caller was a dressy blonde who said you were to ring this number." He read it out while Armstrong made a note of it, then added, maliciously, "The charming Claire has a poor opinion of cooing towheads who toss you their numbers."

"Burn that slip. I'll call you again fairly soon." He cut off without giving the other time to argue the matter.

Travelling uptown, he used a booth in Penn Station to try the number. A blonde appeared in his screen. It was Miriam.

She didn't know whether to look relieved because he was still in the land of the living, or annoyed because once more she was in contact with the cause of all the trouble.

"Top of the morning, Goldilocks!" he greeted.

She sniffed disdainfully. "You can call Lexington 501–17 at two o'clock or at four-thirty, promptly. It'll be no use unless you ring dead on time. That's all." Without further ado she severed the connection.

Short and sweet. Evidently she didn't like big, heavy men.

Or else she didn't care overmuch for the events which followed in his wake.

After having dinner, he called Lexington 501–17 at precisely two o'clock. A neat little switchboard operator answered him, smiled like a toothpaste ad, plugged him through to an extension when he asked for Hansen.

The agent showed on the screen. "I've been trying to regain touch with you the last couple of days. I suppose you know that half your street is burned down?"

"I was there when it started."

"We'll cut this short," Hansen clipped. "One never knows who's listening to what, these days. Remember where we met after you'd asked me to sing you a lullaby?"

"Yes, I remember."

"Same place in one hour's time. Can you make it?"

"Sure! I'll meet you."

The screen blanked. Evidently Hansen no longer was prepared to trust even his own mother. He had adopted the flea technique—that of keeping on the hop.

Business was poor at what was an early hour for Longchamps. Arriving exactly at the sixtieth minute, Hansen found Armstrong at a table in the half-empty room. The agent had brought someone with him, a dapper individual with pale face and glassy eyes, a sort of sartorial zombie.

Seating himself, Hansen introduced his companion with, "Meet Jake—one of my boys. His other name doesn't matter. Just Jake will do." Armstrong nodded sociably and Jake responded with the cold stare of an imprisoned goldfish as Hansen went on. "I've had to jump out of the office. I've slept in different beds three nights running. The alternative is to sleep on a slab. That sort of caper plays hell with my business connections. How can clients find me if they don't know where I am?"

"You should worry about that while you can't be found by others whose payments won't be in cash!" said Armstrong. "The cops want us too, and the longer we're missing, the more they'll want us."

"Not me they won't."

"Why not?"

"All they require is official evidence. I've mailed them a sworn affidavit."

"Is that sufficient?" Armstrong's brows quirked in surprise.

"It may be in this case. There were police witnesses too, weren't there? My spiel's a mere formality. At least, it will cover me against any further charge of contempt."

"You beat me to it there. I hadn't thought of that stunt. Guess I'd better go swear one myself and mail it in."

Jake chipped in hoarsely with: "Whenna we going ta drink?"

"They're coming up now," Armstrong soothed. "I ordered before you arrived." He studied the marbles Jake used for eyes, and added, "Doubles."

"Hokay," said Jake.

Impatiently, Hansen put in, "Take no notice of this booze-lapper. I employ him because I'm weak." His lean face was serious as he looked at Armstrong. "Remember Pete?"

"Of course."

"He kicked off last night."

"Kicked off? You mean——?" Putting back the tobacco pouch he was taking from his pocket, Armstrong looked at his hands. They were steady. His voice was steady as he asked: "How?"

"He was at home having supper and talking to his wife. Suddenly he stopped talking. He looked at her like he'd never seen her before. Then he slid under the table. He was out of this world by the time they got the doctor to him."

"Just when was that?"

"Around midnight. I heard of it this morning."

"Was there anything wrong with him, anything from which he had been suffering a long time?"

"Not that I know about—he appeared to have the constitution of a prize bull." The drinks came up; Hansen handled his as if it failed to interest him. "Maybe it's sheer coincidence. Or maybe it's not. We'll gain a better idea when we learn what brought him down."

"I know what you're thinking."

"Yeah—who's next?"

Armstrong nodded solemnly. "You or me. Companions of the deathwatch. Skiddin' with my shiver-kid!"

"I'm nobody's shiver-kid." Hansen sipped his drink without

tasting it. "You got us into this fix. It's up to you to think a way out." He regarded the other levelly. "Spending the rest of my life keeping clear of homicidal maniacs isn't my idea of fun. Something will have to be done about it. You dumped them on our tails—see if you can get them off."

Placing a coin on the table between them, Armstrong said: "There's one solution."

"How come?"

"So long as we race around too fast for them to catch us, so long are we unable to catch them. I blotted two of them myself, by the simple process of squatting enticingly in the middle of the target. I'm not averse to trying it again." He poked the coin nearer to Hansen. "One of us can sit tight where he's sure to be found. The other sticks around with the boys in readiness to trap the trappers. Toss you for it."

"Is that all you can think of?" Hansen showed his disgust.

"No—but it will provide the action for which you crave."

"This stuff ain't any peppier for being dished out in a snootery," opined Jake, putting down his empty glass. "I drunk better along the waterfront." Raising his voice, he yelled across the room, "Hey, you! T'ree again!" His marble eyes stared stonily at Hansen as if defying that worthy to comment.

Frowning his displeasure, Hansen ignored him, said to Armstrong: "I don't object to becoming the bleating lamb in the lion pit as a last, desperate resource. What else can you offer?"

"Some routine work. Go see Claire Mandle and get a list of the people who've been questioning her about me, find out what you can about them. After that, make contact with a guy named Carson, at the Norman Club, see if you can discover how badly he wants me, and why. Tell him I've gone by plane to Nicaragua, but you can catch me immediately I return. Probably he'll clam up. If he does prove talkative—which is most unlikely—dig out any information he can give you regarding this other mob which is gunning for us."

"Why Nicaragua?" Hansen inquired.

"Oh, tell him that's where rocket number nineteen is being built."

Hansen's jaw dropped. "How'd you learn that?"

"I haven't learned it. I invented the fact. It's being con-

165

structed in Poona, Pekin or Ploughkeepsie for all I know. Nicaragua will be good enough for this Carson, if he asks."

Shrugging, Hansen said: "All right. Anything to keep busy. Just for the book, what are you going to do in the meantime, and how are we going to make contact again?"

"I'll tell you." His voice lowered. "Lindle and Womersley whipped up senatorial opposition to further rocket expenditure. Ten to one most of their following consists of political representatives of the Norman Club. But more dough was granted despite them. Why?"

"You tell me."

"Because the crowd in favour of rockets temporarily proved the stronger. They want Mars and they intend to get it. They're going my way! They've enough political pull, if only for the moment. So they are powerful allies, unless——"

"Unless they're adherents of this gang of crazy coots who're after our skins," Hansen finished for him. "In which case your attempt to interview them will be as useful as sticking your noggin under a guillotine."

"That's a chance I've got to take."

"Do you want any flowers?"

"Neither flowers nor music. Just a plain, cheap funeral without any fuss." He grinned at the other. "If I dared to admit that I'd like a bouquet or two, you'd present me with the bill right now."

"I'm not *that* tight-fisted," Hansen complained.

"Now me, I'll take you up on that." Jake shoved his empty glass towards the agent. "It's your turn, ain't it? Come on—divvy up!"

Looking pained, Hansen repeated their order.

"I'm going to fish around," Armstrong went on. "I'm going to Washington, and I'll call Miriam on Saturday, at five o'clock. Leave any message with her."

"That's no use. Miriam's hopping around like a scared kangaroo."

"Darn!" Armstrong thought a moment. "When I return I'll give a number to Norton, at the *Herald*. Ask him for it."

"I guess that will do." Rising, Hansen snapped at Jake, "Come on, Tosspot—we're back in working hours."

"Suits me. I get tired of leaning on things." Swigging the last

166

of his drink, he gave Armstrong the glass-eye. "Nice meeting you."

The pair departed, Hansen first, Jake following close behind. Armstrong gave them five minutes to get clear. He had a cautious look around the room before he made for the exit.

A comprehensive report of the debate on rocket expenditure was in the library's file of the Washington *Record*. It showed that the argument had been more prolonged and bitter than other Press stories had indicated. Elsewhere, for unknown reasons, the debate had been played down.

Lindle and Womersley and their redoubtable following had almost succeeded in forcing a cut calculated to put an end to construction for a long time to come, and those in favour of getting on with the job had gained victory only by the skin of their teeth. It had been touch and go.

Armstrong examined the report carefully, even the smallest details. This was where he must employ his knowledge of psychology to the utmost, analysing the speeches of those whose aims appeared to parallel his own and, as far as possible, determining the real motives behind them. Double trouble would be his reward for approaching some pro-rocket nut animated by delusions of Martianism. How could one divine from speeches the secret thoughts of the speechmakers? It was well-nigh impossible, but it had to be attempted.

Three times he absorbed the data, determined to miss nothing. This senatorial flare-up was startling evidence of how much more crazily complicated the always complicated world situation had become. Had it been possible to view the picture in plain, straightforward blacks and whites it would have been easy to get the hang of it. But it was far from being a simple case of these individuals on this side and those on that, every person being readily classifiable as in one camp or the other. On the contrary, it was an opposition of uneasy alliances. Any two of these political figures might be in momentary harmony from totally different motives.

Desperately trying to prevent or at least delay space-conquest were Lindle and Womersley and their supporting cohorts in or out of government. Probably the majority of these conceived themselves as the little flock, the nation's elect, the world's élite, the sane ones of Earth, and were as fanatically pro-Martian as any Shintoist is pro-Mikado. Also there were some—an elusive percentage—who knew nothing and cared less about Lindle's cynical creed, who were quite ignorant of the Norman Club's existence, but who genuinely thought all rocket shots a wicked waste of hard-earned money. And, finally, a still smaller percentage of cranks of various sorts, some believing that space ventures were contrary to God's will; some that the cash would be better spent in providing free vitamin-pills for destitute Chinese; some that rockets would lead to new colonial adventures breeding new wars; and a few —outwardly the very soul of patriotism but inwardly the opposite—who secretly desired another nation to get there first.

Those vociferously supporting rocket expenditure were fully as motley a mob and animated by as many differing motives. The huge steel interests were well represented, being mindful of juicy profits both present and prospective. And if Sandy-hair's organization had only one quarter of the political connections enjoyed by Lindle's there must be some senatorial voters clinging to the belief that they were deported Martians. The military were in evidence, too, for cogent reasons, as also were the mining and chemical interests. Here and there were viewpoints apparently based on old-fashioned forms of jingoism; others who gave support on grounds of the inevitability of Martian exploration—"America might as well be the first" —others whose support for rocket projects rested on no more than open enmity for certain parties on the opposing side.

How to sort out one from another? How to divide them into the wits, the half-wits and the witless? Or, more accurately, into the square-dealing, the underhand-dealing—and the death-dealing?

Searching through later copies of the *Record* for any further data hidden therein, his eyes opened wide when he scanned the morning edition of two days before. Harvey G. Anderson had led the boosters who wanted Mars. Harvey G. Anderson had thwarted the Lindle–Womersley combine. Now Anderson was dead! According to the *Record*, he had "passed away unexpectedly but peacefully at the age of sixty-seven." From outside the library, he called the *Record* office.

"I've just heard of the death of Harvey Anderson. Could you tell me the cause?"

The girl at the other end went away from the lens and after

a little while a young man appeared in her place. He looked at the caller inquisitively.

"You a friend of Anderson?"

"The dead have no friends."

"No, I suppose not." The young man mulled it a moment, as if it were a profound thought. "He died of heart trouble."

"Can you be more specific?"

The other became impatient. "It was valvular disease of the heart. He'd had it a long time and was liable to drop dead at any moment."

"Who says so?"

"Now see here, mister, I've given you all we've got. If you want to make a fight of it, go argue with Doctor Poynter."

"That's exactly what I wanted to know—who said so," Armstrong pointed out. "Thanks a lot for the information."

"Always glad to oblige," lied the other, slightly miffed.

Returning to the library, he looked through the medical section of the classified directory. There was no Dr. Poynter. This brought him back to the phone. Calling the Medical Centre, he inquired about Poynter and would have laid a hundred to one that they'd deny all knowledge of that individual. He'd have lost his money. After keeping him waiting five minutes, they came back with the surprising news that Poynter was a New York physician at present staying with Senator Womersley. He felt his back hairs rising as he left the booth.

Putting this matter aside for future reference, he gave final consideration to his data, decided that of all the weird assortment of political rocket-boosters General Luther Gregory was the most promising prospect. That hoary warrior was obsessed by the military value of Mars. Whoever controlled Mars, he had told the senatorial audience for the hundredth time, controlled the Solar system. It was a telling point which had been the main urge behind rocket experimentation all over the world, and had kept it going despite sabotage and misfortune. It was an old and oft-told point which lost nothing by its constant repeating. It served admirably to move the masses who were not interested in political wrangling or scientific lectures but did desire to preserve whole skins. Lastly, it was a point which held no hint of crackpot prejudices.

Apart from such occasional performances, General Gregory made no capers on the political stage. His career, his speeches, his personality and his lack of affiliations made him obviously the one—perhaps the only one—motivated by considerations that were sound from Armstrong's viewpoint even if not sane from the viewpoint of Martians or pseudo-Martians. Moreover, he lived in Washington. His home was less than one mile away.

Armstrong was at the general's house within ten minutes.

The old warhorse was pacing restlessly up and down his study twiddling his visitor's card between thumb and forefinger, his leathery, grey-moustached features authoritative, stern.

Tramping heavy-footed into the room, Armstrong said: "This is a great favour, General. I hope you won't throw me out before I'm through."

Gregory cast a calculating and approving eye over the other's great bulk. "It's no favour to see me. For forty years I've seen everyone who wanted an interview with me, within the limits of my time, from privates upward. On the whole, it has paid me."

"I'm obliged to you, all the same."

"Never mind that, man. If you've something to say, get it off your chest as quickly as possible."

"Well, General, I've urgent, in fact, desperate reasons for inflicting upon you the craziest story you've ever heard. I'll cut it as short as I can to save your time. I ask only one thing of you."

"What may that be?"

"That, having heard it, you don't dismiss it as too absurd to be worthy of consideration. Use all the influence you've got and check the facts before you reach a decision."

"And why does all this concern *me* in particular?"

"Because you've all the authority which I lack."

"So have hundreds of others in this city," declared the General. "Some have more!"

"And because," continued Armstrong, doggedly, "I feel that you would use authority rather than abuse it."

"Oh." He was not flattered. He studied Armstrong as if about to order him to button up his jacket and get a haircut. "Have you approached anyone else before coming to me?"

"No, sir."

General Gregory resumed his pacing up and down the carpet. He glanced at the electric clock, then said: "I have heard plenty of peculiar things in my time, and I doubt whether you can tell me anything queerer. But go ahead—make it as short as you can." He stopped, and his moustache bristled. "All the hosts of heaven won't save you if you end up trying to sell me something!"

Armstrong smiled. "General, have you ever heard of the Norman Club?" He watched the other keenly.

There was no noteworthy reaction. Gregory pondered awhile, said indifferently: "The name sounds faintly familiar, but I can't place it offhand. What of the Norman Club?"

The tale took an hour, during which the General listened without interruption or change of expression. Much encouraged, Armstrong went on, ending the story by detailing his arrival in Washington.

"There you are," he concluded. "The entire world is divided by a secret creed. An invisible empire cuts right across frontiers and oceans, undermining all loyalties, making mock of all flags, menacing every form of national independence. This creed may have no better basis in fact than has Mohammedanism—for which the Mahdi and thousands of his followers gladly surrendered their lives. No better than Hinduism—for which millions have died or are yet to die. It doesn't matter how incredibly ancient its roots may be, whether they be true or false, fact or fancy, it is the modern fanaticism. No longer are we believers or unbelievers. No longer are we either the faithful or the heretics. By virtue of a legendary purge, and by the arbitrary decision of the psychotron, we are now either the sane or the insane!"

The soldier's hard gaze had not shifted from his face during the entire recital. Neither had any expression appeared upon the weather-worn features.

"This is fantastic," he declared. "I'll give you that! Without implying that I think your story untrue, I must say that it is too far-fetched to accept without evidence, considerable evidence! You realize exactly what your account means?"

"I've studied every aspect of it," Armstrong told him.

"It means that you impeach that proportion of the controls running this country."

"And every other country."

"Let's stick to this one. Your yarn means the condemnation

171

of our Intelligence Service, the F.B.I., the police, the National Guard, an incalculable number of the most important people, almost every powerful interest, almost all our channels of information and our means of propaganda. It means that we are not one country, but two!"

"Precisely! The sane and the insane!" He faced the General's steady stare. "As for the Intelligence Service, I don't think it necessarily condemned."

"Why not?"

"Think over the facts: the authorities are building rocket number eighteen down there in New Mexico, getting on with it very slowly, and giving it all the publicity that's going. Meanwhile, they're progressing in secret with two more rockets at other sites. Why should they do that? The answer is obvious. They're satisfied that rockets really are being sabotaged even though they've not been able to identify the culprits. But they've got evidence of sabotage, and the Intelligence Service has provided it. So number eighteen is merely a decoy duck, a bait to attract the saboteurs and draw their attention from what is happening elsewhere."

"Go on."

Wagging an emphatic finger, Armstrong said: "The idea was a good one. It might have worked. But it didn't. Somebody has discovered that they're being fooled. That means that somebody else among the higher-ups has been a blabbermouth. Sandy-hair and his regiment of so-called Martian deportees know of these rockets and would skin me if it would get them the details. Ten to one the Norman Club also knows about them. Ten to one they've got all the dirt, location included. Unless we can find some way to jump on the entire crowd those two rockets will go to blazes exactly as have all the others!"

"You've dumped a red-hot one in my lap!" Gregory started his to and fro marching again. "Naturally, I'm sceptical about all this. But if it's only half true, it's bad enough!" He pulled worriedly at his moustache. "It comes at a time when there's trouble enough already."

"Trouble?"

Gregory faced him squarely, legs braced apart. "The news will be out this afternoon, in the four o'clock editions, and on the radio-vision circuits. Russia has announced the result of her investigation of that atomic plant disaster in the Urals. She says the job was fixed by Russian-speaking Germans whom she accuses of being members of the revived Illuminati, subsidized by France. Some hard words are being said behind the scenes, and the international situation is deteriorating rapidly."

A chill ran down Armstrong's spine. He glanced at the clock. "It has gone four now."

Crossing to his television receiver, Gregory switched it on. The big screen flooded with light, revealed an announcer gabbling away as fast as he could go.

". . . confessed to receiving the detonating apparatus at the Polska Hotel, Warsaw, from one Aristides Duquesne, a citizen of France. The French Government has denied all knowledge of this individual. In an interview given this morning, Monsieur Jules Lefevre, Minister of Defence, declared that France has no reason to interfere with the scientific progress of a country with whom she has a pact of alliance, and that any suggestion to the contrary must be rejected most energetically. He also denied that France has encouraged a revival of the German Illuminati."

For the first time, General Gregory sat down. Leaning back in his chair, he toyed with his moustache while the announcer continued to talk fast.

"The French Government has invited the Russian Government to place its evidence before a committee of the United Nations, and a reply is now awaited. Meanwhile, the cross-examination of Mihael Kihrov and his fellow conspirators continues in Moscow." He paused for breath, then went on. "In an official announcement given by the War Office today, the British state that the annual large-scale manœuvres of their Territorial Army will for the first time be held on French soil. This is in accordance with Franco-British military agreements made last year."

Switching off, Gregory said, coolly: "There are other items not yet to be made public. They are significant and menacing. You can take it from me that the world is lucky to be still at peace—and it is problematical how much longer peace can be maintained."

"Which means that if war should break out, all building of Mars-rockets will cease, here and everywhere else?"

"Of course! Everyone will be too busy struggling for survival to bother about such matters." His hand massaged his chin thoughtfully. "How does all this look to you in the light of this Norman Club business?"

"It's a picture we'd have the devil's own job persuading anyone to see—and the Norman Club knows it! Years of cunning propaganda have instilled deep-rooted prejudices in the masses of both sides, and those prejudices will blind them to the truth. As I see it, Russian members of the Norman Club are working with French members to stir up a third world war and thus set things back by at least a couple of decades. If they succeed, their fellow members in every other country will do their darnedest to spread the conflagration and make it last as long as possible. They've done it twice before—and they can do it again, maybe. But on the two previous occasions they didn't go far enough."

"What d'you mean?"

"Anxious not to wreck this planet completely, they called off the wardogs before it became too late. They blundered there, for while those wars retarded the whole world sociologically, they gave it an immense boost scientifically. You and I and everyone else knows that it was the last world-wide free-for-all which caused a mighty jump in progress with rockets, apart from other items." He stared moodily at the blank screen. "They'll have learned their lesson from that! It'll be different next time. They'll make a proper job of it—if they can. They'll carry it through to the bitter end when all the results of accelerated scientific progress are dust among the ruins, when surviving members of the Norman Club have the only remaining guns and the rest of the world's scattered tribes have bows and arrows. They're maniacs, I tell you—maniacs with delusions of sanity!"

"Well, your obvious sincerity impresses me as much as your story," Gregory observed, candidly. "So I'm going to make some pointed inquiries of my own before committing myself one way or the other. Can you see me again this time tomorrow?"

"I can." Armstrong prepared to leave. "I suppose you've got a record of this conversation?"

Gregory pointed to a wall stud. He was a little apologetic as he spoke. "That controls a Blattnerphone in the next room. All your talk is held there in a reel of wire. You will understand that——"

"I understand perfectly," Armstrong chipped in. "In your position, I'd record every unknown petitioner. It's a wise precaution."

The General looked grateful as he showed his visitor out.

Walking rapidly down the street, Armstrong reviewed the conversation. How far had it got him? Even supposing that he became convinced, how much could the General do, what could he achieve?

Fat, black thunderheads were rolling over the Potomac. They seemed symbolic of the international situation. The few passers-by reflected the morbid atmosphere, they were quiet, serious, preoccupied. If all the knights and bishops on fifty chessboards combined in phony opposition, could they clear the boards of all other major pieces, leaving only a few futile pawns?

Large raindrops began to fall squashily. A ragged line flashed blue and brilliant over the darkening horizon. There followed the sound of clouds being ripped apart.

Taking shelter in an arcade, he waited for the downpour to pass. The window by his elbow was that of a recorder-agent; it held a display of simple press-sheet reproducers like his own, and a few dual-purpose television models like Gregory's. The demonstration model in the foreground was of the former type, and switched on, its screen filled with the front page of the Washington *Post*.

Woe, woe was the theme-song of this page. It is said that France was about to order five classes to the Colours. It is said that Russia has withheld certain secrets of bacteriological warfare from the United Nations Disarmament Commission. It is said that a new and still more powerful Germany was waiting to arise—unless America stepped in to prevent it. The Washington *Post* omitted to mention by whom these things were said, neither did it bother to identify the mysterious "official circles" whom it quoted. The general effect was the same regardless of whether the cause was fact or fancy—it conditioned the minds of the mob in readiness for the coming storm.

His brow was as thunderous as the sky above as his eyes sought less important items in the right-hand column.

ROCKET PILOT WANTED FOR MURDER

Gallup, N.M. Local police are seeking George Quinn, official pilot of R.18 now under construction fifty miles to the north. Quinn is alleged to have slain Ambrose Fothergill, technical director of the rocket site, after a heated argument.

Armstrong's big hands clenched, his fingers curling and digging into the palms. He had no chance to absorb this news fully, for his gaze involuntarily wandered on and discovered another item.

WOMAN SCIENTIST VANISHES

Tarrytown, N.Y. Claire Mandle, physicist sister of the late Professor Robert Mandle, disappeared from her home this morning in circumstances said to be mysterious. Herbert Walthall, F.B.I. agent, admits that his organization is now looking for Miss Mandle, but he says that no information can be given at present.

Disregarding the rain, the thunder, the streaks of blue fire flashing continually, Armstrong whirled into the street and began to run.

CHAPTER THIRTEEN

The address shown in the telephone directory proved to be that of a colonial mansion standing within high-walled grounds. A barbed and electrified wire fence ran along the top of this wall. There was a small, solidly built lodge at front, another at back, and each flanked a pair of enormous steel gates behind which lounged some decidedly hard-looking eggs. Other equally tough mugs could be seen patrolling the grounds beyond the gates. The whole set-up suggested that Senator Womersley rated as a person of considerable importance.

It was obvious to Armstrong that he must discard his vague notions of busting into the dump by means of any handy door or window. Nor was there a chance of anyone bulling his way in without getting lead in the liver for his pains. This was a situation requiring guile.

"Softly, softly, catchee monkey!" he quoted to himself as he approached the front gates.

The guards alerted when they saw him nearing. He put on his face an expression which felt stupid but was intended to be ingratiating. One of the guards responded by spitting contemptuously at a fly on the lodge wall.

Holding his card through the thick bars of the gate, Armstrong spoke as agreeably as possible. "Would you mind inquiring whether Senator Womersley is willing to see me?"

Taking the pasteboard, one of the guards glanced at it, demanded, "You got an appointment?"

"No."

"What d'you want to see him about?"

"A matter referred to me by Senator Lindle."

"O.K." He turned towards the lodge. "You wait there."

The wait lasted half an hour during which he stamped impatiently around and wondered how many wires were humming with questions about him. Eventually the guard came back, surlily unlocked the gate.

"He'll see you now."

Going through, Armstrong followed the other to the house. The gates clanged behind them; it was an ominous sound, the sort of metallic clamour which heralds the beginning of twenty years in Sing Sing. Another patrolling guard crossed their path; he was being dragged at the end of an anchor-chain by a dog half the size of a horse.

Gaining the building, they waited another five minutes in a gloomy, oak-panelled hall from one wall of which the dusty, moth-eaten head of a moose stared lugubriously down at them. There were four guards stationed in this hall and all looked as if they'd been affected by long association with the moose.

Finally he was shown into a lounge where Womersley posed by the french windows. The senator turned to examine his caller, revealing himself as a portly and somewhat pompous personage with ruddy cheeks and long white hair of the kind politely called distinguished.

"So you're Mr. Armstrong?" he enunciated, pontifically. Taking a high-backed chair, he seated himself carefully and importantly, as if about to declare this meeting open. "What can I do for you?" Tapping his teeth with a silver pencil, he regarded his visitor with a faint air of patronage.

"Not so long ago our mutual friend Randolph Lindle treated me to a taste of the psychotron." He eyed Womersley sharply. "Doubtless you know about that?"

Womersley smiled slowly and went on tapping his teeth. He said: "Please proceed."

"You refuse to say?" He shrugged his shoulders. "Oh, well, I guess it doesn't matter. I assume that you do know of it."

"I am interested only in facts," Womersley observed. "Your assumptions fail to divert me."

"Facts interest me likewise—especially the fact that you and Lindle appear to be the leading lights of the Norman Club in this country."

Still playing with the silver pencil, Womersley smiled again, made no reply.

"The Norman Club viewed me as a natural," Armstrong went on. "Having given me the works, they assured me that I'd come back to them, voluntarily, of my own accord. I'm sane, you see? I'm bound eventually to think as they think— because great minds think alike." He paused reflectively. "At that time I disagreed with them most emphatically, and I felt certain that I'd never see things their way, not if I lived another million years. But I was wrong."

"Ah!" Womersley rammed the pencil into his pocket, clasped his hands together, put on an I-told-you-so expression.

"They were right and I was wrong." He faced the senator squarely, his manner deceptively frank. "It's not so much that I've had time to think as the fact that events have compelled me to think. Sandy-hair's gang has given me plenty of food for thought."

"Sandy-hair's?" Womersley was mystified.

"I'm being hunted by a crazy crowd who claim to be Martians lately deported from Mars."

"Hu-mans," defined Womersley. He made a clicking noise with his tongue. "What they lack in numbers they make up for in capabilities. This place of mine is well guarded because you're not the only one they'd like to get at."

"Anyway, they convinced me where Lindle failed. So I've come back."

In silence, Womersley studied him for a while. Then he turned round in his chair, flipped a little lever set in the wall. For the first time, Armstrong noticed that there was a diamond pattern of small perforations in the wall beneath the lever and a small lens above it.

"Well?" said Womersley to the wall.

"It's him all right," assured a tinny voice from the perforated diamond.

"Thanks!" Reversing the lever, the senator turned back and faced his visitor.

"New York identification?" Armstrong suggested.

"Certainly!" He contemplated the ceiling while he continued speaking. "The psychotron identifies sanity. No more than that. It does not classify opinions. Even the sane may hold differing opinions about some things—though not those opinions peculiar to the insane. You realize that, of course?"

"Yes, I do."

"Therefore you will also realize that you can't just jump aboard the bandwagon the moment you consider yourself entitled to do so. A declaration of change of heart is not sufficient for us. It is far from sufficient."

"I had guessed that in advance. You will want me to prove that my notions really are what they purport to be. I shall have to assassinate the President or do something equally desperate."

"You are not without perspicacity," Womersley conceded.

179

"That is to be expected, considering that you are a Nor-man by nature. It now remains to be seen whether you are also one by inclination. We can find you a task the satisfactory performance of which——"

"You need not bother about concocting a test of my loyalty," Armstrong put in swiftly. "The second reason why I wished to see you is because I now have the proof ready and prepared."

Womersley's eyes glowed, and his voice lost its suavity. "What will be acceptable will be that which corresponds with *our* definition of proof—not yours!"

"Maybe. But in this instance the proof is something you'll have to take up whether you like it or not. You can't afford to let it go. To let it pass would send even the psychotron daffy!"

Standing up, his posture irefully important, Womersley snapped: "Be more explicit!"

"They're building rocket eighteen in New Mexico. It's cheese in the mousetrap, as you most certainly know. It's a decoy to draw certain parties away from nineteen and twenty which are being built elsewhere."

"So far, you have told me nothing."

"I'll tell you something now—all three of those rockets might as well be tossed on the scrap-heap."

The senator's face was cold as he said: "Is that all?"

"Not by a long shot!" He grinned his satisfaction. "You shouldn't make assumptions yourself, you know! I didn't mean that they're useless because the Norman Club is going to bust them when the time is ripe. On the contrary, they're no better than scrap because they're hopelessly outdated."

"Eh?" Womersley breathed heavily. "What d'you mean by that?"

"Somehow . . . I don't know how . . . one of those Martian nuts got himself deported along with plans of a super-dooper scout job." He watched with pleasure as the other's florid complexion deepened and his eyes widened in incredulity. "You can understand why he did it, seeing that every one of them is itching to get back home. It's a seven-man-crew contraption, and it's umpteen centuries ahead of anything we've got. He claims that it can be constructed in ten weeks, given the facilities. We can be on Mars sooner than you think!"

Womersley's face was now a dull purple. His breath

180

wheezed deeply. The fury boiling within him was amazing for one of his appearance.

Controlling himself with an effort, he rasped: "Where did you get all this?"

"It was offered me for two reasons. Firstly, it was known that I'm violently in favour of going places as fast as possible. Secondly, it was believed that I might be able to pull enough strings to get the facilities necessary for building the ship. If I can't, or won't, the escapee takes his plans to Britain, France, Russia or anywhere else where he can get co-operation."

"Go on," Womersley ordered, grimly.

"This guy has reneged on his gang—Sandy-hair's gang. Or maybe odd deportees have failed to contact other, better organized ones. He's looking after himself, see? He wants help to build a scout job. He's got the plans—and he's got a price for them."

"What is it?"

"A firm guarantee that he'll be taken to Mars, will be released immediately on arrival, and that no mention will be made of him to the Martians." He made an explanatory gesture. "The boy is homesick."

"Where are the plans now?"

"He's sticking to them."

Gazing at him steadily and deliberately, eye to eye. Womersley harshed, "All this could be true. Yes, it could be—knowing what I do know. What I'm far from satisfied about is why you opposed us so long before you come to us running."

"I dismissed the Norman Club because I couldn't believe all this Martian-origin stuff. It was contrary to everything I'd learned, everything I knew." He stood up, shoved his hands into his pockets. "But now I've learned a lot more. I've been sniped at and I'm still being gunned for, so that for me the whole affair is no longer a matter of truth or untruth, but rather of life or death."

"Yes, but——"

"The snag I'm up against now is that of convincing this fellow holding the plans that I've got political connections powerful enough to get his rocket built in double-quick time. If I don't convince him, off go the plans heaven knows where—and somebody's sure to use them. So this is where you come in."

"Me?"

"Yes. He knows of you as a considerable political influence in Washington. He doesn't know about the Norman Club, much less your connection with it. Being a Hu-man, he'd be mighty leery of Nor-mans, anyway. Having taken a chance on me, he'll take one on any big enough political figure standing behind me. You've got to tell him you can find a million dollars to splurge on his rocket. You've got to persuade him to hand over those plans."

A conflict of emotions twisted the senator's plump features. Apprehension, suspicion, desire—all were there. He paraded several times up and down the room before speaking.

"Where and in what circumstances can you make contact with this individual?"

"He's going to phone my New York apartment before twelve tomorrow."

"Your apartment is burned down."

Oh, so you know that! thought Armstrong. Gibly, he said: "I've got another, of course. D'you think I'd sleep in the fields?"

"What if he has phoned already, while you are here?"

"He'll get no reply and will call again later. But when he does, you had better be there too! Or Lindle. I don't care which of you it may be, so long as it's one or the other. To bring this fish in needs better bait on the hook than I can provide."

"Armstrong," pronounced Womersley, with sudden decision, "I'm enough of a political picture to be framed. In fact, some have tried it—to their everlasting regret!" He stuck out his chest as if he'd have beaten it if only he'd been adorned in a tiger-skin. "So take warning—any funny business will be liable to boomerang on you! I'm going to come in with you on this plan-question, not because I fully believe you, but solely because it could be true and, if it is, it's far too momentous to ignore. We just can't afford to ignore it!"

"That's what I thought."

"And that's what I know you've been thinking!" Womersley retorted. "Therefore, I'm coming in my way, and not yours! If this story proves to be an elaborate gag"—he paused, his face hard—"it will be your last such one on this world or any other!"

"And if it's not a gag, if it proves genuine, the Norman Club takes me to its collective bosom?"

"Yes." Ringing a desk-bell, Womersley spoke to the guard who responded. "Have Mercer get the car ready. Tell Jackson, Hardacre and Wills that they're coming with me to New York pronto." He waited until the other had gone, then said to Armstrong. "Those four will accompany us. They're so touchy they start shooting if someone grits his teeth. Bear that in mind!"

"I won't forget," Armstrong promised.

He resumed his seat while Womersley made ready for departure. His broad, heavy face held a hungry look. As a crocodile, he'd put over a good imitation of a log!

They piled into a big, silver-grey Cadillac with Mercer behind the wheel and Jackson sitting by his side. Armstrong's large pants pressed the middle of the back seat where he was jammed between Womersley and Wills. The folding occasional seat facing the rear three was taken by Hardacre, a craggy personage who obviously regarded his position as strategical and viewed the passenger as a prisoner. He favoured the latter with a belligerent stare. Armstrong stared back at him, sniffed a couple of times, then sneezed.

Pulling away from the fortresslike estate, the powerful machine swooped northwards. Armstrong sniffed at frequent intervals, sneezed a couple more times. Pressed closely against him, Womersley fidgeted with distaste but made no remark. Hardacre eyed him as if the free distribution of germs were a hostile act.

"Got plenty wet in that storm," Armstrong mourned to nobody in particular. "I'll be dead with pneumonia before we get there . . . *A-a-arshoo!*" He jerked with the violence of his sneeze, leaned hard on Wills, struggled to extract a handkerchief from his right-hand pocket.

Hardacre's eyes glittered as he waited for the handkerchief to appear. He seemed to be expecting the sufferer to produce anything from a rattlesnake to a field howitzer. Emitting an irritated grunt, Womersley edged away, giving the heaving Armstrong room to get at the pocket.

Drawing out the handkerchief with a triumphant flourish, Armstrong wrapped it around his nose and bugled vigorously. At the same moment, a tiny metal cylinder slid up his right nostril. Holding the handkerchief on his lap, he blinked owlishly at Hardacre.

After another ten miles, he resumed his sniffing, doing it through the nostril yet unblocked. Then he coughed, gobbled like a turkeycock and hurriedly employed the handkerchief to choke another sneeze. The second cylinder slid up the other nostril. Hardacre's gaze remained fixed upon him. He gasped a couple of times, coughed again, leaned on Womersley while he fought to get at his left-hand pocket.

Hardacre snapped at Wills: "I don't like this song and dance. See what he's diving for now."

Raising himself clumsily in the swaying car, Wills forced a hairy hand into the pocket, dragged out another handkerchief and a bunch of keys. Hardacre registered acute disappointment.

Hoarsely murmuring, "Thanks!" Armstrong mopped his nose with the second handkerchief, jingled the keys, smiled broadly at Hardacre. That worthy scowled, turned his gaze away for the first time, and stared out of the window.

Armstrong sighed, began to scratch his knees. He did it absent-mindedly, sniffing and wheezing at intervals, while the others continued pointedly to ignore him. His fingers scratched and tapped and played nervously until finally he got the phial loose from its knee-strap and felt it slide down the leg of his pants. The slender glass tube fell silently on to the carpeted floor and none heard the sound of it as it splintered under his heel.

The Cad rushed onwards and covered eight more miles in nine minutes before things began to happen. Womersley, who had slowly slumped in his seat, suddenly made loud bubbling noises through pursed lips. At the opposite end of the seat, Wills lolled against Armstrong and swayed helplessly with the motion of the car.

With a sharp preliminary swerve, the big machine commenced to wander at high speed all over the road. With vague alarm battling the urge to slumber, Hardacre fought to awake and make action. His hands moved slothfully and uncertainly as they sought for his gun.

Lifting a columnar leg, Armstrong put his big foot on Hardacre's stomach and shoved. The breath whooshed out of the other. He fell forward, sobbed for air on the carpet. Fumes rising from the crystals on the floor filled his lungs.

Leaning over him, Armstrong snatched the nodding Mercer bodily from under the wheel, tossed him on to Womersley's lap. The Cadillac yawed, headed towards a bank. Bending further forward, he grabbed the wheel, straightened the onrushing machine. He held it thus a moment, knowing that with no foot on the accelerator its automatic gears had slipped into neutral. It slowed. In the seat beside that lately warmed by Mercer, the semi-drugged Jackson pawed at him feebly. Still holding the wheel with his left hand, he slugged Jackson behind the ear with his right.

Reluctantly the Cad drifted to a stop. Putting on the handbrake, he got out, closed the door behind him, sat on the bank and enjoyed a cigarette while the supine passengers continued to stew in the fumes. Once Wills rolled his head lackadaisically; once Womersley made a feeble gesture in his sleep, but after five more minutes they resembled a load of corpses.

With the little filters out of his nose and back in his handkerchief, Armstrong opened all the doors, let the wind clear the car. He swept out a few undissolved crystals. Keeping a careful watch on the road lest he be subjected to the unwelcome attention of other motorists, he lifted out all but Womersley, bore them swiftly one by one up the bank, parked them side by side where they'd be out of sight from the highway. As an afterthought, he picked a convenient weed, placed it in Hardacre's hand. Returning to the car, he rolled Womersley on to the floor, closed and locked the rear doors, got into the front seat and drove onwards at top speed.

His mad pace would have interested the police had he not slowed down twice in precisely the right places. He rushed the Cad as if every second were costing him a thousand dollars. Three times he stopped; once for gas, once to send a wire postponing his appointment with the General, and once to quiet his slowly reviving passenger. All these pauses meant trouble. He had to shoo off a nosey gas-station attendant. He had to tell a tale of drunkenness to a passer-by near the post office. As for the last, Womersley's dim awakening indicated that the tricked guards likewise would be recovering and that the hue and cry would begin as soon as they could start it.

Womersley settled down under a second dose of dope. He

gave the senator a long shot of it, enough to keep him peaceful for most of the night. The rest of the journey was covered without mishap, and he tooled the car through New Jersey with a feeling of satisfaction which grew as he neared Drake's home.

Ed Drake answered the door, took one look, exclaimed, "Jeepers! I thought you'd been buried!"

"I'm in trouble, Ed. I want you to help me out."

"What's wrong now?" His wandering eyes suddenly found Womersley reposing in the back of the car and pain sprang into his lean features. "Hey, are you carrying a stiff?"

"No—he's all out. I'd like you to take him off my hands for a short while." Unlocking the rear door he proceeded to lug the senator from the car. He handed the body to the surprised Drake as if bestowing a gift. "Toss him on a bed and let him snore until I return. I'll be back before long—I'll explain everything then."

Holding the sagging Womersley with difficulty and without enthusiasm, Drake said: "I hope this is on the up and up?"

"Don't worry, Ed. Put him out of sight until I return. You'll be all right. You know me."

"Yeah, I know you—that's what's got me worried." Drake walked backwards through the door, dragging the senator with him.

The Cadillac started up, and Armstrong whirled it away. He took the bottom corner on two wheels. Behind him, Ed Drake peered sourly from the door until the fast-moving car was out of sight. Then he shrugged, closed the door, lugged his unconscious visitor upstairs.

It was four hours and twenty minutes later when Armstrong reappeared. Heavy-footed and tired, he lumbered in, dumped a big black box on the floor, glanced at the clock which showed the hour of midnight.

"Has that body become animated yet?"

"No," said Drake. "He's sleeping like he'd been drugged."

"Which he has."

"Eh?" Drake let his mouth dangle. "Who drugged him?"

"Me." He smiled at the other's expression. "I had to do it to get him all to myself." He sighed, looked at the clock again. "I could have been back an hour ago if it hadn't been necessary to dump his car in New York where they'll be sure to find it. I had to skip from one taxi to another to return."

"You dumped his car?" Ed Drake's voice went up in pitch. "D'you mean it was hot? Have you kidnapped this guy? What the heck's going on around here?"

"Take it easy, Ed. The gentleman is Senator Womersley, and he's paying us an involuntary visit."

Drake jumped. "Womersley! I thought his fat face looked familiar!" He waved worried hands. "Hell's bells, John, they'll give you life for this. What the deuce possessed you to snatch a guy like him? Why drag me into it?"

"You'll see." His foot poked the heavy box he'd brought in. "That is one of the only ten electronic schizophrasers in existence. I had to borrow it at short notice, and after plenty of argument, from old Professor Shawbury, at Columbia. The original model is still in my lab at Hartford—but I can't go there to collect it."

"Why not?"

"Because, brother, I suspect that traps await me at every one of my old-time haunts. That's one reason why I've had to come to you. I've seen you about four times in the last seven years, and this house of yours never was a regular calling-place of mine." He studied the mystified Drake keenly. "The other reason is that after some thought I've decided that I trust you —as far as anyone can be trusted these crazy times."

"That's nice! That's very nice! When I'm doing my twenty years in the cell next to yours, it'll be good to remember that at least you trusted me!"

Armstrong said, harshly: "Ed, if I don't get to the bottom of this, neither you nor I nor millions of others may live long enough to do twenty years any place." He made an impatient gesture. "Where's the body?"

"Upstairs on the front bed." Drake trailed after him moodily, helped him carry the senator down. He made no attempt to conceal his doubt and apprehension as he watched the other tie the victim in a chair.

Moving with businesslike efficiency, Armstrong opened the box, pulled from it a compact piece of apparatus resembling a portable short-wave therapy set. It had a tiny silver-tube antenna and a similar half-wave reflector set on either side of a plastic cup at the end of four yards of coaxial cable.

Putting the cup on Womersley's head, he adjusted the antenna and reflector with great care. Finally satisfied that the two tubes were located precisely where he wanted them with respect to the subject's cranium, he strapped them in position, made sure that no movement of the slumbering senator's head could dislodge them by a fraction.

Next, he connected the apparatus to a power-plug set in the wall, disconnected the coaxial cable, switched on, checked operation. Reconnecting the antenna lead, he fiddled with matching transformers at both ends of it, then switched off. He flopped into a seat, glowered at the unconscious Womersley.

"All we've got to do now is wait for this fat schemer to wake up."

Drake found another chair, lowered himself into it uneasily. "I wish you wouldn't use so much 'we' stuff. This is your play, not mine." He surveyed the apparatus and chewed at his bottom lip. "What will that do to him?"

"Nothing harmful. So far as I'm concerned, it's a sample of tit-for-tat. His crowd put me under a contraption called a psychotron. I'm putting him under this dingbat which, in its own peculiar way, is more efficient."

"Well, what is it?" Drake persisted.

"A microwave schizophraser. A kind of transmitter. It sprays oscillations on the neural band. You know that thoughts are electrical in nature, don't you?"

Drake nodded.

"This thing is no more than a simple jammer of thought-processes. Its beauty is that it can be made to muddle-up only the rationalizing sector of the human brain, leaving the motor ganglions, the memory sector and other parts free to operate spontaneously."

"If I'm right," suggested Drake, "that'll fill the guy with involuntary reactions. It will make him a spasmic. Where's the sense of that?"

"It won't make him a spasmic. It has no permanent effects. The gadget is nothing more than something ten times better than a lie-detector. A person questioned while under its influence is mentaly incapable of refusing, concealing or distorting whatever information is lying latent in his memory sector. When asked, he cannot help but respond with what he knows to be the truth or sincerely believes to be the truth. If he hasn't got the answer, he doesn't reply—he can't substitute a false or misleading item of information." He waved a reassuring hand. "The worst that can happen to this political specimen is that for once in his life he may blurt out some awkward facts. Not so very terrible, is it?"

"He'll take off your hide for it, all the same. He'll make you die the death of a thousand cuts first chance he gets." Drake had another go at his bottom lip while he stared at the senator. His eyes grew round. "Look, he's waking now!"

Going across to the chair, Armstrong slapped Womersley's face gently but firmly. The senator snorted, mumbled, half-opened his eyes, closed them, opened them again. Taking his hands, Armstrong rubbed them vigorously. Womersley gulped, yawned, tried to move within his bonds, looked slightly stupefied when he found himself tied down. Pulling his hands out of Armstrong's grasp, he muttered peevishly:

"Where . . . am I? What's happening?"

Switching on the apparatus, Armstrong watched the politician's florid features. Drake likewise studied them, his own expressing anxiety.

Womersley put out a dry tongue, drew it in again, gaped around with optics which gradually grew dazed. He tried to lift his hands and failed. A few seconds later, his stare was as comprehending as that of a village idiot.

In a loud, clear voice, Armstrong snapped at him: "Who killed Ambrose Fothergill?"

Womersley was silent a moment, then croaked: "Muller."

"On whose orders?"

Again the silence. Womersley seemed to be having a psychic battle within himself despite the jamming of his reasoning processes. Instinct was substituting here—the ancient law of self-preservation. He blinked at his questioner as if he couldn't see him.

"Mine," he said. "Mine . . . mine!"

"Jerusalem!" breathed Drake, looking on.

Sternly, Armstrong continued: "Then why did George Quinn take it on the run? Was he framed? Did he realize that he'd been framed?"

Womersley made no reply.

Putting it in a different way, Armstrong demanded: "Did you give any orders concerning Quinn?"

"Yes."

"What were they?"

"He was to be taken away."

"By whom? By Muller?"

"By Muller, Healy and Jacques."

"This always is somewhat tedious," Armstrong observed to Drake, "because he's conditioned to answer only the bare question and he won't volunteer anything more. I'll have to drag data out of him item by item." Then, to Womersley: "Why did you order them to take Quinn away?"

"It did two jobs at one stroke."

"What were they?"

"It made it look as if Quinn had lammed and therefore was guilty. And it got rid of him."

"Why did you want to get rid of Quinn?"

"He was the official pilot."

"To what place has he been taken?" Armstrong's hard optics were fixed on the senator as he waited for the response.

There was no response.

"Don't you know?"

"No."

Taking a deep breath, he tried it another way. "To whom has he been taken?"

"To Singleton."

"Who is Singleton?"

"The Norman Club director in Kansas City," Womersley murmured. His head lolled forward, was brought up sluggishly.

"Do you know where Singleton has hidden him?"

"No."

"Do you know whether he is alive or dead?"

"No."

"Why did you order Fothergill's death?"

"He was one of us—a Nor-man. He was sane. But he lacked courage. He let us down."

"So?"

Womersley said nothing. He appeared to be in a semi-slumber.

Between his teeth, Armstrong gave forth: "Enough of that. We'll jump to the next subject." In louder voice, he pressed: "Where is Claire Mandle?"

"I don't know."

"Has the Norman Club any hand in her disappearance?"

"I don't know."

Suppressing his surprise, he continued: "If your New York mob had taken her, would you have been informed of it?"

"Not necessarily."

Frowning, he said to Drake: "We can learn something even from negative responses. He doesn't know what Singleton has done with Quinn, nor what Lindle's crowd in New York are up to. He's a pretty fat frog in this Norman Club puddle but isn't informed on everything concerning it. Therefore, big as he is, he's not Mister Big! He's high up—but someone else is higher!"

"Ask him," Drake suggested, with perfect logic.

"Who is the leader of the Norman Club in the United States?"

Womersley sagged in his chair, behaved as if deaf.

"Some gadget," Drake offered, sardonically. "It makes him confess all."

"It can't make him tell what he doesn't know," Armstrong retorted. He questioned the victim in different terms. "Is there a national leader of the Norman Club in this country?"

"No."

He favoured Drake with an I-told-you-so glance before carrying on with: "Who's the Norman Club boss in Washington?"

"Me."

"And in New York?"

"Lindle."

"And Singleton's the boss in Kansas City?"

"Yes."

"Who is the boss in Chicago?"'

"I don't know."

"He doesn't know," Armstrong observed. "You see the significance of that? It's the cell technique! The boss of each cell functions as contact man with two or three other cells, the rest remaining unknown to him. Nobody can betray more than his immediate fellows and maybe another cell or two—whereupon the remainder take revenge. Surviving cells avenge those gone under. The sane maintain discipline in the same manner as the insane, namely, by fear reprisals." He stamped up and down the room. "That means that elsewhere the Norman Clubs don't all function openly as Norman Clubs, and that some are masquerading in other guises—yogi cults, or heavens knows what. I could do with an army, Ed, a veritable army! And it would have to be an international one at that!"

"It sure looks like you're trying to bite off more than you can chew."

"I am—but I've gone too far to withdraw even if I wished to. I'm like a python who's locked his jaws on an antelope ten sizes too large for him—I've got to go on even if I bust!" He tramped backwards and forwards worriedly. "Supposing that in some miraculous manner I bumped this cynical old geezer and all his guards and all his Washington followers—what then? Lindle and his mob continue to function. So do a hundred or more similar cells scattered over this country. So do a thousand or more distributed over the rest of the globe." He screwed his right fist into his left palm. "It's like trying to overthrow international Buddhism in one week. It can't be done —but it's *got* to be done!"

"I don't see why." Drake scowled at the sagging senator, then at the schizophraser, then at the clock. He suppressed a desire to yawn. "If you're yearning for a fight, why don't you get married?"

"This isn't funny, Ed. It's as unfunny as the robot-rocket and the atom bomb. It's as unfunny as bacteriological warfare, starvation, pestilence and the final collapse of civilization." He paused, hot eyes on his listener who looked a little abashed. "If you don't believe it, get a load of this!" Turning to the man in the chair, he said sharply: "Womersley, are the international influences of the world's Norman Clubs striving to bring about a major war?"

"Yes." The speaker's voice was automatic, toneless, and his face was relaxed into near-dopiness.

"Why?"

"We're at the last ditch."

"What d'you mean by that?"

"They'll get . . . they'll get their Mars rockets away." He was mumbling haltingly now. "Maniacs . . . loose in the cosmos . . . congenital maniacs . . . snatching at the stars . . . unless we can start them . . . killing . . . each other." The senator ended with a low gasp and his head sank.

Armstrong leaped forward, switched off the schizophraser. "Brain-strain," he explained to the alarmed Drake. "He's endured the jamming too long and his mind has found refuge in unconsciousness. He'll get over it." Taking the plastic cap from the victim's head, he put the cap on the floor, propped the head with a cushion. "He's out of that drug, but the neural impulses have put him in a haze again. He'll need a little sleep to recover." Discontentedly, he eyed his dead apparatus. "Darn it, I could get ten times as much out of him if only his mind would stand the strain."

"What's all this gabble about the Norman Club, anyway?" Drake inquired.

Armstrong gave him the whole story as swiftly and briefly as he could, and finished, "They have not got complete power in this country—yet! We're a democracy, which means they stand to gain power most any time, when circumstances favour them. Even now, as a strong, influential and ruthless minority they've enough pull to divert our destiny one way or the other. Governmental keyposts are held by their nominees, and departments have a quota of their members. Remember, Ed, that these Norman fanatics can be Democrats, Republicans or even Tibetan lamas; they can operate under any fancy tag which happens to suit their purpose at any given moment— though, all the time, fundamentally, they are Nor-mans, the superiors of Hu-mans!"

"Swami-stuff!" defined Drake, contemptuously. "That's not strong enough to start world-wide wars."

"Don't kid yourself! We aren't alone in this cockeyed world. There are other nations, other peoples animated by other ideas of destiny. In some of them these Nor-mans may have less influence than they have here—but are fighting to get it! In some, they may have more power. In a few, they may be in complete command. And it needs only one country to start a war—not two or more. One country, determined to start a holocaust, can begin the blood-bath. Germany did it under Hitler—and he was as fantastic a visionary as this fat chump or any of his Norman Club buddies. Germany marched into hell and pulled half the world with her—all for the sake of a mighty obsession."

"But——"

"Look, Ed, suppose that Germany's eighty million Nazis had been not a nation but an international cult. Suppose that they'd gained control of two or three countries at least one of which had high military potential. Suppose that they were in near-control of most other countries and formed a gigantic and redoubtable Fifth Column in what part of the world remained —d'you think they might have won their war?"

"They'd still have lost it," Drake declared without hesitation.

"Maybe they would; but they'd have taken a heck of a lot longer to lose it and would have exacted a price infinitely heavier from the world as a whole. However, that's not the point." He tapped Drake's arm to emphasize his words. "The point is that these Norman crackpots cannot lose a war."

"They can't——!" began Drake, irefully.

"Did Orientals lose the last war?"

"A silly question. The last scrap was between the democracies and the totalitarians."

"With the Chinese on our side and the Japs on the other. There were Orientals on *both* sides—so, taking them as a whole, they couldn't lose." His voice slowed down, became more emphatic. "Get it into your head, Eddie, that these Norman cultists are as completely international as short-haired dogs—and have as few real loyalties. Their purpose is to start a war big enough to put an effective brake on what they choose to regard as an undesirable form of progress. Which side nominally wins and which nominally loses matters not a hoot to them so long as the general wreckage is enough for their purpose. Why should they care who stands torn and tattered on the field of battle and claims to be the winner—they're on both sides!"

"I think you credit them with more power than they've got. The world's masses won't rush into uniform and die by the millions merely because an obscure gang of lunatics want them to do so."

"Won't they?" Armstrong's smile was lopsided and lugubrious. "All you have to do is invent a devil with which to scare the millions, use every available channel of propaganda to convince them that said devil exists and that it's an awful thing, and finally persuade them that a fate worse than death awaits them if they don't fight it with all they've got." He clicked his tongue sardonically. "Whereupon they fight like wildcats!"

Drake was indignant. "Are you suggesting that in the last war our boys fought and died for nothing?"

194

"Not at all! Quite the contrary! But for what was the *other* side fighting?"

Drake went silent, thoughtful.

"As I have said," Armstrong persisted, "it needs only one country to start it. The others then have to fight to stop it. And any devil will do to get *some* mob in murderous mood. The Germans fought frenziedly against the imaginery demon called Encirclement. For fifty years or more the Russkis have held themselves ready to battle a fiend called Capitalism. There was a time when Christians fought bloodily against a foe named Islam. If, after due preparation through the world's propaganda-channels, tonight's radio dramatically summoned everyone to prepare to defend themselves against Technocrat invaders from Alpha Centauri, thousands of credulous listeners would reach for their guns. Do you recall those people who wanted to exterminate each other over the question of whether a boiled egg should be cracked at the big end or the little?"

"Shut up!" suggested Drake. "You turn my stomach. You talk like one of these Nor-mans—you're saying that we're all nuts!"

"What if we are? Maybe these Norman cultists are correct; maybe this world is a cosmic madhouse, a sort of dreadful sanctuary for the solar system's idiots—but is that any reason why the inmates should sit and sulk in a corner? Maybe ninety per cent. of we Terrestrials are just plain daffy, but what good will it do us to roam around our cell and mope about it? That's where I and the Norman Club part company. If the loonies can bust out, I say good luck to them!" He pondered a few seconds, added: "Anyway, I'm not satisfied with a psychotron's arbitrary definitions of sanity and insanity, neither am I convinced that Martians, Venusians and Mercurians—if they really exist—are paragons of virtue when compared with us."

"You're selling me. What now?"

"You need to know all these things, Ed, because you've got to help me."

"In what way?"

"I must milk this white-haired old schemer of all he knows even if he collapses ten times during the process. I've got to make contact with some friends lying low in New York. I've got to discover what has happened to Claire Mandle, and I've got to figure some way of getting George Quinn out of bad.

And that's not all, in fact it's not half of it; I must find some way of getting the police and the F.B.I. off my neck. Finally, if it's possible, I've got to pull a fast one on the international Norman Club before they pull a fast one on the world!"

"Three-quarters of which is totally impossible," declared Drake, positively. "You might just as well give yourself up and let matters take their course."

"Not while I've feet in my socks!" He studied Womersley as that individual suddenly commenced to snore. "He's recovering all right. I want you to hang on to him for me, Ed; hang on to him at all costs for at least twenty-four hours. Don't let him get away from you even if you have to bash out his brains!"

"Are you going again?"

"I'm beating it across the river for reinforcements. Have you got a car you can lend me?"

"The Lincoln. It's around the back." Drake gloomed at his sleeping prisoner. "Oh, well—kismet! Reckon I'd better frisk him in case he's carrying something unpleasant."

"I searched him before we got here. He's carrying nothing. If he wakes up and starts bawling about his authority, hammer on his noggin!"

Hastening around the back, he found the Lincoln, took it away fast. It was three-forty in the morning by the clock on the dashboard, and the Moon was riding high as he pointed his bonnet towards the Hudson. "Three-quarters . . . is impossible," Drake had remarked. As one of those concerned with a earlier, ill-fated rocket-shot, Drake tended to be pessimistic. There was another viewpoint, older, better established, namely, that nothing is impossible.

Least of all a cosmic prison-break!

CHAPTER FOURTEEN

The choice lay between two possible contact-points—Norton or Miriam. If Hansen had not yet got in touch with Norton, and if the leery Miriam already had skipped, neither of these points would prove of any use. It was a waste of valuable time trying to think up a third way of finding Hansen without first testing these ready-made alternatives.

Miriam would be best for the first attempt, he decided. Parking the Lincoln near a phone booth, he tried the number which had got through to her on the previous occasion. There was a long wait while the automatic system maintained its persistent *buzz-buzz* at the other end of the line. He listened uneasily, his eyes constantly searching the empty street.

Eventually there came a sharp click, the screen swirled, Miriam appeared in it. She looked dishevelled and liverish—there was no evidence of her afternoon glamour at this hour when dawn was breaking in the east.

" 'Lo, Splendiferous!" he hailed. "How're your poor dogs?"

"What d'you want?" she demanded, showing a mixture of apprehension and irritability. "And why can't it wait?"

"Now, now! Be amiable! I wished only to see what you look like when you've crawled out of bed."

Automatically she primped her hair. Then she gave him a sour look and said: "Say what you want to say, and beat it."

"I called to see if you were still there." He glanced hurriedly through the windows of the booth, looking up and down the street. "I've got to make another call before we can talk turkey, so I'll put it through and ring you again in half an hour's time. Hope you don't mind?"

"It would make a fat lot of difference if I did!"

"I'll call you back from this same booth and will be as quick as I can." He watched her fade out of the screen.

Quickly he returned to the Lincoln, drove it farther up the street, parked it around a corner. He had the bonnet sticking out just enough to enable him to keep watch on the distant booth. With the engine running, and his hands at the controls

197

ready for a fast getaway, he kept the booth under observation for half an hour.

A few early workers appeared, passed him casually. Nothing more noteworthy had happened by the end of the appointed time. Giving up the watch, he drove the Lincoln uptown, found another booth, called Miriam from that.

"I checked your line. Somebody might have been sitting on it—in which case they'd have tried to pick me up forthwith. Evidently they've not traced you yet."

"Would I be here, if they had?" she inquired, scornfully.

"Perhaps, my lovely! They wouldn't remove the bait from the trap, would they?"

"Don't you call me bait!"

"Oh, all right." He wagged his head wearily. "I should have known better than to drag you from your dreams. Tell me where I can find a mutual friend and then you can return to your slumbers."

She babbled an address in Flushing, added hurriedly: "That's until noon tomorrow. Afterwards, he'll be some place else."

"Thanks."

He took the Lincoln across the Triboro at a pace sufficiently sedate to soothe the cops patrolling at both ends. They let him pass with no more than an idle, disinterested glance. Once clear of the bridge he speeded into Long Island, soon found the tumbledown brownstone house which was Hansen's momentary hiding-place.

Hansen peered cautiously around the door. He was barefooted, and his suspenders dangled from his hastily pulled-on pants.

"Did Miriam give you this?" He closed the door quickly behind his visitor.

"Yes. She was anything but sweet—but she gave."

"You were lucky. One more day and you'd have had to whistle for both of us. She's moving tomorrow. Me, too." He dragged the suspenders over his shoulders. "You've got bags like flour sacks under your eyes."

"I know it. I've been up all night."

"Bad habit. It buys you nothing." He padded along the passage and into a rear room. "Squat somewhere while I get the rest of my clothes." His bare feet trudged upstairs. In a short time he came down with the remainder of his attire bundled carelessly under one arm. Proceeding with his dressing, he asked: "What's our next step towards the scaffold?"

"I'll tell you shortly." Armstrong's voice was urgent. "Where's Claire Mandle?"

"Darned if I can tell you. She dropped her shadows and went some place fast."

"Dropped her shadows?"

"Yep. The F.B.I. had her tagged like a jealous father. They've been doing it for weeks—you know that. She kissed them a fond farewell."

"How do you know this?"

Hansen rammed a shoe on his foot, laced it expertly. "Because I helped her."

Waggling his eyebrows, Armstrong rumbled: "You're capable of speech without priming by me."

"I went to see her, and got a list off her like you ordered. She said she could do a lot more to help you if only she could cross the road without trailing a string of bureaucrats behind her. She was convinced that the F.B.I. were the boys following her around, but I wasn't so sure. I lent her a couple of my guys to accompany her into town—just in case."

"And then?"

"She was smart. She got them involved with her trackers and faded out during the argument." He expressed grudging admiration. "It was as slick a piece of work as any I've seen."

"The papers report that she's disappeared, but imply that something has happened to her."

"The papers!" Hansen made a gesture of derision. "When were the papers, the recorders or the newscasts ever concerned with undiluted facts?" He stood up, stamped in his shoes, started putting on his jacket. "The reports didn't mention that two of my men are being held for questioning?"

"No."

"See?"

Armstrong thought it over, then asked: "Did you make a pass at that stooge of Lindle's?"

"Carson? No. I was going after him today."

"Forget him. He doesn't matter now. Things are shaping up —and they're getting mighty hot!"

"*Getting* hot!" Hansen echoed. "What the deuce d'you call it *now*? Out with it—what's your latest crime?"

199

"I'm wanted for snitching a senator."

Hansen paused and stood statuelike while about to knot his tie. Holding the tie straight out, with one tag twisted over the other, he gaped openly.

"Say that again."

"I'm wanted for kidnapping as treacherous a senatorial slob as you'd meet in a month's march," said Armstrong. "Womersley."

"We have had murder, arson, espionage and wholesale sabotage," remarked Hansen, looking prayerfully at the ceiling. "Now he has to add kidnapping." He knotted the tie. "Where have you hidden him?"

"At Eddie Drake's, in New Jersey. I want you to get out there as fast as you can with all the men you've got available. How many have you got?"

"Pete's dead, and the F.B.I. is holding two—that leaves four regulars and five casuals. I can trust the regulars."

"Four plus you and me and Ed. Seven in all. If we can rescue Quinn, that'll make eight."

"Why does Quinn need rescuing? Has he got himself marooned on an iceberg?"

"The Norman yahoos in Kansas City are holding him and are trying to pin the killing of Ambrose Fothergill on him. I think maybe they'll hesitate before they go too far with him; we're quits now—they've got Quinn, but I've got Womersley!"

"Oh, well——!" He reached for his hat. "The day I took you on as a client I stuck my neck out a mile. It was the dopiest thing I've ever done. Sooner or later I'll have to pay for it with the best years of my life." He rammed the hat on his head. "Meanwhile, let's have fun."

"Money is the root of all evil," Armstrong observed. "Whatever happens will serve you right for being greedy. Let it be a lesson to you."

Drake was jittery by the time Armstrong got back. He slammed the door with alacrity, waved his arms around while he declaimed.

"This is the devil's own mess! That stinker upstairs came round about three hours after you'd gone. He had a lot to say, all of it authoritative and ominous. We had a slugging match before I tied him up on the bed. Then the first edition newcast came on—have you seen it?"

"Been too busy. You've got it on the recorder?"

Drake nodded dumbly, crossed the room, switched on his set. The screen filled itself with the front page.

EUROPEAN SHOWDOWN COMING, WARNS LINDLE

Demands supplementary $1,000,000,000.00 for national defence.

Scanning the matter beneath, Armstrong didn't bother to read it thoroughly, contented himself with skipping from phrase to phrase.

"The crisis is approaching . . . we must now pay and pay until it hurts . . . never forget the terrible lessons of the past . . . war clouds looming on the grey and dismal horizon . . . all unnecessary expenditure must be ruthlessly curtailed if we are to shoulder this greater and far more urgent burden . . . no folly more monstrous than that of pouring men, material and money into Mars rockets at such a time as this."

In the adjoining column appeared a small paragraph saying, "Following his interview with the President last night, General L. S. Gregory assured the Press that the fighting forces are ready for any emergency."

Pointing to this, he said to Drake: "I'd gamble my life that Gregory spoke to much greater length than that. The rest of his comments may have been too soothing to suit the propaganda boys. So they left it out, publishing only the bit best calculated to increase public apprehension. One selected part of the truth can be as effective as a downright lie!" He was biting his lip as his eyes suddenly found the right-hand side column.

PUBLIC ENEMY NUMBER ONE

Washington, D.C. A nation-wide hunt is now in progress for John J. Armstrong, thirty-four-year-old New York dabbler in scientific appliances. Armstrong, who stands seventy-five inches and weighs two hundred thirty pounds stripped, is wanted for activities on behalf of a foreign power as well as for several killings and one kidnapping. He is believed to be hiding in the New York metropolitan area, and is known to be armed.

There was not a word about Womersley.

His face calm and expressionless as he switched off, Armstrong commented: "Looks like they've picked up that Cadillac." He gave a shrug of indifference. His eyes were red-rimmed and puffy. There was a strong stubble on his chin. "You lay down for an hour or so, Ed. You need the sleep."

Drake sat in a chair, fumbled with his hands, looked at him wide-eyed. "As if I could snore through this!"

"You're nervous, jumpy. How about a shot of Vitalax?"

"Vitalax!" said Drake, violently.

"And so say some of us—though by no means all!" He took another chair, flopped into it, rubbed his eyes and yawned. Then he closed his mouth and listened. "Someone's coming."

A car whined to a stop in front. Drake came out of his chair like a man in a dream. He stood with his hands dangling at his sides, his whole attention on the door.

Armstrong smiled at him grimly, opened the door, let Hansen in. The agent was followed by three muscle-bound characters, with Miriam bringing up the rear. Armstrong introduced them to Drake.

They spread around the room, and Hansen announced: "We're one down already. Jake got picked up last night. If they'd had the sense to watch his place, they'd have got me when I went for him this morning." He sniffed his contempt for the unfortunate Jake. "He was as drunk as a lord. I don't know what I saw in that guy." He looked at Armstrong. "I had to bring Miriam."

"Of course. You couldn't leave her behind. We'll vote her an angel if she'll set up some sandwiches and coffee." He watched her saunter into the kitchen, said to Drake: "We'd better feed the prisoner, too. Can't let him starve to death."

"He's been fed. I beat him up, then gave him his fodder. He didn't let hard feelings spoil his appetite—he guzzled like a pig."

"Good! Then he ought to be ripe for a further dose of the schizophraser." He tramped heavily upstairs, came down carrying the bound senator like a baby in his arms. He dumped him unceremoniously into a chair.

Glaring around, Womersley pontificated in tones of outraged importance. "You scum needn't think you're going to get away with this." He bestowed the glare on each in turn. "I'll remember each and every one of you, and I'll see that you suffer if it takes the rest of my life!"

Hansen responded, coolly: "And what do you estimate as the rest of your life?"

"Shut up. Leave him alone." Armstrong planted the cup on the furious Womersley's head, tried to strap it accurately into position. Womersley shook his head vigorously and snarled an oath. Carefully and deliberately, Armstrong slapped him in the jaw. The sound of it reverberated around the room. Hansen looked mildly pleased. Womersley rocked back, and Armstrong got the cup fixed to his own satisfaction. He switched on the apparatus.

Breathing heavily, Womersley yelled: "Armstrong, if it's the last——!" His voice petered out. The rage died away from his face which slowly became stupefied.

"What is Singleton's private address?"

Rolling his head to and fro, Womersley mouthed it like an automaton. Hansen pulled out a notebook, noted the address therein.

"But you don't know whether Quin is there?"

"No."

"Singleton alone knows where he's been hidden?"

"Yes."

Rubbing his bristly chin, Armstrong contemplated the semi-comatose politician, and continued inexorably. "Womersley, do you know that someone already is building rockets numbers nineteen and twenty?"

"Yes."

"Who's building them?"

"We are."

Drake exclaimed: "Jeepers!"

"Where are they being built?"

"Yellowknife."

"Both of them?"

"Yes."

"Yellowknife. That's in Canada, way up in the wilds," Armstrong mused. "Is this stunt being pulled in collaboration with the Canadian Government?"

"Of course."

"Are these rockets near completion?"

"Yes."

203

"How near?"

Womersley blinked dopily, seemed to have trouble in making reply, but eventually came out with: "Nineteen is ready for its test flight. Twenty will be ready in two days at most."

"And if both pass their tests they'll be immediately ready for a shot at Mars?"

"Yes."

In an undertone, Armstrong said: *"Phew!* They've gone a lot faster and farther than I'd anticipated." To Womersley: "But neither of these rockets will reach Mars?"

"No."

Moving close to the senator, he harshed: "Why won't they?"

"The fuel coil changes to a critical composition."

"You mean that they're using wire-form fuel fed into the motors from a spool, and that the composition of the wire alters somewhere along its length?"

"Yes."

"Who supplied this fuel?"

"Radiometals Corporation."

"Are they Norman Club adherents?"

"No."

Armstrong looked surprised. He mooched around in a circle, thinking deeply. The audience gave him their full attention. He faced the senator again.

"Are certain of its employees adherents of the Norman Club?"

"Yes."

"Technicians—and inspectors?"

"Yes."

"What are their names?"

"I don't know."

"Without the knowledge of their employers, they are modifying fuel coils in a manner calculated to cause a spontaneous explosion?"

"Yes."

"Do you know how these disruptions are timed—will they be at the beginning, or in the middle or towards the ends of the coils?"

"With maximum delay," Womersley mumbled.

"Meaning towards the ends, when both vessels are close to Mars?"

"Yes."

Drake chipped in viciously: "Somebody ought to cut his fat throat!"

"Be quiet." Armstrong waved him into silence, said to Womersley: "Then the pilots are not Norman Club nominees?"

"No."

"So far as you're concerned, they can both go to blazes along with their vessels?"

"Yes."

Armstrong turned swiftly and pushed Drake back as the latter took an angry step forward.

Carrying on with his cross-examination, he demanded: "Why stir the world to war if you can bust rockets the way you've described?"

"Our psycho-charts show that peace means a rocket-craze which may increase despite failures."

"So?"

"They're planning on sending two together now. It will be four together next year, ten the year after. We can't continue to deal with them all successfully. Only war will change the international psychic patterns."

Snorting his disgust, Armstrong changed the subject. "I told you a story about being offered plans of a scout-vessel by a Martian deportee. You believe that story. Can you locate any such deportees?"

"No."

"Why not?"

"We are notified of them, but they scatter immediately on arrival and we cannot keep track of them. Mad though they are, they're Martians—and very clever."

"You fear them?"

"They regard us as enemies."

"Are they many in number?"

"No. They are very few."

"Do you know anything about this torchlike weapon they've been using?"

"It is an Earth-made model of a vibratory coagulator."

"Has the Norman Club such a weapon?"

"No. We don't know how to manufacture it. Besides, it is forbidden to us."

Armstrong raised his eyebrows. "Forbidden? By whom?"

"By the sane ones of Mars who are in touch with us."

"On *this* planet?"

"Yes."

"Here we go again!" Armstrong looked around beseechingly. "Now we've found *another* gang—sane Martians this time!" He returned his attention to the befuddled Womersley. "Are there many of them?"

"Very few."

"How many?"

"I don't know."

"Are they allies of yours?'

"Not exactly."

"What d'you mean by that?"

"They assist us very little. They refuse to be militant. They maintain a policy of interfering in world affairs no more than is made imperative by circumstances at any given time."

"Name me one of them," Armstrong challenged.

"Horowitz."

"You assert that he is a native-born Martian?"

"Yes."

"How d'you know that?"

"He revealed it when first we invited him to join us. He proved it by providing a psychotron and training certain of our membership as operators of it."

"Some proof!" scoffed Armstrong to the others. "They get hold of Horowitz, give him the old razzmatazz, and promptly he takes 'em up on it. He's a noted physicist with more brains than the lot of them—and as few scruples. He was quick to open the door when opportunity knocked. Getting a load of their Martians obsessions, he says, 'Behold, I am a Martian!' and they fall for it like suckers."

"That doesn't seem credible," Drake ventured.

"No less credible than anything else in this mad affair. Big fleas have little fleas. And besides, any Norman shrewd enough to see that Horowitz was cashing in might argue that a religion needs a saint or two to bolster the faith. Lindle, at least, is cynical enough to accept Horowitz at face value, for reasons of utility rather than real belief." He frowned. "I'll tend to his sainthood once I'm out of this mess."

"Hope springs eternal," recited Drake, in funereal tones.

"We're in to our necks and sinking to our ears. If you can find a way out of this muddle, boy, you're good!"

Hansen stared at him hard-eyed. "You windy?"

"For heaven's sake, quit bickering!" Armstrong scowled around at them. "We're footloose and fancy free, aren't we? We're roaming about fully dressed and in our right minds, and nobody's put chains on us yet. Nobody's going to, either!"

Drake said: "Your self-assurance is magnificent, and I truly wish I could share it. The fact remains that you've got a motley mob of pursuers ten miles long, and how you're going to swallow the lot of them is something I can't make out." He favoured Womersley with a vicious look, and added: "But I'm sticking with you partly because I don't see what else I can do; mostly because I want to see that cold-blooded fish get buried deep down."

"Now you're talking," Hansen approved.

Still frowning, Armstrong spoke to Womersley: "If sane Martians ordered the Norman Club to desist, or even to disband, would it do so?"

"Yes."

"Why would it?"

"They are our superiors and we are loyal to them."

"But they have issued no such order?"

"No."

"Some missionaries!" Armstrong commented, dourly. "They have influenced this world's affairs time and time again, according to Lindle. Do you know of any especial reason why they have refused to intervene in this case?"

"This one is different. It represents an important cross-roads on the path to destiny, and they feel . . . they feel"—he choked, mumbled, proceeded with difficulty—"that this is one time when Earthlings, sane or insane, must . . . work out their own . . . salvation." He choked again, slumped low in his chair.

"He's had enough." Armstrong cut the main-switch, snatched the cup from Womersley's sagging head. "Take him upstairs and dump him on the bed. He'll need hours to sleep it off once more."

Drake and two of Hansen's men lugged the limp senator away. Waiting for their return, Armstrong paraded up and down the room. He was as restless as a caged bear. The others came back; he continued to march up and down the carpet

207

while he addressed his audience. Their eyes followed him to and fro, to and fro, like those of spectators at a tennis tournament.

"Let's take another look at the situation. We're wanted. All of us are wanted in the sense that those not wanted today will be wanted tomorrow or the day after, either as accomplices, or as accessories before or after the fact. The charges against us don't matter much—we'll be saddled with whatever charges can be made to stick. The cops, the F.B.I., the Norman Club, the Martian Hu-mans and, for all I know, the Secret Service and the Navy would give plenty for our scalps." He studied them individually. "Whatever other antics we may perform can't get us in any deeper than we are already."

"The penalty for kidnapping is death," remarked Drake. "I can't imagine going any deeper than nine feet of rope will permit."

Ignoring him, Armstrong went on: "We need all the help we can get—and what we can get is darned little! Apart from those present, there are only four people I feel I can trust, namely, General Gregory, Bill Norton, Claire Mandle and George Quinn. It's not much use me trying to make contact with Gregory again since I can give him little more than he's got already, besides which I'd probably be pinched in the attempt. I caught him in the nick of time, and now it's up to him. As for Claire Mandle, she's out of reach. I'm not worrying about her, seeing that she has disappeared of her own accord. As for Bill Norton, he can't do us much good. Unwittingly, he might do us harm. He hoots with excitement, and we can't afford to be burdened with hooters. That leaves only Quinn."

"And we know who's holding him," Hansen put in, his eyes glittering.

"And we know who's holding him," Armstrong confirmed. "So out next step should be to get Quinn free—at all costs." He paused, then said, "Any other suggestions?"

Drake rubbed his chin thoughtfully before responding. "Don't think I'm criticizing when I ask what Quinn has got that none of us has got. There are seven of us here, counting Miriam. Seven rats on the run! How much better off shall we be when we're eight?"

"We'll be one man stronger."

"I know that. But what good will it do? Look at the situation: you started off by nosing into rocket-flops and that's led you to the present position where you want to face tremendous and world-wide odds in order to prevent a major war. You said yourself that it isn't sufficient for us, as a nation, to be peace-loving, animated by high ideals and a sense of justice, et cetera, because any other nation can start the holocaust. That, in turn, means that even if in some miraculous manner you bust the Norman Club in this country it can still set the world aflame by starting the fire somewhere else, somewhere far beyond your reach—Portugal or Peru, for instance. Then the flags go up, the drums start beating, and everyone sane enough to want to live will be damned as a coward and a traitor, while everyone mad enough to be willing to die will be praised as a hero. The war will be on, the slaughter started, the entire set of circumstances will acquire an impetus which couldn't be controlled by seven millions of us, much less a mere seven. Heck of a lot better off we'll be when we're eight!"

Hansen leaned forward and said, softly: "You'd rather let Quinn stew in his own juice, eh?"

"Don't be so downright stupid!" Drake became angry. "I'm all in favour of getting Quinn out of bad sooner than immediately. He's a rocket-pilot and, as such, I'd give him the privilege of mauling that inhuman specimen upstairs. I'd like to do the mauling myself. *I've a special reason for that!* But I'd forego the pleasure in favour of George because he's a rocket-pilot." His annoyed gaze went from Hansen to Armstrong. "What I'm bawling about is that I don't see any way out of the mess we're in. It's like a quicksand. All we can do is struggle and go down, down, down until we start blowing mud-bubbles. The harder we struggle, the faster we'll sink. That's the way I see it. Maybe you see it differently. Maybe you see something I don't. If so, I'd like to know of it. I could feel I'm going somewhere, and a feeling like that is a great comfort."

"Then you may consider yourself comforted," Armstrong told him. "Our amiable friend Womersley was kind enough to point a way out."

"Eh?" Drake's jaw dropped.

"He said, 'We're at the last ditch!', didn't he? So we'll utilize the ditch—if luck holds out long enough."

"Yeah." Drake looked confused. "Yeah." He passed a hand

uncertainly over his forehead. "This is what comes of being up and about when I ought to be in bed. I'm too dopey to get it." He turned his puzzled face to Hansen. "Do *you* get it?"

"No," replied the agent, unconcernedly. "And I'm not worrying about it. Worry never earned me a dime.' '

"George Quinn knows something we don't, something very useful," Armstrong explained. "He knows when, where and how to blow."

Drake screwed up his eyes as he looked at him. After a while, he gave it up, and said, lugubriously: "Take no notice of me. I'm too far gone even to understand plain English."

"All right. Let's accept that we go after Quinn. That gives us two more problems. Firstly, do we take Miriam with us?"

"Try leaving me behind," snapped Miriam from the kitchen doorway. She used a coffee percolator to gesture towards Hansen. "He's my only alibi. I'm sticking to him."

"There's my answer." Armstrong grinned, and went on, "Do we take Womersley, or shall we leave him here under guard?"

Hansen said: "He's worth his weight in gold to us. I don't believe in parting with gold. Besides, leaving him under guard will cut our number down."

"Keep him in sight," advised Drake. "I like him better in sight. I wouldn't trust him around the corner. I don't trust him upstairs, even if he is unconscious."

"We'll cart him along." Armstrong glanced at his watch. "We've lost too much time already. There are two cars now, Hansen's and Drake's. We've a long run ahead of us and ought to start as soon as we can get ready." He indicated the apparatus on the floor. "And we'd better take all this junk if we can find room for it. It may come in useful if some other canary refuses to chirrup."

"Kansas City, we'll see you soon!" Hansen stood up, and his three men arose with him. "Provided we're not picked up on the way!"

CHAPTER FIFTEEN

Singleton's home stood wide open as if its owner had not one enemy in the world. It posed in amazing contrast with the fortresslike edifice which Womersley needed to feel secure. Evidently Singleton had no cause to share the leeriness of Norman Club leaders farther east, perhaps for the reason that he headed a a cohort smaller, less active, not so deeply involved in the Club's peculiar affairs.

It was an old, rambling but picturesque house standing in carefully tended grounds, and it enjoyed that air of solid, well-established respectability favoured by bankers and the more conservative types of business-men. Viewing it, Armstrong felt considerably heartened. After seeing Womersley's prison he had expected yet another personal Alcatraz.

Sitting in the front car beside Hansen, who lounged at the wheel, and with the second car parked close behind, he said: "That chump Womersley has admitted that Singleton knows him by sight. We also know that Singleton is in that house at this moment. We've been mighty lucky to get this far without incident and I reckon we ought to ride our luck while it's still running. What say we use Womersley as our front—and walk straight in?"

"I like it." Hansen's sharp eyes surveyed the house across the road. "It has always paid me to move fast rather than slow. When you're slow, it gives the other guy time to think."

"Let's go. I'll tell them at back first." Opening the door Armstrong got out. Cautiously, he looked up and down the street. He was careful rather than apprehensive. After many hours of travel, and numberless encounters with all sorts of people—including two cops—none of whom had looked at him with more than casual interest, he was not greatly in fear of recognition. This despite the photograph of him published in yesterday's sheets under an offer of two hundred thousand dollars' reward, dead or alive.

It had been an old and not-too-good reproduction of his beefy pan, blown up to quarter-plate size from a slice of microfilm. Even if it had been good he'd not have been unduly worried. Most folk, he knew, could not remember what they'd read over breakfast let alone what appeared in yesterday's paper. The sharp-eyed exception with an acute memory was his only peril—so carefully he surveyed the street.

It was quiet, undisturbed. Stepping swiftly to the second car, he spoke to one of Hansen's men who was at its wheel.

"We're going straight in. Keep close behind us."

The other nodded, shifted a wad of gum. Armstrong glanced at Womersley, who was jammed in the rear seat between Drake and another of Hansen's men. Womersley glared back at him without remark.

Returning to the leading car, he got in, watched the rear-view mirror as they edged across the road, purred up the semi-circular drive to Singleton's residence. They stopped before the front door, the other car following suit. There were two more cars parked farther around the drive and nearer the exit, but no passengers were in evidence.

With Hansen at his side and the rest behind, Armstrong mounted the ten broad steps leading to the front door, rang the bell. A pert maid responded.

Smiling at her, he raised his hat, said smoothly: "This is Senator Womersley and some friends—we wish to see Mr. Singleton immediately. Please tell him that the subject of our call is a very urgent one."

She smiled back, eyeing the group without suspicion, and chirped: "Please wait a moment." She turned and went away with a flirt of frilly skirts which sent Hansen's eyebrows up an inch. In short time she reappeared. "Mr. Singleton will see you at once."

Stepping aside, Armstrong gave her his hat. His other hand remained inside his pocket, its fingers curled around his ·38. Hansen entered likewise, hat in one hand, hidden gun in the other. So did his three men. With Drake close against his back and Miriam chummily linked on his arm, Womersley went through the door with disgruntled pomposity.

Dumping the hats, the maid led them across a broad hall, opened the door on the farther side. Armstrong paused, signed to Womersley. Looking like a man who had plenty owing to him and intended to collect some day, the senator passed through the doorway, still linked with Miriam, and with Drake still crowding him from behind. The other five followed. Quietly, the maid closed the door.

There were four people in this room, and Armstrong recognized three of them though not the faintest flicker of surprise crossed his heavy face. The first was a little, wizened individual struggling out of a deep armchair. This, he presumed, was Singleton. Near him, already out of his chair and advancing to greet the visitors, was Lindle. Before an empty fireplace, his legs braced apart, his hands behind him, his eyes staring owlishly through thick-lensed spectacles, stood Horowitz. The fourth person was Claire Mandle. She was near a table, one hand braced on its polished surface, the other held to her mouth. Her elfin eyes were enormous as they looked at him.

"Well, well, Eustace," enthused Singleton, in a shrill voice. "This *is* a surprise!" Finding his feet, he advanced towards Womersley with eager cordiality. "I thought——"

"You thought right," snapped Lindle, his voice cutting through the room. He withdrew a couple of steps, his brow thunderous. "And now you've a load of trouble in your lap."

"Huh?" Singleton stopped with one foot in the air, took a long time putting it down. It looked as if he were trying to imitate a slow-motion movie. Turning just as sluggishly, he looked at Lindle. "What d'you mean? Can't you see that Eustace——?"

"Shut up and sit down!" Lindle snarled. "It takes a crazy Daniel to walk right into the den!" His dark eyes focused on Armstrong. "All right, let's have it—what d'you want?"

Armstrong ignored Lindle, Horowitz and Claire Mandle; he kept his full attention on the flustered Singleton as he answered the question in deep, rumbling tones like those of distant thunder.

He said, simply: "George Quinn!" Singleton turned startled eyes upon him, and he caught them and held them as he continued in the same inexorable voice, "And heaven help the lot of you if he's dead!"

Singleton whitened, moved backward.

"Stay where you are." Armstrong strode farther into the room. Out of one corner of his eye he saw Lindle resume his easy-chair and cross his legs with exaggerated unconcern. Claire was still by the table, still regarding him wide-eyed. Horowitz

213

had not moved from the fireplace. He said to Singleton: "Where's George Quinn?"

The other seemed smitten dumb by sheer fright. His gaze roamed dull-wittedly around; feebly he raised his hands, put them down again.

Reaching for a nearby wall-bulb, Armstrong unscrewed it, glanced at it, screwed it back into place. He made a grimace of disgust.

"What's the matter?" inquired Hansen.

"Fifty volts. This dump must have its own generating plant. The schizophraser's no use here—it's got to have a hundred and ten."

"We can take him some place else and pick him to bits at our ease. This isn't the only——" Hansen stopped as Drake nudged him.

"You look after this slob," suggested Drake, meaning the irate Womersley. He moved out as Hansen took over, started walking slowly and deliberately towards Singleton. His face was strangely pale and little beads of perspiration lay across his forehead. "I'll tend to this," he gritted. The others watched him fascinatedly. Going right up to Singleton, he said, quietly but clearly: "I've got a personal bone to pick with you -you dirty little rat!"

Flapping his hands again, Singleton slumped backwards into his chair. Drake towered over him, went on in the same quiet tones: "Remember that last one that blew apart on the deck, before it even could take off? It killed sixty, didn't it? One of them was a synchronics engineer named Tony Drake—my brother! *I saw him go!*" His voice went up in tone and became louder. "That was according to plan—*your* plan, you shrinking louse!" His hand whipped out of his pocket and flashed a gleam of metallic blue. "Here's *my* plan! You've got ten seconds to say what you've done with George Quinn. So help me, if you don't give—and give quick—I'll splash your snake-brains over the wall—and this'll show you I mean business!"

The gun roared with sudden and unexpected viciousness that shocked the room. Singleton emitted a squeal of pain that penetrated the reverberations still bouncing from wall to wall. Dragging up his left foot, he tried to get it into his lap. His face was so colourless that it held a curious quality of transparency.

As Armstrong moved forward, his big face taut, Drake was breathing into the agonized Singleton's features: "Five, six, seven, eight." The gun came up.

"Out at Keefer's! He's out at Keefer's, I tell you!" Singleton shrieked.

The door opened, the maid looked in anxiously. Nobody had heard her knock. One of Hansen's men grasped her arm, drew her into the room, planted his broad back against the closed door.

"Alive?" insisted Drake. His optics were afire with hate as he kept them fixed on his victim.

"Oh, my foot!" moaned Singleton. He got it on to his knee. Blood dripped from his shoe, made little, glutinous splashes on the carpet. "Oh, my foot!"

"Alive?" Drake motioned with his gun. His mouth was all lopsided. "When I ask you something you'd better reply fast! I'm not like *you*, see? I'm not *sane*!" He gave a queer, unnatural laugh. "I'm daffy. I'm so daffy that I can do almost anything . . . anything . . . especially to you!" Bending forward, he bawled right into Singleton's face. *"Is Quinn alive?"*

Singleton hooted for breath, then yelped frantically: "Yes, he's alive. He's at Keefer's, I tell you! And he's alive!"

"Where's Keefer's?"

In cool, sardonic tones, Lindle cut in with: "The place to which that pathetic weakling refers is half an hour's drive from here. It has a telephone. It would save you a lot of trouble, not to mention a modicum of melodrama, if Singleton called and ordered them to bring Quinn to you here."

For some weird reason, this infuriated Drake. He turned his savage eyes to Lindle, swung the gun towards him as well. "Who asked you to open your trap? This is the lily-livered specimen who's going to provide the answers, and when——"

"Easy, Ed!" Armstrong made a swift snatch which got him Drake's gun. "Cool down, will you? Cool down!"

Drake shouted: "But——"

"Take it easy!" Armstrong held him, eye to eye. "Quinn first. We want to get George, don't we? Business before pleasure!"

Slowly, very slowly, Drake deflated. Finally he said: "All right. Let that louse ring Keefer's. That'll be the signal for them to dump Quinn in the river before they come on the run for us."

"We'll take a chance on that." He studied the moaning Singleton. "And I don't think we'll be taking much of a chance —this guy won't sign his own death warrant." To Singleton, he said: "There's the phone. Tell 'em you want Quinn brought here at once."

"My foot!" complained Singleton, whiningly. He pulled the shoe off, revealed a saturated sock. "Let me bandage it first. I'll bleed to death!"

"Bleed to death!" Armstrong's smile was grim as he noted the other's appalled expression. "Millions are going to bleed to death if you and your kind get their way. Fat lot you care about that—and a fat lot we care about you!" He shoved the phone into Singleton's hands. "Go ahead. Say anything you like. Yell for help if you want—it may reach you if you're slow in dying!"

"John!" Claire Mandle took a tentative step forward. She was shaken, uncertain. Lindle watched her with acid amusement. Horowitz turned his lenses towards her, his expression inscrutable. Armstrong ignored her.

"Go ahead," he urged Singleton.

Claire withdrew her step, sat down. Her bottom lip trembled.

Singleton, on the telephone, ironed the quavers out of his voice, and said with passable authority: "Bring Quinn in. Yes, at once!" Putting down the instrument, he started to peel off his sock.

Armstrong sent out the maid, guarded by one of Hansen's men. She came back with bandages; he sat on the arm of a chair and watched her tend to Singleton's wound.

"The incurable sentimentalist." Lindle studied him from across the room. "So far as I know, you're the first certifiably sane one who's proved too spiritually lazy to discipline his own emotions. And look where it's got you." His chuckle was self-assured. "Two hundred grand reward, alive or dead!" He shook his well-groomed head in mock sorrow. "Remember what I said to you once—see how you like the madhouse now?"

He got no response. Armstrong stared at him with sphinx-like lack of expression.

"It'll be a darned sight madder before long," Lindle prophesied. "I shall always remain amazed that anyone so fundamentally sane should choose to support the world's lunatics. I have been lost for an explanation of this contradiction. It seems to me that either the psychotron was out of order and made a wrong diagnosis of you—which our friend Horowitz, a psychotron expert, denies most emphatically—or else we never did succeed in convincing you of the facts of history past and present. Personally, I lean to the latter theory. You are sane—but an incurable sceptic. I think your bullheaded actions since we last saw each other are entirely due to your inability to appreciate what you're up against. You don't believe even your own eyes!" He sat more erect in his chair. "It wouldn't do you any harm to put some trust in them for once—and allow me to remind you that there is always time to repent."

Armstrong's face remained blank; his lips did not part.

"Our power is such," boasted Lindle, determined to make some use of the waiting-time, "that if we wished we could withdraw all charges against you and your companions today. We could make you public heroes tomorrow—and wealthy men the day after."

"What d'you mean by wealthy?" put in Hansen, displaying sudden interest.

Lindle's dark, sardonic eyes shifted to the agent. "We're no pikers. A hundred grand per man."

"Not enough." Hansen gestured to the impassive Armstrong. "He's promised me half a million. He's a better liar even than you!"

Miriam giggled. Lindle became sour. Armstrong watched Lindle steadily, still said nothing.

The surly and silent Womersley unexpectedly woke up and growled at Lindle: "You're wasting your breath. They're all completely unbalanced no matter what your psychotron said." He puffed like an angry frog. "Leave them alone and let them wait what's coming to them."

Claire Mandle stood up again, spoke hesitantly: "John, I tried to help. Believe me, I——"

"Be silent, Claire!" Horowitz was authoritative, severe. "I have told you repeatedly that assistance and interference are totally different things. The first is permitted, the second is not! Positively not!"

His heavy spectacles turned on Armstrong. Obviously he expected a retort. Silent and brooding, Armstrong sat like a huge, cumbersome bear, his eyes hard and cold as they watched Lindle. Horowitz surveyed him as if he were a curious specimen nailed to a board.

"This man," he pronounced carefully, "knows quite well what might be done and intends to see if it can be done. If he fails, it is fate. If he succeeds, it is fate likewise." He shrugged his drooping shoulders. "And that is all there is to it!"

"Are you going as loony as the rest?" demanded Lindle, heatedly. His eyes held little red lights. "Nothing can be done, absolutely nothing!"

"Do you dare talk to *me* like that?" Horowitz put the question calmly, evenly, but its effect was surprising.

The lights faded from Lindle's optics and he appeared to shrink in his seat. Licking his lips, he apologized: "I am sorry. It is not for us to question your ideas."

A bell shrilled loudly in the hall. The maid threw a scared glance at Singleton, who promptly passed it along to Armstrong. The latter nodded to Hansen.

"You look after it. Take a couple of your boys."

Hansen lounged out followed by two of his men. Lindle assumed a look of helpless resignation, tilted back in his chair. His eyes were aimed at the ceiling with the air of one bored beyond telling, and he rocked the chair slightly, its front feet off the floor, then began to tilt it farther.

Coldly and deliberately, Armstrong blew a lump of Lindle's skull away before the back of the chair could contact the stud set in the wall behind. The body kicked twice, slid to the floor. Miriam began to emit curious mewing noises. Claire buried her face in her hands.

In the second of eternity that followed, Armstrong caught a momentary glimpse of Horowitz gravely removing his glasses. He had no time to note more. Singleton, squeaking with frenzied fear, was coming up with something which had been hidden in the cushion of his chair, and Drake was making for him unarmed. He could hear Drake snuffling like a boxer as he shuffled forward.

There was an uproar in the hall, two fast explosions, more noises from Miriam, and the stumbling of feet close behind him. He swung his gun to deal with Singleton, found Drake blocking his line of fire. Dropping the gun, he rose from the arm of the chair on which he'd been sitting, swivelled round on one heel, snatched Womersley out of the grasp of Hansen's man behind him, grunted as he swung the senator's heavy body into reverse and bounced it on its cranium. Womersley yelled, flailed, went limp.

Another gun went off in the hall, then two more. Miriam began to perform a crazy jig, with her mouth wide open. Yet another explosion sounded within the room and Drake collapsed across Singleton's chair. Singleton shoved the body off, stood up on one foot, turned his gun towards Armstrong. He was yipping hysterically and his hand was shaking so badly that the gun's muzzle wavered erratically. He had a moment of fearful indecision as his eyes went from the advancing Armstrong to the Hansen-agent sidling around at one side, and that was his undoing.

The body of Drake shot out a dying hand, snatched Singleton's good foot from under him, brought him down, grabbed at and got his gun. The gun spat low in the carpet and Singleton screeched like a trapped cat. He doubled up violently, straightened out, doubled and straightened again, writhed around with his hands to his middle.

Down on the carpet, Drake coughed some blood, said in a weak, faraway voice: "That's a law . . . good enough for any . . . darned Martians—an eye for an eye!" He strove to lift the gun once more. Armstrong stooped over him to take it from him as it came up, but he was too late. With horrible deliberation, Drake planted a heavy slug behind the jerking Singleton's right ear. "Job worth doing," he wheezed, "is worth doing well." Something gurgled liquidly in his throat. He released his hold on the weapon, laid his head on his bent left arm and quietly ceased to breathe.

Armstrong looked around. Horowitz was standing by the fireplace in exactly the same pose as he'd held from the start, and his expression still was completely impassive. Claire was in her chair, her face hidden in her hands. Lindle, Singleton and Drake sprawled dead upon the floor. To one side, Hansen's agent was surveying the bodies gloomily, while near the door Miriam stood like one in a dream.

Hansen himself suddenly appeared in the doorway. He urged the maid ahead of him, while George Quinn and another of his men followed him in.

"One of my boys is finished," he announced. "We got two of

their men." His dark, hawklike eyes studied the frightened maid. "She gave them the high-sign somehow—I don't how—immediately they got through the door. They went for their guns. She tried to beat it while we were busy. She'd have had the entire town on our necks if she'd got away. Quinn stopped her."

"Good work, George," Armstrong approved.

"It won't look so good mighty soon," opined Quinn, taking in the scene. "They're phoning from Keefer's in twenty minutes to make sure everything's O.K." He turned his worried gaze to Armstrong. "I know you folk have done all this for me, but——"

"Let's cut out the speeches." Armstrong made a gesture of impatience, discovered that his hand was still holding a gun. He shoved the weapon into his pocket. "We want to get out. We've got to move fast. We'll leave the bodies and take the rest."

"All of them?" Hansen counted them, Horowitz, the maid, Claire Mandle and the semi-conscious Womersley, now beginning to stir upon the floor. "That means four more!"

"We can't leave one to start the pursuit. If we take 'em, it may delay things, and we need the best lead we can get. We've four cars available now. We'll take all the cars and all the living." He looked at Horowitz. "You for a start—come on!"

Claire uncovered her face and said: "John, I guessed that you wanted Quinn, and why you wanted him, and I——"

"Later," he told her, gently, "later on. Not now." He motioned Horowitz forward. Obediently, that glassy-eyed individual paced towards the door. Somehow, he didn't hate Horowitz any longer. He'd been satiated by Drake's dying spasm of vengeance, and now he felt only cold, cold, colder even than the dead, the multi-millions of dead who soon were to litter the earth—if planet-wide plotting could not be thwarted at one stroke. His voice was sympathetic of his coldness; a frigid-toned thing that said to Horowitz, "March!" and caused him to march without hesitation or quibble.

They locked the front door, loaded the four cars and sped away. Horowitz's own machine, a long, low-slung job, took the lead with Hansen at its wheel. It held a short-wave radio which Hansen switched on, but there had been no howl of alarm over the police-band an hour later when they rolled into a skyport, made a deceitfully sedate cavalcade across its tarmac towards the control tower.

Either Keefer's had failed to check or, getting no reply to their call, they were investigating with considerable caution. That portion of the Norman gang would be likely to probe the unexpected mess with the careful respect due to Martian Hu-mans whom they'd assume to be the cause of it. They did not fear Armstrong, but they were naturally leery of the Hu-mans and especially of their potent coagulators. The time their care was costing them was all to the good from the viewpoint of the fugitives. The ether was still clear nearly another hour later when their hired twelve-seater, low-wing jet-plane was ready for them.

Obtaining the plane had proved absurdly easy. Faced by a sudden request for a hire-and-drive-yourself passenger job, fully fuelled, the skyport's booking officer had felt inclined to jib. He had wavered at sight of a wad of notes and four auto-mobiles to be left as security. George's pilot's certificate had done the rest. He read aloud the last words on the certificate, mouthing them with awe.

". . . including liquid-fuel or wire-fed rockets of meteor-ological or experimental types." He looked up, his eyes bugging. Not one wanted man was on his mind. "First rocket certificate I've seen." Handing it back as if it were the original copy of Magna Carta, he entered the booking without further argu-ment, in fact eagerly.

With the machine waiting for them, its compressors rotating at minimum while they heated up, they climbed in one by one. Horowitz went up the portable steps as blank-faced as an image. Womersley, now on his feet, but rubber-legged and half-stupefied, had to be assisted in. The skyport's onlookers observed him with mild sympathy and total lack of suspicion. The maid turned on the steps as if tempted to yell her head off, but she changed her mind when she looked into the eyes of Hansen mounting close behind her. The rest got aboard with disarming casualness.

George gave his craft the gun, took her up to five thousand feet and headed dead south. This accorded with their declared destination and made their departure look conventional to observers on the skyport. He boosted her speed slowly but steadily. The ether remained silent.

Edging into the co-pilot's seat, Armstrong said to Quinn: "How soon can we turn north without giving ourselves away to the boys behind?"

Narrowing his eyes as he stared through the transpex, Quinn pondered a moment. "They had a rotary hemispherical antenna on the tower. That means they've got radar. Maybe it's used only in times of bad visibility, or at night. On the other hand, perhaps it's in constant use. I don't know. If we want to play safe, we'll have to get below their horizon before we change course, and then we'll have to make the full turn still below it. That means a pretty wide sweep. If we're being sought for, ground observers will spot us elsewhere."

"We're not being sought for yet." Armstrong fiddled with the controls of the radio. "I don't know why they're so slow at starting a hue and cry. I think this Singleton's mob must be a small and unimportant one compared with those we've got east." Meditatively he rubbed his chin. There was a stiff bristle on it again. "What happened to Fothergill?"

"I haven't got the full story, but I reckon you were right in one respect—he knew something. Either he bleated it or was about to do so. I heard an argument in his office, followed by a shot. Stupidly, I barged straight in, found Muller there, gun in hand, watching Fothergill die at his desk. Muller looked at me as if I were of no consequence whatsoever. He didn't bother even to turn his gun my way. Before I could recover my wits I heard a quick step right behind me and someone handed me a skull-splitter."

"Tough luck."

"I woke up travelling fast in a lorry which eventually dumped me at Keefer's, and I've been there under guard ever since. They let me read their news-recorder, so I soon learned that I'd been saddled with the killing and was wanted by the authorities. I knew also that you were wanted for everything up to massacre." He threw his listener a sidewise glance. "When Singleton sent his call for me I decided that this was it; my time had come. Nobody was more surprised than I when the guys I thought were his men proved to be your men and opened up on my guard."

"The said guards were more surprised," Armstrong guessed. His smile was hard and craggy. "I've learned something long known to people more worldly-wise than I—the aggressor

222

always has the advantage. That is what enabled guerrilla movements to keep functioning despite German and Jap occupation—the old strike-and-vanish technique. That is what has kept us going successfully—so far." He studied the rolling countryside as the plane dipped and swung. "Turn north when you think it's safe, George. We're making for Yellowknife."

"Yellowknife?" Quinn was mystified. "What the deuce is there?"

"Mate in one move," said Armstrong. "If the luck of Old Nick enables us to make it!'"

Leaving the co-pilot's seat, he went back along the cabin, joined Claire Mandle. "We're going to drop you off some place."

"Why?"

"We're fugitives from justice," he pointed out. "It wouldn't do you any good to be found associating with us voluntarily."

"But, John, this can't go on for ever. You can't spend the rest of your natural life running around like a hunted crook. Why don't you——?"

"Why don't I give myself up and let the wolves eat me?" he finished for her.

"They don't punish innocent men," she protested.

He regarded her calmly, knowing that she did not believe her own words. Then he said: "We're going to put you down on our way. If you want to help, you can do so by saying nothing whatever about us for several days afterwards."

She was slightly flushed, her mind full of arguments, her lips unable to voice them. After a while, she murmured: "We may never meet again—never!"

"Just ships that pass in the night," he agreed. He was watching her closely. She found an absurd little handkerchief, held it to her mouth. Her eyes were faraway and moist. Gently squeezing her arm, he went on: "Or we may meet again in the sunrise—if we can persuade Old Man Sun to come up. We're going to have a darned good try, anyway."

"You're bucking a task as tough as that of trying to boss the Sun around." Her voice was low, muffled. "You're trying to divert forces infinitely beyond your power. I know it— I tried to help you and found it futile."

"Tell me," he invited.

She was quiet for a time, toying with her handkerchief while she regained composure. Eventually, she said: "I put together all that you had told me and it made a picture of a sort. When I read about George Quinn's disappearance I deduced that it would be a major blow to you. I guessed that you wanted him, that you needed him badly."

"You know why?"

"I think so."

"And then?"

"I realized that all lines led to the Norman Club. I remembered that they had made overtures to Bob. If they were interested in Bob, they might be equally interested in his sister —and when people get friendly they sometimes talk too much." He nodded understandingly as she went on: "There seemed some slight chance of gaining their confidence sufficiently to discover whether they were responsible for Quinn's vanishing and, if so, what they had done with him. One of the men who had been pestering me for information regarding you was Carson, who described himself as Senator Lindle's secretary. I threw my shadows, went along to see Lindle."

"Go on," he urged.

"Lindle was away. Carson transferred me to Horowitz, who said that Lindle had gone to Kansas City. Horowitz cross-examined me to great length about Bob's work and also about your activities, but I professed ignorance. I don't think he believed me."

"He wouldn't," Armstrong asserted. "Being so expert a liar himself."

She smiled and said: "He assured me that he's a Martian with this world under his thumb."

"By this time, he believes it himself—he's told the tale so often."

"He had a most peculiar attitude towards me, I can describe it only as speculative cordiality. There was something in his mind, his shrewd, fast-thinking mind, which told him I could be useful to him—as an ally, or a hostage, or both. I could tell that much, but I don't think he realized that I could. Having got me there, he didn't want to detain me by force, neither did he want me to go. I think he suspected that compulsory detention might bring out the unpleasant fact that I was bait provided by the F.B.I. On the other hand, he didn't want to lose me.

He found a way out by offering to escort me to Kansas City to see Lindle in person. I took him up on that."

"A nice example of angels rushing in where fools fear to tread," Armstrong commented. "You'll have to change your reckless ways at some date I've got in mind."

"You're the one to talk!" she riposted. Her eyes surveyed him from their tilted corners before she went on. "I used what wiles I possess to persuade Horowitz to give forth during our journey. I've never met a man who can be so boastful without really saying anything. All I could do was read between the lines and draw conclusions."

"At which you're too good for my future comfort," he suggested.

She smiled again. "I decided that he is a very clever man who had a couple of inventions lying around at a moment when a glorious opportunity presented itself. He had the brains to welcome opportunity with both hands. He is another and craftier Hitler—this time with his cohorts underground."

"That's my estimate, too," Armstrong agreed. "And he's made enemies among a few who know too much. They are likewise underground—trying to steal his thunder by claiming Martianhood, even if insane. The insane touch is a nice terror weapon. Humans, bunk!"

"Which is what makes the struggle so crazy," she observed. "It isn't a simple two-sided affray. It's multi-sided. The Normans versus Humans versus you versus uninformed authority. Each smiting the nearest to hand, like an Irish wedding." She pondered momentarily. "In the end, we reached Kansas City, and immediately I found myself practically a prisoner. It served me right, I suppose. But I discovered two more items."

"What were those?"

"Clark Marshall had a taste of the psychotron and got delusions of insanity. He knew enough to be a menace to them. They sought him in vain, and their opponents obligingly did the job for them." She closed her eyes, her voice went lower. "But I think they got Bob. I think Bob played with them, seeking information to pass along to the government—and they found it out."

He squeezed her arm gently. "It's our turn now. Wait and see!"

225

Getting up and going forward, he had a look through the transpex. "How're we doing, George?"

"East-north-east. We'll be heading north pretty soon. Still not a squawk on the short waves." Quinn flipped the radio's band-switch. "Let's try the mediums."

Promptly the radio blared forth, ". . . defined all these accusations of surreptitious military dictatorship as a manifest political manœuvre which should deceive nobody. Continuing, General Gregory said that as newly appointed commander-in-chief of the joint defence services he accepted full responsibility for all orders issued from his headquarters and that the armed forces would be used to maintain internal peace at all costs. It was now his task, he declared, to employ the wide powers granted to him to insure that if world peace were disturbed it would not be disturbed by the United States of America. When asked whether the names of Senators Lindle, Embleton and Womersley would appear on the list which the President has instructed him to prepare, the General snapped briefly, 'I have nothing more to say!' "

Glancing up from his instruments, Quinn found Armstrong's eyes alight with joyous fire.

The radio coughed, beg-pardoned, and went on: "In a dark and foreboding speech made in Clermont Ferrand this afternoon, the French Minister for War reminded France that on two occasions she had been caught unprepared. Announcing the call-up of another three classes to the Colours, he warned his listeners that the present international line-up made the third and final world war well-nigh inevitable. France, he asserted, was determined to preserve her integrity at all costs, and he could tell potential enemies that she now had at her disposal weapons mightier even that the hydrogen bomb. A sensational editorial in today's edition of *Dernieres Nouvelles de Strasbourg* claims that one of these weapons may prove to be a neo-bubonic pandemic."

Again Quinn looked up. Armstrong was scowling heavily.

"It's going to be touch and go, George," he rumbled. "The sands are running out fast." He hooked his brawny leg across the corner of the co-pilot's seat, ran a hand over his forehead wearily. "There's an invisible empire sprawling right across the globe. It's cold and cynical and utterly ruthless and it thinks it can last as long as the accursed principle of divide and rule.

226

But it's got a weak spot!" He massaged his chin bristles vigorously. "Definitely, it has a weak spot! It could be made to collapse like a house of cards. Heaven help the lot of us if we don't bring it down with one blow, at the right time, in the right place. Heaven help the whole of humanity, for their monuments will be a series of those huge, mushroom-shaped clouds rising from a sea of lamentations!"

Looking serious, Quinn juggled his controls as the plane dipped and side-slipped.

"The Four Horsemen," continued Armstrong, speaking to himself, "they shall go forth through the lands and there shall be sounds of weeping wherever breath is drawn. There will be atom bombs and neo-bubonic pandemics—the arrow that flieth by day and the pestilence that stalketh by night!" His voice rasped on Quinn's ears. "Neither can we save ourselves by a world-wide smelling out of witches, for the witches are too many, too scattered, too cleverly disguised." He leaned forward, said to Quinn, "But what if all their witchcraft suddenly becomes ten thousand years behind the times?"

"Eh?" Quinn was startled.

CHAPTER SIXTEEN

Completing their turn, they hit the northbound route at twenty thousand feet above Council Bluffs and from there followed the Missouri up into the Dakotas. Still the ether maintained silence on the short-wave bands. Either the slaughter at Singleton's had not yet been discovered or else the real perpetrators weren't yet suspected. Probably the latter, decided Armstrong, knowing the obsessions of his antagonists. At this very moment, in all probability, they were making futile attempts to identify Drake from their lists of Martian deportees. The longer they continued to bark up the wrong tree, the greater the fugitives' period of grace—and they could do with every hour of it, every minute.

The plane roared on, its jets smoking. The world turned below; the torn world, the worn world, a world split into ideological fragments by autocrats, bureaucrats, theocrats, technocrats and other authoritative kinds of rats. A world without either the room or the patience for the plain, ordinary man's right to mooch along his own personal path with a minimum of interference.

Some book he had read in the long, long ago had pictured what is called civilized existence as a sequence of cataleptic states traceable to an obstruction of the evolutionary process. What was that book? Armstrong had to think for some time before he recalled it as Greiner's "Prelude to Sanity." Oh, well, things might become different if his own intentions were approved in the book of fate. Humanity might open out —like a flower in the sunshine.

But at that exact moment, fifty-thousand steel-studded feet were demonstrating the long forgotten *Passo Romano*, the totalitarian goose-step, along Turin's Via Milano. Nuclear warheads were being loaded on to hydraulic elevators in underground factories in the Urals. A lake of broth, seething with cultures, was being strained at France's Bacteriological Research Station at Lyons. A test-shower of phosphorus pellicules was satisfactorily burning up a field of wheat in Bulgaria. British newspapers were busily hounding out of public life a leading political personality who had dared to say that the road to war is not the path to peace.

Through press-recorders, over the radio and television networks, along each and every conceivable channel of propaganda swelled the flood of lies, half-truths and wilful misrepresentations which, if maintained long enough and made strong enough, would sweep the world's cretins from their precarious hold on individual life and into the sea of death. The chorus of suspicion and hatred slowly but surely was building itself up to the culmination desired by those controlling it—kill or be killed!

Already the smear-technique was dealing with those unwilling to conform. Later, when frenzied masses were psychologically prepared for it, the smear-technique would give way to the blank wall and the firing squad. First make the mob scream for Barabbas—then let them crucify their own! Like dogs salivating to the chime of the Pavlovian bell!

The rolling world was beginning to reel, but over it the solitary plane plummeted on. In London, two swarthy aliens twenty miles apart cautiously unpacked and buried special containers holding plutonium at sixty per cent. of critical mass. In due time they'd be brought together—but not yet, not just yet. In Baltimore, a squad of alert secret service agents seized a cylinder of thorium oxide, killed its owner, made fourteen arrests elsewhere. In Essen, Germany, a retort full of radioactive fluorine blew apart and eighty workers promptly became those for whom the bells tolls. Ten more acquired a new and appallingly virulent form of leprosy, a phenomenon regarded by professional chaos-mongers as of immense help to humanity's backward march along the road to oblivion. But still the plane roared on.

Quinn made a dexterous, one-minute landing on a natural runway near Bismarck, well out of sight of the local skyport. One of Hansen's toughies got out, then Claire, then Horowitz, who stood on the grass blinking owlishly around.

"Maybe you're a native-born Martian, maybe you're not," Armstrong said to the latter, speaking from his vantage-point in the fuselage. "Maybe I'm a pink giraffe, myself. Maybe all this Martian stuff is a lot of malarky. Life's chock-full of maybes, isn't it?" He grinned, showing big, white teeth. "And one more of them is—maybe we'll get where we're planning to go!"

Horowitz offered no reply, but his magnified optics were cold as they regarded the other.

"Keep him out of circulation at least seventy-two hours," Armstrong instructed the Hansen-agent. "After that, toss him to the F.B.I. Whatever you do, don't lose him. Blow his nut off if he gets out of step with you."

"It'll take him all his time to stay alive," promised the escort, dourly.

"Oh, John." Claire looked up, her tip-tilted eyes anxious. "John, I——"

"And maybe I'll be seeing *you* again," he told her, with feeling. He flipped her an envelope which she caught and put in her pocket. "Stay close with the others, and watch his Snake-ship the Martian until he's handed over. Then beat it to Gregory. You'll be all right. Don't worry about us." He studied her as if photographing her piquant features in his mind. " 'Bye, Pixie!"

He closed the fuselage door. Quinn boosted the machine off the ground, gained height rapidly. Sitting beside him, Armstrong frowned thoughtfully through the transpex until the three figures on the ground were lost to sight.

"That goggle-eyed bigbrain is as Martian as my left foot," he said, suddenly. "To use an Irishism, if I'm sane and he's sane then one of us is nuts."

"He can prove he's sane," Quinn pointed out.

"What of it? Suppose we end up by proving him a liar?"

"You've got something there." Quinn mused a moment. "Good liars have changed the course of history, and done it bloodily. They're a menace. I feel it in my bones that he's just such a menace."

"Me, too." Leaving Quinn, he stepped carefully along the fuselage, took the seat by Hansen, said to the saturine agent: "We're crossing the border." He nodded towards the country-side beneath. "Another crime—illegal entry."

Hansen sniffed disdainfully. "That worries me. It's sheer defiance of authority. It's naughty." His eyes keened at the other. "Why did you dump your heart throb?"

"I wanted her out of the way on our last lap. We're gambling —win or sink. I won't risk her sinking with me. So she's taking a letter to Gregory telling him what has happened so far, and what we're aiming to do. He can work out his best moves from

that." Ruminatively, he paused, added, "What's of most importance, though she doesn't realize it, is that I've got her out of
the way before the end comes."

"The end?"

"The end of this chase."

Hansen said, "Oh!" and looked mystified.

In front, Quinn gave the radio another whirl. A brassy blare
came forth: "Skiddin' with My Shiver-Kid." With a pained
expression, he switched to another band, got the tail-end of a
talk on the international situation.

". . . and in themselves the peoples of these countries do not
want war any more than we want war. Like us, they have
troubles enough and desire nothing better than to be left to
solve their own problems in peace. Like us, they believe in the
four freedoms." The speaker's voice hardened. "These are their
natural instincts, the instincts of little people who want to be
left alone. But when they are not permitted to exercise their
natural instincts, when their every channel of information is
poisoned at its source so that they are hopelessly misled about
the sentiments and intentions of their nearest neighbours, when
they are forced to live in a false and illusionary world which
constantly is depicted to them as murderously hostile, then
eventually may they be persuaded to run amok, sword in hand,
willing to die in defence of a way of life which has never been
threatened. Reluctantly, regretfully, with heavy heart but
powerful hand, we, too, shall then be compelled to draw the
sword to protect all those things which we hold dear. There is
no other way out, no other alternative. We must be prepared
to fight—or be prepared to die!"

Cutting off the radio, Quinn twisted around in his seat,
pulled a face at Armstrong. The latter turned and looked at
Womersley glowering two seats behind.

Armstrong said to Hansen: "That speaker was right, of
course. I'd say we've more sane ones in this country than anywhere else, but that won't keep us out of the resulting mêlée
once the rest of the world's lunatics stampede."

"It might be better if the darned world did go haywire," suggested Hansen. "Everyone would then be far too busy to bother
about small fry like us—the F.B.I. and the cops would have
bigger game to pursue."

"You don't mean that. I know you don't mean it. You

231

wouldn't wreck the planet just to insure that you became one of the forgotten."

"No, I reckon I wouldn't. Ultimately I might find myself in a worse fix—a wandering savage, maybe." His dark eyes were meditative. "You know that as a nation we aren't a warmongering crowd. We're not the kind to spill blood and gloat over it. Collectively, we're of a type which enables the President and Gregory and their supporters to have a better chance of keeping things cool than they'd have anywhere else in the world. If anything starts, it won't be us who starts it. Perhaps it's because we're a little less loony or a little more sane than they are elsewhere."

"Perhaps," Armstrong admitted.

"I know that you've got some plan on your mind," Hansen continued, "and I don't doubt that it's so nutty that even the world's imbeciles will know you're mad—and what beats me is how you hope to influence *them*. In America you can summon more plain, ordinary common sense to your side than you could dig up any place else, but what good will it do if you can't cut the ground from under millions of other lunatics? When they stampede, boy, it's going to be some rush!"

"Once when I was a kid I saw a herd of cattle panic," Armstrong said, reminiscently. "About four hundred of them. Black ones, brown ones, white ones, piebald ones; some with long horns, some with short. Cattle of all kinds. They milled around, set their heads the same way, charged off hell-bent for they knew not where. They thundered two hundred yards to a narrow bend, turned it, found two cussing cowpokes fighting like maniacs right in their path. They slowed down, milled a bit, slowed more, then stopped. Finally, they stood around the fighters and watched the battle. By the time it was over they'd forgotten what started them on the run." His elbow dug Hansen gently in the ribs. "Spectacular diversion, see?"

Hansen said: "Uh?"

"Then the boys turned up, urged the steers back to their pasture. Soon the birds were twittering in the trees and all was tranquil once more." He called to Quinn: "Where are we, George?"

"Over Peace River. Not much longer to go."

"Peace River," he said to Hansen. "Do you believe in omens?"

The sun had become a ball of flaming orange low in the west when eventually Quinn called him forward. He stared through the transpex, his face intent, his pulse beating heavily.

Yellowknife lay dimly in the distance a few degrees to starboard. Beneath, copper coloured by the setting sun, sprawled the glistening area of the Great Slave Lake. To one side reared the Horn Mountains, tipped with snow sun-tinged a bright red.

They jetted arrowlike across the lake between Yellowknife and Providence, followed its northward arm towards Rae. This kept them free for a while of direct observation from the ground. Gaining height before they reached the shore, they made a wide sweep east, then south, eventually found the railroad spur running from Yellowknife to Reliance. The rocket assembly plant stood on this spur twelve miles east of Yellowknife.

Approaching from the north, they permitted themselves only the briefest glimpse of the plant. One snatch of recognition was sufficient, and Armstrong snapped quickly: "That's the dump!" Quinn promptly turned his plane around, dropped it earthward in a direction away from the plant. They came down to two hundred feet, spent a quarter of an hour zigzagging over dangerously craggy terrain before finding a suitable landing place. Expertly, Quinn dropped the machine on a half-mile flat, let it trundle to a stop. The assembly plant was now out of sight just over the southern horizon, while Yellowknife was barely visible to the west.

Abandoning his controls with a sigh of relief, Quinn stood up, stretched himself, exercised stiff muscles. "Now to see whether we get a bang on the beak." Opening the fuselage door, he studied the darkening sky with wary eyes. "If there's a radar lookout at that plant, and if it spotted us coming down, something will come buzzing over to examine us mighty soon."

"I know it." Armstrong squeezed past him, got out of the plane, stamped on the hard, cold earth. "But I still think luck is riding with us—and I want to play it to the limit, while it lasts. Heck, we've been lucky even in that it had to be this time of the year—some other time all this would have been ten feet deep in snow."

One of Hansen's men growled from his seat behind the soured and silent Womersley: "Right now I could do with being ten feet deep in hamburgers!"

233

"Me, too!" endorsed the agent.

Womersley licked his lips moodily.

"There's a big lunch-box in the tail." Armstrong told them. "It was put in at the skyport." He smiled as the hungry complainant dived from his seat towards the rear of the fuselage.

Quinn jumped down from the doorway, kept careful watch on the sky. The rim of the sun had now disappeared below the Horn Mountains and a pall of darkness was spreading from the east. The entire southern terrain was grim, silent, devoid of life as far as the eye could see, but there was a faint, primrose glow beyond the horizon where the rocket plant stood, and tiny twinkles of light were beginning to appear in Yellowknife, to the west. No planes came roaring through the twilight, intent on investigating the grounded machine. Either their cautious approach had passed unnoticed, or suspicions had been lulled when they'd turned away.

Bearing a load of sandwiches, Hansen got out of the plane, handed some to the others, munched with them while he observed the onward creep of night. He shivered, spoke around a mouthful of food.

"If this is the far north, give me Miami!" He looked inquiringly at Armstrong. "Now we're here—what next?"

"The remaining step is to take up one or both of those rockets—or die in the attempt," Armstrong replied, slowly and thoughtfully.

Hansen dropped a sandwich, picked it up, bit into it, dirt and all. He bit his thumb as well, swore, transferred the sandwich to his other hand. He ate mechanically, like a man who hardly knows what he is doing. Twice he paused as if about to say something, changed his mind, chewed hurriedly, swallowed with difficulty.

"You serious?" demanded Quinn.

"George, I was never more serious in my life. You know the situation; in every particular it's designed to prevent any rocket getting some place external to Earth. That is the fundamental purpose of the whole set-up, and beside it all other purposes fade into insignificance. So unscrupulous, so determined and so desperate are world-wide machinations aimed at preventing any rocket from reaching Mars that it makes obvious two very important points."

"Go on."

234

"Firstly, it tells us that the saboteurs have satisfied themselves beyond all doubt that the latest types of rockets represent a stage of development where space-travel is in the bag—if the rockets aren't tampered with beforehand. That's something worth knowing, for they've got technical details not available to us, and have some basis for judgment. Secondly, it also tells us that if—despite all their attempts to prevent it—one rocket does get to Mars, it will thus create a new psychic factor of such potency that world circumstances will undergo radical alteration and the world-plot will collapse. It will collapse for the excellent reason that it will have been deprived of its prime purpose. The plotters will disperse, powerless and discredited, like end-of-the-world cultists when their long prophesied Day of Judgment fails to arrive. Their fanatical function has been to stop John Doe and Richard Roe from breaking his bonds, stepping out of this world and into the cosmos." His body loomed huge and bearlike in the gathering dusk. "So it's up to Richard to open the door! As I said before, a rocket on Mars is mate in one move!"

Quinn protested: "I'll give you all that, but how do we know those rockets are ready? And how do we know that they won't be shot off at the appointed time, without any help from us?"

"Womersley blabbed under the schizophraser, when he was in no condition to tell lies. He simply had to tell the truth. He said that one rocket has been officially reported as ready for its test flight. The other was then so nearly prepared that it ought to be ready by now. Test flights and resulting modifications and large dollops of snafu will waste another month or more. If the holocaust starts before then, you know and I know that those two ships will never take off for Mars—they'll be altered and blown somewhere else where they'll do plenty of damage. Moreover, just in case someone does get smart and tries to beat the plotters to the draw, the fuel coils have been fooled with. They're slated to blow apart near Mars."

"So we take 'em up and blow apart with them?"

"Not with fuel for a thirty-thousand miles test flight also on board! Not if we gamble on long odds and take them away *without a test flight!*"

"Yes, ye gods!" admitted Quinn. "That's true enough. If they take off untested, they'll have a ten per cent. fuel overload at the very least. A good margin! And if that explosion point is set at a stage where the remaining fuel represents less than the overload, the ship will have landed before its consumption reaches that point." He flourished his hands in nervous excitement. "But what a risk! What a plain, downright, lunatic gamble! Only the goofiest of galoots would try it!"

"I'm willing."

"Without a preliminary test flight we've no way of knowing whether those boats are really fit to make the long trip. A hundred to one both of them will need modifications of sorts to be discovered only in free flight. How the deuce can a solitary pilot do an engineering job on his vessel when he's half-way to Mars and going faster than zip? Besides, we don't know precisely where that explosion point is. Suppose that it's timed for one hour after take-off—the extra fuel will do no more than postpone the big bang by five or six hours. It'll occur just the same, and down will come cradle, baby and all!"

"I told you the blow-up is due near Mars. It's staged near the end of the fuel coil. The ship should go to blazes on the braking approach, about where most of the others busted. Womersley said so. The extra test flight fuel ought to cover that margin three times over, in my opinion. As for going up without a test, there's no alternative that I can see. If we leave those boats alone, they'll go their own bureaucratic way, wasting weeks while they accord with officially prescribed formula, and eventually getting nowhere. Time is the critical factor. Time waits for no man—and the whole world is betting its collective life on a few potent hours, a few potent minutes. George, we have got to bounce those rockets higher than a kite—either that or we backslide through eternity!"

"*We* bounce them?" Quinn stared around as if seeking a ghost. "Who's the other pilot?"

"Me."

Hansen bolted a piece of sandwich and said: "Now I *know* this world's a madhouse."

"Oh, *you!*" Momentarily, Quinn was lost for words. Then he said: "What d'you know about piloting space rockets?"

"A fair amount theoretically, but my practical experience doesn't exist. It's high time I learned. I'll have to get it from you."

"Mother, listen to him!"

"There are two rockets because they're intended to go together," Armstrong explained, patiently. "That means they'll share a microwave channel. Their pilots can talk to one another. You're going to talk and tell me what to do."

"Boy, I can see myself! Let me tell you, you oversized hunk of stupidity, that handling a space rocket at take-off is worse than riding a drunken comet. Can you imagine me clinging desperately to the controls, juggling with hundreds of tons going up like a bat out of hell, and calmly lecturing you how to do the same?"

"Of course not. So I take off first, under your instructions—you'll be telling me how. When either I've got safely away or have smeared myself over the bottom of a crater, you blow free. If I'm still running, it's up to you to get within talking distance again—if you can."

"It's abetting suicide!" Quinn declared, positively.

"That's exactly how I felt about you when I was concocting those gadgets for number eighteen. What makes you think you're the only guy with a right to break his own neck?"

"You're both batty," opined Hansen, gloomily. "Batty and scatty. Thank heavens there's not a third and fourth boat. You'd have me piloting one and Miriam the other."

"I wish there were," said Armstrong. "You'd be in them!"

"That's what you think! I know I'm sane without needing any psychotrons to tell me!"

"Suppose that I refuse to take part in this crackpot scheme?" Quinn asked.

"You're our key-man. Without you we're sunk. You know that, George. But, sunk or not, I'd go and try it by myself. I've not come this far merely to turn back."

"So you'd step in and snatch all my glory?" Quinn wagged his head sadly. "What a friend, what a friend!" He looked up, grinning. "Not while I'm standing under my hair, you won't!" He sobered, and went on, "For myself, I don't care a hoot—if I did I'd never have been chosen for number eighteen. I don't like the idea of you trying to handle the other boat. You'll crush your thick, stubborn skull, and that will do you no good —and it'll do no one else any good, either."

"Two chances are better than one, even if the second is amateurish and with greater odds against it."

"Yes, I know." Quinn kicked a pebble viciously. "There are two fully qualified pilots somewhere inside that assembly plant and there's a topnotch chance that they're people I know and who know me. I think it would be wiser to get in touch with one of them and persuade him to collaborate."

"A very good idea. Now tell me how we're going to search that place for a pilot without being pinched in the process, and how we're going to persuade him—all before dawn."

"Dawn?" Quinn gaped. "Are you thinking of taking off tonight?"

"If we can get into those ships without mishap."

Solemnly, Quinn extracted from his pocket a heavy automatic which he'd acquired during the fraças at Singleton's. Ejecting its magazine, he made sure that it was full, rammed it back into place, returned it to his pocket.

"Give me another sandwich and I'm ready."

Hansen gave him one, said hoarsely to Armstrong: "Where do I feature in this daffy performance?"

"I want Miriam to guard Womersley and the maid until you return. I want you and the other man to help us bust into the plant and reach those ships."

"And after that?"

"Beat it back here if you can. You'll manage it, I think. If one or both of those ships suddenly blow free, it'll cause such a hullabaloo that a dozen could march out of the plant without being noticed. When you get back here, collect the rest, make for Yellowknife, put a call through to Gregory, tell him everything you know, and leave it to him to protect you. If one of us gets away safely, and makes it to Mars, Gregory will be in a powerful position. He'll be able to whitewash you so that your own mother won't know you."

"If this, if that and if the other," said Hansen, with open scepticism. "What if you don't blow free?"

"We'll all be in the soup, and said soup will be red-hot." His laugh was harsh. "We're in it already, aren't we, so what's the difference? This is our only out!"

"You win!" Hansen went to the plane, issued instructions to Miriam, came back with the other.

No further words were spoken as the four tramped steadily towards the southward glow. A cold wind blew briskly across the rocky ground; the sky was now devoid of any random gleam from the buried sun, but brilliant starlight and a sickle Moon served to make clear their way. They were grim as they marched onward, each occupied with his own thoughts. The glow on the horizon grew stronger as they neared.

The rocket assembly plant covered considerable acreage, had a ten-foot-high wire fence around it, and was patrolled on the outside by armed sentries. At one end of the huge compound lay the administrative buildings surmounted by a large flagpole on which no flag could be seen by the shifting light of wind-tossed arcs; at the other end bulked machine shops, test shops and stores. In the great space between, half a mile apart, soared the tremendous finned and tubed cylinders which were Mars-rockets number nineteen and twenty.

A long, narrow elevator-gantry stood beside the nearest rocket whose entry port was closed. Keeping well out of sight of the sentries, the four sneaked around the area to the opposite side, found a similar elevator mounted against the other rocket.

There were several entrances through that intervening fence which, in the dim, uncertain light, looked as if it might be electrified. Large gates, heavily guarded, broke the fence on two sides where the railroad spur entered and left the forbidden territory. Four very small gates were set in the fence at its corners. At regular intervals of twenty minutes, each sentry went through one of these small gates, pressed a button set on a post within the compound, re-locked the gate and resumed his beat.

Lying low in the semi-darkness, the four watched the sentries for more than an hour while they gained a proper understanding of the routine. Pairs of sentries started from each corner, patrolled at fast pace to the centre of each side, turned back when within recognition-distance of each other, pressed the button on reaching the corner, and started all over again. Each individual made regular contact with two others, one on the corner and one at the middle, and this meant that the knocking out of any one of them automatically would alarm all the rest within a few minutes.

"There are eight altogether, not counting those at the rail-road gates," Armstrong whispered to the others. "We can't flatten the lot of them. The only thing to do is to deal with a pair of them at a corner, just after they've stabbed the security button. It'd take the others about ten minutes to reach the middle and find nobody to meet them, maybe another three minutes to race back to a corner gate and sound the alarm.

That gives us say thirteen minutes to reach those ships and get into the pilot's seat. It could be done easily to the nearest one. The farthest means an extra half-mile sprint. I reckon I can make it if nobody stops me in full gallop."

"Stops you?" hissed Quinn, in low tones. "Who said you're taking the farthest one?"

"My legs say, Shorty. They're twice the length of yours."

Quinn emitted a disgruntled: "Humph!"

"Let's get round to that corner and snake up as near as we can get while those patrols are near the middle. We'll give them time to prod the button, then rush them." He grasped Hansen's arm in the gloom. "See that those guys don't utter a squeak after they've been downed. Sit on them until the other sentries start whooping—then beat it yourselves as fast as you can go. Don't wait to see what happens to George and me—shift your dogs as if you're after a million dollars!"

Wraithlike, they stole through the shadows to the corner, waited for the sentries to near the middle, slipped to within twenty yards of the fence and lay flat among the boulders. Twenty minutes later the sentries returned. Armstrong watched them unlock the gate, press the button on the post. Decidedly those corner gates were weak spots, but for the double locks needing two keys they might have been able to bust in without rushing anyone. The sentries came out, began to close the gate. Despite the cold wind his body was strangely warm as he arose, poised on his feet.

That twenty yards seemed like fifty, and the pounding of his shoes on the hard rock sounded like warning thunder. Someone was snorting beside him, two more hammering noisily to his left. The sentries were amazingly slow of hearing. He'd got to within jumping distance of one of them before the fellow turned and blinked uncertainly into the darkness. He hit the sentry like a runaway elephant, knocking him flat. The other was still fiddling with a key in the gate when Hansen and Quinn fell on him simultaneously.

Armstrong didn't wait. Leaving his victim to Hansen's man, he reversed the key, shouldered the gate open, grabbed Quinn, lugged him through.

"Quick, George—take the nearest!"

Lifting big, pistonlike arms to his sides, he hurled his great body along beneath the waving arcs. Quinn was five yards behind him when he passed the first rocket.

No alarm yet had sounded, no voice had bellowed warningly when Quinn reached the elevator. He engaged the control lever and started to rise. The little pilot was talking to himself as he went up.

"Let that lock be open! Let it not be fastened!"

He glanced aside when fifty feet up, saw the dim outline of Armstrong's burly figure plunging onward in the distance. There were few people about. Three men were talking outside the administrative building apparently quite unconscious of what was going on. Two more were standing under an arc a hundred yards away and staring bemusedly after the running Armstrong. From a large steel building to the north came sounds of music and much laughter. A camp concert.

Two men in grey denims were passing the base of the second rocket as Armstrong raced up to it. They gaped at him, blinked uncertainly, gaped again. With delayed presence of mind, one of them stepped into his path.

"Hey, you, what's the hurry? What d'you think you're——?"

Armstrong handed him a haymaker. The fellow arced backwards under the powerful blow, his feet leaving the ground. Armstrong whirled sideways, swerved and ducked elusively before the other man, found that the fellow's startled confusion had made him easy meat. Giving him no time to gather his wits, he laid him out like a corpse, scrambled frantically into the elevator.

Hell broke loose as he reached the half-way mark. A chorus of enraged shouts and several shots sounded beyond the fence. Pink gouts spurted in the distant darkness and something whined shrilly off the administrative building's steel roof. The three talkers outside of it promptly dropped and scrambled for safety on all fours. Auxiliary lights flooded the entire camp and an alarm gong began its clamour.

At one corner of the assembly station a thirty-inch searchlight shot its beam skyward, lowered it, swung it over surrounding terrain. The shooting had now ceased. Men, shouting and gesticulating, were pouring from the main doors of the concert building. Five more, two of them bearing automatic rifles, raced at top speed past the base of the rocket without looking upwards. The two he had bowled over had now regained their feet and were gazing after the five runners.

The searchlight swung right round, its beam passing directly over him, spotlighting the moving elevator for a second. Still he was not noticed. All attention remained on that far fence. A second searchlight opened up, then a third. When the elevator stopped, he shoved frantically at the closed door of the lock. It opened.

Thankfully, he writhed through the small, circular hole. Temporarily he was out of sight of those below and therefore out of mind. He pressed the button of the elevator and heard it clatter noisily to the ground. Sooner or later that would draw attention to the ship as nothing else had done. But getting him out now that he was in would be a tougher task. In effect, he was in a vault, or a cylindrical fortress.

Finding the pilot's seat, he fastened himself in it, fixed the headphones on his head, pressed a stud marked: *Intercom*. The phones livened up.

"You there, George?" he murmured into his larynx-mike.

"Yes, I'm here."

"Can they hear us on this?"

"I don't think so. There's a stud marked *Ground* on the board. That's their channel. We've got one of our own, to cut out interference." Quinn paused, then said: "You were a deuce of a time! I thought you'd fail to make it."

"Time goes mighty slow when you're waiting and jumpy—like at the dentist's. All right, George—I'm ready. Start talking."

"Take it easy and keep cool," advised Quinn. "You could squat there for weeks and keep them at arm's length. Blow your stern jets whenever they come near and you'll scald their feet off."

"I don't want to burn anyone's dogs. I've nothing against them. Say your piece and let me blast off."

"O.K." Quinn's voice had a metallic timbre in the phones. "Lever on your right, marked *F.F.*, is the fuel-feed control. Move it one notch. Detonate with the red stud immediately in front of you. Your tubes will start blowing at minimum power and they'll need a full two minutes to warm up. Watch the chronometer—it won't be safe to give them any less."

Phlegmatically, Armstrong did as instructed. His foam-rubber seat began to quiver under him. The whole fabric of the vessel developed a rhythmic tremble from end to end. Dust rose from the ground, obscured the observation port over his head. He could imagine a tremendous sensation throughout the camp, with much scurrying around, much bawling of hasty orders, but he could see nothing, hear nothing.

Quinn went on talking, his tones calm, even, unhurried. Armstrong lengthened the blast. His hands, his hair and the back of his neck were warm and wet when Quinn suddenly shouted, ". . . . and for the love of heaven keep that swing-indicator centralized! Now—*boost*!"

He rammed the control over to boost point. The ship produced an organlike and eerie moan, rose slowly, very slowly. The cloud thickened over the observation port. The moan grew louder and half a note higher. The ship seemed almost to crawl through the cloud. Quinn was gabbling fifty to the dozen.

"Ignore the port. Ignore the sky. Keep your eyes on those instruments. Correct the side-swings. Don't let her drift away from the perpendicular. *Watch that swing indicator!*"

The sluggish upward creep ceased all of a sudden, and the vessel increased speed perceptibly. It rose faster, faster. It was going up like an elevator. It was going up like a jet fighter. It was going up like a rocket!

In the phones, Quinn's voice began to fade gradually as he continued: "Keep her going that way. Don't reduce power on any sternpipe. Maintain the full blast. *Watch that swing!*" He stopped, then his voice returned very weakly. "Can you still hear me, John?"

"Only just."

"All right. My turn now, I'm taking off."

Silence for a long time. Armstrong sat heavy-pressed in his seat while the ship shuddered and moaned. He kept his whole attention on his instruments, avoided looking at the increasingly brilliant glitters in the sky.

The swing indicator registered a two degree tilt. He corrected it by swift angling of the stern-steam stabilizer vanes. Gradually the tilt came back, slid to three and a half degrees. He corrected it again with an overboost on the appropriate tubes. The ship ran straight for a while, resumed its tilt. He compensated once more.

After a full hour, Quinn's voice speared into the ether. "Are

you with me, John? I'm up, way up. Can you hear me?"
Silence while the moments crawled by, then, sharply: "John,
can you hear me? Are you still running?" A long lull, followed
by: "I can't see you, John. What's the matter? For Pete's sake
don't start acting funny at this time! If you can hear me, come
back, will you? John . . . John . . . are you all right? Are you
still moving? Have I got this . . . all to myself?" Nothing responded, nothing. The steady moan of his own ship was the
only detectable sound in the whole of creation. Finally, Quinn
said, "Oh, heavens!" His voice vanished from the ether as he
released his stud and closed the channel.

CHAPTER SEVENTEEN

Leaving the telephone, General Gregory marched restlessly up and down his carpet. Seated in a deep chair, not reposefully, but erect and taut, Claire Mandle watched him with wide, tip-tilted eyes.

"That was Hansen. Whether I can clear him and his aides—and all the others for that matter—depends entirely on what happens next. Senator Womersley is the crux of my problem; Womersley and the mob he represents both in this country and out of it. If he chooses to make yet more trouble, as is likely, he can make plenty. He and his tribe can make more than I can cool down despite the support given by the President and certain influential members of the government. This Norman gang is all over the place, and our jurisdiction doesn't extend everywhere. That makes things tough." He gnawed his moustache savagely. "But if this crazy venture of Armstrong's comes off, well, Womersley's crowd won't be able to find hiding-places quickly enough. Armstrong, Quinn, Hansen and the rest automatically would be cleared. World opinion would demand it." He looked at her, smiled reassuringly. "No matter what laws may say, or how they may be written, public heroes cannot be burned at the stake. There are times when the law must give way to expediency—because the people say so, with one voice!"

"What did Hansen say?" she asked.

"He's in the calaboose at Yellowknife along with his secretary and one of his men. Womersley is stamping around breathing fire and fury and reciting a long list of charges against all and sundry. Womersley won't like it when he finds I've got Hansen out and have ordered a plane to bring him here."

"What did he say about the rocket-ships?" she persisted.

"They got away."

"Is that all?"

"Isn't that enough, young lady?"

She nodded reluctantly. "I suppose it is. Can't we find out what has happened to them? Are they really on their way, both of them? How far have they got? They've been gone three weeks. How soon shall we know whether——?"

"As soon as I can learn anything definite, I'll tell you," he promised.

"But surely we should know something by now? They should be about a third of the way there if——" She stopped, her expression pathetic.

"If they've been lucky," he finished for her. "There is nothing on the newscasts and won't be anything unless it's too spectacular to suppress. Those rockets were rather secret, see? Admittedly, how secret has become a matter of considerable doubt, but for reasons of high policy we don't want to advertise them before it is necessary."

"Don't the observatories know how they're progressing?"

"What the observatories know they will keep to themselves until it becomes something well worth telling. All news will be withheld as long as possible. That's just in case we're unfortunate and have two flops dumped in our lap—there's a small chance that they'll pass unmentioned, unnoticed."

She regarded him levelly, her discontent obvious. "Would it matter if the public knew that those two men had tried and failed?"

"In present difficult circumstances, I'm afraid that it might matter a great deal. Some of our jingoists would be swift to blame foreigners for the disaster, and their foreign prototypes would reciprocate by whipping up more antagonistic feelings against us, suggesting that because we built in secret we had an ulterior and probably treacherous motive. There may be even an organized outcry against the completion of number eighteen in New Mexico. All is grist to the propaganda mill when the war gods are sharpening their swords. When world-wide hysteria mounts steadily it is because those unseen forces manipulating international channels of opinion are utilizing every circumstance and craftily exploiting them to the utmost." He resumed his restless pacing on the carpet. "The world is a powder barrel with people prancing around it waving lighted candles. It's taking all we've got to postpone the big bang, and eventually it may come somewhere else in spite of us. Only the attention-diverting roar of rockets on the surface of Mars can change the situation. Armstrong was right in that supposition, though sometimes I suspect him of being as mad as anyone."

Ceasing his pacing, he faced her. "Call it insanity, stupidity, an obsession, or plain, ornery pig-headedness—it's inspiring and not without a certain amount of logic. He is trying to counter madness with madness, like fighting fire with fire."

"That was one of the arguments Horowitz gave me—who is to say what is rational and what is not?" she commented. "Does the end justify the means, or the means the end?"

"Horowitz!" he scoffed. "Already it has been discovered that he was born in Linz—and Linz isn't on Mars!" His moustache bristled as he added, "And we've a shrewd notion of what we've yet to discover—that he's a newer, craftier, more inventive version of Hitler, the self-appointed Messiah of a revived Germania."

She consulted her watch. "The noon newscast should be on the air now. Could we hear it?"

General Gregory flipped the wall switch, watched the screen glow to life. He was a little late, for the announcer was partway through his newscast.

". . . from Concepcion, bound for Wellington, radioed that an immense rocket descended from a clear sky at dawn, at bearings given at 37 50 S by 80 OW, this being about three hundred miles south of the island of Juan Fernandez, better known as Robinson Crusoe's Island. The *Southern Trader* reports that the object swept into a shallow curve which caused it to strike the sea at a tangent. Ricocheting like a flipped stone, the alleged rocket skipped across the surface of the ocean at tremendous pace and eventually disappeared over the south-east horizon." Finishing that item, he started with: "An uproar at this morning's meeting of the new Pan-European League resulted when M. Pierre Dieudonné, the French——"

Clair Mandle was standing up, her hands clasping and unclasping. Stony-faced, Gregory switched off, turned to the phone. He was on it some time, putting through five calls. Finally, he turned to her, faced her questioning eyes.

"The *Southern Trader*'s report came in only twenty minutes ago. It should have been kept off the air. Somebody blundered—or someone is being awkward. Anyway, nothing more is known except that the Chilean Government is investigating. One of our carriers, the *Jefferson*, is at Valparaiso. It has been ordered south to search the area."

"Then, you think——?"

He nodded gravely. "I'm afraid that one of them is down. There's no point in deluding ourselves with false hopes, my dear. It's almost certain that one of them is down."

"Which one?" she said. "Oh, if only we knew which one!" Her look at him was appealing. "And if only we knew about the other."

"All in good time." He patted her shoulder with fatherly confidence. "A little waiting, and the rainbow comes!"

"Can't we *do* anything?"

"No more than we're doing now." He led her towards the door. "Go out, have a look around the shops, buy yourself a pretty hat. Forget all about this for another twenty-four hours. No amount of worrying will make the slightest difference. As soon as news comes through, I'll phone you."

She left, for an hour wandered aimlessly around. Her eyes looked at shop windows without seeing what was in them. Buy yourself a pretty hat—tomorrow pretty hats may not be there to buy. How futile! Which one was down, nineteen or twenty? Who was its pilot? Where was the other boat, and who was piloting that?

She couldn't stand it any longer. Hastening to her hotel, she spent a fruitless afternoon waiting by the news recorder. And all evening. And half the night. There was still no news with the dawn radiocast, no *real* news. Heavy rioting in Afghanistan, massacres in India, fighting on the Turco-Syrian border, a mystery explosion in the naval port of Ferrol, Spain. But no news about rockets—nothing.

Is no news good news? Or bad news? Or even what it purports to be, namely, news?

Gregory's promised phone call drew her eagerly from her breakfast table at precisely nine o'clock.

"A stratosphere jet plane is waiting for you at the skyport, my dear," he told her. "It will take you to New Orleans. You will find some of your friends already on board. Take a taxi and get there just as fast as you can."

"But, General, why——?"

He had cut off. A quick utterance of words, and he'd gone. She gazed at the phone, a little dazed by events, then moved fast. Doing little more than snatch up her hat and handbag, she was out of the hotel and into a taxi in short time.

The three awaiting her in the plane were Hansen, Miriam and Bill Norton. The latter helped her as she entered breathlessly, and the plane took off immediately.

Hansen grinned at her. "Quite a welcoming committee, aren't we?"

"I don't know a thing. What has happened?"

"We got in from Yellowknife, under escort, late last night, had a long talk with Gregory and the F.B.I. This morning they dug us out, rushed us here. Gregory thinks that for the next few hours we'd be safer some place else. Having said all there is to say, we've become a liability—so we're going with you and Norton."

"Going where?"

"To meet Armstrong," Norton put in. He had the expansive air of one well satisfied with life. "Didn't General Gregory tell you that?"

"Then he's safe? He's not hurt?"

"He's a bit damaged, and maybe his dignity is hurt," said Norton, offhandedly. "Beautiful women will find him even more repulsive than he used to be. Otherwise, he's all right."

"Thank goodness!" she breathed.

Norton raised an eyebrow. "He's not such a bad ape," he conceded, weighing her up, "despite that he's so big and so stupid." He expanded his chest. "Gregory is permitting him to talk to one reporter only—all others warned off. Armstrong nominated me. That's friendship. He doesn't forget old friends."

"No, I suppose not," she murmured, her mind in a whirl.

"And I hope he continues to remember them in the future," Norton added, pointedly. He eyed her again. "Can you cook?"

She was taken aback. "Cook? Can I cook?"

"Steak smothered with button mushrooms, and stuff like that." He licked his lips.

"Of course."

"That's fine. That's real fine." He patted his stomach. "I see no reason to withhold my approval."

Hansen and Miriam swapped significant glances, and the latter said to Norton: "That's mighty white of you, Roderick."

"The name is not Roderick," Norton reproved, glowering at her.

Claire put in: "Just what happened to John? Why are we going to New Orleans?"

"They're flying him here," Norton told her. "As I've got it, he skidded across half the Pacific Ocean and thumped into Chile, wrecking his ship and distorting his own profile at the same time. Planes from one of our carriers found him. We should be in New Orleans about an hour ahead of him, and will meet him when he lands."

"I see." Peeking through the window, she watched the landscape rolling far below. Her thoughts were elsewhere.

Hansen said: "Well, that's one floppo. Maybe Quinn's another, some place far from the beaten track, and——"

"What's Quinn doing?" Norton demanded. His eyes were sharp and curious. "I thought the cops wanted him. I thought he was on the run. What's he up to now?"

"Don't you know?"

"Would I be asking you if I did?"

"Then I won't tell you," Hansen said, easily.

Leaning sideways, Norton scowled at him and spoke between set teeth. "Come on—give! What's all this about Quinn?"

Studying him calculatingly, Miriam baited him with: "What is it worth? Is it worth a mink?"

Waving outraged hands, Norton argued with her while Hansen grinned sardonically and Claire continued to gaze absently through the window. The argument was still in full swing and had become slightly acid when the plane touched down at its destination.

The Navy courier arrived ninety minutes later. With jets spouting long columns of mist, it hit the runway, trundled to a stop. Armstrong was first out.

He limped awkwardly down the ladder, his left arm in a sling, his beefy face crisscrossed with strips of plaster, a heavy bandage around his head. His hair stuck out of the bandage in a weird fringe of spikes. His smile was lugubrious and lopsided as he met them, and the plaster crinkled on that side of his features.

"This is what's left," he announced. "Worn but serviceable." He took Claire's cool, slender hand in his huge paw.

"Didn't expect to find you here, Pixie. Who arranged it—Gregory?"

She nodded, looking at him and saying nothing.

Sniffing the air, he gazed around appreciatively. "Though I say it myself, it's good to be back in the madhouse. Let's go some place where we can eat as well as talk." Calling a taxi, he helped Claire into it, climbed after her with one or two painful grunts.

Seated at a table, with Hansen and Miriam listening intently, Claire watching him slant-eyed, and Norton busily scribbling, he said: "I'm sort of on parole until they learn where Quinn's got to. If he has failed, they won't be able to pinch me fast enough! I've Gregory to thank for these few hours of freedom and peace—I'll have George Quinn to thank if I stay free. It all depends on him."

"You did your best," Claire comforted.

"Maybe I didn't do so bad. Maybe I stopped George picking the wrong ship. I got a wobbler. It wasn't quite ready, and I picked it. That was the point where my luck ran out. I don't know what was wrong. It seemed like a couple of tubes hadn't been fitted with linings. They held up a few hours before they burned out. I turned into a huge parabola. I carried on into space and then fell back to Earth. " He rubbed one side of his face, winced visibly. "I entered Earth's atmosphere hell-busting for the South Pacific with my heart trying to squeeze itself between my ears. I guess I could never have been torched by Sandy-hair and his gang. The capers I've indulged in would have pumped a clot ten times around my system by now. I thought I was a goner in any case."

"You're reserved for the hangman," Norton assured. "Carry on."

"I managed to blow her into a shallow curve just before she struck. She whacked the sea with her belly and hopped like a kangaroo. By heavens, she must have covered about four hundred miles in gigantic, ten-mile leaps! In the end, she walloped an island off the Chilean coast, smiting it so hard that she slid right up the beach and dug her nose into the sandhills. I tried to embed myself in the control panel. I waited for someone to hand me a harp, but after a while some planes came zooming around and a gang of Navy boys broke in and lugged me out." Picking up his cup of coffee, he sipped it awkwardly but with

251

gusto. "Reckon that's where my luck came up with one final spurt. I'm the luckiest guy on this crazy planet!"

Norton said: "You never did know the difference between being lucky and being downright bullheaded! Now what's this stuff about Quinn? Where is he?"

"Yes, George," Armstrong murmured, his tones low, anxious. "Now that I've made a mess of it, he's our last bet. If he's sunk, we're all sunk. But if he makes it, and lives to say so, it'll prove beyond all shadow of doubt that this Martian clap-trap is a lot of neo-Nazi hooey."

"Prove it?" Norton looked disatisfied.

"You bet! Look, sonny, if, as these Normans assert, a gang of Martians have been visiting this world repeatedly for centuries, you can accept one certainty—they're going to button the lip of the first guy who lands on Mars. So if anyone lands and talks—there aren't any Martians! You couldn't have proof more conclusive!" His bothered gaze went to the great clock on the wall, noted that it said four-thirty. "We ought to have heard of him by this time. If he's down, he may be unidentifiable, or the news of his crash has been suppressed, or he's busted himself some place far from anywhere." His fingers started tapping nervously on the table. "I wish we knew, one way of the other."

"Perhaps he's still going," suggested Claire.

"I like to think so, but it's not probable because he ought to have made it by now. His flight-duration is such that if he hasn't reached there yet, he'll never get there."

"Get where?" yelped Norton, almost beside himself. "Is this half-pint Quinn up in another rocket? Where did he obtain the darned thing? How many rockets are floating around? If you took up number eighteen and converted it into scrap, how the deuce did Quinn——?"

A big wall-recorder interrupted him. Its huge screen lit up, flickered wildly, cleared, revealed massed military bands. The recorder's matched loud-speakers blared forth a rousing air. Automatically, everyone stood up, heads erect, shoulders squared. Armstrong arose beside Claire, stood with all his weight on one foot, his hand supporting him against the table. Norton was erect as if on parade, a puzzled expression on his features. Hansen looked serious. Miriam was apprehensive.

Something special coming. Massed bands, and the flag under uniformed escort, and the sounding of the anthem. Prelude to war? The dour warning, the appeal to unity, the affirmation of aims? Something very special coming! The marching bands faded out of the screen as the tune ended with a martial flourish of trumpets. An announcer loomed large. Everyone sat down, nervously, attentively.

The announcer for once had lost his suavity and sangfroid. There were papers in his hand, and the hand was shaking slightly but visibly.

"Emergency news bulletin," he enunciated. "Forty-seven minutes ago, for the first time in human history, a voice spoke to us from Mars! It was the voice of George Vincent Quinn, an American citizen, and the official pilot of rocket number nineteen, which took off from a secret starting-point without any publicity!"

Claire felt the powerful grasp of Armstrong's heavy fingers on her wrist. Her eyes were shining. His were fixed with burning intensity on the screen.

"Quinn's vessel does not bear fuel sufficient for a return journey, but Washington experts state that it is now a comparatively simple matter to send a robot-piloted vessel which Quinn can land by remote control and from which he can obtain the necessary supplies. Instructions have already been issued that number eighteen, our rocket in New Mexico, be modified for automatic operation with all possible speed, and it is confidently expected that the vessel will be ready to land within seven weeks. Meanwhile, Pilot Quinn has all the facilities needed to preserve life for six months."

Glancing at his papers, and obviously agitated by the importance of the occasion, he continued: "Amateur radio stations, picking up Quinn's calls, were first to disseminate this epoch-making news which already is electrifying the civilized world. Messages of congratulation have started to arrive from foreign governments and from a host of individuals. Some of the former were accompanied by offers of partly constructed rockets suitable for swift conversion to relief vessels. Commenting on these offers, Columnist Henry Coulthard says in his current review of affairs, 'Yesterday, we were being threatened with rockets by all and sundry. Today, we're being offered them as gifts, freely, willingly, by people quick to realize that the world

253

has changed beyond recognition in a few tremendous minutes. The scientific worth of Pilot Quinn's triumphant trip is as nothing to the psychological value thereof. The trumpet of peace has been sounded effectively—in a distant and lonely crater!' "

Armstrong said, softly, reverently: "Good boy! I'm glad he made it. It was meant for him, and not for a ham like me. It was George's job right from the start."

"Further information will be broadcast as it comes through, but"—the announcer made a dramatic gesture—"before we go on to the next item we bring you the voice of Pilot Quinn speaking from Mars!"

The screen blanked. The speakers coughed, emitted scratching noises, spoke harshly through a haze of static.

". . . am getting your strength fine . . . undamaged." A long, noisy pause, followed by, "Glad he's safe. Tell him . . . bigger they come the harder . . . fall."

The distorted voice and the static cut off abruptly. The announcer came back. "The last part was a reference to John J. Armstrong, official pilot of Quinn's companion rocket number twenty, which made a forced landing off the coast of South America. Armstrong, recently listed as a public enemy, is now revealed as having been engaged in highly confidential work under command of General Gregory, and the F.B.I. has announced that all calls for him have been withdrawn." Switching papers, he went on, "Working in concert, police and armed forces of several countries are raiding the haunts of an international band of saboteurs known as the Norman Club who were fanatically opposed to space-flight, and it is reported that——"

"Finish!" remarked Armstrong, not listening any further. "They'll catch some, not others, but the escapees will be impotent. Time has passed them by." He massaged his jowls thoughtfully. "I hope they don't overlook any remnants of Sandy-hair's mob, either. That crowd represented the inevitable schism which always occurs in a cult. Maybe they didn't like Horowitz. Or maybe he overdid it with his psychotron, convincing them that they were indeed mad Martians. Or more likely they had the monopoly of this new-fangled coagulator, thought it made them the élite of the élite, fell out when they refused to hand over its secret to the rank and file." He sighed reminiscently. "History repeats itself. Horowitz had his enemies on his own territory—just like Hitler. And like Hitler, he's come to the end of the trail."

Hansen jerked a disparaging thumb towards the screen on which the announcer was still gabbling. "Wasn't he sweet? He cleared your character absolutely—but said nothing of mine."

"Nor mine," supported Miriam. She mooned at her boss. "I've never been out of trouble since I entered your employ. Some day, I'll get used to it, I guess."

Grinning with the unplastered side of his face, Armstrong said to Claire: "Do you dance?"

"You can't. Not with that leg," she pointed out.

"As the Man on Mars said, the harder they fall. I've tumbled for keeps." Impudently, he ate her with his eyes.

She pinked a little.

"My scoop!" moaned Norton, viewing them with disgust. "My scoop gets shot to blazes—and you two have to sit and coo!" He wiped his lips with a handkerchief, making an insulting ceremony of it. "*Pfah!* you make me sick!"

Leaning across the table, Armstrong jibed: "Square roots, eh?"

"All right, all right—take her." Norton waved an airy, disinterested hand. "I can find my own." His sour stare shifted to Miriam, became speculative. "Do you dance, Fair One?"

Linking an arm through Hansen's, she thinned her lips, regarded him with distaste. "I read the papers—and sometimes I wonder."

"Wonder what?" Norton invited.

Miriam said, nastily: "How you know you're sane."